Praise for the Novels of Laura E. Reeve

Peacekeeper

"An excellent debut novel. *Peacekeeper* is full of exciting, complex characters in a truly byzantine universe where everything hangs in the balance. I can't wait for Reeve's next book."

—*Mike Shepherd, Bestselling Author of the Kris Longknife Series*

"Former USAF officer Reeve channels her flight experience into this crisp military SF debut... Reeve drives the story at a breakneck pace, providing a fine mix of derring-do, honor and courage, and the familial bickering and affection of a close-knit crew."

—*Publishers Weekly*

"Ms. Reeve shows great promise as an author, with her military knowledge lending a believable component to her fictional tales."

—*Darque Reviews*

Vigilante

"Thanks to an intriguing ensemble cast and their varied takes on the nicely complex universe, readers who missed 2008's *Peacekeeper* will find it easy to catch up in this entertaining second military SF adventure for Ariane Kedros."

—*Publishers Weekly*

"It is rare that a sequel is as compelling as the first book in a series, but *Vigilante* by Laura E. Reeve is that rare exception."

—*Iriarte Files—Writer's Nightmare*

Pathfinder

"*Pathfinder* is a riveting, action-packed space adventure which I highly recommend. Peopled with interesting characters, unusual political situations, and twists and turns, this book will keep the reader enthralled."

—*Fresh Fiction*

"Laura is a great world builder."

—*Cybermage*

A CHARM FOR DRAIUS
A NOVEL OF THE BROKEN KASKEA

Laura E. Reeve

Cajun Coyote Media
MONUMENT, COLORADO

Cajun Coyote Media
P.O. Box 1063
Monument, CO 80132-1063
USA
www.ccm.ancestralstars.com

This is a work of fiction. Names, characters, places, and incidents are a product of the author's imagination. Locales and public names are sometimes used for atmospheric purposes. Any resemblance to actual people, living or dead, or to businesses, companies, events, institutions, or locales is completely coincidental.

Interior Layout by BookDesignTemplates.com
Cover by Laura E. Reeve

A Charm For Draius/ Laura E. Reeve — 1st ed.
ISBN 978-0-9891358-3-2

For Dee

Acknowledgments

I began creating the world of the Phrenii when I was in college, long before the character Draius existed, so I apologize if I forget anyone in these acknowledgments. First, I thank my parents and my sister for having the patience to read my many stories. In addition, thank you, Wendy, for doing early copyediting on this story and others. Thank you, Dad, for working with me on the logical progression of technology. In the decades that followed, I began to piece together the first book that would be the story of Draius. I am grateful for the critiques and encouragement from many writing groups: Jim Ciletti's workshops, the Pikes Peak Writers, and the Rocky Mountain Fiction Writers. Thanks also go to the many writer friends who gave up their time to critique parts of this book or its entirety: Daniel "Bear" Kelley, Jodie Kelley, John Britten, Robin Widmar, Summer Ficarrotta, and Scott Cowan, who also wrestled with the final editing of this version. I'm grateful to my agent, Jennifer Jackson, who had faith in the initial manuscript and championed it in a market where it just wouldn't fit; and to my husband, who has forever been my steady advocate and supporter. Finally, thank you, Dee, for giving me kind encouragement to publish this while suffering through your own tragic loss.

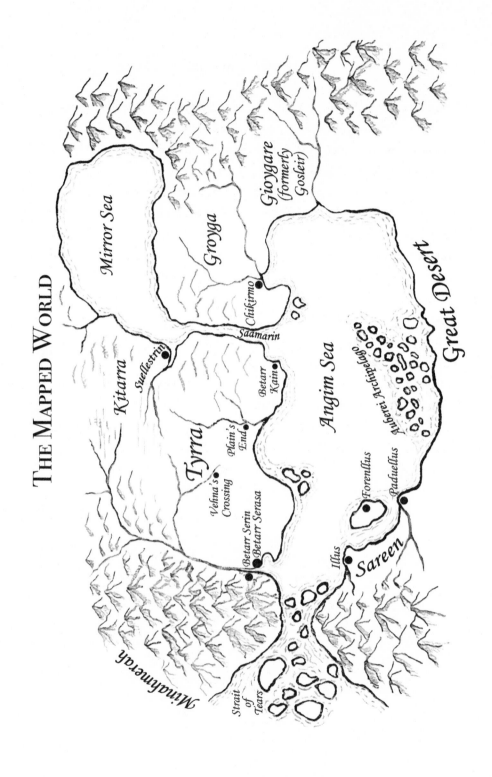

THE MAPPED WORLD

Mirror Sea

Groyga

Gioygare
(formerly
Gosleir)

Great Desert

Kitarra

Snellestrin

Chikirmo

Saamarin

Betarr
Kain

Angim Sea

Tyrra

Plain's
End

Vehna's
Crossing

Auberei Archipelago

Betarr Serin
Betarr Serasa

Forenllus

Paduellus

Illus

Sareen

Minalmerah

Strait
of
Tears

CHAPTER ONE

The North Dibrean Valley

Death magic and life-light are antagonistic; neither can suffer the other to exist. When Nherissa created *necromancy*, it was turned against the five elemental Phrenii, the life-light creatures who protect our children and our spiritual path to the Stars. This is why King Kotiin made the practice of necromancy punishable by slow death on the wheel and ordered all written research and records destroyed. In hindsight, many consider this a superstitious overreaction.

—Royal Librarian Pettaja-Viisi Keri, in Tyrran Year (T.Y.) 1109

D raius ached to be home, yet couldn't face what waited there. Maybe she shouldn't have let her pride take lead. Maybe she shouldn't have filed that formal complaint. Had she been a coward, to push it under Lady Anja's door just before leaving on patrol? Her jaw tightened.

She put the spyglass to her eye—*for the twenty-seventh time*, her mind whispered—and examined the maelstrom sitting on the mouth of the Whitewater. From her vantage point high upstream, she saw starlight reflecting off the top of the dark whirlpool of clouds hiding her home cities. Lightning flickered at its edge.

That can't be natural. She shook away the profane thought as she watched lightning erupt from the storm, rippling and pushing mist through swollen-budded birches and pines up the valley toward her. She sat more than two days ride away, yet she felt the sound of the storm's thunder hit her breastbone and travel through her body to ground itself in the boulder behind her back.

Sixty-seven... Sixty-eight... Her mind, without encouragement, ticked off each surge of thunder during the watch.

A boot sole scratched on gravel.

She jumped to a crouch, knife in one hand and spyglass in the other. The figure, barely visible in the dawn drizzle, answered her challenge and proved to be Bordas, the leader of this tedious rotation.

"Going on your morning constitutional? Or, perhaps, checking up on me?" She adjusted her oilskin before sitting on the damp ground again.

He waited as another thunderclap washed over them. "Neither. I thought I'd check on Henri. Why are *you* pulling a double watch?" He squatted beside her and watched her face, frowning.

She stayed silent, enduring his regard with tight lips. Although she was the same rank, she was technically under his command; Bordas was King's Guard and she was filling the auxiliary City Guard position on his patrol. He could order her to speak but when she agreed to take Henri's watch, she'd promised her silence. A promise she regretted.

"As long as Henri didn't pull his old dodge of gripes and pukes. Remember, I'm Meran-Kolme. I watched him in lessons. I've seen him heave up his food, without purging brew, just to be excused from schoolwork." He waited.

When she shrugged, Bordas sighed and held out his hand. "How's the storm?"

"Exactly where we left it six days ago." She slapped the spyglass into his outstretched palm.

He did exactly as she had done, focusing tightly upon the sister cities, or rather the darkness that engulfed them. He jumped backward when fingers of lightning spurted and strained northward toward them. She silently counted to twenty before the thunder pounded them, then incremented the number of thunderclaps.

He handed back the spyglass. "It can't be the same storm. If my opinion mattered, I'd say it's—"

"Don't." Her throat tightened, but not from the cool air. "If it's natural, the Phrenii can nudge it out to sea. But if elemental magic can't move it..." She swallowed. *Necromancy. An evil that exists only in nightmares and children's stories.*

"Whatever it is, it's beyond this poor soldier's grasp. If we push the horses, we can check the northern villages and get to the sister cities in two days." He stood and scraped mud off his boots before climbing up to the campsite.

Bordas rousted the sleeping patrol while Draius stayed in her spot, leaning against the boulder. From behind, she heard jingling, flapping, boot steps, hooves stamping, all punctuated with brusque calls and the puffing of horses excited by the frenetic breaking of camp. She was already packed, so she continued to watch the vortex as daylight pushed in from the east. There was little wind at the top of this valley, and she could see her breath in the chill morning air. The gentler weather of false-spring was held in abeyance while that whorled grey and black chaos sat at the mouth of the river.

Seventy-one... Seventy-two...

Down in the cities hidden by the maelstrom, her son Peri and her husband Jan waited. Thinking of them twisted her stomach. Was Peri safe? He was protected by Lady Anja and sheltered inside her house. How would Jan turn the storm to his advantage? She could hope that he was too busy to whisper in his matriarch's ear or visit his lover.

Worry and humiliation swirled inside, nauseating her. She felt ready to vomit bile onto her boots. Just like Henri had.

CHAPTER TWO

Third Kingday, Erin Two, T.Y. 1471

I bound the old man's wrists and ankles, because I was the only one who accepted what had to be done. I felt the lodestone's desire, like the fleeting touch of a lover, as I attached the pulley hook to the bonds around his wrists. After I hoisted him to hang with his toes touching the floor, I moved to stand behind him, where I could no longer feel the lodestone.

Then I spoke into his ear. The roar of rain on the warehouse roof hid my words from my cohorts, but not from the old man. His eyes widened as he heard me recite the customary blessing to relieve dumb beasts of their souls before sacrifice. I looked away from the fear in his faded eyes, which were nearly blind from rum and suffering. My chest tightened. I told myself he was *less* than a beggar, because even panhandlers had names, family, and lineage. This man was *nunetton*, one of the "forgotten nameless" who would never be missed. In the eyes of the Tyrran matriarchs, he didn't exist.

I pushed his quivering body, using the overhead conveyor, to within an arm-span of the lodestone's crate. Careful to keep him between the crate and me, I gave one final push and stepped back. The others huddled several paces behind me. We watched the lodestone take his mind. He whimpered and drooled, imploring to be freed, until his cries turned to mad babble. Still we waited, listening for a change in the storm outside.

"By the Horn, put that nameless bastard out of his misery."

4

I knew the voice, but I dared not name any of the cloaked figures, even in my thoughts. My employer nodded his agreement, but his eyes flickered in the shadow of his hood. Perhaps the oath angered him, or perhaps he feared a mere reference to the Phrenii might attract their attention—as if the lodestone's antagonistic magic hadn't already put us at risk.

"The documents were clear," I said. "Satiating the lodestone should sooth it, help hide it from the Phrenii."

We all flinched at the crack of thunder and flash of lightning radiating from the narrow windows above us. A pounding roar on the roof heralded the return of cherry-sized pellets of ice which had broken windows all over the sister cities. I glanced up at the mullioned panes, hoping their narrow shape and the overhang of the roof would protect them.

"Let's not argue about theory while we drown. Finish this," my employer's fingers twitched to indicate the beggar. "If it doesn't work, we'll try something else."

Holding down my resentment, I stepped behind him and sliced his throat. A surge of hunger, no longer just hazy desire, clutched at me. I jumped backward to safety.

Silence. The deluge stopped, as if a sluice gate fell before the source. Behind me, I heard breaths drawn in hope—*maybe the storm will end*—and trail into sighs of disappointment as a light patter began again. This was an expensive price, paid in blood, for such little effect.

Even though the experiment failed, I still had observations for my journal. I couldn't examine the lodestone because it was hidden inside a crate and we carefully avoided shining light into the opening, for *our* protection. After losing several workers during the excavation of the stone, we'd learned to be careful. As I watched, the beggar's body had its life sucked away, and soon, all I'd pull away with the rack hook would be a wrinkled husk.

Behind me, the tired argument began again.

"It's going to tear apart the cities. That's if the Guard doesn't find us first." The voice was panicked and I didn't recognize it, although the sentiment that we were mere minutes away from a death sentence under the King's Law was becoming a common refrain.

"It's the Phrenii." The wine merchant, with her exotic and cultured voice, wasn't afraid to identify the problem.

"They haven't detected us—"

"As far as we *know*. They're the embodiment of life-light magic; we might as well try storing gunpowder beside a furnace. We must put distance between them and the lodestone." The woman's logic was flawless, and punctuated by a ground quake that caused the entire upper level to tremble.

"The Groygan offer is generous. Their payment would finance more experiments and research," the politician said. My employer called him a traitor, but never to his face.

"Sending the lodestone east will risk the attention of pirates," said the dry voice of the gentleman scholar.

The members of our secret society continued to debate whether to send the lodestone south or east, and if east, how we might avoid the piracy around the Auberei Archipelago. I walked to the edge of upper level and watched the water rising on the lower floor of the warehouse. A surge of mildew and rot overwhelmed my nose. Whatever was in the bottom layer of crates was now worthless, although that wasn't my concern. Below, the accountant stepped carefully in the ankle-high flood, but dropped his robes into the fetid soup drink to grip the ladder.

"What about the Sareenian desert tribe?" my employer asked. He was still loyal to Tyrra and resisted sending the artifact to our traditional enemies.

"I told you, they are treacherous and too poor to come through on their offer." The Sareenian ship owner had a thick accent that made him as recognizable as the female wine merchant.

I ignored the discussion. I don't carry a thirst for revenge, as does my employer. He's a dangerous man with deep, hidden passions that are unseemly for this venture, but as long as our goals coincide, I render my services to him in a professional manner. Neither am I influenced by Groygan gold, as are the Sareenian ship owner and the traitorous politician. I hope, through study and experiment, to recover the roots of magic for mankind. Wherever the lodestone goes, I will find the means to follow it.

"The storm isn't moving." The accountant panted as he finished the climb to our level. "The Phrenii are protecting the dikes about the river and the bridge, but the canals are rising in the lower city."

The bass rumblings of a rebuilding storm followed his words. Obviously, there weren't enough nunetton in the sister cities to keep the lodestone satiated—and I knew no other method of preventing its magic from clashing with the Phrenii. I turned to face my cohorts in their soggy robes.

"Gentlemen." My address was general, considering our motley membership. "We have no other avenues. If we don't want a disaster, we should move the lodestone away. Perhaps arrange a temporary situation?"

My employer's barrel chest deflated with defeat, but his voice was implacable. "I won't allow the Groygans to have it, even for a short period."

"Perhaps that desert tribe can be useful, after all. We might be able to ship it south tomorrow." The Sareenian ship owner glanced at the traitor.

At the time, I was the only one who noticed the surreptitious look they exchanged.

CHAPTER THREE

Murder at the Sea Serpent

Consider what we were before the Phrenii came: savage tribes fighting with Groygans to the east, and living nomadic lives in tents. The Phrenii helped us establish Tyrra out of chaos, but what price have we paid? Undoubtedly, we are the most advanced society in the Mapped World, but we can no longer wield the magic of our ancestors. Today, the only remaining evidence of life-light magic is the existence of the elemental Phrenii themselves.

—*Andreas, editor of The Horn & Herald, First Hireday, Erin Two, T.Y. 1471*

Mid-morning on Farmday, wind began moving in the valley. With no view of the sister cities, Bordas needed someone to climb a tall pine and provide a report. He picked Henri and Draius looked away to hide her smile as the crafty young man balked.

"Obviously, ser, the storm moved out to sea." Henri glanced upward. "The clouds are moving south now."

"*Obviously?* I'm not making assumptions. Up the tree, soldier!" Bordas made a crude, upward motion with his hand.

Henri jumped for the lowest branch of the pine. As he climbed, needles, twigs, and colorful oaths filtered down to the ground. Once he reported clear skies breaking over the cities to the south, everyone relaxed.

With Henri back down on the ground, sulkily wiping pitch from his hands, Bordas decided to continue with a normal patrol schedule. That meant they came back to the sister cities at the end of their eight-day rotation—just in time to watch the Phrenii lower the dikes that held back the wrathful Whitewater.

They were caught in a press of crowds at Bridge Square, where four major roads joined at the one bridge that connected the two cities. Draius had to stand in her stirrups to get a clear view of the Whitewater Bridge. It shone as only Tyrran marble could in the afternoon sunlight. Two single-horned creatures, Phrenii, loomed high on either end of the bridge; multi-colored walls of mist swirled and hid the river.

The ringing that accompanied phrenic elemental magic began resonating through the cities. The tones vibrated inside her skull and she squinted as the Phrenii became transparent and elemental, shining with a brilliance that forced her watering eyes closed. When she opened them, all that remained was a bridge crossing a swollen grey river. The Phrenii had shrunk to the size of deer.

This exhibition of power wasn't common to the crowd that gathered on the Betarr Serasa side of the bridge. Carriages stopped, while both drivers and occupants stared at the spectacle. When the dikes disappeared, a murmur swelled from the crowd. Draius frowned when she heard the vulgar term "unicornis" muttered with foreign inflections; ten years ago there wouldn't have been so many foreigners in the crowd.

After the Phrenii returned to their normal size, tradeschildren poured out from the crowd. They surrounded the creatures, stroking them, grabbing their manes, even tugging on their tails. Adults stood back as awe battled with other feelings on their faces: longing, shame, and regret. They'd probably forgotten the power of the Phrenii—it was too easy to focus on the discomfort they bring to adults.

Dahni was the phrenic element for water, and the aspect for healing. It stood on the near side of the river and now turned toward its audience. Immediately, adults at the front of the crowd shrank back, drivers started whipping their horses, and onlookers began dissolving away. Draius and other members of the patrol hunched, hoping to avoid drawing attention as faceted green eyes glanced over them. Dahni began to move south along Canal Street with an entourage of children, and they all breathed easier.

Bordas turned around as Draius pulled her horse aside. "Til next time, Serasa-Kolme Draius," he said, formally dismissing her.

"Meran-Kolme Bordas." She returned his salute and kept her tone neutral. She hoped it'd be more than three erins before she did another patrol. She swung her leg over Chisel's hindquarters and slowly slid off the tall chestnut horse. She almost groaned when she hit the muddy ground, the thud of *home* going from her heels up to her teeth. Her leg muscles felt strange, like they were unfamiliar with walking or standing.

Pride, however, kept her posture stiff and tall until the patrol turned to go. No one else in the patrol bid goodbye to her, the only City Guard member. Instead, the six stained and grimy members of the King's Guard clattered away over the Whitewater Bridge, climbing toward the high shining spires of Betarr Serin. *After an entire patrol together, I'm still common watch to them.* Even to Henri, who had to know by now that she'd seen through his jokes and schemes. Sadly, marriage had improved her sense for detecting deception.

She turned to the streets of Betarr Serasa, the lower city where commerce occurred. It was a mess. The results of the "worst false-spring storms ever recorded," to quote the passing crier, were broken windows, the smell of mold, and mud puddles galore. Every now and then, she saw burned thatch where lightning had hit, and the fire had been suppressed.

The populace was recovering. Shops bustled with afternoon customers, while glaziers fit new glass into storefront windows. Carriages clambered in and out of potholes, widening them and spreading mud about the cobblestones.

She fastened her sword on her saddle, took off her garrison cap and neck guard, stuffed them in a saddlebag, and scratched her head and neck. She loosened the saddle cinch and her horse sighed.

"Come on, Chisel." She jiggled the reins. Side by side, she and the horse trudged along the street, their heads down. Neither of them made an attempt to dodge splashes from the wheels of passing carriages.

The City Guard stables were only five blocks east of the Whitewater Bridge. The stable manager, Horsehead, stood waiting at the gates.

"I thought patrols only lasted an eight-day. You're wearing at least an erin's worth of mud." Horsehead directed his assessment, as usual, toward the horse. "Who knew we'd get such storms in false-spring?"

"I'm fine, thank you. Have you seen Peri today?" Now that she was back, she ached to wrap her arms around her son.

"That rain was something, wasn't it? The Phrenii have been mum about the cause, which has the streets rife with rumors about—" Horsehead cut his ramblings short as her eyes narrowed. "And—ah—Peri's well. Safe and sound. He stopped by today before lessons with his cousins. He looks like he's fitting in just fine. You shouldn't worry about *him*."

She nodded, catching his implication. Her son was adjusting to the sister cities, as opposed to her and Jan. Peri was experiencing a normal Fairday, sitting through the same old routine of afternoon lessons with his cousins, while his father, mother, and matriarch struggled to patch the growing cracks in a marriage contract. She tried not to think about Jan pleading his case with Lady Anja while she was gone on patrol.

Pressing her lips together, she took the tack, saddlebags, and weapons off Chisel and let two young stable hands take him toward the wash rack. Chisel, however, had other plans and dragged the children toward his stall and food. Horsehead motioned to an older apprentice to help with the large gelding.

"Now then, let's have it," she said.

Horsehead bent his head to scratch behind his ear, avoiding her gaze. "Have what?"

"Some news you'd rather not tell me?" She kept her attention on the task of brushing dried mud from her clothing. When he didn't answer, she added, "Wouldn't bad news be better coming from you, than from someone who's less than a friend?"

"Don't know about that." He grunted, perhaps not willing to admit friendship after all those early years as her riding master. Then he dropped the words like an axe, quick and merciful. "Meran-Kolme Erik announced his choice for Deputy Officer of Investigation. It's going to be Jan."

Her hands stopped moving.

"Most of us know you're the one with the right experience. But Erik opened up the appointment and you know how Jan is..."

Yes, she knew how ambitious, competitive, and ruthless Jan could be. "Did he say why he picked Jan?"

"He doesn't have to justify himself to anyone but the captain." Horsehead looked uneasy. "Even though you're one of the best riders I've ever taught, man or woman, you know that Erik prefers to work with men."

"Women number one in twelve within the City Guard."

"But that's not the ratio of *officers*." He grinned. "That's more like, um, ah—"

"One in thirty." She felt deflated. She knew the numbers, as well the low odds of Erik promoting her. "But selecting *Jan*? That's a slap in my face."

"I told you to go into the King's Guard when you could, didn't I? I warned you about the politics in the City Guard. You weren't wining and dining Erik, nor slapping him on the back and buying him drinks, were you?"

She reluctantly had to admit he was right and shook her head. Horsehead seemed relieved, no doubt figuring his unpleasant duty was finished. He leaned over the riding ring fence, ready to gossip. "Who went on this patrol rotation?"

"Bordas commanded, and I was the only City Guard. The others were King's Guard entrants on their first patrol. Rather full of themselves, too." Her voice took on a perfectly clipped upper-city intonation. "Oh, Father was *so* proud of my score—top ten percent—but my cousin didn't make the cut and had to find a position in the City Guard." Her nasal pronouncement made "City Guard" sound worse than street beggar.

He chuckled. "You didn't tell them you had the chance to wear the green and silver."

"They were young twits. All uncontracted males. They'll learn respect soon enough." Draius shrugged.

"They certainly will, once their matriarch starts checking their balls like a bull for stud."

Horsehead's irreverence made her laugh. She could picture every matriarch she'd ever met, even the young Lady Anja, holding a cattle prod. The image seemed so natural.

"By the Horn, they made *me* feel old," she added.

"You're not yet twenty-eight by my feeble reckoning. Wait 'til you get to my age. You'll be ancient in their eyes."

"If my ancestral stars allow." She could only hope to be as active at his age. Horsehead was hale enough to handle and ride horses, but rumors put him at more than a hundred and fifty years. Only matriarchal records could prove otherwise. He had run the City Guard stables and armory for as long as anyone could remember.

This reminded her that she had a powder weapon to return. The King's Law forbade the carrying of powder weapons inside the sister cities, except by the watch. "Here's the musket I was issued. Put it back into the armory, where it'll be more useful."

The long weapon rested against the fence and she handed it over. Its weight required her to use both arms.

He examined the weapon critically, moving the serpentine matchlock back and forth. "Oiled and clean. How many times was it fired?"

"Thirty times, total. I can hit a tree at twenty paces as long as I'm aiming at a forest. Just don't specify a particular tree."

"Next time you'll get one of the new muskets. The smithies have a better boring process and slower burning wicks. Should help the aim but not the kick. They'll still need to be braced."

"Then they can't be used on horseback. Just give me a saber and let me charge; I'll cut down anyone shooting powder at me."

"The sentiment of all cavalry. Glad to see I didn't waste all that training." He laughed and slapped her on the back, which was as sentimental as he got. "Now go. I'll take care of the tack and weapon."

She said goodbye, hefted her personal belongings over her shoulders, and walked toward home and the promise of a wash. Her scalp itched from her long silver hair being bound in braids and pressed down about her head from the garrison cap. The skin on her cheekbones and nose felt raw from wind and rain. The saddlebags weighed heavily on her left shoulder while her sword belt looped over the other. The sheathed sword hit her in the back of her right leg with every other step, no matter how she tried to control her lanky stride. She might have the coin for a carriage, but the thought of taking the bags off her shoulder and rummaging through them on the muddy street kept her slogging forward. She'd attained a numb equilibrium and didn't want to stop.

Four blocks from the main square, she passed the Sea Serpent Pub. It was a respectable establishment catering to varied clientele: King's Guard and council members mingled with City Guard, ship owners, and shopkeepers. It'd been in business for more than four hundred years.

Noise tumbled out of the tavern door. She paused and listened to the joyful racket of those who were looking forward to the end of the eight-day. The spring sunlight felt warm upon her back. She counted the chimes of the clock on Bridge Square and figured she could do with food and drink. Particularly drink, given Horsehead's news that her vocation as a City Guard officer was foundering. Besides, Peri was still in lessons and she didn't want to face the matriarch waiting for her at "home." At least, not yet. She strode into the Sea Serpent.

Rays of sunlight burned through slatted windows, crossing the floor-boards while the corners and upper gallery of the large room receded into comfortable gloom. A few lit pipes made enough haze for the sunlight to become solid in the air. The aroma of the pipe smoke harmonized with the smell of potato soup and the hops and malts used in Tyrran beers and ales. Her mouth watered.

"Draius, b'my ancestors, are you back already?" The familiar roar came from the foot of the stairs. A shape lunged up from a chair. Berin sported an untrimmed beard and short bushy hair, contrary to current Tyrran styles. Not that he'd ever followed fashions for as long as she'd known him.

"Greet's, Draius." He laid a beefy arm around her shoulders. Draius was tall, but she barely reached Berin's chin. "Stinky, dirty, and ready for a beer? I'll have to say that in all the time I've known you, I've never seen you looking worse."

"Thank you. And greetings to you too, Berin."

He laughed in his resonant bass and guided her to his table, helping her stow her items. Berin owned warehouses that sheltered goods sent in and out of the harbor and he frequented the Sea Serpent several times an eight-day. Draius sat down next to Berin's assistant, Wendell, with her back against the gallery stairs.

Wendell greeted her and re-clasped his drink with hands spotted with ink from keeping tallies in the warehouses. As usual, the corner of his mouth was smudged where he held his pen while he worked. Beside Wendell sat a City Guard lieutenant Draius didn't recognize.

"This is Lornis, he's new Guard and I'm buying him a Fairday drink. Always like to be on good terms with the Guard." Berin winked. Down here in Betarr Serasa, "Guard" meant City Guard, not King's Guard.

"Greetings, Lornis." The lieutenant appeared to be about her age. "You're a little old to be entrant, aren't you? Where'd you transfer from?" She wasn't usually so blunt, but her social skills were rusty after an eight-day of rough living.

Lornis's eyebrows rose, but his bright brown eyes held humor. *Honest* humor, because she saw crinkling at the corners, quickly deepening into lines. The edges around Jan's eyes never crinkled, which had been the first hint to realizing all the expressions on his pliable face were carefully molded. In contrast, Lornis had a face of sincere angles and high cheekbones, narrowing to a chin that was almost, but not quite, sharp. He wore his light brown hair pulled back in a clasp, which caused it to fall in a shining cascade down his back to his waist—the classic style of the Tyrran plains tribes, who only braided their hair for battle.

Berin laughed and clapped Lornis on the back. "I told you. Drives straight to the hilt, doesn't she?"

"I'm not a transfer. My grandmother finally admitted I was never meant to be a goldsmith, so she gave her approval to apply to the City Guard. They let me test through to lieutenant." Lornis adjusted his sleeves so the green displayed just enough white through the slashes. His sleeves were new and his collar crackled with starch. His buff jerkin was new and unstained, making Lornis as bright as a new coin.

His attention to his uniform seemed a bit excessive, and what was this option to "test through" to lieutenant? She'd never heard of anyone avoiding erins of training to jump into the Guard officer corps.

"More beer!" Berin roared, startling her. The prospect of smooth, light Tyrran beer distracted her and her stomach started rumbling.

"I'd also like soup." She looked longingly at the empty bowl in front of Lornis.

"And soup," Berin called to the serving girl, his voice cutting through the noise in the common room.

She looked down at her field uniform, stained and bearing no rank, which was customary for patrols. Her uniform sleeves were woven and plain. She wore breeches, acceptable for working women, but they showed considerable wear. She didn't look too bad for having lived in mud for an eight-day, but she felt awkward sitting near the new dandy lieutenant. She rested her hands in her lap, fingers curled to hide her ragged, broken nails. Unfortunately, her light pewter-colored skin, the result of diluted blood from silver-skinned ancestors, wasn't dark enough to hide the dirt embedded into creases and small cuts.

"Was it raining on the eastern plains?" Lornis asked her.

"No." Remembering the maelstrom she saw from her perch at the northern point of the Dibrean Valley, she asked, "Any word on what caused the storm?"

"Oh, everyone has an opinion, ranging from Nherissa rising after five hundred years to steal our blood, our souls, or maybe our silver, to our ancestors punishing us for slighting them." Lornis grinned, his eyes sparkling. "Alms at the reliquaries are up and everyone's singing at evening star-rise, it seems."

She shivered. "What do the Phrenii say? Surely the King asked them?"

"They've kept mum, which doesn't help us sleep better. Of course, we'd have more damage if the Phrenii hadn't conjured up those clever things to keep the river tamed."

"At least the creatures are good for something," Berin muttered. When they looked at him, he added, "They didn't protect the warehouses from the rising canal waters. *We* constructed a shunt to divert the runoff and *we* saved our goods, not the Phrenii."

Draius watched Berin grimace. When she moved back from Betarr Kain, she noticed her old friend had a darker, sharper edge to him. The Fevers had changed everyone, particularly Berin. Now he was prone to uncharacteristic moments of sullenness.

Lornis waved to a tall broad-shouldered Guard officer entering the common room. "Jan! Over here!"

The entering officer had an innocent and slightly rounded face, making him look younger than his real age. Falling over his shoulders in soft waves, his hair had glimmers of gold in the late afternoon light. Unlike Draius, Jan's hair had never tended toward the silver of their Meran ancestors. His dark blue eyes searched the room, ignoring the female heads that turned in admiration.

Lornis saw the expressions of disapproval at the table and bewilderment lined his forehead. Jan approached their table.

"Greetings—Lornis, Wendell, Berin." Jan clapped Wendell on the shoulder. Berin nodded, avoiding eye contact.

Jan turned to his wife last. "How was the patrol rotation?"

"Fine." Conscious of her chapped face and dirty clothes, she took a sip of beer and tried to concentrate on the flavor. She clenched her other hand, still lying in her lap.

Jan's angelic smile changed; he carefully balanced welcome with concern. "I'm glad you're back. Peri's been unhappy lately, having bad dreams."

Her eyes narrowed. From someone else, those simple sentences could be taken at face value. Jan had managed to convey accusation, as if it could only be her fault. *I'm too tired to play "impress the audience."* She still had a few unbroken fingernails, and she dug them into her palm. "Not now, Jan. We can talk later."

"Certainly." Jan's tone and smile were vague. He was up to something, but she couldn't summon the effort to care.

Jan scanned the room for a seat, apparently not willing to sit in the open seat between Lornis and Draius. By the windows, market stall owners were whittling down their earnings by drinking and dicing. At the next table, a councilman notorious for his womanizing worked on his next conquest, a barmaid. Across the common room was a table of mixed guard members, both King and City. Meran-Kolme Erik, Officer in Charge of Investigation, was just sitting down with them. Erik was currently Draius's commander, but not for much longer. If he preferred her husband as his deputy, then she would soon be re-assigned. Again.

Jan said goodbye and like any politic bootlicker, headed straight for his new superior officer.

"I should get home to Peri." Draius started to stand up.

Berin laid his large hand on her shoulder and gently pushed her back into her seat. "Now, now. Last I knew, there wasn't a school-master alive that let his students out early on Fairday." Berin pointed at the clock standing by the fireplace, which marked four hours past noon.

Draius relaxed. Peri was still at afternoon lessons.

"Honestly, Draius, he manipulates you like a puppet!" Berin tried to use a low tone, but everyone at the table heard him. Wendell and Lornis studied their empty glasses.

She pressed her lips together tightly, hoping not to hear the same old refrain. When she was nineteen, her matriarch suggested a contract with the Serasa-Kolme, pairing her with the handsome Jan, of whom she knew very little. Did she have any objections? With her mother gone from the Fevers and her father barely interested in his daughter's future, she turned to cousins and friends for opinions. Almost everyone approved of the Serasa-Kolme, a long-established lineage responsible for the construction of the original walls for Betarr Serin and Betarr Serasa.

Berin, however, was ten years older than her and the lone dissenting voice. "Self-serving, controlling, and a political climber" had been the phrase he'd used to describe Jan. "You're Meran-Viisi, King's lineage, you can do better than him." She went forward with the contract anyway, brushing off his warnings as over-protective.

Berin's refrain now added, "I warned you, didn't I?" At this point, he thought she should petition Lady Anja for dissolution, but he didn't know the depths that Jan's revenge could go.

"Finish your drink." The big hand on her shoulder loosened and patted her back.

So there wasn't going to be a public scolding. Grateful for small favors, she sipped her beer and enjoyed one of her favorite pastimes: watching people. Unfortunately, she could hear Wendell whispering in the new lieutenant's ear. "Another woman in the Guard... no comfort clause... matriarch's his aunt..."

By the Healing Horn, why don't I just hire a crier? In a society of arranged marriages infidelity wasn't unusual. What *was* unusual; she'd just brought a formal complaint against Jan before their matriarch, because no comfort clause was built into their contract. She and Jan had resisted such a clause, against his grandmother's advice. That seemed so long ago, so many deceits ago.

The Sea Serpent's common room was crowded. It was Fairday and everyone was celebrating the last working day of the eight-day. Tomorrow there would be little, if any, business done in Betarr Serasa.

The barmaid plunked down another pitcher. She'd forgotten the soup and Draius opened her mouth to mention that, but the barmaid whirled and waved at someone at the top of the stairs.

Draius looked up over her head to see Councilman Reggis leaning out from the gallery that accessed the upstairs "meeting rooms." Reggis made signs for the barmaid to join him in the third room off the gallery. The barmaid responded with a toss of her blond curls that could mean either yes or no, and she moved to other tables before Draius could mention the soup.

Draius turned her attention to the group of mixed guard members across the room. Sitting next to Jan, Erik put away another dark ale and slapped her husband on the back. A life of excessive drinking was taking a toll; Erik's puffy face displayed a spider web of red veins spreading outward from his nose, and he was only starting his fifties. He'd been promoted from deputy commander to OIC of Investigation a year ago, and so began her own slide into professional darkness.

"Draius, what do you think?" Berin asked.

She jerked her attention back to her own table as Wendell repeated the latest news: the *Horn & Herald* was extorting loyal Tyrrans to boycott Groygan silk to protest their privateering and piracy.

"Only a fool believes the *H&H*. There's no proof the Groygans are financing privateers, or that they're connected to Rhobar." She raised her voice to be heard above the din.

"Groygans can't be trusted. Those skirmishes near the Saamarin—"

Berin's deep voice was sliced apart by the shriek from above, a high shrill sound that went on and on. Babble in the common room died down, overwhelmed. Wendell's face went white and he glanced at Berin, who looked up at the gallery, trying to pinpoint the source of the noise.

Draius sat closest to the foot of the stairs. She grabbed her sheathed sword, took the stairs two at a time and ran toward the barmaid standing at the last door on the gallery. She stopped so suddenly at the doorjamb that Lornis bumped into her. The lieutenant gagged, and Draius gritted her teeth at the smell of blood.

CHAPTER FOUR

Third Fairday, Erin Two, T.Y. 1471

Powerful men make fatal misjudgments because they underestimate everyone but themselves. The traitor had realized his deadly mistake, when he first felt the drug.

"Why?" he whispered as he lost control of his cup. Wine soaked his vest and the hammered goblet ended up on the floor planks, lightly ringing as it rolled from side to side.

I called my apprentice to catch him because I alone couldn't handle his weight. Then, after we moved him between rooms, I needed help to lay him out. The boy blanched when I drove nails to fix his hands and feet to the floor.

"Don't worry, he's already dead," I lied. There was no need to expose Nherissa's secrets to my apprentice. "And there's so much noise below, no one can hear. Go stand watch at the window."

After the boy left the room, I answered the traitor's question. I leaned down to his ear and whispered, "We know you sold the lodestone to the Groygans; we've checked on the ship. Now you're our next experiment in Nherissa's art."

A quiver was his only possible response. The combination of drugs I'd used had paralyzed him and started slowing his breath and heart. I opened his vest and shirt and made my first cut, according to the instructions I'd read. Since I'd planned everything and rehearsed each surgical procedure,

I barely had time to appreciate the results before we were out of the room and down the ladder.

I can savor the details now. An hour later, my hands still tingle from the sensuality of the procedure. There was beauty in the sharp blade as it sliced into his body, exploring deeper and deeper. Although the heart had stopped, the warm blood welled up like velvet and was nearly sufficient to complete the rite. I could sense the powerful death magic as I captured it within the circle and focused it into the amulets. The feeling became arousing, almost unbearable so, as the flesh was removed.

Beyond the magic, I discovered I also delight in danger. I refer not to the necromantic rite, which has its own risks if the power isn't directed correctly, but of performing such a rite over the heads of the Tyrran Guard. While those arrogant members drank and ate with others who hold up their lineal names like shields, a nunetton (but *forgotten* and *nameless* by my own choice) killed someone they were honor-bound to protect.

CHAPTER FIVE

Insubordination

We've entered the age of the scientific method, so I ask what need has mankind for magic? The Society for Restoration of Sorcery appeals only to romantic fools and I, for one, think there is no place for magic in this world. Even if the King can control the Phrenii, they are no longer needed.

[Editor's note: The views expressed by Rista are not the views of this paper, which expresses gratitude to the Phrenii for their protection during the recent floods.]

—*Khalna-Nelja Rista, in Letters to the Editor, The Horn & Herald, Third Fairday, Erin Two, T.Y. 1471*

The barmaid kept shrieking and Draius had to grab her by the shoulders. She hiccuped and started breathing with deep, wrenching gasps while her eyes stayed wide. Looking bewildered, she held out a key.

"Was the room locked?" Draius asked, taking the key from her limp hand.

The woman's mouth worked, but nothing came out.

"Get a statement, written and signed, if you can." Draius handed Lornis the key and pushed the woman toward him. The barmaid latched onto Lornis and, to his credit, he efficiently hustled her into the next room.

Draius looked over her shoulder and saw an overwhelming mass of people coming up the stairs to the gallery. A few of the quicker patrons had already made it to the doorway where she stood and most turned away, retching.

She had developed a strong stomach during her work with the Office of Investigation, but she'd never seen so much blood in one place. Meran-Nelja Reggis, popular member of the King's Council, had been nailed to the floor by his hands and feet, and eviscerated. Strange symbols were drawn with blood on the floorboards and walls. With so much of his inner torso spread about and that amount of blood loss, he couldn't still be alive. There was no possibility of phrenic healing.

With no more time to examine the room, she dealt with the surge of people pushing toward her. She drew her sword and held it high, causing those at the front of the crowd to scramble backward.

"You!" She grabbed a market stall owner she recognized. "Go to City Guard Headquarters at Number Ten High Cerinas Street. Tell the desk to send the watch to the Sea Serpent. Go!"

She raised her voice to be heard above the din. "This is Guard business now, people. I want all of you to go downstairs and wait, because you may be questioned."

Prodding, yelling, and gesturing with her sword started turning back some of the clientele. The creaking of the gallery from the weight of the crowd convinced others they would be safer downstairs. As people began moving back down the staircase, she saw Jan and Erik wading toward her against the current. When they reached her, she was giving instructions to Mainos, manager of the Sea Serpent, regarding the sealing of the room. Erik held onto Jan's shoulder and swayed.

"I'll give the orders here, Draius. You're overstepping your authority," he said.

"The room's secured, ser. Did you post someone at the exits to keep all these witnesses contained?" She looked down at the common area to avoid facing Erik. Below her was a boiling mass of people and she couldn't see the doors.

Erik drew a deep breath; his face became redder and his voice more pompous and slurred. "This is why you're not promotable, Draius. You have no sense for the conventions of rank. It's *your* place to take care of such details."

She glanced at her husband standing behind Erik. As the incoming deputy, this was Jan's responsibility. His eyes slid away and wouldn't meet hers. No help was coming from him. She leaned toward Erik and said, in as low a tone as she could manage, "Have you had too much to drink, ser? The captain himself will be arriving soon, considering who's in that room. Go home, and I'll have all the details you'll need tomorrow."

"You want me to leave so you get more time with the captain? At my expense, no doubt." Erik enunciated his words.

Draius was grimly amused. Erik worried about schemes to take his position as OIC and his paranoia always focused on her. Now he'd given the deputy commander position to Jan, who had the natural male inclination toward politics and the talent to flatter and manipulate. If Erik worried about subordinates climbing over him, then he'd just given his worst threat a perfect position.

"Ser, maybe she's right. If the captain is coming and you're not in top shape, Draius can manage the scene." Jan put exactly the right nuances in his words, now appearing to only reluctantly support his wife.

"I'm quite sensible and *I* haven't just come off patrol!" Erik glared at her.

She returned the glare. Caustic comments fought to get out of her mouth. When she finally spoke, though, her tone was cool. "Commander, a member of the King's Council is dead and you have a possible witness in the next room, but are you sober enough to question her?"

As Erik's face turned purple, she knew she'd made a mistake.

"Curse you with phrenic madness!" Erik shouted, spittle flying. "If you don't leave right now, Draius, I'll have you thrown out! Be assured that I'll be filing insubordination charges tomorrow."

"Fine. Good evening to you, ser." She punctuated her words with the whine of sheathing her sword.

She hoped Erik saw his ale a second time when he went into that room. She pushed through the crowd on the stairs and on the bottom floor. As she suspected, no one had been posted to control the exits. Her saddlebags had been trampled and shoved under the table. She didn't know where Berin and Wendell had gone, or the multitude of witnesses who were inside the tavern at the time the body was discovered.

Outside the Sea Serpent, she took deep breaths of fresh air. She hadn't realized how pervading that cloying metallic scent had been, sticking at the back of her throat like bad food. And there'd been too much blood—

"Draius, wait!"

Jan had followed her out of the pub. She looked up and mentally asked her ancestors, now visible in the evening stars, for patience.

"What is it? Shouldn't you be inside, showing Erik what kind of deputy you'll make?"

"He'll be fine. Besides, I won't be deputy until the new erin begins on Markday. Technically, I have no authority."

"Erik should go home and sleep it off. He's going to trip right over his own balls, and in front—" She circled to her right, and Jan turned with her so that the light from the tavern windows lit his carefully expressionless face. He was taller and she had to look up to meet his eyes.

"You're *hoping* he'll mess up in front of Captain Rhaffus," she added.

She was rarely surprised by his maneuvers any more. City Guard and King's Guard positions were stepping-stones to political positions, which was why there were few women in the Guard. After all, "women have the mind for business, while men have the passion for politics," went the saying. Her husband, however, could be as cold and reasoning as any matriarch when planning his career moves.

"Commander Erik's career is in his own hands, not mine," he said.

"A deputy should ensure his commander doesn't humiliate himself. Afterward, the commander is grateful and indebted to the deputy. Isn't that how the game is played?" She'd given up on playing at politics. Instead, she worked as efficiently as possible with the hope of pleasing her commander, but all she managed to do was antagonize Erik. In the past year, he'd taken her off every case in Investigation and changed her tasks to drudgery that rarely impacted their duties. This wasn't the first time he'd ordered her away from an investigative scene, but they'd never before ended up in public argument.

"Erik's focus is on your insubordination. You made a mistake by losing your temper."

"Which you'll never let Erik forget. Is that what you wanted to tell me?" She suddenly felt exhausted. The surge of energy from finding the councilman's body had drained away.

"No. I have a request for my wife." Jan came closer and raised his hand to gently stroke her along her jaw line. It was an intimate gesture, from another time when she believed his gestures were spontaneous. Now she knew the gesture was calculated. *Was he ever honestly attracted to me?* Unwilling as her thoughts were, her body still responded and she was repulsed.

"Yes?" She stepped backward and out of his reach.

His hand dropped. "I'm asking you to withdraw your complaint, for your sake and for Peri's. You're only marking yourself as a troublemaker, and our son as well."

"Has Lady Anja said that?" She watched his face carefully.

"She's my aunt, I know her. She'll do anything to keep our son."

Draius was relieved. By the way he sidestepped her question, she knew nothing had changed while she was gone. His statement about Peri was true: no matriarch would willingly give up children to another lineage, not with the dwindling Tyrran birth rate. However, he'd also just told her that Lady Anja hadn't rejected her formal complaint as trivial.

She shouldn't be talking with him right now, not when she was tired. Jan lived by controlling others. He influenced his fellow Guard members to further his career, he easily swayed the emotions of his son and wife, and he'd even made the mistake of trying to manipulate a matriarch. She still remembered his face when he realized he couldn't influence Lady Anja. He might have occupied a special place in his grandmother's heart when she was matriarch of the Serasa-Kolme, but this was not the case with his aunt.

"Go back inside. Erik needs your help controlling the rabble." She turned on her heel and left.

...

"I know Groygan eyes when I see them," Skuva said, his voice sullen and defensive.

Haversar watched the boy silently. He didn't like Skuva's tone, but he had to make allowances. Even *his* gut twisted at the bruises on Skuva's head, neck, arms, and legs. The left side of Skuva's face had swelled to black, purple, and barely recognizable. This evening, he'd been beaten until unconscious, then left like a bundle of trash in an alley in Betarr Serin, the upper city. Haversar's men had found Skuva, and brought him "home" to the bolthole near the Betarr Serasa docks, where Haversar ran his organization.

He flicked his fingers, and someone hurried to put a wet cloth on the boy's face and tend his wounds. Everyone relaxed. Skuva's knees gave way as he was helped into a chair. He was a rarity: a true nunetton, a child who had slipped through the grasp of the matriarchs and their records, to be raised anonymously on the streets by Haversar.

"Why did you choose this mark?" Haversar asked Skuva.

"Dapper enough to carry gold, and walking like a gentleman who'd tipped back too much drink." Late on Fairday evening, Skuva made the most obvious conclusion. He'd earned the elite position of working the streets of Betarr Serin with his light touch and quick fingers.

"What happened then?"

"I followed him a couple blocks, then got close enough to cut the strings on his purse." Skuva gulped. "He was quick as a cat. Grabbed me by the collar and arm, so I couldn't twist away."

"Did he say anything? Did he have an accent?" Haversar asked.

"He said, 'What ho, boy,' and he sounded Tyrran as you or me. Then his hood fell back. He might have been Tyrran, 'cept his eyes. They shone bright in the gaslight." Skuva tried to shake his head, and winced.

Haversar believed Skuva, even though there weren't more than ten Groygans inside the sister cities. Skuva was only twelve, and looked even younger because of his size—a Tyrran couldn't hurt a child like that. An outraged Tyrran gentleman would have done no more than drag Skuva to the nearest watch post or give the boy a lecture; the offended adult thought their words could change the wayward child. Haversar had taught Skuva to listen respectfully and promise to set his ways straight. The boy took his training seriously because he couldn't get afternoon lessons or apprenticeships; only Haversar could provide him with a future.

"So, at that point, he knew you'd outed him as Groygan?" Haversar asked.

"Yes, 'cause I tried to get away. His grip turned to iron and his face—well, he got serious. He pulled me into the alley and started hitting me. I couldn't do nothing 'bout it, I swear by the Horn. He was too strong."

"Did he say anything else?"

Skuva's eyes went wide as he remembered, and one of his pupils appeared larger than the other. "Something 'bout taking a message."

Haversar understood. He waved at the two people who were trying to apply rudimentary first aid to Skuva. "Let him rest, but watch him. If he worsens, drop him off at the Betarra Hospital."

There was murmured surprise at his words, but he frowned back and eyes dropped. He motioned Johtu over to his side. "Something's afoot at the Groygan embassy, and we've been warned to back off."

"Why? What have we done to the Groygans?" Johtu might be a little slow, but this time he'd gotten to the crux as fast as Haversar.

"I'm not sure. Perhaps we've seen something we shouldn't. Talk to everyone assigned to Betarr Serin yesterday. See if anything strange—stranger than normal—has been happening." Haversar chose the people he placed in the upper city carefully, to avoid drawing unwanted attention. The King and his counselors lived up there, but more importantly, so did the matriarchs of the most powerful lineages in Tyrra. He stepped lightly around matriarchs, because they had the resources to put him out of business if he became too much of a nuisance.

"Where, do you suppose, were the Phrenii? They wouldn't let this happen."

"You're being Tyrran, assuming the boy is under their protection. *You* wouldn't take the chance that they'd be close enough to sense his distress." Yet another reason Haversar believed a *Groygan* had attacked Skuva. A Tyrran adult wouldn't chance the madness they'd suffer if the Phrenii found them hurting a child.

"Well, the boy's lucky he didn't get his throat cut." Johtu fingered his own knife hanging on his belt.

There it was again, the little twisting in Haversar's gut. He was definitely too invested in Skuva. After a deep breath, he said, "Keep a quiet eye on the Groygan embassy. I want to know when they're going in and out, and how—although I expect all the tunnels have been blocked."

Johtu nodded, and left to disseminate orders. Folklore said the Betarr Serin houses occupied by the matriarchs had entrances to ancient tunnels, reputedly running throughout the plateau. At one time, these tunnels supported intrigue and surreptitious meetings between lineages. Supposedly there was no way out of the upper city or off the plateau through the tunnels, but Haversar made no assumptions. He wondered whether he should pass Jan any advice, perhaps a warning; did these hunches qualify as payment of life-debt? No, this was purely *personal* right now.

•••

Draius filed a report with the watch, so it was long after supper hour when she quietly let herself into the house. Jan's aunt Anja, who became matriarch of the Serasa-Kolme after his grandmother started her path to the Stars, owned this stately bluestone house with marble architrave about the main door and front windows. The Serasa-Kolme also had a house up in Betarr Serin, but the new matriarch preferred to stay in Betarr Serasa, loaning the upper-city house to Jan's sister.

When she married, Draius changed her lineal name to Serasa-Kolme, so now Lady Serasa-Kolme Anja alone considered the complaint of Jan's infidelity. Draius hadn't met Anja before she took the chance of exposing her marital problems. Their original contract was a standard, simple one that didn't allow for infidelity. At this point, Jan probably regretted not getting the additional clauses that allowed one to seek comfort outside the marriage, sometimes needed to make arranged marriages bearable.

Anja was new to her position, but had been trained well. The matriarch needed to know how Jan felt toward his son, and whether there was a chance for more children from Jan and Draius. Anja had listened intently to the story and then asked, "Does Jan fulfill his duties as father and husband?"

"Peri adores his father, and Jan's very attentive." Draius could be confident about this, even if she no longer knew whether Jan could *love* anyone.

The matriarch's questions became pointed and persistent, as well as embarrassing. "Do you still share a bed? Do you allow him to touch you?"

She'd flushed and stammered, and the truth came out. By the time she and Jan returned from Betarr Kain, they rarely slept together. Jan accused her of changing, becoming colder. His argument became self-fulfilling as he sought discrete dalliances, and she withdrew further.

But the last affair, after they came back to the sister cities, was different. It was *public*, and it was *serious*—Draius was aghast to learn how long he'd been seeing Netta and how open they'd been. She was humiliated and furious. When she first spoke to Lady Anja about it, she wanted retribution and satisfaction for her wounded pride. Matriarchs often meted out punishment: the term was "matriarchal justice for lineal matters."

"Any action I take must be for the good of the family line. The *children*. So what can I do to mend your relationship?" Anja asked. "What could happen to allow Jan back in your bed?"

Draius had no answer. Matriarchal theory stated that children rarely resulted from unwilling or unhappy women. Tyrran women lived in the paradoxical world of arranged marriages where they were supposed to be content and satisfied. With the falling birth rate since the Fevers, it was no wonder that more contracts had comfort clauses and the taking of lovers had become common.

Anja decided to see if time could shrink the chasms between Draius and Jan. Her decisions were swift: Draius and Peri would move in with Anja, while Jan would live separately and without his lineal stipend. Jan had been livid and for once, he couldn't hide his anger. But Anja stood firm. Since he couldn't afford to rent a decent house with only his Guard salary and he wasn't on good terms with his sister, Jan took officer rooms at the barracks rather than lease accommodations.

Draius quietly closed the large front door. This was a beautiful house, but after an erin it still didn't feel like home. Living under Anja's scrutiny made her uncomfortable. She suspected Anja wanted some decisions from her, but she felt ambivalent, rudderless and, worst of all, *responsible*. Time had frozen—everyone became motionless while they looked to her—as if she had the answers! So she had finally upped the stakes and made the complaint formal. She'd pushed her letter under Lady Anja's parlor door when she'd departed for patrol duty, so early in the morning that no one else stirred within the house.

"You're late," Anja said, coming down the stairs. "Have you eaten? I can rouse Nin. She put some lamb aside for left-over."

Lady Serasa-Kolme Anja was young for a matriarch. She appeared to be near Draius's age and strangely, she was unmarried. Her high cheekbones and sharply sculpted nose were typical Tyrran. Like Jan, her eyes were unusually dark blue, but her silver-blond hair and eyebrows were definitely Meran, and so light they looked white in the lamplight. She had the same Serasa-Kolme inscrutability as Jan, but not the ability for displaying a mask of contrived emotion. Anja was dressed in her bedclothes, her hair tied back for the night. The lamp she carried threw her shadow back up the stairs to the second floor.

"No, please don't bother. I lost my appetite at the Sea Serpent."

"I heard the news from the crier. It's all over town," Anja said. "And a runner stopped by with a message from Captain Rhaffus. You're to report to him tomorrow."

On Ringday? Draius wearily nodded. She should have the day off. Instead, she'd be paying for this evening's fit of temper and facing Erik's insubordination charges. She pushed her dark thoughts aside and asked, "Is Peri in bed?"

"Yes, although he wanted to stay up for you. But Fairday or no, I want him in bed at a regular hour."

"I spoke with Jan tonight. What has he been saying to Peri—and to what purpose?" The words came out harsher than Draius intended.

"I think he was talking about how you could be reunited. Peri became apprehensive, it seemed." Anja made no attempt to qualify Jan's secondary, and subtler, motives. Her own expression was impassive as she paused, searching Draius's face in the lamplight.

When Draius didn't reply, Anja lifted her shoulders in a shrug. "I won't keep him from his son. Jan has his parental rights, as do you."

Her jaw was rigid with anger, but Draius managed a polite goodnight. After she stepped past the matriarch she realized that neither of them had mentioned the written complaint. She went to Peri's room and, as usual, the boy was sleeping light.

"Ma?" The silver-blond head turned.

"I'm back, Peri. How ya doing?" She hugged him. "How was your eight-day?"

"Afternoon lessons have been so boring, I'm starting angles and calculations. Yesterday, I followed the unicorn—"

"Where'd you learn that word?"

"Ilke said it." His gray eyes went wide. Peri's cousin Ilke was precocious and bossy for nine years, but then, Draius had been the same at that age. *Before the Fevers.*

"Well, that's a vulgar word. Ilke shouldn't use that word for a phrenic element. They're 'the Phrenii' and they're not individuals."

"They have names—we were with Dahni."

"Their names are only for our convenience. Did you touch it?" A shadow passed over her heart. When would he be too old?

"Sure. Dahni showed us the northwest canal."

"Don't *ever* touch them if you don't feel like it." Of course, adult warnings weren't necessary; everyone knew when he or she shouldn't touch the Phrenii any more.

"I won't." He leaned against her for a few moments and she thought he had gone back to sleep. She marveled at his seven-year-old body: one moment he was awake and the next he was asleep.

He wasn't asleep. "Da came to visit every morning."

"I heard."

"He says maybe we should move back to Betarr Kain. Then everything will be alright." Peri ended with a lilt of question. He hadn't been happy in Betarr Kain, where there were fewer children his age and only one Serasa-Kolme cousin, a much older boy.

"This doesn't have anything to do with where we live."

"But you came back here because of *me*—" Tears formed in her son's eyes.

"Shush. Your Da and me—it has nothing to do with you or moving back to the sister cities." She put a finger on his lips, while cold rage built into a rock of ice in her chest. Jan wasn't above letting his own son feel guilty about his estrangement, particularly when he knew Draius would be compelled to step in and take the blame. *Because it's my fault, isn't it? I had to bring it up with Lady Anja, and I was so angry that I wanted to punish Jan. Now he's pushing back on all fronts.*

Peri didn't say anything. He turned away, his body tense. He didn't believe her empty assurances. Spending a moment in thought, she realized that Jan hadn't noticed how happy Peri became after they'd moved here.

"Betarr Kain isn't a fun place to grow up. After all, there was only your Da and me and you and cousin Jenni and her son. That's not a *family*, is it?" She poked him lightly in the side to get a response.

He snorted. "I suppose not."

"No, because you should grow up within the Serasa-Kolme. Think of all the things that Lady Anja and the sister cities can provide. The Pettaja tutor for you and your cousins. Your classroom. The canals. And we have the Serasa-Kolme offices and houses, as well as more horses and coaches—"

"And the markets. And Nin. She's such a good cook." Peri turned back, his expression lighter.

She started stroking his head. "Don't forget the security of the Phrenii. Even though Jahri or Famri visited Betarr Kain once in a while, we always have two elements in the cities. Honestly, don't you like it here better?"

"Sure, but Da—"

"Your Da is angry with me, and *only* me. We're having grown-up problems—which makes for really boring arguments, believe me."

"He's angry with Lady Anja, too. About his stipend." Peri yawned, drifting into sleep.

Her eyebrows rose. Perhaps she'd underestimated her son, although this could be the result of Peri having his older cousins about him. The vision of bossy, lanky Ilke, standing a head taller than Peri, made Draius remember her young years in the cities, running after the Phrenii with her Meran-Viisi cousins. She'd spent her afternoon lessons with two future kings and hadn't they gossiped about the marriages and affairs of older cousins and parents? But that was too long ago. Her memories felt strangely remote, like they'd happened to a different Draius.

She kept stroking his head until he fell asleep. After kissing his forehead and inhaling the scent of his hair, she left for her room.

She hoped she wouldn't toss about and relive the hurtful words she and Jan flung at each other. But after she snuggled into the featherbed, she dreamed about the Sea Serpent. Repeatedly, she ran down the gallery toward that bloody room, only to be whisked to the end of the gallery and run its length again.

CHAPTER SIX

Third Ringday, Erin Two, T.Y. 1471

U nfortunately, every step we take to save our tattered plans takes us deeper. We've gone past the point of no return.

I rousted my apprentice again. The clock rang three hours past midnight, when only Star Watchers were awake as they plot their precise maps of our ancestors. My employer knew where the double-dealing Sareenian ship owner could be found, and he dictated the time.

We were betrayed for Groygan gold, but what did it buy? We suspect the lodestone has gone beyond anyone's control, and we will confirm this with the Sareenian. If I were a superstitious sort, I might believe our bad luck is due to a malevolent spell but my charms, unsophisticated but functional, indicate we've not been touched by any type of magic.

Yet bad luck hounds us. Our inept City Guard didn't find the carefully planted evidence that proves Reggis a traitor and implicates the Groygans. We cannot turn the ship around, we cannot protect her from pirates, and we cannot prevent storms from hounding her—although we figure they become milder the further away from the Phrenii she sails. Most worrisome of all, is her valuable cargo still sound? Perhaps the ship owner can tell us more.

For me, this long night held even more disappointment. The ecstasy from the councilman's death didn't carry through to my next experiment. Alone, as my apprentice slept, I dared to try activating it: the shard of the Kaskea that should give me entry to the Void and the secrets of the Phrenii. After channeling such power this evening, I thought my blood might carry enough magic to cause an effect. Nothing happened. The small shard lay quiescent, covered with drops of my blood and mocking me, proving my common lineage better than any matriarch. I wrapped and hid it under the floorboards again, trying to put it out of my mind.

I busied myself with checking my blades and tools in the valise. I heard my apprentice struggling into his coat, already tight across his growing shoulders.

"Come along, we've work to do," I called, as I snapped the valise shut.

CHAPTER SEVEN

The Office of Investigation

*COUNCILMAN MERAN–NELJA REGGIS BIZARRELY BUTCH-
ERED! IS MAGICAL MURDER TOO MUCH FOR OUR BUNGLING
CITY GUARD?*

Chaos reigned last night at the Sea Serpent where Councilman
Reggis was found brutally murdered. City Guard responded immediately, but didn't control the ensuing confusion as looting and damage
occurred in the Sea Serpent. City Guard Officer Meran-Kolme Erik admitted he was baffled (perhaps by the ale, being far into his cups?) He
couldn't explain how the councilman was disemboweled in a room with
a locked door and no windows...

—*The Horn & Herald, Third Ringday, Erin Two, T.Y. 1471*

O n any other Ringday the City Guard Headquarters would be quiet
and minimally manned, but this morning it bustled with activity.
Several watchmen sat at the front desk and the heavy oak benches were
filled with bleary-eyed people. The lucky ones had staked out enough
room on their bench to lie down, while others slept in sitting positions.

Looking them over, Draius recognized faces and realized the watch
was still collecting statements from the Sea Serpent's clientele. The scents
of stale beer and unwashed bodies drifted about. She walked past the desk
and down the cool stone hallway to the captain's office.

"Take a seat, Draius," said Rhaffus, the captain of the City Guard. He was a large man, filling the room with his presence. His hair had been dark at one time, but now it mingled with white and was cut to rest upon his shoulders, as dictated by current fashion. He had a precisely trimmed mustache and beard on his lined face, a face that indicated many hard years of service. It was impossible to tell whether he had spent a sleepless night, but she suspected he had.

The gaslight hissed comfortably and kept the office bright, and the small stove in the corner threw off enough heat to warm the stone room. Captain Rhaffus sat at his desk, his Guard officer sword and scabbard hung on the wall behind him.

The only other person in the room was Lornis, the new lieutenant, sitting quietly and writing. One hand rubbed his impeccably trimmed beard, and again, his uniform was spotless. She glanced down at her own and breathed deeply with relief. Someone had pressed her sleeves and brushed her jerkin. She couldn't measure up to the dandy Lornis, but she was presentable; Anja's household staff must have ensured this.

"I fired Erik last night," Rhaffus said. "He's no longer Officer in Charge of Investigation."

The news lifted a weight from her, but she wasn't too surprised. Jan's plans were unfolding faster than she expected, but at least she needn't worry about insubordination charges.

"I have no problem with my officers having a drink, but I expect them to be competent when called to duty. At the least, he could have turned the matter over to other officers. Instead, he let a drunken crowd trample the evidence!"

"Yes, ser." She pictured Jan explaining to the captain, "I suggested Commander Erik should go home, ser, but he insisted on staying." This had worked out well for Jan.

"Take a look at the greeting I had this morning." Rhaffus tossed a folded *Horn & Herald* at her.

Draius opened the sheet that supposedly provided Tyrrans with the most relevant information from the sister cities. The smell of the ink was strong, so she handled it gingerly.

"COUNCILMAN MERAN-NELJA REGGIS BIZARRELY BUTCH-ERED," screamed the top headline. She skimmed through the text until the end, where she read aloud, "Could this foul play be magical, as proposed by the Society for the Restoration of Sorcery? Even the City Guard won't rule out this possibility!"

She snorted and put aside the flier. "Magical murder? Bungling Guard? Too bad the crass sensationalism doesn't hide our own, er, inefficiency."

"You mean *incompetence*, don't you? This time, Erik went beyond embarrassing his Meran-Kolme ancestors. The Guard has been humiliated in front of King and country!" Rhaffus slammed his large hand down upon his desk with a loud smack. Both she and Lornis jerked in surprise.

"I've sent a message to Andreas, telling him he's gone too far. Using this murder to advance his ridiculous society is unethical and he'll only hamper our investigation."

Andreas, the editor of the *H&H*, was known for his lack of taste and tact, as well as his unending quest for "truth." Only an edict from the King could stop him, as some embarrassed King's Council members discovered. Rhaffus considered Andreas a thorn in the side of the King's Law.

"Too bad his only competition is *The Recorder*." Lornis referred to the other publication in the sister cities, which printed a dry rendering of births, deaths, marriage contracts, import and export shipments, production figures, and currency rates. *The Recorder* was published once an eight-day, as opposed to the daily *H&H*.

Although many Tyrrans disapproved of Andreas's operation, the *H&H* was widely read and no one volunteered to produce a different daily paper. Rumor said Andreas couldn't cover his costs printing the *H&H* and while this might be a fine hobby for a gentleman with means, Draius didn't think a daily publication could ever turn a profit.

"There's nothing to be done about what Andreas prints, Captain, unless you petition a magistrate," she said. "If you're patient, he'll pauper himself and close down. Surely you didn't call me in on Ringday morning to talk about the *H&H*."

"Of course not. Since they mucked up the scene before I arrived, I'd like you to recall everything you saw in the room."

"I put in a summary report—"

"I need a *picture* of the crime scene. Now." Rhaffus picked up his pen, expectant.

Having done this before, when Rhaffus was only a commander and the OIC of Investigation, Draius closed her eyes and began.

"Councilman Reggis is lying across the center of the room, his feet pointing toward the door. His hands and feet are pinned to the floor with nails and there's a deep incision lengthwise down his abdomen. He's been disemboweled, and his fingers cut off. I didn't see those separated members anywhere. There's so much blood." She swallowed. "Blood on the floor and walls. Too much blood for one man, it seems."

"You're right. We've found something that looks like pig hair in the blood on the walls. Go on."

"A circle of blood is painted around the body, with filled circles at each hand and foot. A sign is drawn in blood on the wall facing the door, so it aligns over the head of the body."

"Was this it?" Rhaffus held up a hand-drawn diagram of concentric circles with a scribed letter "N" in the center. He laid it in front of her, with a pen.

"I think there was more of a tail on the 'N' at the bottom, so that it entwined with the inner circle." After leaning forward to adjust the diagram, she sat back and closed her eyes again.

"There's a low table to the right of the body. On it is arranged, from left to right: a change purse, a stoppered glass vial with something black in it, a similar vial with something white in it, and two folded pieces of parchment. A chair against the right wall has a folded cloak on it, the same color as the cloak he was wearing in the common room. On the floor are scattered coins."

"How many?"

"Hmm." Her eyes stayed closed. "I see six halves and two tenths, but the blood could be covering more."

"Most of that evidence disappeared." The captain's voice was grim. "The vials were found on the floor, cracked, but with their contents intact. The coins, change-purse, and documents, if they were documents, are gone. When I reached the Sea Serpent, Erik was puking on the gallery floor, the crowd had moved the body downstairs, and the staff was cleaning up the room. Can you believe it?"

Captain Rhaffus barged on, not expecting an answer. "Reggis must have been knocked out with a quick-acting poison prior to his death, because no one heard screams. He was unconscious or deceased by the time they started cutting him up—and they had little more than half an hour to do their butchering. Do you remember anything more, Draius?"

After a pause, she shook her head and opened her eyes. "I only had a few seconds to look about."

Lornis stared at her open-mouthed, while Rhaffus laughed. "What did I tell you, Lieutenant? A memory that paints a picture."

Lornis looked down at his notes. "From my own—inadequate—memory, I've written down what I saw and what the barmaid told me. She claimed she was meeting Reggis after her shift and used the key he gave her to get into the locked room. She insisted, multiple times, that this was a tryst of the heart and no money was involved."

"When did you last see the councilman alive, Draius?" asked Rhaffus.

She pictured Councilman Reggis at the top of the stairs, leaning over the balustrade and gesturing to the barmaid, pointing to the *third* room!

"Ser!" She sat straight up in her chair. "You've got to examine the third room on the gallery. He intended to meet the girl in that room, yet we found his body in the *fourth* room."

Captain Rhaffus stood up and shouted for his aide, who appeared at the door. Rhaffus gave him orders to seal off the whole gallery of rooms at the Sea Serpent.

"I never thought to ask *where* she expected to meet the councilman. I figured their appointment was in the room where his body was found." Lornis made another note.

"By now there won't be anything left to find." Rhaffus cursed Erik, mumbling, but clearly enough for her to hear. He stomped back to his desk and sat down, making the chair creak. "I didn't call you here solely to get your view of the room. I'm offering you Officer in Charge of Investigation."

She was speechless.

"You've earned the position," Rhaffus said. "You've got the experience. I made a mistake when I promoted Erik, by not going with my instinct—which says you're the one for this job."

"But I'm only a lieutenant commander." Full commanders usually filled Officer in Charge (OIC) positions.

"Well, this case could bring an early promotion for you. Or, it could bring an early end to your career." The captain's eyes glinted.

Draius caught the implication as well as the threat, but the deputy position worried her more. Erik had already selected Jan and after seeing him climb over most of his commanders, she didn't know if she could work with him. Trying to find another name, of *any* other suitable candidate, she mentally ticked off the roster of Guard officers in Betarr Serasa. Unfortunately, with Erik gone, the only officers left with any investigative experience were Captain Rhaffus and herself.

Using a neutral tone, she asked, "Will Jan still be deputy?"

"No, I'm moving Jan to Deputy of City Defense. After all, he's Serasa-Kolme, and they built most of our city walls."

Jan wouldn't be penalized, since that was a lateral move, but he wouldn't be grateful. He'd obviously hoped to move into OIC of Investigation, which was a crucial position for career advancement. Every captain of the City Guard had done a stint as OIC of Investigation, including the one sitting before her. In fact, Rhaffus had gone straight to the captaincy from it.

"What do you say, Draius?"

She hesitated. She'd always let her career be subordinate to Jan's. She'd been offered a position in the King's Guard immediately after her marriage to Jan, but he had to take a post with the Betarr Kain City Guard. She moved with him to Betarr Kain, where Peri was born. When Peri was old enough for afternoon lessons, Jan managed to get a post in Betarr Serasa. Once they'd moved back to the sister cities she didn't reapply to the King's Guard, which would mean continual patrols outside the sister cities, and always being away from her son and her husband. Instead, she took work with the City Guard in the Office of Budget and Analysis, which was considered a dead-end position.

From Budget she quickly moved to Investigation, which was a rewarding job under Rhaffus. When Rhaffus was promoted and replaced by Erik, however, the Office of Investigation became a place of drudgery. Now she was being rewarded with the offer of a good position, one that promised advancement in the Guard. If she accepted, the bad news was that every ambitious officer, including Jan, would be angling to replace her. To stay in this position, she'd have to be politically astute and dodge any negative publicity—Erik being the cautionary example.

"Well? You shouldn't turn this down in favor of Jan," Rhaffus added. "In my opinion, he's just not right for this position. If you don't accept, I'll find a different officer."

Rhaffus couldn't know the reason she hesitated; she knew what Jan was capable of when he felt wronged. She remembered the officer in the Betarr Kain Guard whom he felt had been promoted, unfairly, ahead of him. He'd methodically ruined the man, exploiting a gambling weakness until his rival resigned in disgrace and killed himself. Jan never expressed any remorse, even when she confronted him, and she'd never mentioned it to anyone. She wondered if that was all that held them together: his confidence in her discretion, and her obligation to strengthen his conscience. She took a deep breath.

"I'll take the position," she said. *I can't live in fear of my own husband. What can he do to me that he hasn't done already?* She felt a surge of satisfaction, but whether it came from the retribution against Jan or from honest fulfillment, she didn't know.

"Good! I'm going to try Lornis here as your deputy. You'll have two watchmen and a clerk, although you'll share the clerk with the Offices of Budget and Analysis."

She glanced over at Lornis who was, even at his age, an inexperienced lieutenant. "Ah, ser?"

"Yes?" Rhaffus was looking down at his notes, obviously finished with their discussion.

"Can we talk about my staff, ser? Perhaps in private?" Out of the corner of her eye, she saw Lornis look down and flush. Rhaffus frowned, but she plowed onward, "Shouldn't I have a more experienced staff? The Councilman's murder is high priority."

"I'm giving you Ponteva, who has plenty of experience. As for Lornis, I'm sure you'll find him more than adequate." The captain's tone sounded final.

"Yes, ser. Thank you."

"Make the most of this opportunity, Draius, and don't disappoint me. This has received Meran-Viisi attention because a member of the King's Council was murdered. You'll have to provide reports directly to the King, starting first thing tomorrow." He made a motion of dismissal.

Yes, she had the opportunity of a lifetime, as critical eyes watched her take a position meant for a man with political aspirations. Failure would mean resignation, voluntary or not, just like what happened to Erik. She set her jaw and saluted Captain Rhaffus.

•••

The Office of Investigation resided in merely two rooms: a large outer office with a table and several chairs, and an inner, smaller office for the OIC.

The entire staff had been called in for duty and was waiting for her. The clerk, Usko, was a small man who vibrated with precision and efficiency. Usko started working for the Office of Investigation under Erik, so while she'd exchanged pleasantries with him each day, her tasks had required little interaction with the clerk. Now he showed her the records on the Reggis murder: initial reports from the coroner, statements the watch had collected from witnesses, etc. The physical evidence, including the key Draius had taken from the barmaid, was locked away.

"Very efficient," she said, making Usko beam. "Officer Lornis and I will have to go over all of this in detail."

She glanced at her second-in-command, who watched the small clerk with a small smile. The captain obviously favored him, but she didn't know why Lornis rated special treatment. *If I'm going to be saddled with him as my deputy, I hope he's got a brain in that pretty head.*

The two watchmen assigned to staff duty had their watch cycle reduced to three shifts an eight-day, and the rest of the eight-day they were devoted to supporting the Office of Investigation. They were opposite sides of a coin: Ponteva, a grizzled watch commander, and Miina, a young trainee who had recently graduated to Entrant rank. Miina's dark hair was shorter than fashionable, but could still be tied back. Her hair made her look very young and she bubbled with child-like enthusiasm, making Draius wonder if she could still touch the Phrenii. It was unusual, but not unwarranted, to assign such a young watchman to staff duty.

"What's our first assignment, ser?" Ponteva had the ease of many years of experience, and a stillness about him that reminded Draius of a hundred-year-old oak. Solid.

She handed Ponteva the background that had been compiled for Councilman Reggis. "Get started on the interviews. You'll need to question relatives, friends, and associates, and find out who might have a grudge against the councilman. Identify anyone with a motive."

"We'll have a long list. He was popular with the women." Ponteva was blunt.

"Then you better get started," she said.

The two watchmen sat down at the conference table and laid the background information in front of them. Ponteva started giving Miina names, which she wrote down in an order that would make their traversal of the cities easier. Miina obviously had a logical mind, and by all indications, she and Ponteva would work well together.

Draius turned to Lornis, examining the files with Usko. Although the lieutenant was the same height as Draius, he towered over the clerk, who seemed frail by comparison. His hair cascaded down his back and looked like a shining mane, while the clerk's glasses and wispy hair reminded her of a marsh bird. Draius suddenly had a disturbing sense of predator and prey, standing together.

"Ser?" Lornis looked her quizzically.

"Let's go over the witness statements." She motioned for him to follow her, but paused before entering the inner room for the *Officer in Charge of Investigation*, savoring the moment. This was *her* office. No longer Erik's, and not Jan's.

The thought of Jan soured her. This position might sound the death knell for their contract. This murder case would end one of two ways: failure would end her career, but success would end her marriage.

CHAPTER EIGHT

First Markday, Erin Three, T.Y. 1471

O n Markday morning, the clear light didn't erase the memories of the previous night. Eventually I must write down the specifics of how the Sareenian died, how wondrous our bodies can be, and how much violation they can suffer before expiring. My employer, however, was more interested in the information the Sareenian divulged in an effort to save his life: the ship was to sail to the ports of Chikirmo, not Illus, as my employer instructed. Of course, we already knew that, but not the fact the Sareenian registered the ship and cargo with underwriters.

I focused on capturing the energy of pain and death. The magic streamed through my bloodstream and pounded in my heart, so I paid no heed to the Sareenian's screams, pleas, or eventual prayers. Being careful, I sealed the power into the pieces of flesh using purified silver and ensured the circle and signs were drawn correctly.

During cleanup, my employer blocked my view of the room with his bulk. I thought he wanted my attention. "Any suggestions, Taalo? What can be done, if the Groygans have the lodestone?"

"You're assuming the ship arrived safely in Chikirmo with its cargo." The Sareenian's death still sang in my head, so my voice had a slight tremor. I caressed the cold metal of my tools as I cleaned and reluctantly packed them away. Their surfaces, smooth and sharp, made my skin tingle.

"Do you know otherwise?" My employer's voice was sharp.

"I suggest we wait for the news from our contacts in Chikirmo. If the lodestone is lost, we've got a bigger problem."

My employer rubbed the side of his head. "I hate to do nothing but take the defensive."

"We can always talk to the Groygan. We can confront him with his bribery, and warn him that no one can yet control the lodestone."

"Humph." My employer obviously couldn't admit this might be our only option.

There was a muffled yelp and the scuffling of boot heels on the floor. I leaned sideways, around him, to see one of his men roughly forcing my apprentice out the door.

"What's happening?" I moved to interfere, but my employer blocked me. Being large and brawny, he can easily best me.

"He's outlived his usefulness."

"But he's *my* apprentice. You're not allowed to touch him."

"Not allowed?" His bushy eyebrows arched higher. "You gave me permission the moment you involved him in our rites of power."

You mean my rites. You have done nothing but issue orders, which weren't even obeyed. With effort, I held my tongue. It would be undignified to struggle with my employer over a pubescent pimpled boy, so I tried reason. "I need him in the shop. I can't afford to train another, not at this time."

"He's too young, too much of a risk—believe me, he does better service as a floater, blamed on Haversar. We need a diversion for the City Guard's investigation. If you need help preparing the rite, I've learned enough to assist you."

I winced, for several reasons: I now knew how my apprentice would die, and I never like to hear that name. Everyone knew that someone ran the darker side of this city, someone who commanded the criminals, the disaffected, and any nunetton who might not yet qualify as one of the former. His name shouldn't be uttered, not out loud and not near the wharves.

The boy struggled, but he wasn't strong enough to prevent the men from binding his arms behind his back and lowering a hood over his head. Before I turned away, the hope died in his eyes. I grappled for control, reached for the cold protection of dispassion that I've cultivated in my heart. I concentrated on my employer's last sentence. "Are you mad? Suggesting we do another rite, so soon? You've already cautioned us about the new Officer of Investigation."

"This Sareenian went to underwriters and may have said too much about the cargo. More purging is necessary to remove the stench of betrayal. Why aren't you, of all people, champing at the bit to do more? Didn't you say you needed more magic for working charms?"

"Yes, but we risk death if the Guard connects us to these rites. Not a quick death, but death by the rack."

"I'm aware of the price." His enigmatic answer was the end of our conversation as we quit the dockside office where we'd left bloody havoc.

Now, in the bright morning light of Markday, I look about my empty shop and I can't bear to open it. I leave it shuttered and go back to bed. I lost my apprentice in order to divert the new OIC of Investigation. Meran-Kolme Erik's replacement won't be as easy to sidetrack, according to my employer.

I can convince myself I'm not emotionally affected. I can run the shop without the boy—but the morning doesn't feel right when he's not clattering about and breaking my precious glassware. I close my eyes to will away the memories.

CHAPTER NINE

The Meran-Viisi Household

As Erin Three starts, the Rauta-Nelja attempt to contract our King in marriage, and we wonder why he tarries. The Pettaja-Kolme bookseller near the square will offer Avo Cabaran's "To Have and Hold Power," which is banned in every Sareenian City-State. The bookseller cautions that copies are limited. Disagreements between the Meran-Kolme and the Vakuutis-Nelja continue, regarding debts incurred by Meran-Kolme Erik, who has quietly left for lineal holdings in the plains. Meran-Kolme Erik is replaced by Serasa-Kolme Draius—can she direct our lumbering City Guard in finding the murderer of Councilman Reggis? And, while his seat remains empty, the King's Council addresses yet another tax for financing new naval ships.

—*News Around and About the Sister Cities, The Horn & Herald, First Markday, Erin Three, T.Y. 1471*

Draius would rather have given the report by herself. Visiting Betarr Serin and seeing familiar places and faces, including her cousin, might be painful. She didn't want a stranger along. Unfortunately, the order stated that all officers working this case should present their findings to the King.

"Much too nice a morning to deal with murder," Lornis said as they crossed Bridge Square, empty of traffic this early in the day. His voice held underlying chirps of joy.

She frowned to discourage any more chatter. Her mood didn't improve, but a glance about proved Lornis correct. Markday was living up to its name for starting a new eight-day. The sky was clear, crisp, and clean, with no echo of the previous eight-day's weather.

They trotted their horses across the Whitewater, where bridge and river marked the edge of Betarr Serasa. Stopping momentarily, they both looked up toward Betarr Serin, sitting at the top of a winding road with switchbacks crawling up the plateau.

The steep grade was hard for the horses, so they slowed to a firm walk halfway up the trail. Lornis rode with stolid horsemanship, while her seat was more elegant, gracefully teaming with Chisel. She reminded herself that few others had the benefit of her teachers and tutors. Her father had spared no expense getting her the best education and training.

At the top, they dismounted and led the horses. Two King's Guard, fitted in flashing silver and green, nodded to them as they passed through the gate to Betarr Serin. She glanced up at the cannon stationed on the walls. No projectile heavy enough to harm the walls could reach them from sea level, even using modern powder. However, those cannon could accurately sight the harbor below, where ships looked like toys and the docks seemed to team with ants.

They turned onto the main thoroughfare, walking on white marble, smoothly rippled from many years of use. Grey stone residences were walled off from the streets, their courtyard gardens spilling over the walls in waves of spring-flowering vines such as fuchsia and white chaste-flowers. Sweet scents wafted through open gates, which exposed fountains shaded by spring greenery, tempting the pedestrian out of the sunshine.

Past those gates were the long-established lineages of Tyrra, maintained by the schemes of matriarchs who planned each marriage and named each child. Someone had to develop the next generation, and the responsibility fell to the same women who controlled the lineal assets, investments, and legacies.

They met hardly any traffic and walked up the sloping stone street in silence. Draius glanced into the Serasa-Kolme courtyard as they passed, eyeing the residence, stable, and carriage house occupied by Jan's sister. The plantings weren't well maintained and no doubt Taru would hear about that from Lady Anja. The estate continued beyond the house. Accessible from the street, the Serasa-Kolme reliquary rose beyond the other buildings. The seven-hundred-year-old structure was made of meticulous Serasa-Kolme stonework, with ornamental scrolls carved on the lintels and above the pillars, distinguishing it as architecture of the Fourth Era.

As Draius and Lornis crossed the street that ran in front of the Groygan Embassy, they both studied the gate that dripped with red and yellow streamers. The bright silk ribbons floated in the breeze. Groygan guards stood at the courtyard entrance and above them flew the Groygan flag, displaying a red, cat-like creature that most Tyrrans had never seen. Ambassador Velenare Be Glotta, had been in place almost six years, longer than any other Groygan ambassador. Intelligence collected by the King's Guard was contradictory: the extensive post might indicate Glotta was out of favor with the Council of Lords (since Groygans considered living in Tyrra a hardship), or he might be extremely favored (from gathering better intelligence than previous ambassadors).

Lornis hesitated, but Draius kept walking. "No time to trade taunts with the Groygans," she said, speaking of one of the rites of passage into the Guard.

Two blocks later the sound of children's laughter came from a side street. A clear voice rose above the others, singing an old rhyme.

> *"Era, Erins,*
> *Mark the fifth season,*
> *Even as the Phrenii reason.*

Ashen, Ashes,

Count the five portals,

Men may rest as they are mortals."

It was a meaningless verse every Tyrran child learned. The sound of the children combined with a high tinkling vibration that couldn't be reproduced by man-made instruments. Scholars named this "ringing" and said it was caused by the life-light magic within the Phrenii. To adults, the ringing stood as warning. *Stand back.* Draius and Lornis hastily drew their horses to the side and backed against the wall.

One of the Phrenii turned onto the street toward them, dancing on cloven feet. Its spiral horn sparkled in the clear spring sunlight. Children ranging from three to twelve years of age surrounded the creature. They skipped beside the mottled and translucent being, twining their fingers in its mane and petting its coat. A small girl, no more than four years old, ran out from a gate across the street and skittered in front of the creature. She squealed and held her arms up, stopping the Phrenii. A head larger than half the size of her body, with jaws that could snap her bones, lowered to her level. She threw her arms around the creature's neck, avoiding the razor-sharp spirals of the horn.

Draius smiled at the girl's enraptured expression. She was safer than any child could be at the moment. No Tyrran adult would break her fantasy and delight; it would be broken soon enough when she reached adulthood and left her innocence behind.

If Draius reached toward the creature, she knew that guilt, from her smallest transgression to her largest trespass, would crash down upon her. She'd relive her worst moments, her hand would drip with blood, and Groygan eyes would fade and become dull with dust. It didn't matter that she'd been ambushed and had protected herself—her actions were not compatible with the Phrenii.

Adults never talked about the shameful moments they experienced, over and over again, when the creatures came near. Along the path to adulthood, everyone gave up the joyous feeling of touching the creatures, but she didn't know the exact moment it happened. By the time she was arguing with her father about the merits of a boy with whom she was enamored, she'd drifted into puberty and the Phrenii were making her uncomfortable.

Of course, anyone foolish enough to raise a weapon against the Phrenii would become a gibbering maniac. The "phrenic madness" protected these creatures from adults—or vice versa.

Staring at the creature's translucent body, she saw whirling clouds that seemed to pull at her. Suddenly dizzy, she averted her gaze before the Phrenii's attention could fall on her. The scent of a sea breeze wafted past. The sound of hooves stopped. She looked up to see faceted blue eyes directed toward Lornis while children circled and skipped about.

"Welcome to the sister cities, Lornis, where you belong." The words from the creature hung in the air accompanied by a tone. Draius caught her breath. This element of the Phrenii, named Jhari, represented air and prescience.

Lornis coughed and bowed. Jhari appeared to take this as a response; it turned away and led the children right at the next intersection. The voices and ringing faded. Lornis avoided making eye contact with Draius as they continued up the slow incline of the main street.

"This is the second time I've encountered Jhari." His voice seemed bitter. His shoulders slumped, a tiny movement that only she might have noticed.

"Sounds like you have a phrenic prophecy hanging over your head."

Lornis shrugged and opened his mouth.

"No." She stopped him. "Don't tell me anything. I'd rather stay oblivious, if you don't mind."

"That was my opinion, too. No one but my grandmother knows."

She said nothing more. *Poor soul—a reading from the Phrenii placed some sort of destiny upon him.* Most Tyrrans resisted asking the Phrenii for a reading, only resorting to phrenic prescience when absolutely necessary. Their readings rarely satisfied the questioner and caused a lifetime of fear.

"Better to believe you're at the helm and living free, than with the dagger of destiny at one's back," went the Tyrran saying.

After several more intersections, they arrived at their destination near the northern edge of the plateau. Here the street ended, leaving them facing the Meran-Viisi reliquary, the oldest in all of Tyrra. To their left was a residence with the address of Number One Betarr Serin. It stretched to the cliff face on the west and the Dahn Serin Falls in the far northwest corner of the city. The gates were heavy and wooden, without decoration.

Draius's critical eye saw the flecks of rust on one of the hinges. The gates were shabby, even shameful, for the House of the Meran-Viisi. It was the King's residence, and the place where *her own mother* grew up. The wide marble stairs to the grandiose building across the street overshadowed the entrance to Number One.

She glanced up the stone staircase to her right, overwhelmed with memories, having a vivid sense of climbing the stairs beside her father. After the Fevers, she was ten and he had been too lost in his own pain to pay attention to the funeral of a king, the crowning of another, or his own grieving daughter. Eight years later, she had helped her ailing father up those steps so he could officiate as her younger cousin Perinon was quickly installed as King.

The stairs led to the Palace of Stars, in which the Tyrran government functioned. It held reception halls, offices for the King's Guard, and chambers for the King's Council. One elected and one appointed member represented each borough on the council. Reggis had been an elected member.

"Ser?" Lornis caught her attention. "Where are we to be received?"

She shook her head to clear it. Stepping to the entrance to the grounds, she pulled on the bell and it jingled inside the courtyard. They heard someone approaching the gate.

"At least this should be quick," Lornis said.

"Why?"

"Well, you being Meran-Viisi, his cousin and all—" He stopped at her expression.

Her mouth and tongue felt like they'd been deadened. "You've been looking into my background?"

"Yes, ser." Color flared and disappeared on his sharp cheekbones. "As a deputy, I should know my commanding officer."

"Well, I'm not Meran-Viisi any more. I won't be getting any special treatment. Of that, I'm sure." She pressed her lips together to bring sensation back. No need to educate Lornis in lineal politics, or the fact her father had withdrawn from his family-by-contract after her mother died.

Of all the King's Guard to be on personal duty to the King, it had to be Henri who opened the gate. His eyebrows went up as he looked them over. "Yes?"

"The City Guard Officer of Investigation and her deputy, to report to the King," Draius said stiffly.

"Of course, *Lieutenant* Commander." Henri smirked and motioned for a stable hand.

After being admitted to a tidy square that contained a fountain, their horses were taken aside and they were shown into a room that opened onto a terrace. The terrace faced the Dahn Serin Falls where the waters fell from the mountains and then flowed off the plateau.

Then they waited.

•••

When Perinon reached the door to the small east parlor, he paused and sighed. He was King of Tyrra, Bearer of the Kaskea, Holder of the Phrenii's Promise, High Commander of the King's Guard, Starlight Wielder for the Meran-Viisi, and yet he quailed at entering the parlor late for his Markday breakfast with his aunt.

Lady Aracia, matriarch of the Meran-Viisi, looked up from pouring her tea when he opened the door. She didn't stand as he entered, perhaps to remind Perinon that he remained her nephew and she controlled all the Meran-Viisi assets.

"Did you oversleep?" Her tone was pleasant.

All the same, he bristled. "No. Instead of getting a full night's sleep, I had to speak with the Phrenii." Mahri had awakened him early to give him a history lesson.

"What about? Anything of relevance?" She poured Perinon some tea.

"Not yet." The lecture would be relevant someday. Unfortunately, phrenic prescience wasn't useful. Compounding the frustrating ambiguity of their readings, they would often merge the future with the past, forgetting their place in the present day.

The steward dished up his breakfast and he dug into the eggs and potatoes. The morning service of china and silver was neatly arranged, shining in the light coming through watery panes of glass. The *Horn & Herald* and *The Recorder* lay to one side on a platter.

"By the way, Lady Rauta-Nelja wishes to present her favored grandchild to you today."

He was too tired to handle her blindsiding attack. His jaw hardened and he pointedly laid his hand on the table, the one that carried the ring that held the Kaskea shard. The ladies were always favored grandchildren, always beautiful, and always very young. The Rauta-Nelja were an offshoot of the Meran-Nelja, rising to a four star constellation about two hundred years ago. He supposed this might be a suitable contract but, as usual, he wouldn't have anything in common with this young lady.

Aracia set her mouth into a thin line. "Rapport with the Phrenii shouldn't prevent the King from doing his duty."

Duty meant fathering children, the primary function matriarchs expected from males. She made no secret of her opinions: he avoided his responsibilities to the Meran-Viisi and his people. Of course, she couldn't understand the burden of the Kaskea.

Perinon became King at the age of sixteen, when his brother Valos died in the currents of the Whitewater north of the sister cities. Very few had been bound to the Kaskea at such a young age. There were legends of the effects of being in rapport with the Phrenii—not without historical support, because rapport could cause madness. Personal quirks exhibited by a king were often attributed to the Kaskea.

"Don't worry, I'll be marriageable for at least the next sixty years. I won't retire from society and waste away." His words were harsh, bitter, and immediately regretted.

A spasm crossed her face. When the Phrenii were near, Perinon saw light and darkness entwine into unbending strength within Aracia. The darkness was self-serving pride, but the light of her service and loyalty made her an excellent matriarch for the most powerful lineage in Tyrra. She'd been raised to always consider what was best for the Meran-Viisi, and she was only doing her duty.

"I'm sorry," he said. "I should never have implied that I would go the way of my mother."

"My sister was already broken by her losses from the Fevers. You are stronger, and I expect you to start considering a contract. The people expect this also." She nodded toward the *H&H*.

"Need I remind you that bearers of the Kaskea have always had childless contracts, unless they're allowed to choose their own spouse?"

"I'm not forcing a choice on you, I'm merely exposing you to possibilities." Her mouth twisted into a prim expression.

"Well, I don't have time for *exposure* this morning. I have to deal with the Reggis murder."

"That's only a matter of setting dates for an election. Surely you have time this afternoon." She continued to push him.

"Fine—check with my secretary and schedule it." He made his escape. His secretary couldn't stand up to Aracia either; the poor man got a tic in his face whenever he dealt with the matriarch. Perinon had no doubt he'd see the Rauta-Nelja prospect this afternoon.

He was late entering the small reception room in his residence. His secretary started going through a pile of petitions. The first was from a man who claimed a milk cart had frightened his horse, causing damage to his buggy. He wanted compensation from the milk vendor, but the magistrate who handled the original complaint thought the training of the horse was deficient. The petitioner hadn't agreed with the magistrate's decision, so he exercised his right to appeal directly to the King.

"Sire, there's City Guard here from the Office of Investigation. They're waiting for an audience," said one of the ubiquitous green and silver uniformed Guards who paced the corridors. The young man's voice carried an undertone of disdain.

Happy to lay aside milk stands and buggies, he asked, "When did they arrive?"

"An hour ago."

"What? I should have been notified *at that time*. Get them in here."

The young Guard's eyes widened. He left to find the officers while Perinon and his secretary waited. Inside this room, the roar of the Dahn Serin Falls was muted and the faint chords of a harpsichord wafted in from the marble hall. Soitto, Aracia's second daughter, was practicing in the music room. Onni, Aracia's eldest daughter, wasn't allowed the trivialities of music because she was training to succeed Aracia as matriarch of the Meran-Viisi. There were reasons why the matriarchy was passed to daughters only as a last resort: Onni resented having this responsibility pushed on her and there'd been dissonant mother-daughter clashes in the household that made him wish he were anywhere else.

But today the household was peaceful and he rubbed his beard with relief, belatedly noting he hadn't had it trimmed this morning.

Two City Guard officers were shown in, and he was pleasantly surprised to see one was his cousin Draius. Actually, their mothers had been true cousins and when they were alive, he and Draius played and learned together. They took lessons with other Meran-Viisi children of their generation, all traditionally called "cousins." He hadn't seen her since the Fevers abruptly ended their childhood, but he recognized her in the woman who faced him. The family resemblance was unmistakable and he could have been looking in a mirror: she had his same lanky bones, silver-blond hair, gray eyes, and the dusky, almost pewter-colored Meran complexion.

She and her companion bent their knees, but he motioned for them to stand.

"Welcome, cousin." He crossed the room and gave Draius a kinsmen kiss on the cheek. He kept his hands on her shoulders as a surge of happiness flowed through his chest, something he hadn't felt in a while. His face broke into an easy and genuine smile.

"A cousin removed, Sire." She bent her head and then returned a cool and tight smile, which quickly faded.

"As you wish." He dropped his hands from her shoulders.

So it was true: she didn't care to keep her name or her connection to her lineage, as was customary among the Meran-Viisi. The lineages of children were negotiated differently for each marriage contract and Perinon suspected her children, if she had any, were Serasa-Kolme. She'd given up everything her lineage could offer, which was substantial, and she'd become so—so unfamiliar. He wondered how the vivacious and loyal girl he knew had turned into this distant, controlled woman.

In the flicker of an eyelid, he suddenly felt the sun on his face and smelled the cold water of the northern canals. He saw the eight-year-old Draius, diving fearlessly into the water, then bobbing up and calling to him. *We are Meran-Viisi, Peri. We are never afraid*, she'd said that day, trying to convince him to take his first jump off the canal bridge. Had the Fevers changed her so much? Perhaps marriage had changed her.

"I'm reporting for the Office of Investigation, with my deputy commander, Lornis." She didn't provide the lineal name of her assistant. In theory, matriarchs planned unique names within each generation, so it was Tyrran custom to go by primary names.

Perinon went back to his desk and sat, placing his hands on the smooth, cool marble surface. Everyone in the room started to look like transparent shells around writhing light and dark veins. The air became brighter and fresher: he was reminded of sun shining on wet grass.

Mahri had silently entered the room and now stood behind his shoulder. His secretary backed away from the desk to stand at the wall; he knew when Perinon needed distance.

"This crime has high visibility, Officer Draius. A member of the King's Council has been murdered. We can't have the people losing faith in their leadership, or in their City Guard. The City Guard must use whatever resources necessary to find this killer." This speech, however pompous and trite it sounded, fulfilled his monarchal duties.

"Sire, we'll do everything in our power." Draius gave him the rote answer, glancing at the creature standing behind him.

Adults outside the King's presence rarely saw Mahri. The element of Spirit, with golden eyes, was the keystone and the controller of the phrenic circle. Mahri stepped forward and Perinon reached up, almost brushing the luminescent mane that framed the creature's head like the nimbus of a star. Like any other adult, he couldn't touch the Phrenii and his fingers stopped a hand-span away from the creature's hair. He sensed Draius stiffen.

Some Tyrrans loved their King being exposed to the Phrenii and their magic, while others thought it unhealthy; apparently Draius was of the latter opinion. Perinon watched her struggle briefly with her distaste, then shrug it aside. Few Tyrrans could begrudge a relationship that made their King stronger than any other ruler in the Mapped World. Supposedly, "he who is bound to the Kaskea can command the Phrenii," and no one knew the limits of their power.

That was legend, because Perinon knew he couldn't command the Phrenii to do anything against their will, not any more. The original Kaskea had been shattered more than five hundred years ago and only one shard was fixed in the ring he wore. The broken Kaskea held only a faint echo of its original power.

"I'd like updates on your progress every eight-day, preferably in person. How goes it so far?" he asked, breaking the silence.

He watched his cousin summarize the relevant aspects of the crime. Draius had the strong light of duty and loyalty to her King and country. With that light intermingled dark wisps of stubbornness and pride. The pride was tinged with pain and perhaps his cousin had already paid the price for her Darkness.

He turned his attention to Lornis, saw a curious spark of light within the man and heard Mahri whisper in his mind, *the ancestors have marked this one.* So the Stars show a destiny for this man? He knew he wouldn't get straight answers from Mahri, and instead concentrated upon Draius's report. When she came to the sign painted in blood on the wall, he stopped her.

"Do you have a drawing of this symbol? The Phrenii might understand its significance." Because they avoided the creatures, adults easily forgot the Phrenii were sources of historical information.

Lieutenant Lornis opened his satchel, pulled out a drawing, and held it up. Perinon saw two concentric circles with an "N" drawn within them. The tail of the "N" dipped into the concentric circles and entwined them. Before he could frame a question, a charge ran through him, a chilling vibration from the entire phrenic circle. Perinon gasped, unable to breathe—

"Sire? Sire?"

He looked up. He was sprawled across his desk and his secretary was beside him, trying to help him back into his chair. The City Guard officers were leaning over the desk in concern. Mahri stood behind him, still as stone. He was wheezing and managed to choke out a few words. "Just need air."

The concerned mortals in the room backed away, making a semi-circle in front of his desk. Even the King's Guard stood with the others. Soitto was peering in from the hallway. How long had he been fighting for air? Finally able to speak in a normal tone, he sat back in his chair and drew another deep breath. "I'm fine. Attend to your posts, please."

While everyone went back to his or her assorted places and the guards shooed away the twelve-year-old girl at the doorway, Perinon went as deeply into rapport with Mahri as he could, without actually entering the Void. What went through the Phrenii was *fear*: raw, naked *fear*. There had been another time they felt such fear, when they were facing destruction. So this was the reason for the morning history lesson.

"Mahri, tell the officers about this symbol," he said.

Mahri responded, using the circle to summon up memories from the Phrenii.

"The concentric circles combine to make a sign used in necromancy, a proscribed and evil art. Necromancy can bind power into inanimate objects, and that power might look like true magic to the ignorant. The 'N' is a reference to Nherissa, the sorcerer who developed this art." Mahri's voice had musical tones, but was neither high nor low, neither male nor female. After the Phrenii spoke, no one could ever fully describe their voice.

There was silence. The tales of the sorcerers Nherissa and Cessina were well known but had become children's bedtime stories, obscured by time and multiple tellings. It was easy to forget that the Phrenii had lived during those times.

"We are speaking *hypothetically*?" Draius cautiously directed her question to the Phrenii. "Mankind might have used this art once, but can't use it any more?"

"Nherissa was the last mortal known to use necromancy and he was consumed by the souls he imprisoned. He was one of the last men who had the ability to attain the rank of sorcerer."

"But Nherissa's art died with him. Our murderers did *not* use magic; this is man-made butchery." Draius's voice was clipped, almost sharp. "Sire, I should think torture, murder, and mutilation, whichever came first, to be the primary points here."

Perinon hid a smile: he remembered how stubborn his cousin could be.

"Necromancy is the only crime on the books that still rates death on the wheel. Attempted necromancy can be punished with the same, or life imprisonment, if the magistrate deems mercy is deserved. Signed by King Kotiin in the year 998 and never rescinded." Lornis looked sideways at Draius and finished sheepishly, "I just took the exams."

"I know the King's Law and I can quote that paragraph, too, but it's unlikely to ever be enforced." Draius looked at Lornis coldly, then turned back to Perinon. "Sire, I cannot support the hysteria being whipped up by the *H&H*. If this case cannot be solved by methods that have stood us good stead for years, then perhaps I'm not the best—"

"Officer Draius is correct." Mahri's voice, though soft and melodious, cut across her words like a knife. She stopped, looking confused at the unexpected support. "Mortal weapons and mortal evil killed those men."

In Perinon's head the Phrenii whispered, *her Meran blood will play a part we cannot yet see. In this, we are certain.* The added phrase indicated they had a clear prescient flash of the future. He rubbed the temples of his forehead. He already had a headache, and the day was only at mid-morning.

A messenger came to the door and Perinon waved him over. The young man gave him a note, which he opened and read. His heart sank. He waved the note toward Draius.

"Well, Lieutenant Commander Draius, you've got your work cut out for you. There's been another murder and it sounds similar." His head started to pound as he felt the agitation from the Phrenii.

He watched Draius read the note and saw compassion and anger wash through her body. She truly *cared*, though she gave little outward sign of her emotions. Her loyalty, her sense of responsibility, and even her stubbornness would serve him. She would hunt down these murderers with implacable justice and logic, and she would never give up until she found them.

CHAPTER TEN

Murder by the Docks

I believe my master Cessina fully intended to break the Kaskea, not just weaken it. At the time, he thought Tyrra's ruler would never again need to command the Phrenii. He also thought the lodestone of souls would stay forever hidden and the Phrenii would always be safe. On his deathbed, in that flash of insight many sorcerers have when it is too late, he realized he was wrong on all accounts.

—*From the notes of Sorceress-Apprentice Lahna, tentatively dated T.Y. 1014 (New Calendar)*

When Draius and Lornis arrived at the office near the docks, the similarities to the murder of Councilman Reggis were obvious. Symbols had been painted in blood on the floor around the body, while two concentric circles with a scripted 'N' were drawn on the wall. The dead man in the middle of the room had been eviscerated. The deep incision twisted a bit across his torso, maybe made incrementally, one section at a time. This time, she didn't doubt the blood on the floor and walls belonged to the victim.

She studied him. She never forgot a face, but features frozen in agonizing death weren't always recognizable. Trying to imagine the countenance without the mask of terror and brutality from his slow death, she was fairly sure she'd never seen this man before.

The victim was Danelo Torna Tellina, an importer and owner of multiple ships. As his name indicated, he was Sareenian. Several years ago he'd moved his operations to the port of Betarr Serasa from Illus, a Sareenian City-State. The victim's clerk unlocked the office this morning and discovered the carnage. He immediately notified the watch. This time no one had been allowed into the room, except those with authorization.

"Over here, Draius." Norsis bent over the body, making notes and clicking his tongue in concentration. He was the City Guard Coroner, complementing his regular mortician business. Coroner work didn't normally provide full time employment, but this eight-day was disproving that theory.

"He's been here a while." Norsis clicked his tongue again.

"How long?" she asked. They'd arrived just past noon and she hadn't had lunch yet. Despite the stomach-churning sights in this room, she was hungry.

"Maybe a day, maybe longer. It'll be difficult to decide time of death—not like Reggis."

"Speaking of Reggis, where's your full report?"

"On your desk, Lieutenant Commander, as we speak." The coroner's voice was muffled since his cheek pressed against the floor on the other side of the body. He heaved an exasperated sigh and sat up, rocking backwards onto his heels. "If *anyone* would like to help, I still have fingers unaccounted for."

She rolled her eyes at Lornis, who gave her a weak smile. Perhaps he needed a break. "Lornis, why don't you go outside and collect statements while I help Norsis."

"Yes, ser." He promptly made for the door.

"Thinking he'll break when we go hunting for body parts?" Norsis asked.

"Not everyone can handle this. At least, not initially."

"You did fine when you started. Erik went through at least four floaters before he could keep his food down." The term "floater" was slang for bodies found floating in the canals near the wharves. "I bet your pretty lieutenant is heaving outside right now."

"Perhaps he is, but it's normal. Not everyone is as *lucky* as we are." She put a sarcastic tweak on her words, getting a grin from the thin coroner.

She helped him in his gruesome, but necessary, task. It became a difficult dance, moving about the body, avoiding the blood to keep from messing up the odious artwork. In the end, they had to list six fingers as missing from the scene. More absent body parts, similar to the other murder. Were they gruesome mementos?

Otherwise, there was little physical evidence of interest. This time there were no vials, no change purse, no parchment left beside the victim—thinking back upon those items, she remembered them arranged neatly, almost obsessively lined up by height and *demanding to be noticed...* Unsure where her mind was traipsing, she filed this thought away for later.

Tellina had been murdered in his own stark and functional shipping office. When it was closed, he usually kept the office locked, although several employees had keys. She didn't touch the piles of folders on his desktop, probably paperwork for running his ships and imports. Searching the desk drawers, she found a locked cash box.

"Did you find a key on the body?" she asked.

Norsis rummaged in a bag and produced a small key. She opened the cash box with it. Inside was more than a tyr in small change, probably his petty cash. It could feed someone for an erin, if they were careful. She searched the desk further and found a gold brooch in the shape of a butterfly, placed inside a small, carved wooden box. A normal criminal would never have left such prizes. She kept the box aside to give to his family.

Norsis had the body loaded on a stretcher and carried out to the coroner's wagon that waited outside. She followed him outside and stood on the creaking, weathered stairs to the office. Lornis stood beside the steps, blinking, his eyes watering. He wouldn't have been the first to lose his stomach contents at this scene, but she hoped he'd been discreet.

There was commotion on the other side of the wagon. A watchman dragged Andreas, editor of the *H&H*, over to stand in front of Draius.

"He tried to get a look at the body, ser."

Andreas sputtered and his shirtsleeve had come untied while he struggled against the City Guard that outweighed him by a couple of stones. The editor was short and obviously not acquainted with physical exercise.

"I have a right to give the public information about this murder." Andreas squirmed in the Guard's grip, his face red.

"Yes, you do," she replied, motioning to the Guard to release the editor.

Mollified, Andreas straightened his clothes. "Then I can look inside the office?"

"No. While you can publish anything you want, you're not allowed access to the body or the murder scene. You can apply for a copy of the coroner's report down at Headquarters. That is proper written procedure, *under the King's Law.*" She raised her voice to ride over his protests.

"Can you at least give me a statement, Officer Draius?" Andreas's tone was sullen.

"This is our statement: The City Guard is following several leads, but we cannot yet reveal our suspicions."

The editor snickered. "And the connection between the two murders?"

"No comment."

"Any use of magic?"

"No. That's ridiculous."

"Was he gutted like the councilman? Left inside a locked room?" He was coatless and tugged on his vest, perhaps in unconscious memory of the watchmen's rough handling. His sleeves were worn and stained with ink. At one time Andreas employed several tailors, but he no longer had the funds to stay on the cutting edge of fashion.

"No comment. You'll have to look at the reports when they're released."

"That'll be days from now. Erik used to give me exclusive information."

"I doubt it," she said. "If that were true, you shouldn't have killed his career."

"I'm flattered that you attribute such power to me, Officer Draius, but Erik was responsible for the decline of his own reputation. I merely printed the facts."

Privately, she agreed that Erik caused his own fate, but she was in the mood to cut down Andreas. "Well, we'll see how long you can afford to print your *facts*. How deep are your pockets, or should I ask how deep do your lineal funds run?"

Instead of having the desired effect, Andreas grinned at her spiteful words. "I'll be here a while. I've found patrons. The bookseller I recently mentioned has been besieged by customers and she's willing to pay for more attention. Other merchants may follow."

"Where is your *truth*, then, if it is paid for?" she asked.

Andreas only shrugged. "About the body—"

"Escort him out of here." She summarily gestured to the Guards. Andreas gave her a resentful look as the two burly City Guard trotted him down the street and to a bridge that led away from the docks.

"Are you sure that was wise?" Lornis asked in a quiet undertone, leaning toward her. His breath was acrid from vomit.

Draius suddenly felt oppressed; everywhere she turned, she was hemmed in by the smell of vomit, blood, or canal water stinking of decay. She rubbed her temples. "It's best if Andreas thinks we're incompetent. I want the guilty parties to feel they have us stumped."

"Are we stumped?" At least his eyes were looking bright again.

"No. At least, I'll never admit that. Come on, let's go through the rest of the office."

They skimmed through the documents and found nothing unusual in the cargo declarations and shipping manifests, but they didn't have experience in shipping, importing, or exporting. In case they missed something important, she closed off the office with a seal of the King's Law. Besides, it might flush out the next of kin who'd need to remove the seal.

Outside, she glanced at the low sun. "Ready for an early supper?"

"I don't think so." Lornis looked uneasy. "I never thought I'd *ever* say this, but I'm not hungry."

"You'll get used to it." She pulled out her spring watch, one of the few expensive gifts from her father that she'd kept. The time was five hours past noon. "It's too late to examine the rooms at the Sea Serpent; the evening crowd is starting. Let's make a stop by the Royal Library and save the pub for tomorrow."

It was time to do a little research on a long-dead sorcerer named Nherissa.

• • •

Draius turned the bound sheet of parchment, which was in surprisingly good condition. She had directly gone to the section titled "ERA FOUR: In which Tyrran expansion and control of the Mapped World rises, while her sorcerers dwindle." In the shelves marked for Cessina there were few documents, and these were the only pages she found that referred to Nherissa.

> *I write this entry tonight with a heavy heart. Based upon these notes I've read, I'm convinced Nherissa has become so embroiled in this evil art that he cannot be saved. I cautioned him, specifically, against this line of study.*
>
> *"The dead do not give up their secrets lightly," I told him. "You might not want to pay their price."*
>
> *He laughed at me. "Don't you wonder why the Phrenii hide the death magic from us? Perhaps this is a way to spur talent in mankind."*

Draius shivered from the cold draft that went through the cavernous marble library, raising scents of old leather, parchment, and linen. Where was Lornis? A sign said they should ask the Royal Librarian for assistance and she'd sent Lornis to do exactly that. She didn't expect to find any documents or papers by Nherissa himself, since all those materials had been destroyed long ago, but there should be plenty of notes left by Cessina.

Looking back down the aisle of shelves to the center of the library, she saw a few students hunched over their studies and wearing cloaks against the chill. This library was maintained through royal grants and she supposed those grants included private Meran-Viisi funding as well, but that wasn't her business.

The pages were written in blocked handwriting because the inks of that era required slow, methodical lettering, and careful blotting. She continued reading.

> *I know Nherissa is obsessed by the loss of our magical talents. I am also concerned, because I am rarely able to walk the Void any more.*
>
> *"How long since you've seen a child with talent, with the ability to touch the Void?" Nherissa asked me. "You and I may be the last living men who can use elemental magic from that realm."*
>
> *I didn't tell him I had found a child with a small amount of talent, because I had no intention of exposing her to him.*
>
> *"There are still those with the Sight," I said.*
>
> *"The Sight! You think to rely upon the dreams of those who stumble about the Blindness? Might as well depend upon the ramblings of old women," he scoffed.*
>
> *"Mankind might not be meant to have elemental magic." I spoke from my own fears, from dreams that showed me mankind would suffer greatly before any man or woman held talent again.*
>
> *At my words, Nherissa became incensed. "Why should the Phrenii alone be able to use the elements? Why should they be set above mankind, when they are nothing? They are only portals. While we are real, they are merely starlight and dust."*

After that conversation, I watched his jealousy of the Phrenii grow. I followed his work as closely as I could, and his experiments began to take an alarming turn. First he attempted to coerce secrets from the dead, using large amounts of animal and human blood with his incantations.

With the mention of blood, Draius paid more attention.

Then he discovered that torture and death have power. What followed were more heinous acts, such as torturing animals and humans in ceremonies to bind that power into objects.

His research has progressed to evil conclusions. I have read his notes and, by his own words and hand, Nherissa has shown himself.

There was no more in Cessina's hand, but all Tyrrans knew the explosive conclusion. At the bottom of the page, other handwriting caught her eye. It was darker, written with modern ink in a running style. Draius squinted to read the small letters.

"Necromancy," she read, "was first formed as Nherissa's attempt to communicate with the dead. He expanded it into a mechanism for collecting power, but collection must be done carefully, so as to protect the practitioner. See Nherissa's notes, Year 180 of the Sixth Era, O.C."

She frowned. How could *Nherissa's* notes be cross-referenced in modern script when they were all destroyed after his death? Hearing footsteps, she stepped out from the scroll and loose paper archival storage. Lornis and the Royal Librarian were coming down the hall. Lornis walked with a cat-like, graceful step. He slipped through the air currents untouched, while the librarian's green robes billowed. On the librarian's chest was embroidered a candle, the Tyrran symbol for wisdom. Around the walls of the library assistants were lighting the gas, as the building had been recently modernized.

"Greetings, Officer Draius. I am Nokka, at your service."

"Greetings. We'll need your assistance, ser, in examining archival manuscripts—" she did a quick calculation, looking down at the scribbled note on the bottom of the page in her hand, "Around year 930, by the New Calendar."

There was silence. She looked up. Lornis had an odd look on his face, while Nokka's face twitched with anger and wariness.

"It appears there was a robbery," Lornis said.

"When?"

"Last summer, around Erin Six. The archives. It was a staggering loss—those items were donated by the Meran-Viisi eras ago." Nokka's mustache twitched with a life of its own.

"This good ser thought we were following up on his report, which he made to the Office of Investigation." Lornis raised his eyebrows and when she glanced down at the reference she held, he added, "There's no inventory of the missing items, although they're sure that none of Cessina's materials were taken."

She chewed her lip thoughtfully, noting the puzzlement in Lornis's eyes.

"I've received no response from the City Guard since the robbery and it's almost been a year." Nokka's outrage was obvious in his tone, as well as his mustache. Erin Six would be at the beginning of last summer, after Erik became OIC of Investigation and insisting on handling each case himself. Even though this happened under Erik's watch, she didn't think Nokka cared about the distinction and she agreed. But, something was wrong here...

She held the key in her hand. This document held a recent cross-reference to Nherissa's notes, which *should not exist*, not under the King's Law. Added to this was the robbery of items the Library was loath to enumerate. Erik might have perceived these inconsistencies but probably ignored the robbery, thus avoiding a confrontation with the Royal Library and the powerful Pettaja-Viisi. Luckily, she had no compunctions about offending librarians, nor any worries about saving a professional reputation.

She made a quick bow of apology. "I'm new to my job, and I apologize for failing to look over the current case load. The recent murders have taken all my attention, to the detriment of current investigations."

"Of course, the murder of Councilman Reggis," Nokka said, mollified. "I must apologize also, Officer. I forgot."

"However, you *must* provide an inventory of everything stolen from the library last year." Her tone was suddenly clipped and commanding, using her upper-city education and intonation.

Nokka's eyes widened. "Bu—but we don't have such a list. I couldn't provide it when I originally reported the robbery and—"

"Ridiculous! I've had the finest Meran-Viisi tutelage, and I'm well aware of the record-keeping done by the Royal Library and Archives." She didn't mention she sat elbow-to-elbow at afternoon lessons with the future King Perinon, while watching her older cousin Valos, another future King, struggle with his calculations at another table.

Nokka looked indecisive. Instead of the common watchman or City Guard he expected, he was faced with someone who must be Meran-Viisi, of the King's lineage.

Draius pressed on. "I can prove Nherissa's notes still existed, far into the New Calendar. No one would have referenced the Old Calendar until well after the year 1000." She held up the page with the note penned in the margin.

"By the Horn, no one should be marring Cessina's work!" Nokka reached for the paper, his face reddening, his lip and mouth working as if he were having a fit.

"I'm confiscating these." She yanked the papers out of his reach. "If they're not about necromancy, they'll be returned. You're also going to give me a detailed list of all the proscribed items you're holding, as well as those stolen from the Library. I suspect they're one and the same."

"Are you suggesting the Royal Library ban works that contain heretical ideas?" Nokka's voice sounded tense, like an overstretched mandolin string. "That would make us no better than the Sareenians. We offer the new work by Cabaran, while the Sareenians are frightened of it. If the works you refer to are offensive, well and fine—but I know the King, and the Meran-Viisi, support my efforts to keep an open library."

"Officer Draius is referring to the *King's Law*, which required the destruction of all materials concerning necromancy, or authored by Nherissa," Lornis said.

"Oh, I suspect Nokka is quite familiar with the King's Law." Draius gave the librarian a tight smile.

"That is archaic law, built upon ancient superstitions, and I question your *interpretation*," said Nokka. "We're no longer a society that runs away from mere ideas, even when they conflict with our view of the soul's sacred journey."

Draius shook her head. "We're investigating two murders, Nokka, both of which can be put on the doorstep of necromancy. What would have guided such butchery, other than historical papers of *ideas?*"

"Oh." Nokka was taken aback. "I don't know."

"I have the authority, under the King's Law, to examine your records. So, are you going to give me those lists, or do we march in front of a magistrate for a ruling on my *interpretation* of the edict against necromancy?"

"Well, if you're going to resort to threats." Nokka converted his outrage to justified huffiness. "Of course, I'll have to report this to—"

"Report this to whomever you like," she said.

"You'll have to wait while I have a copy penned. I only have one list."

"No need to make a copy. I can look over your original and memorize it." She jerked her head sideways, trying to get him moving. Nokka looked dubious, but he went off to find one of his assistants, leaving her and Lornis alone.

"We're going to have to go through all the closed cases," she muttered.

"I suppose so." Lornis spoke quietly as his eyes glanced around, in warning, at the echoing stone library. "Even *I* can remember there were only two open cases when you took over: the jeweler's robbery and the councilman's murder."

"Three now, counting the Sareenian's murder." Her jaw tightened. "I want you to sit down with Usko and go through all the cases closed under Erik. He could keep me working petty crimes, away from the substantial cases, but I can't believe he closed cases without Usko's knowledge."

"It'll take time."

"It has to be done."

Lornis sighed. "Should we also get statements from the librarians tonight, regarding the robbery?"

"No, their memories will have drifted." She lowered her voice to a whisper as she saw Nokka coming back. "Let's hope their statements are written and still on file."

"This is everything that was stolen." Nokka was holding three sheets, but he paused as a door opened across the large hall. Loud and angry voices came from the room as a small man with fuzzy, gray hair popped out. The door slammed behind him. The door's sign, hanging from a peg, swayed and rattled. The sign read "Meeting of the Royal Academy of Science."

"What, Taalo, kicked out again?" Nokka turned toward the small man eagerly, but Draius wasn't about to let the librarian divert her. She snatched the sheets out of Nokka's hand. He stroked his mustache and beard with his hand, trying to cover his frown.

She read the entries penned on the first sheet, noting such titles as "Principles Based on the Process of Necromancy," "Binding of Power Through Death," and "Concerning Cruelty and its Residual Magic in Tissues." The entries were dated in New Calendar years, written toward the end of Era Four in the years 850 to 999. *All of these documents should have been destroyed per King Kotiin's edict of 998.*

The dates also fit within the last part of Nherissa's lifetime. When mankind could use magic, the lives of the practitioners—sorcerers and sorceresses—were extended. Cessina was supposed to have lived several hundred years, if records could be believed. He might even have been present at the making of the Kaskea, albeit as an apprentice.

She tallied the entries; there were twenty written works by Nherissa and Cessina identified on the first page. She read through the second page, and gasped at the short list on the third page. "These were stolen also?"

"I said we suffered a *staggering* loss, Officer. They took one of the shards of the Kaskea left in our keeping, though only our ancestral stars would know why. The tapestry of the last stand between Nherissa and Cessina was, of course, priceless. Irreplaceable. The same can be said for the original Meran Sword of Starlight."

She felt a flash of anger, tinged with surprise. These artifacts were part of her heritage. She'd never considered their monetary worth. "Darkness and Fury," she swore under her breath, then asked aloud, "Why would anyone take these?"

"When I said the tapestry and sword were priceless, I wasn't making a joke," Nokka said. "All the items are valuable, as well as having historical significance. I'm sure buyers could be found for everything except the Kaskea shard."

"Why no buyers for the shard?"

"Not useable by anyone but the King, of course—as if anyone would *want* to use it." Nokka shuddered and wrapped his arms around his chest. "All the shards look like common pieces of slate with lines engraved. How would anyone prove their authenticity?"

"I don't suppose they can ask the King to hand over his ring so they can compare them." Lornis made an attempt at humor, but Draius wasn't amused. Inside, she was building herself up to a cold rage, and rather enjoying the process.

"So this is how the Pettaja do their duty as caretakers?" Her voice was cold.

"We're sworn to protect *knowledge*, not precious artifacts. These items—"

"Many of which are supposed to be destroyed. A king requested—no, *ordered* your ancestors to destroy these items, and they didn't comply.

Am I to assume the thieves took all the documents proscribed under the King's Law?"

"Yes, that's all of them." Nokka was responding, in kind, to her anger. "But it's ridiculous to expect a modern library to enforce such ancient and superstitious—"

"What's your lineal name?"

Nokka stopped, shocked at her impertinent question. Even Lornis looked shaken by her bad manners, but she asked again. "Your lineal name, your *specific* lineage?"

"Pettaja-Viisi." Nokka drew himself up to his full height, his mustache twitching.

Well, well. She was in the process of personally offending the second oldest and most powerful lineage in Tyrra, after the Meran-Viisi. The Royal Library had been formed to keep records of the Meran-Viisi and their rule of Tyrra. The librarian in charge would be the five star lineage, hence the tag of Viisi.

She pressed on. "You may think this trivial, a minor matter of the King's Law, but it isn't. Tell your matriarch that I will avoid reporting this to the magistrates, because this has become a lineal matter. My report will go straight to King Perinon and the Meran-Viisi. After that, it's up to them."

Even though five hundred years had passed, the Pettaja-Viisi had still failed in their duties to the Meran-Viisi King. Nokka's face paled, and Draius figured he'd run directly to his matriarch when she left. As they walked away from the librarian, down the long center of the library, Lornis was quiet. She had a moment of regret; in retrospect, she could have been more politic. Regardless, it was done. She'd write the specifics up for Perinon and bypass the King's Law magistrates, something the captain might not approve. As for Perinon, after seeing his reaction to the necromantic symbols, she doubted he'd let this alone.

"Officer Draius. May I presume?"

She started, abruptly pulled from her thoughts. The little man, identified as Taalo by Nokka, stepped out from the entrance alcove, as if he had been waiting for them.

The first word that came to mind when she looked at Taalo was *gray*. His eyes were blandly gray, his mustache and beard were gray, the unbraided fuzzy hair coming from his head was gray, and his skin was a dusty shade of gray, a parody of the fluid silver Meran coloring. He reminded her of the dust balls under the beds that Anja's maid Maricie was forever battling.

"Yes?" She remembered her name had been used in the *H&H*, giving her notoriety of a sort, and Taalo could have easily overheard her conversation with the librarian.

"Can we help you?" Lornis asked.

Taalo's mouth stretched, presumably in a smile, to reveal gray teeth. He bowed, and presented Draius with a card.

Draius gingerly took the card from his hand, avoiding his discolored fingertips. The card read, "Taalo, Apothecary, using the latest Scientific techniques of Chemistry, to be found at 62 Silta Street."

"Greetings, Taalo." She bowed quickly and handed the card to Lornis. "Do I have need of an apothecary?"

Frustration crossed Taalo's face. He nodded his head toward the closed door in the library, toward the meeting room he had left. "I am forever trying to change the perception that Science is a gentlemanly pursuit of study with no practical purpose. I can make no progress with the Academy, who enjoy their useless and expensive experiments, but perhaps I can convince the City Guard."

"Chemistry?" Lornis looked thoughtful. "You've abandoned the tenets of alchemy?"

"Of course, Officer. Pekon proved the transmutation of metals to be impossible in thirteen-forty-seven." Taalo stretched his mouth again.

Lornis nodded. "Certainly he did, but not independently. The Phrenii were steering everyone away from the dangerous metal therapies of his day."

Taalo's eyes narrowed. "There's no mention of the Phrenii in Pekon's work, ser. Mankind forges our own progress forward."

Lornis shrugged, perhaps wanting to continue, but Draius had more work to do this evening. She looked pointedly at the door, her escape from the strange little man. "Ser, are you offering advice?"

"I'm suggesting the City Guard has need of *chemistry*. Have you not run across mysterious items in your investigations? What if I could supply you with an analysis of such materials, an *identification*, perhaps?"

"I will consider your suggestion, Taalo." She grabbed the card from Lornis and made a show of putting it in her pocket. "Good evening, ser."

She pushed past the little man.

•••

They left their horses at the Guard stables and walked through the damp streets. It was dinner hour, when recently lit streetlights cast wavering shadows and there were few pedestrians about. They took a short-cut to City Guard Headquarters, going through a long, dark alley. Their footsteps echoed and Draius loosened her knife, just in case. Brandishing weapons, in a confident and competent manner, could frighten off thugs.

"Are you going to officially link the murders?" Lornis asked.

"I might as well, before the *H&H* does it for me," she said. "I'll talk to Andreas again, but this time *I'll* be asking the questions."

"You suspect his Society for the Restoration of Sorcery?"

"I think these murderers pretend to sorcery, even though it's all a sham, so Andreas may know some likely suspects." Her voice bounced off the smothering walls of the alley.

"He might be involved himself."

She was about to reply when she heard the footfall at the alley opening behind them. She touched Lornis's arm and he was alert enough to pull up against the wall right beside her. They stood absolutely still, shoulder to shoulder, with their backs against the wall. There were no more sounds at the end of the alley. After what seemed like a long stretch of time, she motioned to him and they moved on, but neither of them said anything more in the streets.

They stopped at the watch desk when they got to Headquarters, and asked about progress on Tellina. No family had been identified for the dead ship owner. Since he was Sareenian, contacting the matriarch for the lineage was out of the question. In searching Tellina's home, the City Guard found no information regarding family members in the sister cities. They sent a notice of his death and a request for information to Illus, but it would be several days before any response arrived.

Once they were in the warmth and light of her office, Lornis mentioned the sound they heard in the alley. "Do you think we were being followed?"

"No. It was probably a cat, or worse, some rats."

He shrugged. "I suppose it would be melodramatic to assume otherwise. I'll ask Usko for last year's cases."

Usko was still in the outside office, and he gave Lornis a pile of files. Lornis worked quietly at the other desk in the inner office while Draius penned a note to Perinon. She called a messenger to carry it up to Betarr Serin. Then she wrote up her report on the Tellina crime scene, which she had Lornis verify.

He shook his head while she read her report. After she finished, he said, "I wish I had your memory."

"Sometimes it's useful. But there are events I wish I didn't remember with such clarity."

"I never thought of the disadvantages."

"Believe me, there are drawbacks. How's the review going?" She gestured at the stacks on his desk.

"I think these are the *legitimately* closed cases from last year." He pointed at the largest stack, to her relief. He handed her a small sheaf. "These three files, however, are reports you should probably read. They're the robbery of the Royal Archive, and two reports from farmers."

"Farmers?"

"They found their livestock gutted—with symbols painted on the ground with blood. Although the victims were animals, the madness is painfully familiar."

"Not madness. They use method and precision," she mused. "In both of our murders, the exact same fingers were missing. The victims were oriented with their heads pointed directly toward the middle of the circular symbols drawn on the walls, and their limbs were arranged in exactly the same configuration. The wounds down the torsos were precisely done with an extremely sharp knife, their intestines were pulled out in—"

She stopped as she saw Lornis's face, his lip curling as he attempted a queasy smile. Perhaps she should focus on other details. "Two unmarked vials with powders were left at the first scene, but not the second. And what was on the parchment that disappeared from the first scene? No one's turned it in, and it might be able to answer some of our questions as to *why* they murdered the councilman. The only thing we know for sure is they came prepared to perform their ceremony."

"So the murders were ceremonies?"

"Someone wants us to believe that." She tapped the desk pensively, then reached into her pocket, pulled out Taalo's card and turned it over thoughtfully. "Perhaps they're performing experiments, but we don't recognize them as such?"

Lornis raised an eyebrow. "I doubt that little man can provide practical advice."

She shrugged. She was now the OIC and if she wanted to try radical techniques, this would be the time. "Are you still here, Usko?" she called, thinking he'd gone home.

She was wrong. The clerk was quickly standing in the doorway, his face red. "Yes, ser?"

"Have you ever heard of this man?" She handed him the card.

She asked a simple enough question, but Usko stammered his answer. "N—no, not really. Well, yes—I've heard of him, but I don't know him. He's supposedly a good apothecary. What do you want from him, ser?"

"He says he can identify unknown materials. Have we heard of anyone else that would attempt this, at least in a methodical manner?" She looked at Usko and Lornis, who both shook their heads. This was new territory, indeed, for the City Guard.

"Then Taalo must be our choice. Usko, tomorrow you will take the two powders found at the councilman's murder to this apothecary and commission him to do his analysis. We will *pay* him to identify these powders for us."

"Are you sure, ser?" Usko wiped his glasses. "How much should we pay him?"

"The watch has informants. We have standard payments for information, don't we? Why not pay this apothecary the same sort of fee?"

Usko left, after fussing about and neatening his workspace. Draius also got ready to leave, reaching for a packet on her desk which she hadn't touched.

"You're going to take the coroner's report, perhaps as a little light reading before bed?" Lornis raised his eyebrows. "You *are* the right person for this job."

She laughed as she turned off the gaslight and closed up the office. On the way out they said goodbye to the incoming watch, who were playing dice and waiting for their shift. Outside, she pulled her cloak tighter against the chilly spring night.

"Until tomorrow, then." She faced Lornis.

Lornis laid his hands on her shoulders. She felt the warmth of his hands through the fabric of her clothes. He was about the same height as she was, so she looked straight into his face. She was suddenly intensely aware of him, his warm brown eyes, his shining cascade of hair, and exactly how close his chest, hips, and thighs were to hers.

"You look tired. You should try to get some sleep, rather than reading reports." His hands squeezed her shoulders before he turned away.

She could only nod, astonished at her reaction. Then she slowly turned and walked the other way, smiling a little. As she rounded the street corner, a shadow moved away from the wall. She grabbed her knife hilt and a hand clamped on her wrist to forestall her.

CHAPTER ELEVEN

First Hireday, Erin Three, T.Y. 1471

T his evening, my employer wanted me present when he met with the
Groygan ambassador's lackey.

We met him in a suitably neutral and neglected workshop in the port
canal district, where the buildings loom close and the sea breeze can't
clear away the odors. Contrary to Betarr Serasa's northern canals where
the waters run clear, these are fetid, slow, and dark. Every now and then,
debris bobs to the surface and one needs a strong stomach to investigate
its nature, which explains why nobody hauls it out unless absolutely necessary. I remembered my poor apprentice and a spike of anger struck my
temples. I rubbed my head and looked away from my employer, concentrating instead on Orze Be Lottagre, who was the first Groygan I'd ever
met.

"I cannot help you, ser, if the *Danilo Ana*'s captain took my advice and
sailed for Chikirmo." Lottagre smiled. He sounded as Tyrran as any five-
star nobleman, instead of an "Honored Sword" for Groygan Ambassador
Velenare Be Glotta. His eyes denounced him, however, with narrow pupils and irises that glinted and reflected light in the dark like an animal's.
That might only be Tyrran myth and I wondered what I could learn from
dissecting those eyes. My fingers twitched, then stilled when he glanced
at me.

"He took your gold, not your words, to heart. You bribed a shipmaster to violate the course he filed with the harbormaster." My employer's tone made me shiver. He was most dangerous when he was quiet.

Lottagre's smile faded. "As embassy personnel, we cannot be charged under your King's Law. Besides, you couldn't accuse us without revealing your own crimes, which have been deliciously recounted in your *Horn & Herald*. So I'll ask you—how soon before the City Guard is banging on *your* door?"

I watched Lottagre carefully, not quite convinced he was bluffing. The Groygans were more dangerous than I realized; how did they get their information?

"I'm more concerned with finding the ship than worrying about the City Guard," my employer said. "More than five days have passed since the ship sailed and my contacts in Chikirmo report that the *Danilo Ana* has not arrived. It appears we've both lost our money, as well as a powerful artifact."

Lottagre's eyes flashed at the mention of "contacts in Chikirmo," but he didn't say anything. He probably had the same reports within his embassy. A ship could sail from Betarr Serin to Chikirmo within three to four days during false-spring, when the winds are better for west-to-east sailing. By now the *Danilo Ana* should have reached the city.

"What about pirates?" I asked, carefully watching Lottagre's face. The *H&H* voiced the opinion of most Tyrran and Sareenian sailors: that the piracy committed by Rhobar about the Auberei Archipelago was actually privateering for Groyga. That archipelago, jutting into and violating the Angim, allows pirates to lie in waiting for honest cargo ships. Avoiding piracy was the main reason our group voted to send the lodestone to Illus.

Lottagre shook his head. "That galley carried a bombard of iron weighing several tons and the new centerline cannon was the best that gold can buy. The crew was well armed and if they had a modicum of competency, they could easily defend themselves against boarders. More likely, the crew betrayed you or the ship was blown off-course by storms. Perhaps she's lost, gone to the bottom."

That wasn't what we wanted to hear. Navigational issues and storms were certainly possible, of course, despite the distance the ship put between the lodestone and the phrenic elements. Another worry, which I couldn't voice in front of the Groygan, was that we didn't know the full extent of the lodestone's powers. Being both a prison and amalgam of cursed souls, the lodestone itself might have taken action to affect its own fate.

Where is that ship?

CHAPTER TWELVE

Husbands, Lovers, and Maids

If our children are our lifeblood, then Tyrra's life is draining away. Since the Fevers our pregnancies and live births have dropped. The Phrenii say they cannot make an infertile woman fertile again, but they can increase a man's ability to father children. But sadly, no one will volunteer for phrenic healing, given the superstitions. So while our men avoid reality and indulge their passions, our women buy useless potions or powders, and we matriarchs frantically search our records for viable matches. Perhaps all that's needed is time, but can Tyrra afford any delay?

—*Entry in Meran-Viisi matriarchal records by Lady Aracia, T.Y. 1469*

"Jan, what are you doing?" Draius tensed but didn't draw her knife once she recognized her husband.

"I was going to ask you the same question." He continued to tightly hold her wrist.

"Have you been following me?" She thought of the sounds in the alley and twisted her arm out of his grip.

"What were you doing with him?" Jan used a light, curious tone and wore his perpetually pleasant smile, but she could sense he wasn't in a good mood.

"Lornis *works* for me, as you well know."

"Are you going to take him as a lover?"

She gaped for a moment. He knew, quite well, how she felt about honoring the clauses in their marriage contract. He was attempting to sidetrack her. Collecting herself, she decided she was too tired to do anything but play by the same rules. "Are you judging me by *your* behavior? You know I'll honor our contract, in the manner and intent it was written."

"No, you'd never involve yourself with someone for trivial reasons." His voice was quiet and he looked searchingly at her face. "I'd advise against this dandy, pretty as he is."

"Why?" She lifted her chin. Guard protocols forbid superior officers from becoming involved with someone under their command. They both knew this, just as they both knew she'd never involve herself with Lornis, so why were they talking about it?

Jan seemed to be carefully considering his next words. "If Peri is hurt by this, I'll make sure he understands that you're to blame."

He was doing it again: jumping around and twisting the argument, keeping her off-balance with vague threats. And why did he always pick a time when she was exhausted? "Peri's life needn't change unless *you* change it. You were never so concerned about our son before this."

The lineal matriarch was the keystone in the nurture and development of Tyrran children. She arranged for tutors and trainers, as well as spending time herself each day teaching the children the ethics, traditions, and history of the lineage. Half-brothers, half-sisters, and cousins, whether true, removed, or distant, sat together at their lessons because the lineage meant everything. The original parentage of children wasn't as relevant as the lineal name that sustained them, sheltered them, clothed them, and paid for their schooling. In Tyrra, the word "bastard" had no sting, unless the hurled insult was "*nameless* bastard." Then there might be a fight.

"I've realized how much the boy means to me. Do you think he'll ever forgive you?"

"Why is this my fault? It's about you and Netta."

The memories of confronting him about Netta were still raw and painful. At the time, he tried to act as if he was revealing everything on his own volition, ignoring the fact that she'd discovered everything in a public and demeaning manner.

"I need to get this off my chest so I can start fresh," he had said, when confronted. "What I've done shouldn't impact *us*."

"How can this not have any impact?" It sounded like they were talking about other people: another Draius, another Jan, living far away in a distant land.

"It can't, because I haven't allowed it. Besides, it's over. I've had the good faith to end it and now we can start again. Fresh."

Yes, he might be ready to start over, but Draius wasn't. She'd contacted Netta regarding the affair and learned more than she expected—if Netta told the truth. According to her, *she* ended their relationship, even though she had comfort clauses in her marriage contract.

And if Netta hadn't ended it, would Jan still be her lover? This was the question Draius desperately wanted answered. Even though the betrayal was blunted by previous infidelities, this affair had been different. Learning where Jan's true feelings lay, however, was no small task when he was a master of deception.

"What if I asked the captain to transfer Netta? Send her to Betarr Kain for four years?" she asked suddenly.

His mask slipped. For a second, she saw something in his eyes, something she'd seen only once through the crack of a door. Netta had been honest. Under Jan's façade, deep and buried in his soul, he had feelings for that woman. She saw, again, the flash of passion and tenderness he'd never shown toward her.

He laughed, his mask of invulnerability perfect again. "You wouldn't do that. You're devoted to objectivity, to keeping your emotions from affecting your work for the Guard. Remember, I know you well."

True, her threat was empty. And now, her life was empty. She retreated into Darkness, all hope gone. She could never go back to the time when she felt secure. When she thought she was *loved*. That innocence and trust could never be regained. She stepped away from him while he waited for her to reply.

"I could forgive another dalliance, but I'll never forgive or forget your feelings for Netta—no, don't deny it. Consider this when you make your case to Lady Anja: the Stars will fall into Darkness before I *ever* let you into my bed again, regardless of where our contract stands."

Her tirade took all her breath, and now her chest heaved in silent sobs. He stayed quiet while she turned and left.

Why was she always the one who walked away? Because Jan never walked away from something, or someone, he thought belonged to him.

•••

The next morning, the sun was barely licking the white peaks of the Cen Cerinas and turning them to rosy flames when she went downstairs. Nin had started breakfast, inferred by smells and sounds from the kitchen. Maricie, Anja's maid, barely old enough to be out of afternoon lessons by Tyrran standards, was laying the breakfast service out in the morning room.

Maricie's family had come from Sareen looking for employment, which Tyrra had in abundance. Sareenians flowed into the sister cities from Illus, Paduellus, and especially Forenllas, seeping into holes and cracks left in Tyrran society after the Fevers. Sareenians provided eager and cheap labor for the many vacant jobs.

"Good morning, Mistress," Maricie said as she breezed around the table placing china. "Breakfast will be a few minutes, but tea is ready. Oh, that'll be the news." She bustled out toward the front door as they heard the belled cart go by.

Draius poured herself a cup of tea. She stood in open double doors to enjoy the view of the back garden. Anja's garden glowed in the morning when the sun hit the back wall and the dew picked up the light. Spring had arrived and bulb flowers were beginning to bloom, while vines and perennials peeked up through the soil. She could almost convince herself that last night's argument with Jan had never happened.

Peri's footsteps banged down the stairs and came to a stop in the hall. "What's wrong, Maricie?" she heard him ask. "Here, I'll take the papers. Are you well?"

Maricie's answer was unintelligible, but she heard the maid go up the stairs with unsteady footsteps.

Peri laid the *Horn & Herald* on the sideboard as he walked through the morning room. "Maricie's taken ill. I'll go tell Cook." He vanished again, but his footfalls danced in the kitchen while Nin admonished him to stay away from her food.

"Without Maricie, Nin will need help at the market." Anja stood in the doorway.

"Peri can go before his lessons. He's finished his assignments," Draius said. Peri was big enough to carry sacks and be a set of helping hands, which was all Nin needed.

"Good, because I wanted to have Cerin turn over the vegetable beds today—what's this in the paper?" Anja had picked up the *H&H* and was staring at the front page.

"We uncovered another gruesome murder yesterday."

"That's not what I mean." Anja laid the paper down in front of Draius.

The top headline on the flier read "GROYGA THREATENS TO RECALL AMBASSADOR." Below that article was the Tellina murder. Apparently the murder of a Sareenian shipper wasn't big enough news by itself, so the headline read: "OFFICER MERAN-VIISI DRAIUS IN CHARGE OF INVESTIGATING MAGICAL MURDERS! IS THIS A PROMOTION TO PERILOUS DUTY?"

Draius was annoyed on several counts. First, she'd changed her lineal name to Serasa-Kolme when she married Jan. Matriarchs of both lineages had approved the change, and duly changed their records. Andreas was trying to give his article more appeal by throwing the King's lineage in the headline. Second, Tellina's full name was only mentioned once. Third, the article made much ado about connections to the Reggis murder and the "magical" signs left in locked rooms. While the suppositions were silly, the details were correct. Andreas must have gotten information from someone inside the City Guard.

She read the entire article carefully and realized that instead of following up on the "perilous duty" in the headline, the article insinuated she was incompetent! Andreas used his words carefully, but the implications were clear. Draius tossed the paper back on the table and told herself not to take it personally.

"Are you in some sort of danger?" Anja watched her steadily.

She carefully phrased her answer. "Jan and I have jobs where we encounter more danger than the ordinary citizen would face. However, what I'm doing this erin is no more dangerous than what I was doing last erin. You have no cause to worry for Peri's sake."

"I could be worried for your sake," Anja said.

There was the Serasa-Kolme inscrutability again: Anja's words might be a rebuke, a caution, or an expression of concern, but there was no clue from her face.

"Well, don't worry about me," Draius said. "I'm not taking the traditional path for a woman, but I'm good at what I do. I'm not in any danger."

"But you could be so much *more*. With your memory and your mind for facts and figures, I could use you within the Serasa-Kolme. You could start managing the smaller construction projects, which would bring in more money than that small salary you earn—"

Peri came back in, chattering about his plans for the day. Anja stopped, but her face said that they would be speaking about this again.

"Perinon, will you help Nin at the market this morning?" Anja asked Peri as he settled on his chair.

Peri ducked his head. He hated the use of his full name, and Draius gave Anja a warning glance as she laid her arm across her son's small shoulders.

"It'll get you out of helping Cerin dig the beds," she said in a conspiratorial whisper. "I'd jump at this chance to escape, if I were you."

A small smile started on Peri's face. He nodded. Draius knew he'd have more fun at the market than helping Cerin in the garden; sometimes jugglers, or even the Phrenii, could be at the market in the mornings.

Peri finished his breakfast and was away from the table quicker than Draius would have liked, because he left her alone with Lady Anja. She tried to concentrate on her breakfast, afraid that Anja would renew their previous conversation.

"I've received a complaint from the Pettaja-Viisi," Anja said, breaking the silence first. "Apparently your behavior at the Royal Library yesterday wasn't well received."

Draius continued to chew on the bacon that Nin had sliced and cooked perfectly; it was thick and crunchy, with just enough fat. There was nothing she could say in her defense, and she was only surprised by the speed with which the complaint had arrived. How did the matriarchs exchange information so quickly?

"If you're serious about this *non-traditional* path you've chosen, then you must learn to be more politic, especially when dealing with men." Anja poured herself more tea and put a small amount of sugar into the cup. She stirred carefully before continuing, and the chink of the spoon on the china sounded clear and cold. "Handling men's passions requires *both* shrewdness and tact: talents you should develop."

Draius sighed and wiped the grease off her lips, remembering to dab with the napkin. She kept her gaze on the young matriarch's face. "If a formal apology is necessary, Lady, then I will make one. But I will only apologize for my manner, not my actions."

"Who said anything about an apology? I trust your judgment enough to believe your manner was warranted."

Draius blinked, then looked down at her plate in confusion.

"But I give you fair warning." Anja's tone became severe. "Lately, you've been the topic of our discussions far too often. This is understandable, given the unconventional way your father raised you, but you should try to avoid matriarchal attention in the future."

Draius gulped. It was one thing for Jan to say she'd marked herself as a "troublemaker," but quite another for a matriarch to advise her to keep her head down and stay out of trouble. The latter was far more serious.

After excusing herself from the table, she spent some time reading in the garden. Before she left for work, she quietly climbed up the back stairs to the third story to check on Maricie. As she suspected, the maid was not in her room.

• • •

"I can't stand it anymore, the grunting and panting. Surely I've suffered enough!" Onni faced her mother and her hands moved in emphatic jerks.

"Have you been taking the powder I gave you in your drink before bedtime?" Aracia was attempting a soothing tone; instead, it felt like cool steel running against one's skin.

"Of course, but the Phrenii say it can't help. They say it's—"

"They say it's only superstition. But the powder can be relaxing, if nothing more. Too bad the Phrenii can't *heal* women's infertility, like they can supposedly do for men. I fear this is the price we pay as women." Contrary to her words, the matriarch was unemotional, as immovable as stone.

Onni stared at her mother. "You think *that's* the price we pay? No, our price is to be handled, night after night, with no end in sight. How long must I do this?"

"Your contract is a valuable connection to the northern Viljella-Viisi. We can't afford to dissolve it."

"There won't be any child. It's been six years, and I've tried and tried. All for you and the Meran-Viisi. I can't—"

"Then take a lover," Aracia interrupted Onni before she could whip her emotions into full gallop again. Mother and daughter faced each other, their profiles identical.

"It's quite the fashion, and I made sure you have the appropriate clauses," Aracia continued. "You've seen the records. You know how we record parentage, unvarnished and accurate. It doesn't matter as long as you choose the father carefully."

Perinon stood in the doorway to the library, unnoticed by the women. His secretary had been standing behind him, but no longer, having fled back to his office at the sound of the women's raised voices. He wondered if he should have followed as he cautiously cleared his throat.

Both women turned toward him. Onni flushed scarlet.

"Sire," Onni murmured, bowing her head. After he acknowledged her, she rushed past him to get out of the library.

Perinon sympathized with his cousin, thrust into duties she never wanted, but he said nothing as she left. He and Onni had never spoken to each other about their particular responsibilities to the Meran-Viisi.

Aracia waited, an immovable pillar in the middle of the room. He held up the matriarch's latest recommendation, penned on vellum stamped at the top with the Meran-Viisi crest.

"You suggest I appoint Muusa to my Council? He hasn't any experience—" Having no more polite words, Perinon chose bluntness and raised his voice. "He's an idiot, a hedonistic buffoon of the worst kind. It pains me to call him cousin. What's wrong with Runos, my first choice?"

"I spoke with Runos," Aracia said. "She wishes to continue with her business interests, and leave politics to men."

"Must we hold to tradition so blindly? 'Men have no mind for business and women don't dabble in politics,' at least, until they want something." He made no attempt to hide his sarcasm. They both knew how much matriarchal counsel drove Tyrran political affairs.

"Muusa is only temporary, until a replacement for Reggis is elected." Aracia's tone sounded just like it had when she attempted to placate her daughter.

"By the Horn, *Lady*, this is not matchmaking!" Perinon emphasized her matriarchal title. "We're talking about an appointment to the King's Council."

"Yes, we are. Muusa needs experience, as you've seen, if he's ever to rise in politics. He's still young, pliable, and eager to please, which you can turn to your advantage. If I'm not clear enough, *Sire*, then I suggest you read that book by the Sareenian."

Aracia turned, her skirts swishing in the silence as she walked over to the bell cord and pulled it. Faint jangling tones sounded down the hall in the direction of the kitchen. "Would you like mid-morning tea?"

Perinon tried to determine whether he'd been insulted, and failed. Sometimes she could be as obscure as the Phrenii. Despite the widespread adult belief that the creatures were both soulless and heartless, Perinon sometimes felt intense emotion from them through the bond made by the broken Kaskea. In contrast, he'd never felt a whisper of emotion from Aracia. As the only person in Tyrra who could actually perceive the emotions of others—when the Phrenii were near—he knew the true heartless beings in Tyrra were the matriarchs. Was it the training, or Tyrran society, that beat all compassion and empathy out of them?

"I'll appoint Muusa to the temporary position," he said. "But if he gives me cause to regret this, I'll hold you responsible."

"And morning tea?" She turned toward the steward who was warily entering the room. She was calm and collected, as if their raised voices couldn't carry outside the library and down the marble halls.

"No, thank you." Perinon tried to set aside his resentment at being manipulated, as he watched Aracia's smug smile. He didn't want to be distracted from the work he had to do this morning. Next on the enormous pile on his desk was a report from Draius. He turned on his heel and left the library, wondering when he would see that same calculating look on Onni's face.

•••

Lornis's face lit with a radiant smile when she walked into her office, the corners of his eyes crinkling. Draius smiled back, now uncomfortably aware of his beauty. Inwardly, she cursed Jan, wondering if she'd ever again be able to look at Lornis objectively.

"I see you got some sleep last night," Lornis said.

"Some," she allowed. She'd finished the coroner's report this morning, taking advantage of the quiet garden.

"Seen the news?" Lornis tossed an *H&H* onto her desk.

"Yes, and I want some words with Andreas."

"I hope to see that. It should be entertaining."

She glanced up to see if he was being facetious, catching his gaze. He lounged in a chair beside her desk, where he'd laid out some records. He'd brought in another chair and had his feet up on it. His hair was bound in a silver clasp and his finely chiseled face radiated intensity. She looked away, breaking eye contact.

"You look comfortable." Her tone was dry. "Did Ponteva and Miina find out anything interesting yesterday?"

Lornis motioned at the stacks beside him. "We're collecting backgrounds and interviewing forty people, men and women, who have some reason to be upset with the councilman's recent exploits—mostly sexual."

"My, he was a busy man."

"Yes," Lornis said, musing. He looked at a list in his hand. "Reggis seemed able to move in all circles, from barmaid to Lady of three-star, even four-star lineages. It doesn't feel right."

"I know." Draius moved around her deck to sit. "I never understood his appeal."

"No, I didn't mean that. I mean his murder doesn't feel related to his womanizing."

She smiled. "Your instinct is right. This murder doesn't have the signature of a personal vendetta or sexual jealousy. In those cases, there is often disfigurement of the face or genitals. Remember, this is no crime of passion and that's why you can't read the emotion or motives."

"You've said that before. So why do Ponteva and Miina have to grind through all these interviews?"

"Because one thing I learned from Rhaffus was to be thorough. No lead should be left to dangle, because there's always the chance that the unlikely person may be your culprit. And we might learn something useful from these interviews that helps us close this case."

"But you're not bothering to follow these leads yourself."

"No. I trust Ponteva's determination to close them out for me, and I can follow the more interesting, unconventional leads."

"Speaking of which, I reviewed the files regarding the robbery at the Royal Library." Lornis spoke in a neutral tone. If he questioned her actions yesterday, then he was keeping his doubts to himself. But, if he started gossiping about her treatment of the librarian, and talk of her *sidestepping* the magistrates to go straight to the King came to the captain's ears…

Draius suddenly realized how tenuous her position really was. She wondered how savvy Lornis could be; would he take advantage of her mistakes and ruin her? He was different from Jan, not as politic or ambitious. Certainly, he'd not yet showed the ruthlessness she'd seen in her husband. She watched his bright, alert face as he talked, looking for secondary motives.

"Erik took statements from librarians, clerks, and students that had visited the Royal Archives for an eight-day before the robbery was discovered. Unfortunately, no one knows when the materials were stolen, only when the theft was discovered." He appeared to be totally immersed in this case, and nothing else. How did such a political innocent jump to the rank of lieutenant, and gain the captain's trust?

"Can you tell why the case was closed? Did Usko say anything?" She kept her voice low.

"There were no suspects. Usko says Erik closed the case as 'unsolvable' after two erins, over his objections."

Something in his face made her ask, "But you don't believe him?"

He looked uneasy. She stepped to the door and looked into the outer office, which was empty. After she nodded, he said, "I just can't put my finger on it, but something doesn't feel right. Granted, Erik ran this office with an iron hand and Usko couldn't complain to you or anyone else."

She didn't know Usko very well, either, since the clerk had been attached to the Office of Investigation after Erik took over. However, she was beginning to trust Lornis's perception and intuition; perhaps this was his talent, and the reason the captain had assigned him as her deputy.

"Keep an unobtrusive eye on our clerk, when you can," she said. "And I'll need your help to go through all the pub's rooms today."

Lornis smiled, jumping to his feet with sinuous grace. "It's close enough, the weather's nice, so I assume we'll walk?"

"Yes, it's a beautiful day for a quiet stroll."

Lornis took the hint. He was silent as she took the lead, setting a stiff pace with her long legs. Without any unnecessary chatter, they dodged carriages and made their way to the pub in less than half an hour.

They sat in the common room, exactly where they'd been sitting the evening of the murder. About half the other tables had customers who were ordering and consuming the modest mid-day meal offered by the tavern.

Mainos, the manager of the Sea Serpent, hurried over to their table. "Officer Draius, you're hurting my business. Keeping those rooms closed is costing me in gold every day!" He wrung his hands melodramatically.

"I have a hard time believing you count your daily earnings in tyr." She looked about. The interior of the pub looked significantly shabbier in the mid-day sunlight.

Mainos offered them a meal at a discount, and while Draius refused both the discount and the meal, Lornis bought a bowl of stew and put it down in record time. He ordered a second bowl while she talked with Mainos, who tried to convince her of the hardships he suffered.

"I rent those rooms out hourly—not for what you think," he added hastily, seeing her expression. "I rent them for private card games and meetings. For instance, Andreas and his Society for the Restoration of Sorcery were supposed to meet here this afternoon, but now I'll lose that rent."

"Do they meet here often? How many people?" Draius was intrigued.

"These are only the top members, usually five or six of them." Mainos leaned forward and added in a low voice, "Andreas says it's business for the society, but I think all they really do is play cards."

"Well, we only need to examine the last two rooms, so I'll let you open the others if we can use one of those rooms for our interviews."

"Anything to help the Guard." Mainos brightened at the prospect of having at least a few rooms to let.

Two rooms were opened and Draius used one to take a second statement from Mainos. Although it was much too late to get accurate information, she hoped something new might present itself. He recounted everything he remembered from the night of the murder, but his memory was already blurring. She heard nothing remarkable in his account of Fairday night, so she moved on to the subject of Tellina, hoping to find some connection between the murders.

"Yes, I met Tellina on the day Reggis was murdered," Mainos said. "He came in for a meal."

"Do you remember where Tellina was when the body was discovered?" Lornis asked, eagerly jumping into the interview.

"Oh, he was long gone by then. Tellina left right after taking the midday meal."

"Did you rent the third room again that day, before the councilman took it?" Draius asked.

"Twice." Mainos provided the names of the clients.

She continued her questions while Lornis made notes. Had Mainos ever seen Reggis and Tellina together? No. Did he know if they had a business, or personal, relationship? No. Had he seen Tellina after Councilman Reggis was murdered? No. Draius sighed. So far there was no connection between the victims, aside from their patronage of the Sea Serpent.

"Can you send the barmaid up to speak with us?" she asked.

"Certainly, Raivata's just come on shift."

"Have her bring me some tea," called Draius as Mainos left the room. Thinking over her small collection of clues, Draius got up and went to the window. She stared down at the alley between the buildings.

"My, my. What pretty hair." The voice was sultry. Draius unconsciously touched her long braids as she turned, then realized the compliment wasn't meant for her.

Raivata stood in the doorway, holding a cup of tea. She bore little resemblance to the weeping, screeching ball of misery that Draius threw toward Lornis on the night of the murder. She seemed taller, more statuesque. Right now, she ogled Lornis with frank appreciation.

Lornis looked up from his seat at the table and smiled back. He sat sideways to the door, and his hair divided across his shoulder in shining cascades. Raivata threw back her shoulders, causing her breasts to mound higher, and sashayed smoothly across the room to flounce into the chair facing Lornis. She didn't spill a drop of tea, which she set down in front of him.

Draius cleared her throat. "The tea is for me," she said, getting barely a glance from the barmaid.

"You look like 'The Hunter Chieftain,'" Raivata said. She leaned close to Lornis and her breasts threatened to fall out of her bodice.

Draius's eyebrows rose so high she felt her eyelids stretch. Looking at Lornis in a new light, she suddenly saw his resemblance to the mosaic the barmaid referred to. It ran across one wall of the Palace of Stars, and its source was older than the building itself. When the Palace had been built, an artist created the mosaic from an ancient tapestry woven by one of the original Tyrran tribes. The faded and frayed tapestry pre-dated the arrival of the Phrenii and the Meran blood introduced into their ancestry.

On the wall, the artist used chips of stone to form a hunter galloping on his horse over the Tyrran plains, carrying a spear. The hunter had brown hair streaming behind him, his angular face narrowed to a sharp chin, and his eyes were a warm brown. If Lornis put a silver circlet on his brow, he would have been the exact image of the Hunter Chieftain.

Lornis's smile broadened. The barmaid's hand moved to cover his, but he smoothly transferred his right hand to the teacup and slid it toward Draius, his gaze never leaving Raivata. "About the murder...?"

The barmaid looked blank.

"We'd like to talk about the murder of the councilman," said Lornis.

Raivata pouted. Her knees touched his. "I'd really like to forget about that. I must've told the watch the story three times already."

"I'd appreciate it if you'd tell me what happened, one more time." Lornis patted her knee, which seemed to mollify her. She launched into her story, playing up the drama.

Draius reached for her tea and sipped it. Lornis was handling Raivata well, deftly sidestepping her advances and bringing her back to her story, trying to find new details, checking consistency. *I guess I get to be the aggressive interrogator.* Guard training covered the passive-aggressive roles that they played when questioning witnesses or suspects, and Lornis seemed to have a natural talent for interviewing.

Raivata finished her story, providing no new information. After she finished, she reached forward and carefully selected a lock of long shiny hair resting on Lornis's chest. She started winding it about her finger, but there was still an arms-length between them. Lornis seemed entirely unconcerned with her gradually shortening that distance. Draius knew his attitude would only encourage the barmaid, but did he know?

Lornis looked up from his notes and smiled at Raivata. *Of course he knows his effect on women.* The lock of hair was starting to tighten.

"Why did you go to the fourth room Fairday evening?" he asked pleasantly.

The barmaid blinked and stopped twisting the lock.

"Weren't you supposed to meet the councilman in the *third* room that night?" Lornis asked. His voice was still affable, but there was an unyielding quality in it. Raivata dropped the lock of hair. The pout came back on her face.

Draius felt it was time for her to take up the aggressive role and distract the barmaid. "The King's Law requires that you be truthful with us. If we find you've lied to us, we can charge you with obstructing our duty."

Raivata finally acknowledged Draius by shooting her a sharp look, but quickly regained her composure. She took some time to smooth her long curls about her face before saying, "Yes, we were to meet in the third room, but he was in the fourth room. What does that matter?"

"So Mainos doesn't know you have a master key." Lornis gave her a conspiratorial smile.

A quick, guarded look flashed across Raivata's face. "You won't be telling him, will you?"

"If you tell us why Reggis was in the fourth room that night, I won't be telling Mainos anything."

Raivata's answer wasn't very illuminating. Apparently Reggis was in the habit of renting both the third and fourth rooms at the same time. Raivata had checked the third room first, but when he wasn't there, she tried the fourth room to find it locked. She had quietly pulled out her master key and opened the door.

"So the councilman never told you why he would rent two rooms. Didn't he confide in you?" Lornis asked.

"Of course." The maid sounded a bit miffed. "He needed my advice. He said I provided him with pers—perspective. He said I had sharp insight."

Draius looked down quickly at her tea and concentrated on not smiling, coughing, snorting, or making any other sound that might be construed as derogatory.

Lornis ignored the insinuation that Raivata provided the King's Councilman with vital information. "Anything particular on his mind this past two eight-days?"

"Oh, yes," Raivata replied. "There was the vote for raising taxes on imports from Groyga, how to handle the Groygan ambassador, and some trade he was involved in—I guess it wasn't going well."

"Can you remember the specifics of that? Was this some sort of commerce? Shipping, perhaps?" Lornis jumped on this point that might connect Tellina and Reggis. Also, it was unusual for a King's Council member, an established politician, to be involved in trade. Managing business was normally the work of women.

Raivata frowned while she thought, and Draius hoped she wouldn't overtax herself.

"I think it had to do with shipping foodstuffs. Reggis thought it was too soon to ship them because the goods would spoil." The maid's face cleared, directing a smile to Lornis. Apparently she wasn't familiar with how foodstuffs spoiled.

Draius looked down at her tea again.

"Of course." Lornis smiled.

Raivata didn't know much about the councilman's trysts outside of her time spent with him, and couldn't provide information about his other relationships. Lornis thanked her for her cooperation

"Anything to help, Lieutenant. You can interview me any time." Raivata leaned over as she got up, nearly catching Lornis's nose in her cleavage. As she walked around his chair she trailed her fingers along his sleeve. "I hope to speak with you again."

"I'm certain you will." Lornis replied brightly, but he turned back to his notes and did not watch the barmaid's swaying hips as she left the room.

There was no sound in the room except for the scratching of Lornis's pen. Draius finished her tea and set it down on the saucer with a clink. Lornis looked up.

"Well, you managed her well. I had no idea of your skills with women."

Lornis put down his pen and gave her a hard, direct look. "I know how to play the game. But it's just a game."

"As long as you're not likely to be distracted by a pretty face." *Now why did I say that?*

"Not likely; it takes more than a fine face and figure to catch my eye. I know what sort of woman interests me, and I won't find her serving in a pub." Lornis went back to his notes.

Draius was uncomfortable with the direction of this conversation even though she had initiated it, so she changed the subject. "We still can't establish a connection between Tellina and Reggis."

"What about the 'goods' Reggis was shipping?"

"The councilman's name didn't appear on any of Tellina's invoices and there are many shipping companies in this port. Still, it's a possibility." She motioned at the door. "Let's go over that third room, the one where he was supposed to meet the girl."

The third room was multi-functional like the one they just left, with a small table, four chairs, a sideboard, a wardrobe, and a lounge that could double as a bed. The room was crowded with furniture as it attempted to be both proper parlor and clandestine bedchamber. It had a window, while the fourth room, where the body was found, did not.

"Supposedly no one has been in this room since the morning after the murder," she said. "But it was open for an entire night, so anything could have been removed during that time."

"This was where I interviewed Raivata, the night of the murder." Lornis shuffled through his notes.

Draius looked around. There was a rumpled sheet on top of the lounge chair. On the sideboard were a flask and two glasses, with what looked like a dried puddle of wine. There were muddy footprints and dirt on the wooden floor near the door, probably from the overflow of the crowd that night. Beside the door was a chamber pot. The entire room reeked of sweat, urine, mud, and vomit. She wrinkled her nose and sighed.

"Anything you noticed that evening, that might seem out of the ordinary?" she asked Lornis.

He looked carefully around the room. "Unfortunately, I don't have your eye for detail nor your memory. Raivata threw up into the chamber pot—twice," he added helpfully, then his eyes moved to the sideboard. He paused. "I considered ordering spirits to steady her, but there was just too much chaos that evening. I looked over at the sideboard for something to give her, and I'm sure that spill of wine was fresh."

"Norsis suspects a very fast-acting poison. The poison could have been administered in the wine."

"If he was poisoned in here, how did he get to the next room? Someone would have noticed the incapacitated councilman being hauled around on the open gallery," Lornis said.

She stared at the wardrobe. "Do you realize the wardrobe in the next room is placed against the wall directly in line with this one?"

Their eyes met, and they both went to the wardrobe. Lornis pushed against its tall side, but it appeared to be attached to the wall. She opened the double doors. The back of the wardrobe looked solid.

Lornis knocked and felt around the edges. "Ah." There was a click, and he pushed on the back wall of the cabinet. It pivoted to reveal another wardrobe interior. He reached and pushed outward on the other set of doors, then stepped through the opening and down into the fourth room.

"Get Mainos," Draius said. "He knows about this door."

CHAPTER THIRTEEN

First Millday, Erin Three, T.Y. 1471

Even though I don't yet understand how Nherissa created the lodestone, I can piece together the philosophy and craft behind the making of small charms. I have recorded the practicum:

> Use Pekon's instructions to make aqua regis from vitriol, sal armoniac, sal niter, sal gemmai, and alumen crudum. Take, with proper reverence, a button of noble silver recently made from cupellation. Dissolve the silver into as small an amount of liquid as possible, taking care to not breathe the fumes. Seal the flask, and put it aside.
>
> Select slivers of power-bound flesh and an item possessed by the same source, such as a trinket or threads from clothing they wore.
>
> Develop a recipe for the antithesis of charm's effect. This charm will cause the direct opposite of healthy breath—so prepare the normal remedy for congested lungs: comfrey, calamint, liquorice, and hyssop, pulverized in a poultice.
>
> Cover the flesh and belongings with vinegar in a retort. Distill off the vinegar, then take clear water and wash away all sharpness. Combine items with the poultice and wrap tightly together in a small pouch.

Pour a circle of fresh blood around the pouch. Ensure the circle is at least an arm-span across in diameter. Place the gemstones ruby, sapphire, emerald, and garnet on the circle at their respective positions of east, north, west, and south. The gems must be touched by blood. Now take the silver in aqua regis and carefully pour it over the circle of blood, while chanting the precise instructions.

The resulting charm performed admirably by asphyxiating a rat when it stepped outside its cage. Of course, this charm was given simple directives.

I then experimented with more abstract instructions, designing a charm to control the City Guard Officer who's in charge of Investigation. I told my employer what I overheard in the library, but he still thinks he has her under control.

I disagree. She's too close to the truth.

CHAPTER FOURTEEN

The Apothecary and the Editor

GROYGA THREATENS TO RECALL AMBASSADOR

The Groygan Lords have given an ultimatum to our King's Council: reduce import taxes on Groygan silk or Ambassador Velenare Be Glotta will be recalled, thereby crippling all negotiation. The Council has no comment at this difficult time while they scramble to replace Council-man Meran-Nelja Reggis, who was our primary negotiator. Tension has been rising between our two countries and rumors of skirmishes near the Saamarin grow every day.

—*The Horn & Herald, First Millday, Erin Three, T.Y. 1471*

Mainos entered the room in front of Lornis. When he saw Draius standing in front of the open wardrobe, he tried to turn away. Lornis grabbed the bulky tavern keeper about the shoulders and kept him in place.

"Well, to think there was a door between the rooms," Mainos said half-heartedly, with a little nervous laugh. His shoulders slumped and Lornis let him go.

Draius glared and Mainos added hastily, "I'll be honest. I knew about it. Maybe, in bygone eras, it was used to fleece sleeping customers, but I've never used it for that. I swear by the Healing Horn! I forgot all about it."

"Certainly you remembered it when the councilman was murdered?"

"Yes," Mainos mumbled. Draius had to lean close to hear him. "I was worried about the reputation of the pub. Then, when the 'magical murders' started being touted by the H&H, I couldn't say anything about it, you see? Besides, all that ballyhoo pulled in more customers."

"You've got more to worry about than your reputation—do you know the penalty for keeping information from a Guard Officer? Did you think I wouldn't find this door?" Draius almost sputtered. How stupid did Mainos think she was?

"There didn't seem any need to bring it up. When everyone said the windows were locked tight and no one could escape, I figured the door didn't matter."

"We haven't confirmed any of the windows were locked. Besides, it's not up to you to determine relevance," Draius said. "I'll have to report this to the captain but I'll ask him to keep it to a fine. How many of your staff knew about this door?"

"Not many," protested Mainos.

"And Reggis?"

"Well, yes. He knew. He sometimes rented two rooms at a time; to separate business from pleasure, if you catch my drift."

"What about Raivata?" Draius asked.

"No, she doesn't know the rooms are connected." Mainos's voice was firm.

She wondered if she should tell him how much he'd underestimated his barmaid, to the extent that she'd copied or pilfered a master key, but it wasn't relevant to her case—at least right now. She raised her index finger in warning, wagging it in front of the innkeeper's sagging face. "I'm leaving Officer Lornis here to get the names of everyone who knew about the hidden door. He'll be questioning them. We also need to know when Reggis ordered his wine, and who served it. Be sure to give him your full cooperation, Mainos."

Draius put on her cloak. Below, the common room was starting to fill with customers for the late afternoon. Mainos looked like he wanted to be elsewhere while Lornis gave him a quiet lecture. Mainos' face was starting to go white as she left.

She went through the common room quickly and walked around to the alley under the rooms. There were scuffs along the side of the building under the window to the third room, as would be left by the use of a ladder, although they could have been there before the murder.

A ladder could explain the quick exit made by the killers—she now considered the deed done by multiple people—as well as their unnoticed entrance. But the walls were thick and the windowsill deep; they couldn't have easily climbed into the room without Reggis's cooperation. He must have known his murderers, perhaps even expected them. Why did he let them into the room?

• • •

Millday morning came and her staff still slogged through statements of witnesses. There were no sound suspects in sight, although Draius felt she knew the means behind the murders.

She decided to give Lornis a break, taking him with her to visit the apothecary. They found the neatly presented shop on Silta Street, with a sign that read APOTHECARY, SUPPLIES & ANALYSIS.

She pushed open the door, tinkling a bell that hung high on the frame. The inside of the shop was small, with only one counter. The place had a sharp caustic smell, a constant reminder that strange and dangerous compounds could be bought here. Shelves covered every wall from floor to ceiling, containing pouches and small stoneware jars covered with parchment. All the items on the shelves were labeled and organized with precision, almost obsession.

Taalo stood at the counter, marking something on a package.

"Ah, the work for the Office of Investigation. Right this way." Taalo went through the curtain behind the counter, and they followed.

The laboratory was larger than the storefront. It was also warmer, thanks to a small kiln roaring on one wall. Samples were set near the chimney to keep warm. The apothecary probably used the kiln for making custom glassware; many examples could be seen on a long narrow counter nearby.

Draius stopped by a rounded flask with a long thin neck that went up for an arm's length before it curved down into a gentle slope to rest in a smaller flask. The little apothecary paused beside her.

"An alembic," Taalo said, as if that explained everything. "I'm doing a distillation, searching for a particular oil. I once created a jellylike oil and found it particularly explosive. If I can isolate it again, it will change our entire society." His voice grew pompous. "It will be able to propel projectiles with more speed and force than the best corned powder."

Lornis looked at the little man doubtfully.

"I haven't perfected the process yet," Taalo said.

"But if distillation won't separate the oil, then it suffered a character change and must be lost," Lornis said.

The apothecary raised his gray eyebrows. "You have training?"

"My grandfather was an alchemist, and I assisted him for a while. When Pekon disproved the transmutation of metals, my grandfather took the title of Chemist."

"The Academy of Science refused my petition to use that title. Those of us with practical experience aren't considered worthy of it, so your grandfather must have been lucky." The apothecary's tone was spiteful.

"My grandfather is Kulte-Kolme." Lornis acted like his non sequitur explained everything.

The apothecary looked impressed. "Precious metal refining?"

"Yes, I have a little background, at least enough to know when someone's trying to flummox me."

Taalo looked a bit sheepish. "Well, I'm missing something, perhaps a thaumaturgic constituent." His expression turned eager. "As Kulte-Kolme, did you meet the great Pekon?"

"Yes, although we didn't call him *great*. He and my grandfather were cousins. Pekon was considered radical and at the time, we all hoped to transmute less noble metals to silver and gold."

"How would you describe him?"

"Can we speak about the analysis?" Draius asked. By her left elbow, a strange-smelling liquid was starting to a boil. The whole building might blow sky high before she got her information.

"Of course." Taalo's mouth stretched. "The black powder you sent me was a poison, and it quickly killed the mouse I fed it to. Poor thing." He gestured toward the far wall, which held cages of small animals and rodents, lined up by cage size.

"Can you tell what sort of poison?" Draius asked.

"Wolfsbane." Taalo handed her the vial with the original powder. "It can be deadly when prepared properly, using the root of a plant that grows on the slopes of the Cen Cerinas."

"How did you identify it by this powder?" Draius held up the vial and tilted it, looking at the finely ground grains.

"By something of my own invention." Taalo held up a square wire frame over which was stretched an almost transparent paper. When Draius reached to touch it, he pulled it back quickly.

"No, don't touch! Your fingers will contaminate it with oils. This is a fine linen paper made specially for me." His own fingers were permanently discolored and of questionable cleanliness, but she didn't point this out.

Taalo showed her another stretched square that hung vertically over a shallow bath of liquid. The fluid barely touched the bottom of the paper, and was slowly seeping upwards. Above the level of the liquid, there was a horizontal row of little black dots on the paper.

"See those black dots? Those are samples I dissolved in spirits and placed on the paper. The solution in the bath is absorbed vertically up the parchment, and it moves parts of the samples with it. Different plants make different patterns, according to their personality. See, here is your powder beside my sample of wolfbane." He produced a dried paper square showing two identical streaks, each having four blotches of the same shape and color.

She was impressed. "Were you able to do this with the other powder also?"

Taalo hesitated. "No," he said, using a glum tone. He went over to the shelf and took down another square of stretched paper. On it was one long wide smear.

"Why didn't it work?"

"I don't know. Certain materials may lack the personality for this analysis." He brightened. "But I'm fairly sure the second sample is dried, crushed Rowan flowers."

"Why?" Lornis asked.

"Other properties. It smells like Rowan flowers and it's not poisonous. I've written up my analysis, as specified in the work contract."

"Well done," Draius said. "The City Guard will pay your fee."

As she filled out a bank draft with the City Guard seal upon it, she wondered whether this information really had any value. After all, Norsis already concluded that Reggis had been poisoned before his body was mutilated. She handed the draft to Taalo, and started walking out of the laboratory. As she came near the door, she saw a wide cauldron that had a flat mirror set inside.

She stopped and leaned over the cauldron, looking at the mirror. Her image was clear, but quivered. As she watched, her head faded and blurred while at the central part of the mirror, a bright green jewel came into detail. It seemed to be hanging from her neck. So this wasn't a mirror because she wasn't wearing—the surface rippled violently and she jumped back.

Taalo had jiggled the cauldron, and now plunged his hand through the mirror. It looked like a molten metal, yet it wasn't hot. The ripples extended from his hand as he moved it through the shimmering liquid.

"Don't get close to the quicksilver and breathe the fumes," he said. "It might bring on visions or madness."

Draius felt a flush of embarrassment, and tried to compose herself. She turned on the little apothecary. "Would either of those powders be of use in the art of necromancy?"

Taalo looked surprised. Then his mouth stretched and his eyes narrowed as he looked up at her. "What interest would you have in the archaic and illegal practice of necromancy, Officer?"

"Answer my question."

Taalo looked down at the quicksilver and studied it for a moment. When he looked up, his eyes glinted. "I sell dried Rowan flowers as protection from necromantic spells. Some of my customers are superstitious and believe the art is still practiced."

Draius exchanged a look with Lornis. When she turned back to Taalo, he was over in the corner going through a trunk, humming tunelessly. He held up a small pouch on a leather string and walked back to her.

"What is that?" she asked.

"I see danger ahead for you." Taalo cocked his head with almost a pleading expression. "I want to give you a charm for protection."

Taalo reached to put the pouch around her neck but she pulled back. A wounded expression crossed his face, making her feel guilty. It couldn't hurt to humor the little man, could it?

"I'm not one of your customers," she said.

"A charm may be sung, a charm may be said, but most powerful of all, a charm need be made. So I sing a charm for Draius." Taalo used a high dreamy voice as he reached to put the pouch around her neck and this time she let him tie it. It settled on her breastbone. She'd take it off outside, away from his view. "What's in—"

"*San klamek.* Never, never look. Never, never see." Taalo giggled and snapped his fingers.

Draius shook her head. The room felt stuffy; maybe she had breathed in some of the quicksilver fumes. She looked at Lornis, whose brows were knotted as if he had a headache. "What were you saying?"

Lornis shrugged.

"You asked me what purpose the quicksilver had, Officer." Taalo pulled aside the curtain to the storefront and gestured for them to precede him. "Those with the Sight believe it can focus their talent. Again, deep-seated folklore that has never been proven."

Outside the shop, the air was still chilly and the spring sun tried to burn through the clouds.

"What a strange little man," Lornis said.

"I agree." She made a dismissive gesture, as the memory of Taalo's face slipped away like silk falling through her fingers. "I didn't know you were Kulte-Kolme."

"Yes, but I wasn't intended to be a goldsmith. Shall we make that visit to Andreas, as you promised?" Lornis turned and ran gracefully beside the street, his arm up to hail a passing carriage. He had a catlike energy about him, reminding her of a predatory hunter coiled to spring.

The Kulte-Kolme was a long-established and wealthy lineage that owned most of the gold mines in the central and northern Tyrran plains. They had a reputation for being reliable and were not known for taking risks. Some might call them stodgy. Draius had once seen their matriarch, Kulte-Kolme Enkali, and she could imagine the matriarch's bewilderment when trying to place Lornis. The conservative matriarch must have been at her wit's end to figure out what to do with him—especially if he was cursed by a destiny.

"What are you smiling about?" Lornis asked when she climbed into the carriage.

"Oh, nothing." She knocked to tell the driver to proceed. "To the Offices of the *H&H*, please."

• • •

Andreas proved uncooperative. Draius expected some obstinacy, but not this much protest.

"I can assure you that each and every member of the Society for the Restoration of Sorcery is a law abiding citizen. Some are quite respectable, in fact." Andreas pushed his dark hair, mussed and unkempt, away from his eyes. With his rumpled sleeves and stained vest, he had the look of a man too preoccupied by the world's woes to take concern with his appearance, or to answer questions from annoying Guard officers.

"I hope you won't mind if I check your membership myself," she said.

"Actually, I do mind. My word should be good enough."

"And your word is based *on your Honor?*"

Andreas didn't answer her jibe. He sat back down at his neat and tidy desk, a surprising contrast to his appearance. Draius stood directly in front of him, her arms crossed and her long legs spread in an aggressive stance. Behind her, Lornis leaned nonchalantly against the doorframe, effectively blocking the way out. Not intimidated by their tactics, Andreas smugly smiled.

She tried a different approach. "What about Councilman Reggis?"

"What about him?"

"Was he ever a member of your S—R—S?" She knew he didn't like the acronym given to his society.

Andreas hesitated. "Yes, he came to a few meetings. Then he never came back."

"Why?"

"I don't have to tell you that."

She stepped forward so quickly that Andreas jerked back in his chair. She thumped her hands down on the desk, and leaned over so far she crowded him backwards.

"And I don't have to take your insolence. This is a murder investigation and I can have you before a king's magistrate in minutes. By the Horn, I can drag you before the King! So don't make me angry." Her voice was low, almost rasping. She towered over the rotund editor.

"You can't threaten me!" His eyes darted about to light on Lornis, who was examining his fingernails with interest.

There was a moment of silence while the editor squirmed.

"Okay, okay. Back down, Officer." His voice wavered. "I guess there's no reason not to tell the Guard. He wasn't really a member of our Society."

Draius went back to her upright standing position while the editor smoothed both his clothes and his composure. "Reggis thought we were a bunch of play-actors. Called our induction ceremony a sham, can you imagine? He was impatient with our incantation group and only came to three meetings."

"What about Tellina?"

"Never met him. I never heard his name until he was murdered."

"Now, what was so bad about telling us that?" Her voice was still rough, but she stepped back to give the editor some more space. "So why are you calling these the 'magical' murders?"

"Why not?" Andreas regained some of his former confidence: he smiled and spread his hands. "I can recognize the magical symbols used by the perpetrators."

She doubted that, because all reference materials on necromancy were missing. Perhaps Andreas had something to do with the robbery of the Royal Archives? Testing this theory, she said, "Enlighten me. What symbols are being used?"

Andreas sniffed and used a lofty tone. "Years of training are required to understand such things. I can only say that the circles are a reference to true elemental magic, such as the Phrenii use." Apparently Andreas didn't recognize the connection to necromancy, and had doubly shown his ignorance by connecting the symbols to the Phrenii.

"Why did you insinuate I might be in danger?" she asked, referring to the Hireday article.

"You might be."

Draius rolled her eyes. "Do you have any proof, or are you just hoping for a convenient event?"

"I got you to read the article, didn't I? Like the twist on magical murders."

"Well, your twist is no longer valid. There were no locked windows. There's a hidden door to the next room, so a murderer could have left the body locked up, yet escape unseen. We've determined a mundane, not magical, means of committing the murder."

Not only did the disappointment on the editor's face satisfy her, but she could also send a message to the perpetrators. *We know how you murdered Reggis.* Andreas was no fool, and he would print this information. News was news.

A boy pushed past Lornis and charged into the room.

"Cousin Andreas, there's been another murder on High Canal Street—" The boy noticed their City Guard uniforms and closed his mouth.

Lornis was out the door and into their carriage, which they had asked to wait, without a word. Draius followed, but hands clutched at her arm as she started to climb in.

Andreas clung to her, his cloak hanging off one shoulder. "Let me go along."

"No. I can't have anyone messing up evidence."

"I'll stay outside, away from your work. I won't bother you, or any other City Guard, with questions. I swear by the Healing Horn. On my Honor."

Draius relented. There was something almost childlike in the editor's pleading eyes. She allowed Andreas to climb into the carriage with them.

Lornis raised his eyebrows.

Shrugging, she said, "Remember that I can have you arrested if you interfere, Andreas. Don't be troublesome."

CHAPTER FIFTEEN

First Millday, Erin Three, T.Y. 1471

That bitch from the City Guard strides into *my* laboratory and mocks me with her Meran blood and lineage. The insult became unbearable when the quicksilver showed a vision. She reflected as if she could, one day, control the element of water through the Kaskea. All due to the circumstance of her birth!

She has never studied the arts, while I have devoted my life to them and still, the stolen shard spurns my blood. It was time to put the charm on her, regardless of my employer's warnings. Neither she nor her pretty-faced deputy will ever remember it.

My charm was designed to hold back her investigation, although the instructions may be a bit too abstract to be effective. I used flesh from our most powerful victim and an important bauble to give the charm complexity. It will stand any type of scrutiny, even magical, and there is no one who can see through its shield.

CHAPTER SIXTEEN

Warnings

A Minahmeran princess, one of the silver people, was walking in the forest when she happened upon creatures like no other. They were made from starlight, with magic horns that sang clear ringing notes. The princess befriended the creatures and named them Phrenii.

One day she met a Tyrran chieftain while he hunted. They fell in love and when he asked her name, she replied, "You may call me 'beloved of Phrenii,' for where I go, they will go." She married the chieftain and the Tyrran people called her Raka, short for 'beloved.' They united the Tyrran tribes into one, but eventually Raka's health failed. Her soul now shines in the Stars, the brightest in the Meran-Viisi constellation. In his grief, the King asked the Phrenii, "Will you leave us now? She was your beloved, too." The Phrenii replied, "We remain to serve," and they remain to this day.

—Tyrran Children's Tale, Origin Unknown

"It's beautiful when the sun shines through the mist. See the rainbows?" Cella shouted over the roar of the Dahn Serin Falls. Being a practical girl, she didn't lean against the metal railing. Her quiet pragmatism had convinced Perinon to meet with her again.

He beckoned her away from the railing, not willing to shout. Before she stepped back, her hands caressed the ornate metalwork.

125

"That railing is Rauta-Nelja work," Cella said as she walked toward him, pride ringing in her voice.

Her chaperone cleared her throat in warning, but Perinon shook his head at the woman who trailed behind them. Another refreshing aspect about Cella was she forgot to add "Sire" onto everything she said, and she spoke her mind. Behind the chaperone followed his two Guards. Perinon felt like he was leading a parade, rather than courting a girl.

Unfortunately, his mind kept referring to Cella as a girl. He couldn't help it. She certainly possessed the beauty of a young woman, with long silky hair, a small waist, high firm breasts, and athletic hips and legs. She would become more beautiful as she aged, but for now she was a sixteen-year-old girl who needed a chaperone.

Aracia had pointed out that ten years wasn't a significant difference for most marriages, but he knew the real reason Aracia chose them so young: she needed to be certain the girl would be malleable and controllable. The matriarch couldn't afford yet another strong-willed woman in the Meran-Viisi household who might challenge her authority—she was having enough problems with Onni. At first Aracia had chosen passive and docile girls, but when she noted Perinon's distaste for them, she changed her methods.

Perinon wanted a woman closer to his age, someone who could be a lover, friend, and partner he could trust, but he was stymied by his position. He couldn't march through the streets asking to meet women, so he had to make do with Aracia's choices. With every one of her selections came the subtle warning: the sooner he contracted, the better. While he grew older, the prospects would continue to be the same age.

He had insisted upon having Mahri in the room when Cella was presented, much to Aracia's consternation. Aracia had watched him as carefully as he had watched Cella during the reception. With the Phrenii near, Perinon searched Cella for self-centeredness and vanity, but found her lacking in both. She was a girl who truly didn't realize her beauty; she had been raised to run the family business and had been expected to work.

While Aracia didn't have the insight of the Kaskea's phrenic bond, she could tell Cella passed the first hurdle of his fickle tastes, so she pressed for another meeting.

"I've a mind to replace my wooden gates with iron ones." Perinon had chosen this conversation starter in hopes of engaging Cella's interest. Actually, he rather liked the shabby, unimposing, and comfortable wooden gates on the Meran-Viisi residence.

"Your gates fulfill their duty. But ones worked in metal would be easier to open and they'd give your Guard more visibility to the street." Cella's eyes brightened as she considered the possibilities, contrasting with her dusky Meran coloring.

"I hadn't considered the security ramifications." He nodded, grudgingly impressed.

"The Meran-Viisi constellation, worked in silver across twisted iron would be beautiful." Her arms gracefully traced the design in the air. She glanced back at her chaperone and added, "If that appeals, Sire." Her silver-blond hair floated around her waist as she turned her head.

"Yes, it appeals. Especially if you could *personally* design me such a gate. Would you have the time and inclination?"

He was amused that Cella considered the question as if she truly had a choice. She hadn't yet realized the matriarchs were aiming her at him like a crossbow quarrel.

"I'd be honored to design it. I'm certain you'll find our work exceptional," said Cella. Her face became animated, shining with excitement. "We can work a gold edge on the constellation, if you wish, but silver represents both starlight and the Tyrran Crown. After all, the King's Guard is fitted in green and silver."

A cough from the chaperone caused Cella to add "Sire" belatedly onto her last sentence. Perinon gestured abruptly to the woman and she backed away, her eyes down.

Aracia had correctly calculated that her commitment to her family's trade would attract Perinon. Cella was dressed in working clothes: not breeches, but a boot-length soft kirtle under a fitted coat that had sides slit up to her hips. The coat set off her small waist and the clothes looked comfortable. No doubt Aracia and the Rauta-Nelja matriarch had selected Cella's outfit carefully and part of him rebelled at being so manipulated.

But, as he looked down into her eager face, he resigned himself to those manipulations. Cella was already stunning, but she couldn't be married until she was nineteen. Of course, Aracia would push him for a commitment long before that. Even if he decided against a contract, Cella wouldn't be hurt by his decision. Her potential to be contracted could only increase from the King's attention, and he'd noticed his Guards, both men, had followed her figure also.

"I bow to your aesthetics," Perinon said, bending his head closer. "You would make better choices than I, and the design will benefit."

Cella blushed. "Thank you, Sire. I have to—I'll need measurements, before I can draw up the design."

"By all means. The King's Guard will be notified and you'll get whatever access to the gates you need. Would you be able to present your design next Kingday?"

"Certainly." She bowed her head, her eyes taking on a dreamy quality, lost in her vision.

After dismissal, Perinon watched her walk away beside the chaperone, not chattering like a young girl, but contemplative like an artist. It would be a shame to take her away from her artistry to contract her to a King. He sighed. He suspected she'd make a loyal life-long companion and a satisfying lover, but she would never be the soul mate he was looking for. Perhaps he could accept that.

"Sire? The Pettaja matriarchs have been prompt in responding to your summons. Lady Aracia has made preparations and awaits you." His secretary was at his elbow. The tic in the man's face was pronounced today.

"Are the Pettaja-Viisi prepared to relinquish custody of the Kaskea personally?" Perinon asked. "I will not have it handed over by a lackey."

His secretary nodded. "The hall is ready."

Aracia had agreed the King should display every symbol of authority he had to support him in this unpleasant duty, although she wouldn't be prepared for everything he'd planned. He would receive the Pettaja in the hall of the Palace of Stars: much too big for a small group, but sufficiently grand and imposing. Perinon went to his quarters and had his stewards put the entire regalia of his office on his body, minus the Meran Sword of Starlight, which had been stolen due to Pettaja incompetence. As he fanned the ember of anger inside him, he vowed that if his City Guard recovered the sword, he'd never let it gather dust in an archive again.

This was another unintended consequence of his brother's unconventional thinking. Valos's establishment of embassies, open borders, and trade treaties had probably saved the debilitated and wearied population of Tyrra, which had been more than decimated by the Fevers. But Perinon didn't agree with all of his brother's ideology: Valos insisted that a leader no longer needed to be a warrior, only a statesman. Today, Perinon had to be both.

Full regalia included dress armor, which consisted of breastplate over chain mail. The breastplate had been buffed to such a high shine it hurt his eyes. The Meran-Viisi constellation, worked in silver at chest height, glinted. Even the chain shone like liquid silver. Perinon appreciated the efforts of his armorers, given the short notice.

"Good work," he said, when they finished fitting him. The armorers were two young men, probably still in training and probably Rauta-Nelja. That gave him pause; perhaps he had a stronger connection with Cella than he thought.

His manservant put two circlets on his head, one for kingship of Tyrra, and a subordinate one as Starlight Wielder for the Meran-Viisi. When he entered the hall, he noted the startled glance Aracia gave him before she bowed her head and sunk to one knee. Perhaps she had forgotten, as well, what the kingship required of him.

Aracia rose after he gave her a permissive motion. "The Phrenii?"

"They wait in the antechamber, if I need them." Perinon settled himself on the throne. He hadn't told Aracia that he would use the Phrenii; he needed every weapon at his disposal for this coming "battle."

Aracia sat down on her chair below the dais and the Pettaja were announced. Three matriarchs entered the far door: first Pettaja-Viisi, then the subordinate offshoots Pettaja-Nelja and Pettaja-Kolme.

The three women wore court dress, with their hair intricately braided. They seemed calm and prepared, as if they were used to responding to his abrupt orders every day. However, this had been the first time Perinon had issued such a harsh summons, under his seal, in the entire ten years of his reign. The purpose of this summons lay in a small ornate box carried by the Pettaja-Viisi matriarch, held carefully between her two hands and away from her body.

The matriarchs ignored the King's Guard they walked between, keeping their eyes forward. As each matriarch presented herself and went down gracefully in a courtly curtsy, she met Perinon's gaze with cold, distant eyes—instead of bowing her head. Each time, he felt his balls shrink upward, as if fearing for their lives. He let them stay on bended knees for an uncomfortable time. Everyone was silent; no one could speak until he gave leave.

"Rise." He controlled the urge to clear his throat.

The matriarchs looked around after rising, but he had every chair in the room removed, except for his throne and Lady Aracia's chair. The matriarchs would have to remain standing.

"Sire, we respond to your summons." The matriarch for the Pettaja-Viisi, as the oldest lineage, would be their representative. This matriarch was the youngest of the three, the prettiest and, of course, the most dangerous. Her name was Leika and she had the reputation of being a vicious negotiator, even among matriarchs.

But this is no negotiation, Lady Leika. Perinon had removed all signs of dialogue or conciliation. Only Lady Aracia was present, even though he could have called in the other Meran offshoots, the Nelja and Kolme lineages. While there might have been strength in greater numbers, this was really an issue regarding loyalty to the *Crown*, not a matter between lineages.

"Thank you for responding so quickly." At least he would give credit where it was due. "As the most recent Bearer of the Kaskea, in the long continuous line of sovereigns who have done so, I relieve you of your duties as custodian and guardian of the artifact. This will be so noted in the King's Chronicles, in addition to my receipt of the remaining pieces."

There was no sound in the hall, save the scratching of his secretary's pen as the entry was made in today's chronicle. Lady Leika glanced about, perhaps unsure how to proceed. He kept his face frozen, because he didn't know. Never before had the Pettaja been so careless as to have their stewardship questioned and removed. Leika finally decided to step forward and place the box on the dais, in front of his feet.

He fought his wild desire to snatch up the box, an urge that came from the Phrenii. Instead, he spoke as she stepped back in line with her fellow matriarchs. "My City Guard reported the robbery of the Archives and raised other concerns as well. Besides being remiss in your duty to protect artifacts placed in your care, the Pettaja have ignored the King's Law."

"No one regrets the loss of these artifacts more than we do—but the fault lies with the City Guard for not protecting the archives, and for not apprehending the thieves after we reported the robbery." Leika's face looked sad and regretful, but Perinon doubted she felt those emotions, at least honestly.

"This is about the King's Law, not the robbery. I care nothing about the stolen items." His voice was harsh, to hide his lie. He had to weave a fine path: he was in rapport with the Phrenii and had to address their fears foremost, but he had to present their nightmares logically to the matriarchs. Above all, he had to maintain the appearance of sanity and health, because the matriarchy wasn't just entrusted with choosing his successor. The matriarchy, if all five-star lineages agreed, could move to dethrone a king, but only under charges of mental instability. He thanked his ancestral stars that Draius had provided him a well-researched account of what she found in the archives.

He added, "I have a City Guard Officer report that clearly proves Nherissa's knowledge lives on, in violation of King Kotiin's edict of 998."

"You reference an arcane law, enacted over five hundred years ago in a time of fear. One could hardly expect it to apply in these days, Sire." Leika's face dimpled with a sweet smile.

"But it still stands in current King's Law, and it was certainly valid law *when it was issued.* Why didn't the Pettaja-Viisi comply?"

"Are you bringing us to task for the actions of our ancestors, Sire? Surely we cannot be held responsible for the mistakes of those who go before us to the Stars."

"A *Meran-Viisi King,* whom the Pettaja are sworn to obey, issued an edict and the Pettaja ignored it." Perinon's teeth clenched, and he made a physical effort to relax.

"King Kotiin had much to deal with in those days, and the Pettaja-Viisi petitioned to reverse his decision. We should research records of those proceedings, then act accordingly." Leika shrugged. "We can compensate the Meran-Viisi, if you wish, for the materials that were stolen."

"This isn't a lineal matter. Matriarchal justice will not suffice here, when the King's Law has been offended."

"As Pettaja, our duty is to protect knowledge, not destroy it." Leika's words were mechanical, a mantra.

"As Meran-Viisi, our duty is governance." Aracia spoke for the first time and all three Pettaja matriarchs looked at her. Aracia finished cool- ly, "And all lineages must, first and foremost, uphold the Crown and the King's Law. Otherwise, all would be chaos and we would resemble a Groygan council."

Perinon didn't know if matriarchs passed messages with their eyes, but he could tell the balance of power in the room had suddenly tipped in his favor. He didn't need the Phrenii near to read the uncertainty in the

Pettaja-Kolme matriarch's face, or to see that Leika was furiously recalculating her options.

"What would you have us do, Sire?" The Pettaja-Kolme matriarch squeaked out her question and received a sharp look from Leika. The older woman bowed her head, giving the floor back to Lady Pettaja-Viisi Leika.

"Since this falls under the King's Law, then perhaps we should take this up before your magistrates," Leika said.

He suppressed a smile. Leika's threat was false. She wouldn't allow the Pettaja to be seen as offenders of the King's Law, not in the public courts. The Pettaja lineages provided historians, tutors, and researchers of law. But, while Leika was concerned about her lineal reputation, Perinon worried about panic among his people as well as the agitation of the Phrenii. In particular, the Phrenii didn't want their young charges—essentially, all the children of Tyrra—threatened by the dark blot of necromancy. Perinon's dreams were filled with their fears, their experience with Nherissa, as well as with dripping blood, blood on the Kaskea...

With effort, he focused on Leika. "There is nothing to question. The King's Law can be subject to interpretation by my magistrates, but it is *my* understanding that rules. Kotiin's edict stands as written: any materials regarding necromancy are dangerous, and my Guard will make every attempt to collect those works and destroy them. This is for the safety—"

"Aracia, this is ridiculous. Are we to be ruled by old superstitions and legends? Magic is lost, if it ever existed. This is a sham, a mockery of the law—obviously, this is about Meran-Viisi control."

Leika had interrupted him, and turned to Aracia. It was the ultimate rudeness and worse, this was a calculated insult intended to play upon boyhood memories. He'd expected her reaction and attitude toward elemental magic. This was why he'd planned a demonstration, without warning Lady Aracia. The matriarchy needed a reminder of the power of the Phrenii. He fanned the ember inside him, and let his anger take over while, mentally, he called Mahri.

"*Enough!*' he roared, standing up. On the dais, he towered over the matriarchs as the Phrenii flowed out of the anteroom to stand behind him. Perinon could feel them: Mahri, flanked by Dahni and Jhari. Spirit, Water, and Air, easily available.

Wind whipped his cloak about him, and his anger pushed for more. The women standing in front of him staggered as a wave of wind hit them. They raised their arms to shield their faces as rain drove down on them. Wild musical tones played throughout the large room. At the far end, even the King's Guard raised their shields and cloaks to protect themselves from needles of driving water.

"This is about whether life-light or death magic shall hold reign. And, make no mistake, life-light's elemental magic still exists." His voice boomed and the stone floor vibrated. Sahvi, earth and influence, was now in his grasp, even though Sahvi was leagues away. The lamps on the walls flared wildly and were shattered by Famri, also far from this room. Oil dripped down from the broken lamps, floated on top of a layer of water, and suddenly flames danced about.

Every king who had been in rapport with the Phrenii was provided some elemental power, according to which phrenic element he was attuned. Valos was attuned to Dahni, water and healing, making his death by drowning understandable only to someone who had experienced phrenic rapport. Perinon's father had been attuned to Sahvi, giving him influence and control of earth and stone.

Perinon, however, was unique: the only king ever attuned to Mahri, the phrenic element of Spirit. He sensed every element about him and he could control them all. As the power surged through him, he could easily forget that it wasn't his to call at a whim, or his to control. The power belonged to the Phrenii, and could only be used with their cooperation. Today, the Phrenii were willing to support him. No lives would be taken, and only egos would be wounded.

"Necromancy is the antithesis of life-light. Necromancy interferes with the journey of souls and saps life force from the Void." His words shook the hall, clearly heard by all over the wind and tones of magic. The matriarchs had gone to their knees, huddling to protect their bodies and faces. The Pettaja-Kolme matriarch was crying, her hand tightly pressed over her mouth.

Perinon made a sweeping gesture with his arm. The double doors at the end of the room, made from heavy oak planks as thick as a man's hand, shattered into splinters and flew into the outside hall. Luckily, no one had been standing outside, but the effect sobered him. He stopped the power flowing through him.

There was instant silence, except for the sound of oil dripping from lamps and the muffled sobs of the Pettaja-Kolme matriarch as she tried to regain control. Water and oil pooled about the hall but the flames were gone, instantly extinguished. The smell of smoke mingled with the tang of lamp oil. Except for him, everyone in the room was on their knees, wet and bedraggled. His secretary's hair was plastered over the side of his face, covering one eye. The matriarchs' fine clothing clung to their bodies; their court dress was ruined.

Perinon, on the other hand, felt exuberant. The matriarchy always chose the male who would hold the Tyrran Crown. These women had placed Perinon on the throne at too young an age, stripping his life of normalcy and requiring him to bind his lifeblood to the Kaskea. Now they could regret their decision. He had just proven he was no mere puppet, and worth more consideration than the seed between his legs. He couldn't see Leika's face, but Aracia's lips were tightly drawn together and her gaze cast downward.

"This is my ruling, regarding the Pettaja." Out of the corner of his eye, Perinon saw his secretary scrabbling to find something dry to write upon. Leika's head jerked, but he continued relentlessly, "All Pettaja lineages will support the City Guard's attempt to find the proscribed documents. They will open *any and all of their records*, as required by the City Guard. If the City Guard incurs additional expense in finding these documents, the

Pettaja-Viisi will be fined to compensate for their costs. Once the documents are found, the Pettaja will assist in their destruction."

He scooped up the box that contained only three—*there should be four*—shards of the Kaskea, before stepping lightly down from the dais. Moving around the Pettaja matriarchs, he stopped beside Aracia, also on her knees. "Lady Aracia."

She looked up, braided hair dripping, lips pressed tightly in disapproval.

"This hall must be cleaned and repaired."

Her lips became thinner.

"Repairs are to be paid by the Pettaja-Viisi," he added.

Aracia's face relaxed. She nodded and Perinon knew, in this small detail, he had pleased her. He walked out of the receiving hall, followed by the three Phrenii. None of his Guard detail followed him.

• • •

After Draius and Lornis left Andreas on the street with the watch and were going up the stairs to the reported murder scene, Lornis started chuckling. Draius looked at him suspiciously.

"You were pretty scary with Andreas," he said. "I couldn't believe your voice. It gave me chills."

"Well, I think I'm the one with a chill. My throat is scratchy." She coughed.

The murdered man was Purje-Kolme Vanhus and he'd been found above a small office that purported to assess cargo for export, as well as assessing antiques. The Purje-Kolme were entrenched in the exporting business, and provided Tyrra with Naval Guard members. This time, there was lineal support at the scene.

"The body can't be released, not until I make an examination," Norsis was saying to a young woman on the landing.

"It's our right to place his ashes and bones in the reliquary, and with all possible speed." The woman obviously represented the Purje-Kolme.

"Ah, Officer Draius, we just sent for you." Relief softened the coroner's face. After all, it wasn't his job to interface with the family.

"Norsis is correct. I can't release the body until he's examined it, which means he must take the body to the morgue at the hospital." Draius took over, and Norsis went back up the stairs to the rooms. Lornis speedily followed, apparently preferring the examination of a dead body to hassling with a matriarchal agent.

The young woman focused her cool glance on Draius, assessing her as the next troublesome official who had to be handled. She had to be a matriarch in training. "By what authority do you hold Vanhus's body?"

"By the King's Law." Draius stood up straight so she measured a head above the young woman. "Coroner inspection is required in a murder, and the City Guard must control the area, and the body, until the coroner is finished."

"Will they subject his body to heat or fire during this inspection?"

Draius saw the problem: the Purje-Kolme, or at least their matriarch, must be deeply spiritual. They were worried about the release of the soul to the Stars. "Absolutely not," she said. "Norsis will do nothing that would cause release of his soul. You will be given all the remains for the departing pyre."

She didn't think it wise to tell the young woman that Vanhus probably didn't have his appendages any more, or all his organs. It also wasn't spiritually relevant; not every part of the body needed to get to the pyre. Just enough ashes and bones had to be collected to claim a spot inside the walls of the lineal reliquary.

After placating the Purje-Kolme representative, Draius saw the murder scene for herself. There was a difference here from the two previous scenes, because Vanhus knew what was coming. There were signs of a struggle: furniture was broken and plaster had fallen from the ceiling and walls. Vanhus was a big, working man and he put up quite a fight, but the end result was the same for him as for Reggis and Tellina.

Lornis was more comfortable than he had been with the previous murders; he was logging evidence and avoiding the body without turning green.

"Draius, you have to run these people to ground," Norsis said. "I'm becoming overworked. Are we to expect another butchery in two days?"

"I don't know." She tried to respond in the same light tone, but her spirits were flagging. *How will I stop this, when I can't even connect the victims?*

"Well, I hope they're killing their own." Norsis grunted as he rolled the body slightly.

Draius and Lornis exchanged a glance and she knew he was thinking of the SRS, but she couldn't picture them as the murderers. Where Andreas and his cohorts were like children, the people who committed these murders were the adults. Andreas really didn't have a clue about necromancy, but the murderers appeared to be accurately following Nherissa's evil footsteps.

"Vanhus could be connected through Purje-Kolme shipping," she said. "Unfortunately, I expect a struggle with the Purje-Kolme when it comes to getting any business records."

"Someone different made this initial incision." Norsis was closely examining the torso, and Draius crouched over the body to see. Norsis pointed out the beginning and ending points of the eviscerating cut. "The cutter was not as skilled in medical knowledge—the previous victims had the cut starting exactly below the rib cage. This cut was accidentally started too high."

"Perhaps Vanhus struggled more than the other victims." She peered at the mangled torso.

"No, they nailed down his hands and feet securely, and the bruising shows heavy pressure was put on his arms and legs. It took several people to immobilize him."

Lornis made a sound from across the room, but when she looked at him, he was studiously examining the items on a table. He was drawing something, perhaps a diagram, using sharpened charcoal.

"Different murderers. Several people." Draius pondered. She hadn't made information about the previous murders public, so an unrelated set of murderers couldn't be mimicking these details.

After the missing parts of the body were recorded, and Norsis had made all his notes and drawings regarding the orientation of the body, the watch took the body down to the waiting wagon.

"No vials, or anything that looks like poison." Lornis watched her look carefully about the room and memorize the details.

"Yes. When it comes to the use of quick-acting poison, I'm beginning to think the first murder was an anomaly."

"After seeing Vanhus' size, I can't see anyone making him drink or eat anything." Lornis made a few more notes, then stowed everything in a satchel.

Draius lingered, hoping that Andreas had left after the body was loaded and taken to the morgue. She had no doubt he'd manage to get a look at the victim.

"Nothing else to check, so I'll seal the rooms and office. It'll keep the Purje-Kolme from cleaning up before we're ready." She tacked a seal of the King's Law across the doors before going downstairs. Lornis followed.

At the bottom of the stairs, she opened the door to the street and stopped. The streets of Betarr Serasa were now clogged with a thick fog. A light breeze from the sea swirled the mist, but couldn't push it away. Streetlights made a valiant effort to burn against the shroud, but they were losing the battle. More surprising than the weather, however, was the lone Phrenii standing in the street, without any children about it. The creature appeared to be waiting.

"Good eve, Draius. Good eve, Lornis," it said.

Draius tried to answer, almost choked, and coughed instead.

"We wish to speak with you." The fog surged about the creature and she couldn't see the color of its eyes, but she smelled seawater.

"Of course. We're at your convenience," she said.

"We wish to show you Nherissa's tower, from our perspective. Please meet us there at dawn on Farmday."

"Dawn?" She immediately regretted her previous words. The ruin of Nherissa's tower was above the Betarr Serin plateau, sitting on an outcrop of the Cen Cerinas Mountains. At a leisurely pace on horseback, it took two hours to get there, and the Phrenii wanted her to be there at dawn?

The creature cocked its head, waiting. As the mist momentarily cleared about its semi-transparent body, she saw faint green waves crashing—this must be Dahni. Water. But staring at the Phrenii could result in madness, so she glanced away.

"Of course." She tried to make her voice sound confident. *What else can I say?* One can't ignore a request from the Phrenii.

The creature regarded her with brilliant green eyes. "Be careful, Draius. We sense you have been touched by evil."

Her throat felt uncomfortably tight and she raised her hand to... Her fingers went to her hair and she tucked a soggy braid behind her ear. What had she been about to say?

"In this, perhaps we are late." The creature turned away and they lost sight of it in the fog.

"I don't know how to handle all these dire warnings." She attempted a light tone. "First Andreas, now the Phrenii—although I could swear it seemed confused."

"Even though their memory is good, the Phrenii don't see the passing of time like we do. Speaking of memory, I've got everything that happened today written down." Lornis patted the satchel. "I think Tellina is looking like our prime suspect right now."

"Then who murdered him, and how did he murder Vanhus, if he was already dead?"

"I meant he murdered Reggis, then—his accomplice took over."

"You're focusing on the convenient suspect, aren't you? It's easy to suspect the foreigner."

He smiled back, his teeth gleaming in the twilight fog. "I'll keep that in mind. But my current theory is that Tellina and an accomplice used the window in the third room to ambush Reggis. They entered from the alley under the window, of course."

"It's hard to ambush someone when you're crawling through a window. Why didn't Reggis just flee? Better to assume that Reggis knew and trusted the perpetrators. Besides, your theory doesn't extend to the following murders. I think we'll have to make sure we rule out the possible connection to Andreas's Society, even if it seems silly. I wonder what he meant by an 'incantation support group'?"

Lornis laughed and shook his head.

She was starting to look forward to his smile. Impulsively, she asked, "Would you like to have dinner with us tonight? Nin always cooks too much food."

"I'd love to. It'll be better than the barracks kitchen."

Draius was right. Nin had cooked plenty for dinner. When they arrived at Anja's house, it was filled with the deep rich smell of beef and peppers. The dish was one of Nin's specialties. She sliced the beef thin and browned it with fresh Sareenian peppers from the market. The whole mixture, with brown sauce, was poured over thick noodles.

They removed their weapons and cloaks, leaving them with Maricie in the hall. She had recovered from her spell of sickness the previous day and blushed when Lornis thanked her.

"My duty, good ser." Maricie looked down as he gave her one of his brilliant smiles. Draius saw her eyes fix upon his back as he went into the parlor.

Before going to the evening table, Draius introduced Lornis to Lady Anja as a co-worker.

Lornis bowed as Anja offered her hand, saying, "Draius is actually my supervisor. I have much to learn of the investigative process and she's an excellent teacher."

She looked away in embarrassment.

Anja was gracious, but her eyes missed no details. She watched Lornis with the same scrutiny she applied to Draius and, as always, kept her feelings hidden. Her eyes flickered slightly when she asked him to give his matriarch her greetings. The Kulte-Kolme and their wealth were well known in the sister cities.

They sat down to dinner, where everyone but Draius started eating with enthusiasm. Peri was full of questions for Lornis, covering the subjects boys were most fond of: What weapons did he favor? Did he intend to go into politics or be a magistrate?

As Lornis and Peri chatted, she tried to relax. It was a comfortable, quiet dinner, in contrast to the conflict and verbal sparring games that would occur if Jan were present. In fact, this was probably what a family dinner should be like—her throat spasmed. It could be a perfect evening, if she only felt better. Her throat was raw, and she took a small sip of water.

"Are you well, Draius?" asked Anja. "You're not eating."

"I'm fine." She speared a piece of meat and twirled it. She popped it into her mouth, chewed it thoroughly but without interest, and started to swallow. Her eyes opened wide as she felt the meat lodge in her throat. She started gagging.

"Ma?" Peri stood up.

Shaking her head violently, she tried to breathe. Concerned, Lornis pounded her back sharply and the piece of meat flew out. But her chest still heaved, no air would enter.

Lornis stood up.

I'm not choking, I'm being strangled! She felt frantically around her throat for the cause and Lornis pounded her back again, which didn't help. Her ears roared and her vision grayed at the edges. She clawed at her neck. She writhed and ended up on her knees on the floor, pulling at her collar. She was growing faint and rolled over on her side, her hands still scrabbling at her throat.

She felt Lornis down on his knees beside her. He tore away her collar and his fingers caught on a string or lacing—with a sharp yank, he broke it. Something went flying and hit the floor with the sound of marbles scattering.

She drew ragged gulps of air and her vision cleared. On her knees, curled up, she began retching. Lornis had his arms around her, supporting her. A broken pouch and its contents spilled out on the floor in front of her. Indefinable lumps were littered about, but one object was obvious in its fine detail. It was part of a human finger, still wearing a ring, a recognizable one. It was a councilman's ring—and she suddenly *remembered.*

"Arr—arr—rest the dustball," she gasped.

"What?" Lornis still held her securely.

She took a deep, shuddering breath. "Have the watch arrest that cursed apothecary!"

CHAPTER SEVENTEEN

First Kingday, Erin Three, T.Y. 1471

Last night I felt the charm squeeze the breath out of the City Guard officer. I'd never before designed a charm to report back to me and I couldn't help feeling proud, as if I'd sent a child into the world to fulfill its destiny.

The feeling was brief and I suppressed it as hubris, knowing I still have much to learn before I ever come close to the sorcerers of past eras. I felt it best to gather my important belongings and get away from my shop. The charm may no longer be obscured and if so, the Guard would figure out what killed the woman.

Having nowhere else to go, I found my employer near the wharves. That's when I discovered he'd tried to perform a ham-handed necromantic rite without me, taking several others of our group. I was incensed.

"This is not license to exact your revenge," I screamed at him. "Your pieces of flesh from the victim are worthless. Their power is weak from imprecision and ineptness."

Rashly, I told him how I had handled the Guard officer, how the charm had killed her. I was surprised by his intense reaction and loss of control.

"I told you I didn't want her hurt!" His hand moved fast and slapped me on the side of the head, sending me flying. He wouldn't listen to my explanations, but had me locked away in a tiny room with a cot. Luckily, his men dumped my two carpetbags on the floor, leaving me with my belongings. I spent the night there, trying to get meager sleep on the makeshift bed.

This morning I had a visit, early, from my employer. He looked somber and of logical mind.

"I've just received news. The watch tore apart your shop and laboratory, of course, and two Guard officers visited late last night. One of them was Draius, so your charm was ineffective."

"But it triggered! And the trigger was set only for her. Are you sure she's alive?"

"She's hard to miss, Taalo, believe me. Now you've put us all in jeopardy. If you wanted to warn her away, this was the wrong way to go about it. She'll focus her efforts on you, and she's got the tenacity of a hunting dog. We may now lose our source in the Guard."

We both knew our source was expendable, so I went to the crux of our differences. "Like it or not, my charm identified Commander Draius as an obstacle to our goals."

My employer pointed a beefy finger into my face, almost touching my nose. "Don't take that school-master's tone with me. I won't have her hurt."

"That may not be possible. You're not being rational."

"And you're concentrating on the wrong problem. You're supposed to be finding the lodestone. Otherwise, you're of no use to me."

That was an interesting choice of words; I had also come to the conclusion he was of little use to *me* in the long term, but disentangling myself from his schemes would be thorny. I adjusted my collar before answering, needing a wash and a change of clothes. I also needed time.

Using a cautious tone, I said, "We've exhausted all normal methods for finding it, but there might be one possibility left to us."

My employer can be patient. He sat on the cot, making it groan. While he waited, muffled sounds of normal daily business came through the walls: men moving crates, shouting orders, and the scraping of boats against the sides of canals.

I spoke slowly, looking down at my shoes. "I've done some research. No one, not even the Phrenii, suspect the Kaskea can be used by more than one person."

"The Kaskea! I'm spending all my lineal wealth to rid us of those creatures—and you want someone to jump into rapport with them?" My employer stood up and spat out his words. "How will this avenge my family?"

I backed into a corner, but there was no place in the room that he couldn't reach me. He hadn't been pleased when he learned I'd stolen the shard from the archives, but since he thought it useless, he'd let it lie. Now I had to work carefully. My employer wasn't stupid: he knew using the Kaskea would be dangerous.

"Don't worry, you couldn't ever be in rapport, because you don't have enough Meran blood. But that pasty-faced assistant of yours could try," I said.

"Why don't you take the risk yourself?" he jeered.

Cold ran through me, causing me to shiver. He couldn't know that I already tried, could he? While my gray-hued skin, hair, and eyes all insinuate I have Meran blood, the Kaskea still rejected me. Not once, but three times.

"Remember, it's broken." I almost stuttered. "It doesn't have the power it once did."

But he didn't pay attention, even to his own mocking words, lost in his own hate and loathing for the Phrenii. "It would open up all our plans to those—" The big man sputtered, something I'd never seen.

"That's why we should use someone who doesn't know much about our plans." I was pleased that I came up with a good excuse: this was why *I* shouldn't attempt to bind to the Kaskea. "Those creatures are portals; have you forgotten your nursery rhymes?"

"Rhymes?"

"They have basis in fact. The Phrenii are gateways to a place that can provide a wealth of information, called the *Void*. Do you think the kings of Tyrra have risked madness for just a bit of elemental power?"

I've always admired my employer's flexibility. He has strong feelings and motivations, but he's always open to new ideas. I waited while he considered the proposal, against all other possibilities. But he wasn't ready to buy into my proposal just yet. "Why can't we try to get information from the captain of the ship? Like we did with that sorceress, the apprentice to Cessina"

"You're presuming the Sareenian captain is dead, which is probably correct." I grudgingly admired his logic. "But to force a soul away from the path requires us to be near the site where the person died. We had to figure out where Lahna left this life and when it comes to the ship's captain, we can't know."

My employer shook his head. "What risks are there in the Kaskea besides madness? We've come in contact with the lodestone—will they feel that?" It was obvious who *they* were.

At this point, I knew that I had made myself useful again. I fingered the side of my bruised face. "I must do more research. I need to read the sorcerer's notes, find out exactly how the Kaskea allows access to the Void."

So I was allowed to move about, under watchful eyes. After I washed and changed, I retired to my room to study Nherissa's notes, as well as my own. I wasn't stupid enough to leave these precious articles for the City Guard to find. However, I was in a bit of difficulty. I didn't mention to my employer that Nherissa lost contact with the Void, which fueled the sorcerer's anger and jealousy of the Tyrran King and his Kaskea, not to mention the Phrenii. I couldn't find support in all these notes for having the Kaskea assist others to the Void. And the risks are high, because there is always some sort of madness involved with using the Kaskea or getting close to the Phrenii.

My reason was challenged, and I met the challenge with elation. I had to piece together a useful plan for my employer while ensuring my own escape.

CHAPTER EIGHTEEN

The Tale of the Phrenii

When the body of King Valos came home, everyone went into mourning except the Phrenii. The creatures insisted the broken Kaskea be bound immediately to our selected heir to the throne, Valos's younger brother and my only remaining grandson. The binding was done with only the Phrenii present. I was in agony as I waited, fearing Peri was too young and the madness would take him. Luckily, he remained sane, but he's not my Peri any more. The Phrenii were perplexed because he became attuned to Mahri, the keystone. This had never happened. Scholars and Star Watchers rushed to their records, insisting this was a portent of conflict to come during King Perinon's reign. Whatever happens, I hope not to see it. Watching my children and grandchildren die in the Fevers was enough torment for one life.

—Entry in Meran-Viisi matriarchal records by Lady Nuora, T.Y. 1461

Late on Kingday morning, Draius opened the door to the Office of Investigation and found it crowded with people. All the chairs were filled, and people leaned against the walls and sat on the floor. Many toted the identifiable bags of their trade, with papers, pens, and seals. It looked like a constellation of clerks had descended into her office.

She'd taken her time getting to work because she'd been up late into the night. Anja had insisted on calling a physician, but after being examined and considered fit, Draius went to check the apothecary's shop. She stayed only long enough to convince herself that Taalo had shut down his laboratory, packed up, and left. She fingered her throat and looked toward Usko, who was standing in front of his files, as if prepared to defend them against the other clerks. Usko didn't meet her eyes.

Ponteva opened the door to the inner office and motioned to Draius, who pushed through the bodies to get into her office.

"Ser, we're knee-deep in Pettaja-Kolme." He closed the door for privacy. "Not to mention several Pettaja-Nelja and Pettaja-Viisi. They say they're here to *help* and they brought those." He gestured to her desk, where he'd laid three letters.

"Thanks, Ponteva." Her voice was still rough.

He didn't answer, but his sharp eyes flickered to her throat, then back to her face. At first, she'd tried to use powder to hide the bruises that went the entire length of her neck, but it didn't work. Her neck still looked like it had been caught in a vise, much larger than anyone's hands. The bruises showed clearly above her collar.

"Where's Lieutenant Lornis?" she asked as she skimmed through the three letters.

"He's taken Miina and gone back to that shop—says he's going to tear it apart board by board, if he has to. He's burning with purpose, and I can't say I disagree. We can't have attacks on the Guard, however they're done." Ponteva's world consisted of solid people and things; he sounded doubtful of the circumstances of the attack, but he couldn't deny the bruising on her neck.

She was grateful that Lornis was searching the laboratory. Last night she'd felt such loathing for the place, she wasn't sure she'd be able to adequately examine it for evidence. Preferring to focus elsewhere, she said, "Well, well. These letters offer the services of the Pettaja, regarding the robbery of the Royal Archives."

Actually, the letters offered assistance in inverse proportion to their lineal status. The Pettaja-Viisi haughtily insisted their people only be used in tracing "necromantic literature," the Pettaja-Nelja offered assistance in searching for anything related to the robbery of the archives, while the Pettaja-Kolme enthusiastically offered labor for whatever purposes needed by the City Guard. Draius didn't know where, or why, these offers had come her way—but she wasn't about to turn down free labor, and she wasn't going to bother with lineal distinctions.

"Ponteva, have them search for Taalo and any information about who he knows, who he does business with, and where he goes. If they balk, tell them he's the prime suspect in the robbery. Have them look through everything from meetings of the Royal Academy of Science, to the receipts at every bookbinder and bookseller. He's also ordered specific supplies, such as fine linen paper. And it's unlikely he owns his shop—have them search through ownership records. By the Horn, have them look everywhere for that stinking little apothecary."

The day disappeared quickly, lost in the grinding details of coordinating untrained investigators and evaluating all the information that flowed back to her office.

•••

In the twilight before dawn on Farmday, a cold breeze whistled through the remaining stones of Nherissa's tower. The crumpled west walls now stood no higher than a child, and to the east there were no longer any walls at all.

Draius stood with her back to the wind, her cloak whipping around and enfolding her. Her long hair was unbraided and loose, blowing forward across her shoulders and brushing against her face. Impatient, she gathered it together and stuffed it securely under her cloak. She rubbed her bruised neck and shivered, but not from the wind.

"This is where the last two Tyrran sorcerers battled," Mahri said. "We were witnesses."

She'd been surprised to find two creatures waiting for her: both Mahri and Dahni. Speaking to one creature was the same as speaking to all, so why had two come to the tower? Adult Tyrrans seldom faced more than one of the Phrenii, so she and Lornis had kept their distance, just to be safe.

The Phrenii, glowing in the dawn light, stood at the edge of the clearing. They refused to enter the circle of stones. Draius and Lornis tied their horses at the edge and walked into the remains of the tower's foundation.

"There is nothing here but dirt and rocks." She crossed the circle, her boots scuffing through fine dry dust and making it to rise like smoke.

The Phrenii stayed where they were.

Nherissa's tower once stood high on this steep outcropping of the Cen Cerinas. From this point, they could see all Betarr Serin and Betarr Serasa and southward over the Angim Sea. Under the dark skies Betarr Serin looked bleak, no longer a shining jewel. The dawn was now complete, but the sky was still dull with thick clouds. The cities below were stirring beneath the scattered showers and light winds. She could see the morning packet boat starting up the Whitewater, pulled by sturdy mules on the bank.

She turned away from the view and back toward the creatures. She'd come for a tale, one she'd heard many times, and it was time to get on with it.

"Show me your perspective, Phrenii. I am here, as you requested." She leaned against the short wall behind her.

"We tell the tale of the last days of Nherissa and Cessina, and the breaking of the Kaskea." Mahri started, speaking in the style of old story tellers. "This story is never complete and no one knows all the pieces.

"In that time the source of elemental power, life-light magic, was disappearing in mankind as each generation faded into history and started their journey to the Stars. The number of sorcerers waned. Even though the life-light magic lengthened their lifetimes to eras, they were dying out. Suitable apprentices could no longer be found.

"Finally there were only two sorcerers left: Nherissa and Cessina. When the life-light magic began to leave them, they also became concerned, even frightened. Cessina withdrew from society to study, while Nherissa began to quest for different channels of power.

"While magic drifted away from mortals, the King of Tyrra wore the complete Kaskea, fashioned by sorcerers at the beginning of the third Era. The Kaskea was a powerful item, but only useable by Minahmeran descendants: whoever wore the Kaskea had authority over the Phrenii and commanded the loyalty of his men. One had only to witness King Voima defeat the rock giants on the northern moors of Kitarra, to understand the power of the Kaskea.

"The Kaskea was handed down over many generations to King Mielis, who had no son, only a nephew Kotiin whom the matriarchs determined would be his heir. Slowly, so slowly that no mortal noticed, King Mielis started to go mad. He became obsessed with his mortality and, unfortunately, we could not recognize this madness.

"During Mielis's reign, a shadow also fell over Nherissa's heart. His loss of power caused him to be jealous of us, the Phrenii. This jealousy and quest for power led him to invent the dark lore of necromancy. Necromancy derives power from death, draining the Void, and is the antithesis of life-light. It allows practitioners to restrain souls against their will and wrest secrets from them. While it is evil and dangerous to interfere with the journey of souls, Nherissa went even further. He learned how to bind the power of death and pain into objects, eventually becoming powerful enough to even bind souls in this manner.

"We, the Phrenii, were ignorant of Nherissa's jealousies and his intent to undo us. King Mielis and his madness distracted us, which may have been intentional, even instigated, by Nherissa. We watched the King's logic fail as he became paranoid of everyone around him. He gave orders that put his people in unnecessary danger, and he imprisoned his nephew Kotiin because he feared a plot to take his throne. We knew this was wrong, but Mielis, through the Kaskea, commanded our loyalty.

"However, concern for Kotiin did allow us to consult Cessina. In the aspect of Mahri, we searched for him and found him locked away and studying dusty scrolls. When we told him of the ill treatment of Kotiin, Cessina sighed.

"'This is more than I prepared for,' he said. 'I am old and tired—now I have to deal with the Kaskea.'

"Even old and tired, as he claimed, thunderclouds of power gathered when Cessina stormed into the Palace of Stars to stand before the King. Mielis cowered in front of his rage.

"'A gift should be used as it was intended,' Cessina said as he ripped the Kaskea from Mielis's neck. Immediately our eyes cleared and the mortals in the room looked like they woke from a dream. The Phrenii could now feel Nherissa and realize our peril.

"Men ran to free Kotiin without permission. When Mielis saw Kotiin, his own Guard had to hold him back to keep him from killing his nephew. He became a maniac.

"For us, there were more important things to address. We came with Cessina, here, to Nherissa's tower. Kotiin followed with a company of King's Guard, but Cessina bade them to stay back. Weapons and mortal strength would do no good here.

"When reaching this tower, the Phrenii encircled it and attempted to crack the stones, but Nherissa's death power was too strong. He struck at our very hearts, filling us with the dread of mortality. Eventually the Phrenii huddled behind Cessina, a miserable mass of fear. Nherissa appeared at the top of the tower and jeered at us.

"'My brother, why are you doing this?' Cessina asked.

"'You might have forgotten the call of power, but I haven't. Look at your Phrenii! When I make them mortal, they will become my pets.'

"'I warn you, the evil art you created will undo you.' Cessina was shaking from fear, rage, or perhaps weakness.

"For an answer, Nherissa sent his power searing down upon his brother sorcerer. Cessina fought valiantly, while the Phrenii cowered behind him. We could do nothing to help him. The sky filled with the flashes of power. Finally Cessina was knocked down and pushed back along the ground. Kotiin rode up and threw himself off his horse to shield the old sorcerer. The Phrenii were ready to flee into the forests, which shames us to this day.

"'Wait,' Cessina said. 'There is still hope. We need more time.' The strength of his voice caused us to stand fast, and Nherissa paused upon the battlement. A wind rose, circling around the tower with a shrill keening.

"Cessina, with Kotiin's help, struggled to his feet. 'You are destroyed. My cohort is releasing your prisoners.'

"Nherissa heard him over the wind, and his face went white.

"'Who?' was the last word Nherissa spoke. He was torn apart on his own battlements by unseen forces, his limbs flying into the wind, his flesh tearing off his bones. Underneath the shrill sound of the wind, we heard the screaming of voices and knew they were the released souls of the dead. The earth began to shake as the souls hurled themselves upon the tower, tearing it apart with their hatred. The stones began to crack.

"Dust whirled about us and splinters of rock rained down. Cessina pushed his way to the tower on his knees, not strong enough to stand against the stinging debris.

"'I must go inside,' Cessina called, so we struggled to follow. Kotiin joined us as we worked our way to the tower, none of us understanding Cessina's need. He struck the doors with power and they disintegrated, no longer protected by Nherissa.

"We followed him into the stronghold while it was being dismantled. As we went, the old sorcerer searched every niche and corner, and checked every pile of bodies—for there were many. At last, he found what he was looking for: a child dressed as a boy of no more than twelve summers. The child was still alive, with a worn face, spent from fighting a great evil. Cessina quickly covered him with his cloak.

"'The lodestone,' whispered the child, weakly gesturing toward the corner.

"The stone in the corner devoured light and we could barely see it resting in a stand shaped like a giant hand. The Phrenii knew we were looking at our mortal bane. It is the lodestone of souls, perhaps the great-est necromantic charm ever made. An enormous number of deaths gave it power, even after it was forced to release its trapped dead. The lodestone is powerful enough to have a will to exist, and can warp mortals with its evil.

"Cessina chanted a spell of life-light protection and carefully stowed the stone in a large leather sack, which both he and the child had to carry between them. He said the mere touch of the lodestone could kill a mortal.

"'Lahna and I must take care of this evil thing. I don't have much time left,' Cessina said. Only then did the old sorcerer remember the Kaskea he had ripped from Mielis.

"'The Kaskea must never again be misused, even by a king of Tyrra. Now the bearer must step into the mind of the Phrenii and understand their pain.' Cessina held out the Kaskea and Kotiin, mistaking his gesture, reached out to take it. There was a splintering sound as the Kaskea shat-tered into five shards, and Kotiin pulled his hand back as molten metal from the setting and chain dripped from Cessina's hand to the floor. One shard now rests in the ring on King Perinon's hand, and the Kaskea can no longer bend men, or Phrenii, to the wielder's will.

"After breaking the Kaskea, Cessina and the child left, taking with them the lodestone of souls. They left in the Tyrran year 998 by the New Calendar, and the Phrenii did not question what Cessina planned, know-ing he would do his best. If it couldn't be destroyed, he would hide it."

Mahri lowered its head. "We felt Cessina labor toward this end for fifteen years, before he left us to make his way to the Stars."

Silence covered the ruins, save for the wind. Draius looked at Lornis, who raised his eyebrows. She shrugged in response. Neither said any-thing. The breeze lessoned, but continued to sigh through the remaining piles of stone.

Finally, she broke the silence with careful words. "An excellent tell-ing in the ancient tradition. Every Tyrran child knows the story of how

Cessina's apprentice Lahna infiltrated Nherissa's tower in the guise of a young boy."

She paused, almost overwhelmed by a memory of her mother pointing out Cessina in the night sky over the sister cities, the vividness of this childhood memory probably brought on by the nearness of the Phrenii.

Clearing her throat, which still felt sore, she continued. "However, I never heard of this *lodestone of souls*. I would never doubt your telling of these events, but—and I don't mean to be disrespectful—what does this have to do with our current investigation?" She was trying to be diplomatic, which was unfamiliar territory for her. After such a story it would be rude to bluntly ask, *So what's your point?*

Dahni picked up the story. "The child Lahna, whom Nherissa mistook as a boy, grew to be a minor sorceress. She and Cessina withdrew from society and no one knows, including us, what they did with the lodestone. We believe that Cessina resorted to hiding it because he could not destroy it. And we know that in the past false-spring, it has been unearthed and used. In this we are certain."

"This lodestone still exists? What about the souls?" Lornis's jaw stood out in sharp lines.

"The lodestone was emptied of souls by Cessina and his apprentice. Since it was recently unearthed, however, it has entrapped another one or two."

Lornis looked ill and Draius understood how he felt. Even her stomach churned. The journey of souls to the Stars was supposedly inviolate, eased by one's honorable behavior during life and the cleansing fire after death. "Do the Phrenii know where the lodestone is hidden?" she asked.

"No."

"Then how can you be sure it's unearthed?" Her eyebrows lifted. She might as well push them to be specific, for once.

"Life-light and necromancy are antagonistic. When a powerful necromantic charm like the lodestone comes near us, our elements become— unpredictable. Uncontrollable. Hence, the uncomfortable rain, wind, lightning, and earthquakes of the last erin. Even when it was close, we searched and couldn't find its location. Now the lodestone has moved away and our charges in the sister cities are safe."

"Moved away..." Lornis echoed. He pulled out the small sheets that he used for making notes.

"But how does this relate to the murders?" She doggedly tried to turn the conversation back to the mundane. "It seems the lodestone was gone long before those men were killed. And, in the presence of the King, *you* said that no magic was used in these murders."

"Mortal weapons did kill those men, but these events cannot be a coincidence. We felt the lodesone feed. Then Nherissa's art is rekindled, aided by his own records. The murders were used to make necromantic charms. Now someone attempts to use a shard of the Kaskea. This feels like a plan to resurrect necromancy."

Mahri had picked up the conversation from Dahni. This transition was like watching a juggler play sleight of hand with balls. Being elements of the same mind, they disoriented her by passing the debate back and forth. Was this intentional? And why did two of them came to this meeting?

"To what end?" She ground her right foot into the dust, hiding her vexation. "Why would anyone want to resurrect necromancy?"

The creatures said nothing, the equivalent of a phrenic shrug.

"But only the King can use the Kaskea." Lornis pounced on a point she shouldn't have missed. "You're saying someone tried to break his bond? How is that possible?"

"The Kaskea was designed by men, and the binding can only be broken by death. We assumed the broken Kaskea would be wielded the same as before, by one person of Meran blood, but we were mistaken."

Their puzzling answer shook her. Tyrrans had no gods, but the Phrenii are True-Starlight-Below, making them brothers and protectors to the Tyrran ancestors. Tyrrans believed the Phrenii were immortal, they couldn't lie, and they were never *mistaken*. "Does the King know about this?"

"He knows our nightmares," Dahni said. "We feel mortals attempting to touch us through the shard of the Kaskea. We feel blood and death magic, anathema to us."

It might have been a trick of the early morning light, but she thought she saw Dahni shiver. With its brilliant green eyes, the creature looked searchingly at her, as if expecting some response. Locked by its gaze, she struggled to look away.

"Only those of Meran blood can bind to the Kaskea," Mahri said. "A sorcerer helped the King through his first use of the relic—"

"Until the sorcerers were gone," Dahni added.

"Now that the Kaskea is broken, it still requires preparation on our part and by the wielder before it is bound. Last night, when another tried to use it—"

"With blood, pain, death," Dahni added.

"And by avoiding rapport, he risked his own sanity and the sanity of the King," Mahri finished.

"He? Last night?" Draius focused on the points that might, just might, help her. Her mind recorded the words as well as a clerk could write them, but she set most of them aside as gibberish. "Do you know who attempted this?"

"We know he is male and he has some Meran blood. We also glimpse his heart—he is coerced into this and he avoids rapport, which will lead to madness."

"But do you know his *name*?"

"Not yet, but we will know him should he come in contact with us."

Of course, they can't give me anything practical, only intangible myth and madness. Whoever attempted this would be avoiding the Phrenii, but that would make him like any other adult in the sister cities. She turned away and watched the river below, having a momentary insight that disturbed her: *the Phrenii are frightened.* Stepping over each other's words was a behavior she'd never seen, perhaps evidence of panic. The concept of the Phrenii fearing anything or anyone was strange, like the thought of the Phrenii being *wrong*. She walked over to where the edge of the tower had been and pulled her cloak tighter about her while she gazed down at the cities.

"So this person must have Meran blood, yet the use of blood is 'anathema'? I don't understand." Lornis's voice carried thinly on the breeze.

"Neither do he and his cohorts. Perhaps we should use the words lineage or bloodline."

"Oh. So there's no blood involved in bonding to the Kaskea."

"We do not talk about the process of binding, for many reasons. We just say that sufficient need and free will are required from the user. The murderers, however, have assumed the Kaskea resembles a necromantic charm. They taint our bond with blood and pain."

Something in Dahni's voice made Draius shudder and she forced her thoughts back to the *physical* evidence. This reasoning was too tenuous to suit her: necromancy was the only connection between the thefts of the Royal Archives, the murders, and the lodestone, and only because the Phrenii said so. The Phrenii were considered unconventional information sources at best. The King's Justice preferred evidence that could be seen, handled, and heard, from real people. She needed to leave the mysticism behind, she thought, as she turned back to face the creatures.

"Only a mortal with access to Nherissa's notes would be able to fashion the charm that nearly strangled you." Mahri gestured at her with its horn.

"You knew about Taalo's charm?" Did they also know where Taalo had gone? Lornis and Miina, with the help of the watch, spent a day tearing apart the laboratory for clues. They found a false floor, where several circles were burned into the wood. Lornis identified the use of something he called 'aqua regis,' which could dissolve almost anything, given enough time. Otherwise, they found nothing of significance.

"No, we couldn't see the charm because the maker effectively obscured it. We only felt the evil, but we remembered we must warn you." Mahri's tense was garbled, an indication their prescience had mucked up their sense of time. When was the 'present,' for creatures that had lived so many years and not only experienced, but foresaw, the same events over and over again?

She fingered her throat while her heart pounded from the implications. Taalo had managed to *hide* something from the Phrenii. She'd worn the charm right in front of the creatures, yet they merely *felt* something was wrong? It was difficult to accept such imperfections in the Phrenii. Taalo was more than an eccentric murderer, and much more dangerous than she suspected.

"We must examine this charm," Mahri said.

So they knew she still carried it. She unwrapped it and displayed it to the Phrenii, having to get closer to them than she had ever been since childhood. Her hands shook as she held out the pouch, lying upon the cloth wrap. Their noses bent over her hands, and she fought an intense urge to step back—*please, I don't want to see blood on my hands.* She didn't know how they were examining the item. They might have been sniffing, because they closed their eyes, but she wasn't sure they could breathe or smell.

"It is minor death magic. Made by mortals through torture and murder," Mahri said after they were finished and she could step away. "It has been a long time since we felt this. The maker was skilled enough to use a spell of concealment, so even if you happened to notice it, your thoughts would slither away from it."

She wore the pouch the entire day without remembering it or having anyone remark upon it. Not even the Phrenii saw it. "Why did he use the councilman's finger and ring?"

"This charm has, as its source of power, the violent and shameful death of a powerful man," Mahri said.

"Why the symbols, the extra blood?"

Mahri hesitated, perhaps having the entire phrenic mind consider the question. "We do not understand their significance, but we believe rituals help the necromancer focus and tether the power."

Draius wrapped up the charm again in several layers of cloth, tying the bundle firmly with leather lacing. *I'm not frightened of this thing.* She yanked the knots tight.

"The charm was given a command based upon a trigger, so you must present a danger to the necromancer," Mahri said.

She thought back to the moments before the choking episode. There had been no bright enlightenment regarding the case, no dawning awareness, only the comfort of an evening where she had felt safe and secure. Comfort she rarely felt, true, but nothing regarding the case.

She shook her head. "The murderers are only in danger from the King's Law and Justice—if I die, someone else will take my place."

The creatures looked at her as if she had missed their point. She sighed, wanting to end this conversation, but it couldn't hurt to keep an eye out for this lodestone. Perhaps this was the way to uncover the conspiracy. "We know what the Kaskea shards look like—they've been on display for hundreds of years. What about this lodestone? What does it look like?"

She seemed to have stumped the creatures. They cocked their heads and said nothing, their eyes following her as she paced slowly across the foundation of the tower.

"Surely you remember. You described the stand that held it." Her voice was challenging. "How big was it? What color? How heavy? It could be carried by a child of twelve and an old man, correct?"

Finally, after several moments, Mahri answered. "One does not *see* the lodestone. You will *feel* it long before you come close to it. Many mortals will not live through a close encounter with the lodestone. It has been built from death and its purpose remains: our destruction."

The hair rose on the back of her neck. The fear the Phrenii felt for this thing would be a heart-stopping fear for a mortal. She remembered how Perinon had been affected when the Phrenii first saw the necromantic symbol. It wouldn't be good for the Tyrran people to discover that the Phrenii, their immortal protectors, could be so frightened—or that they believed they could be destroyed.

"I think we should keep information about the lodestone between myself, Officer Lornis, and perhaps our captain." She looked at Lornis and their eyes met, his glance as wary as her tone. Perhaps she shouldn't even speak to the captain about the lodestone, since it might not be relevant to the case.

"A wise decision," Mahri said. "And, for the King's safety, the Kaskea shard should be found as soon as possible. Our dreams have been touched, and any madness that occurs within our circle will damage his mind."

She swallowed, hard, picturing Perinon when he was young and happy. When he was just her younger cousin Peri. The warning suddenly hit home.

CHAPTER NINETEEN

First Farmday, Erin Three, T.Y. 1471

I consider last night to be a success, even if my employer doesn't. We bound his assistant's blood to a shard of the Kaskea and had him attempt to walk the Void, using my charms to hide him from the Phrenii.

I can't express my loathing for that milk-and-toast assistant—why can he go where I cannot? The man is weak; he barely hung onto his sanity during the process. We had to tie him down to prevent him from hurting himself. Afterward, he babbled about creatures hunting him; I assume he meant the Phrenii. Luckily, he isn't privy to our plans and can't reveal much more than our identities if the Phrenii catch him and rip open his mind. But that's risk enough, so I put as much power into my charms as possible.

Next we'll try to have him pull me into the Void with him. I'll prepare a charm to assist this, based upon Nherissa's notes.

CHAPTER TWENTY

Families

Orders to Admiral Purje-Nelja Ahjo, given under my hand and the Crown of Tyrra: You are authorized command of fifteen commissioned ships of the Naval Guard, and hereby ordered to subdue and seize all vessels and effects of Frisson Rhobar, operating within the Auberei Archipelago. Should Rhobar produce letters of marque issued by the Groygan Lords Council, treatment and process of persons in Rhobar's command shall fall within the rights of a Power at war, but such letters must be returned to the Crown with all speed.

—Signed by Master of Arms Meran-Kolme Sevoi, Third Markday, Erin Two, T.Y. 1471

The Phrenii left Nherissa's tower, traveling faster than normal horses. Draius and Lornis set a pace that allowed them to get back to Betarr Serasa by mid-day. As they rode and talked, Lornis threw his shoulders back and his hair rippled behind him, giving him that classic look of the nomadic hunter. By contrast, the humid air weighed down both her hair and spirits. She felt disheveled—and irritated at herself for being concerned about her appearance.

They were thoroughly chilled by the time they stopped at the Sea Serpent for mid-day meal. The recent publicity hadn't hurt the tavern's business; in fact, quite the opposite. There wasn't a free table to be found.

Berin hailed them from across the room, inviting them to join him and Wendell. He was in his usual roaring good humor, but Wendell was pale and withdrawn.

"You don't look well," Lornis said to Wendell, after greetings were exchanged. He threw his cloak back, but Draius kept her cloak tightly wrapped about her; the common room wasn't warm enough for her.

Wendell had dark circles under his eyes and his skin looked pale and clammy.

"Oh, he's just tired from celebrating the wage increase I gave him yesterday," said Berin, clapping his large hand on Wendell's back.

"I might have caught a chill last night," Wendell said with dignity, after giving his employer a strange look. While Berin attacked his chunky soup with gusto, Wendell made motions and only sipped the broth.

Raivata took their orders for soup and beer, giving Lornis a quick wink. A large steaming bowl was quickly brought for her deputy, but Draius had to wait. Another batch was heating. She rolled her eyes while Lornis dug into his bowl with enthusiasm.

"You should get a tonic against the Fever," said Lornis between mouthfuls, pointing his spoon as Wendell. "If you worsen, you could consult the Phrenii."

Both Wendell and Draius cringed, knowing what was coming. Berin slammed his hand on the table, his booming voice clearly heard above the other voices in the room.

"Darkness will take the Stars before an employee of mine has to use those creatures for healing! Country farmers might run to the Phrenii every time they stub their toes, but here in the cities we only use them as a last resort! Even then, most refuse the healing."

"I apologize if I offended you." Lornis frankly met Berin's glare. "Your ways may be different. My matriarch might rely on the Phrenii more than others."

"No offense taken." Berin's anger seemed to evaporate, but his voice was still somber. "Everyone thinks the creatures are infallible—but they're not, you know—they couldn't save us from the Fevers." He took a long swig of his beer.

Draius winced, thinking about how fallible she had just found the creatures to be. She knew the real pain behind Berin's bluster, and how hard he'd been hit during the epidemic. Only an adolescent himself, he watched his parents, his twin brother, and his younger sister die. Even worse, he was left without his lineage when the Fevers abated. By some strange twist of fate, the Fevers wiped out all the Tarmo-Nelja down to Berin and one of his cousins. The Tarmo-Nelja stars still shone in the night skies, but no matriarch was left to manage the lineage and their reliquary was empty of the living.

Berin's last living cousin quickly ran for the cover of the Vakuutis-Nelja, marrying an underwriter and changing his lineal name. Several matriarchs offered to contract Berin and take him in, but he refused, not willing to give up the Tarmo-Nelja lineage that was now meaningless—except for the comfort of his ancestors.

Berin offered an apology. "Anyone here will tell you I'm more wind than weather, so to speak." He held out his beefy hand to Lornis. "And when it comes to phrenic 'healing'—I only wonder what *our* physicians could do if the Phrenii would only share their knowledge."

Draius didn't bother to bring up the old argument: the Phrenii tried to train mortal physicians, but the minds of men didn't comprehend the world as seen by the creatures. She and Berin had several heated discussions on this in the past; Berin saw the Phrenii as hoarders of knowledge and there was no swaying him.

Her stew arrived, and another bowl of soup appeared at Lornis's elbow. He dug into it. As she ate, the hot meal began to warm her. She threw back her cloak, forgetting her collar didn't hide her entire neck.

"By the Horn, Draius, what happened to you?" Wendell asked, staring at the bruises.

"I had a small problem with a recalcitrant collar. It must have been starched too heavily."

Wendell watched her, uncertain about her joke. His eyes were wide.

Berin shrugged. "Well, Draius, you may not want to talk about those bruises on your neck, but at least you could explain that little ditty in the H&H this morning."

"I haven't read it. Why?"

They were astounded that she hadn't seen the paper yet. Berin got a copy from Mainos, which he laid before Draius with a flourish. "Under *Letters to the Editor*, submitted anonymously."

She stared at what appeared to be a children's rhyme:

> *Sing a charm for Draius,*
> *A killer's on the loose,*
> *And if she deigns to pay us,*
> *The killer's for the noose.*
> *Make a charm for Draius,*
> *Some magic 'round her neck*
> *And if she won't obey us,*
> *Rein her into check.*

Rolling up the pamphlet and gripping it tight, she looked around the tavern and realized she was the subject of many covert glances, even blatant observation. In a society where matriarchs chose primary names carefully to avoid overlaps within a generation, there was no doubt as to who was being referenced in the rhyme.

"Come on, Lornis, we've got to go." She stood up, sending her chair skittering into Raivata, who shrieked and nearly tipped her tray onto patrons at the nearby table. The shriek caused Draius, as well as others, to flinch. Raivata turned and glared at her.

"Hmm?" Lornis had his mouth full of stew, unfazed by shrieking serving girls or tipping trays. Loath to leave his lunch, he quickly stuffed in more spoonfuls and was still chewing furiously when they mounted their horses.

•••

Guard Headquarters was busy. It was shift change for the watch, which meant inventorying and issuing weapons, checking rosters and rearranging duties: all the normal business of the City Guard.

Draius and Lornis made their way to the captain's office and came face to face with Jan, who was just leaving.

"Greetings, *Lieutenant* Commander." Jan used her full rank, not shortening it to "Commander," as usually done during casual conversation. He ignored Lornis, standing behind her.

"Greetings." She nodded her head in response, but Jan was already turning away in an obvious snit. What had he been doing in the captain's office?

Captain Rhaffus was finishing a meeting with the watch commanders and he motioned Draius into the office. The three watch commanders gave her surreptitious glances as they filed by her. When the captain saw the crumpled pamphlet in Draius's hand, he grinned.

"I had Andreas brought in when I first read the paper. He was screaming to see a magistrate immediately." Rhaffus snorted. "A professional editor wouldn't publish such a thing."

"So you had to question him in front of a magistrate?" Draius asked.

"Yes, he demanded his full rights. He pushes the King's Law as far as possible."

"What did he say?"

"He wouldn't tell us anything about the note other than it was left anonymously, and the magistrate ruled we couldn't imprison him since the poem caused no harm to body or honor."

Lornis was astounded. "What about the strangulation charm? That's the connection, that's the harm!"

The captain wilted Lornis with a glare. "Would *you* want to convince a king's magistrate that an inanimate object could suddenly up and strangle someone?"

"Ah. No, I wouldn't, ser."

"I'm not sure that Andreas knows anything more than he's said." Draius thoughtfully fingered the heavy inked paper in her hands.

"And I'm sure he's involved in this up to his dirty neck. I can't wait for another chance at him." Rhaffus and Andreas had a long history of conflict going back to when Rhaffus was OIC of Investigation and Andreas first took over the small publication that originally catered to poets. Andreas built up the circulation of the *H&H* at the expense of Rhaffus's cases.

"We got the report from Norsis, regarding Tellina's body." Rhaffus gestured them toward the chairs in front of his desk and handed an opened packet to Draius. She eagerly scanned its contents.

"Norsis read Taalo's report and believes the apothecary was correct in his analysis of the poison, because Reggis's body exhibits signs of poisoning by wolfbane. This plant can be lethal and quick acting, depending upon the concentration, how empty the victim's stomach is, and sol-biltee... " Rhaffus waved his hand vaguely, dismissing the technicalities. These days, with scientific discoveries and mechanical marvels buffeting everyone, he left the mental exercises up to his OICs.

"Which begs the question: if Taalo is involved in the murders, why give us an honest evaluation of the poison?" Lornis said.

"Maybe he was compelled by professional obligation." Rhaffus shrugged.

"But Tellina wasn't poisoned." Draius put her finger on the vexing contradiction.

"I figured you'd notice that. Reggis's heart stopped by the time he was eviscerated, but the same was not true for Tellina. Much more blood—he was alive for quite some time."

Rhaffus's teeth showed in his signature aggressive grin, but Lornis grimaced. "Sounds like a public execution in Groyga."

"Which won't sit well with our Sareenian population, even though several of their City-States practice similar barbaric executions. This is yet another detail that can't be made public." The captain's voice was final, closing the subject. He leaned back in his chair, making it creak.

"What's your working theory, Draius?" Rhaffus sounded like her old mentor again.

"I assume multiple people are involved." She slipped into present tense, her gaze unfocused as she pictured the scenario. "They know the councilman has rented both rooms for the evening, and they arrange a meeting with him. They reach the second floor from the alley using a ladder. One of Reggis's conspirators, because I'm sure he's involved in something unseemly, climbs into the third room and he allows himself a glass of friendly wine with them. The wine poisons him within moments. Now the murderer has only a short amount of time. This works better with an accomplice, who comes up the ladder with 'supplies' and helps drag the body through the wardrobe to the next room, which is also locked. They go through their ceremony, for whatever reason, and butcher Reggis.

"They had about fifteen minutes, by my estimate, before the barmaid came to the door. By that time they took off their protective clothing, and probably used it to wrap their tools and mementos. Whether the window in the third room was locked from the inside now seems to be a rumor; Lieutenant Lornis found no proof that it was truly locked."

"What about Tellina?"

"For this to fit, Tellina must be involved with the conspirators somehow. He learns of the murder when the criers take the news to the streets. He might have confronted the others, perhaps he wanted out. Since they were willing to sacrifice him, he must have already fulfilled his purpose."

The captain spread his hands in question. "It makes a good story, but how does the next victim tie in? And what is the goal of this conspiracy you've invented?"

"I don't know, and I don't know what part Vanhus played. He specialized in antiquities, and the Phrenii have suggested— "

"The *Phrenii?*" Rhaffus looked aghast.

"I know they're not considered reliable sources—"

"That's not the point. We can't take this into the Halls of King's Justice, using the Phrenii for our support." Rhaffus rubbed his bearded jaw. "Just think how Andreas would dramatize that. I won't have it."

She swallowed her protests about the bigger problems: the use of a stolen Kaskea shard, use that might break Perinon's mind, and the lodestone that caused the false-spring storms and created such fear in the Phrenii. The captain would say that it wasn't her job to worry about those issues—and he'd be right. She had to solve murders and thefts, perpetrated by mere mortals.

Clearing her throat, she started over. "We're not close to bringing this before a magistrate, ser. I don't have suspects, other than Taalo, and only because he purposely put the councilman's finger and ring into that charm. It's a compelling connection, but it only connects him to Reggis, not the other two victims."

"What about the poem in the *H&H*?" asked Lornis.

"Someone has a bizarre need for publicity." Draius shrugged. "I don't see anything in the poem that gives me better insight."

"Ah, yes, the publicity..." Captain Rhaffus was looking down at his schedule, and Draius thought he was preparing to move on to other business. Instead, he looked up and fixed her with his keen glance.

"I'll be honest, Draius. The *H&H* is reflecting public attitudes and they're not looking upon the Guard kindly, at least with respect to these murders. I've also had complaints from your fellow officers; some think I should have chosen someone with more experience to replace Erik."

She flushed, realizing how perfect Jan's timing had been: he voiced his "complaint" in front of the watch commanders, not in a private session with the captain. She also knew how precise Captain Rhaffus was in his choice of words. If Rhaffus said *multiple* officers had made complaints, then someone other than her husband had also objected to her selection.

"You are each filling positions above your actual rank." The captain's tone was heavy as he looked back down at his desk. "While I have faith in both of you, I may have to accede to this pressure. I have to consider the morale of the City Guard and right now, we all need some results. *Soon.* Do you understand, Commander Draius?"

Draius read the captain's warning perfectly, as well as Jan's. Because he was now the deputy of City Defense, the politics within the Guard would expect Jan to campaign for his commander as a possible replacement for Draius. While the captain probably assumed Jan's motives to be "for the best interests of the Guard," Draius knew her husband better. He preferred her disgraced and no threat to his own career, regardless of what it meant to the City Guard. Of course, Lornis would be similarly tainted when Jan was finished.

"Yes, ser." Draius tried to sound optimistic in spite of the hard knot in her stomach. "We'll get you results."

•••

Draius sent Lornis to pry Vanhus's business records away from the Purje-Kolme. She sent a Pettaja-Viisi clerk along with Lornis, giving him additional support. Ponteva and Miina had departed to interview shop owners and neighbors near Taalo's laboratory, dragging along a reluctant Usko, who protested that he didn't do "field work." All the other Pettaja at her disposal were out trying to find traces of Taalo.

Reluctantly leaving a peaceful and empty office, she hailed a carriage and gave the driver her address. She leaned back in the seat and lost herself in the details of the past few days, details her mind had stored away for later perusal. As the carriage turned down her street, she saw residents strolling about the peaceful neighborhood, enjoying the spring sunshine that had pushed away the morning clouds.

She paid the driver and paused on the steps to Anja's house, enjoying the clean solidity of the stone face and the carving of the wooden window mullions and doors facing the street. As she reached for the handle on one of the double doors, it popped open to reveal a flushed Maricie.

"There you are, Mistress! Just in time, too."

"Excuse me?" She drew back. She'd told no one about her hunch.

"I was about to send a runner for you. Lady Meran-Viisi Aracia is here visiting and she wishes to speak with you."

The matriarch of the Meran-Viisi was here? Draius barely managed to remove her cloak before Maricie hurried her into the parlor, where the two matriarchs waited. Anja was dressed for gardening, wearing a simple kirtle that reached to the midway point of her soft calfskin boots.

Aracia was undoubtedly the most powerful woman in Tyrran society. Not only was she matriarch of the Meran-Viisi, she managed the King's household and assets. She was sister to Perinon's mother, who died of grief after the death of Perinon's brother, King Valos. Even in mid-life, at perhaps sixty years, Aracia was an imposing figure. She was in full visiting dress. Her silvering hair fell down her back in an intricate pattern of tiny braids. Two hairdressers, working at least an hour, were usually required to create such a style.

Draius glanced from older woman to younger woman, trying to gauge the atmosphere of the room, but both matriarchs displayed blank and genteel expressions.

"Greetings to you, Lady Aracia." She made a quick bow by slightly bending at the waist. It was an appropriate gesture because she was dressed in her Guard uniform, but a flicker of distaste wrinkled Aracia's lips and forehead, quickly fading. There was no way to know whether the matriarch disapproved of the uniform, the manly bow, or the visible bruises on her neck.

Aracia was also cousin to Draius's mother and niece to the previous Meran-Viisi matriarch, Nuora. When Draius's mother had died, Nuora had sent a note of condolence. The matriarch hadn't attended the pyre, but there were so many funerals during that dark period of the Fevers. Without the Phrenii and their healing, Tyrra might have lost more than half her population, rather than one in every five. The Fevers were finally defeated about fifteen years ago, but the country was still laboring to recover.

Draius thought if her mother had lived, she might look like Aracia, but less stern. The resemblance stirred up bad memories, her mother insisting she didn't want phrenic healing, her father crying over her mother's unconscious body and sending nine-year-old Draius to the Phrenii, but much too late. The Phrenii heal anyone who appeals for their help, but in the order they ask. There is no partiality for rank or gravity of illness. Not for the King, and not for Draius's mother, who was dead by the time an exhausted Dahni showed up at their door. There were too many sick and dying for only five Phrenii—and no healing, even magical, can pull someone back from death.

"Greetings, Draius," Aracia responded. "I've been remiss in my attention to you, and to your child."

"Not at all," she said, moving to sit in a chair halfway between the two matriarchs. Perhaps Aracia had seen the articles and poem in the *H&H*; she probably disapproved of such publicity for the Meran-Viisi, no matter how removed Draius was from the lineage. "I changed to Serasa-Kolme when I married Jan, and I no longer expect support from the Meran-Viisi."

"But now your marriage contract is in jeopardy," Aracia said bluntly.

This wasn't what she expected. "Well, y-yes," she stammered, looking at the impassive Anja for help.

"I am assessing their contract," Anja said. "I'm sure you'll agree this shouldn't be changed in haste."

Aracia sniffed. "I've heard rumors of drunkenness, gambling, and infidelity. Best not to wait too long."

Draius suppressed a smile at the absurdity of her husband giving up control of his money to gambling. She opened her mouth to say Jan hardly ever gambled or drank to excess—

"The only complaint is infidelity." Anja was surprisingly candid.

"I see." Aracia looked sharply at Draius. Whatever she saw, she undoubtedly didn't approve.

Draius squirmed and felt she had PRIDEFUL stamped across her forehead. She wanted to be any place but that parlor, where the two matriarchs observed her in silence. This uncomfortable aspect of having one's life opened for all to appraise, and having others decide what course one would take, had caused more than one of her Meran-Viisi cousins to flee the country. In a way, Draius appreciated leaving difficult decisions to matriarchs, but young Tyrrans often rebelled at this control and moved to Sareen to live their lives in peace.

"What of the boy?" asked Aracia. "If you dissolve the contract, will he be Serasa-Kolme or Meran-Viisi?"

Of course, she wasn't interested in Draius, but Peri! Draius's mind raced as she reassessed the situation. Aracia might be considering all possible options for continuing the King's lineage, and a young boy with the next-generation name of Perinon, with Meran-Viisi blood, who might be brought back into the Meran-Viisi fold... She suddenly felt out of her depth; these were things that matriarchs handled, not Guard officers.

"It's too soon to tell if the contract will be dissolved, but *if* it is, then this may be a point for negotiation," Anja said.

As the discussion progressed, Draius fidgeted while the two matriarchs maneuvered and made no early commitments. Eventually the visit was over, and Aracia rose to leave. This had been a surprising coincidence—but beneficial, because Draius needed information from Aracia. Unfortunately, when everyone stood, she realized she'd have to make her request in front of Anja.

"Lady Aracia, a request please." She stopped the woman as she prepared to grandly sweep out of the room.

"Yes? What is it?"

"You know what I'm investigating, and that I have both the King's attention and his Law behind me..." Draius hesitated. She'd never heard of a matriarch doing this before, but these were unusual circumstances. "I need records of all the Meran blood-lines."

Both matriarchs looked at her with astonishment.

"That's—that's absurd," Aracia sputtered. "What do you need them for?"

"I'm sorry, I can't tell you that. Except that I'm looking for someone with Meran blood, someone no longer carrying the lineal name." *Quite similar to my situation*—an uncomfortable thought.

"Impossible." Aracia sniffed. "No one with the King's lineage would be involved."

"The Phrenii told me this."

One didn't sniff at the Phrenii. Still Aracia hedged. "You need records of all the Meran bloodlines? That surely involves more than Meran-Viisi."

"I know, but the Meran-Viisi line is the original source of Meran blood. Your records would show the offshoots to Meran-Nelja and Meran-Kolme." Watching Aracia's face carefully, Draius knew that she was right. Aracia probably had the bloodlines of half the sister city population mapped out.

The matriarch's eyes, cold and proud, held her gaze. Draius stood her ground. There was really no other place to find this information and all the women in the room knew it. As they knew it was Aracia's duty to resist this, thereby protecting the privacy and venerability of matriarchal records.

Draius had a duty also. "I could go through the magistrates and use the King's Law to force you to give me the records, but that would be so *public*, wouldn't it? I can even petition the King. Consider those headlines in the *Horn and Herald*: 'King must force his own matriarch to open records. What are the Meran-Viisi hiding?'"

There was a moment of silence. She didn't waver as the older woman glared at her.

"Very well, Officer Draius." Aracia almost frosted the windows with her tone. "How far back do you need records?"

"I can probably find what I need with four generations."

"You will get lineage records covering that period. But no other transaction information will be included." Meaning she wouldn't provide information regarding Meran-Viisi business interests or assets.

She nodded. That was all she needed. After bidding farewell, Aracia's exit was grandly executed and Draius was free to get on with her original business. She went to her cloak and pulled the little box from her pocket. Then she found Maricie in the morning room, polishing some silver.

"Yes, Mistress?" Maricie looked inquiringly at her.

"Hello, Maricie." She quietly closed the door behind her and walked up close to the Sareenian maid, who only reached her shoulder. Tyrran women were tall.

"Can I help you, Mistress?" Maricie's eyes darted about.

She backed away, aware that she had been unconsciously aggressive, as if she were questioning a suspect. She didn't want to frighten Maricie, who had worked for Anja for three years, since the age of thirteen.

The girl relaxed a little, and Draius said, "I'd like to hear what you know about Tellina, and where you went Hireday morning."

Maricie kept her eyes down on the silver in her hands and her motions became more determined, almost frantic.

"I know you were upset by the news in the paper. You pleaded illness, then left the house by the back stairs, didn't you?"

She reached out and stilled the maid's hands. "Maricie, I want to help."

Maricie dropped the silver on the sideboard and wiped her hands on the towel hanging from her apron. She kept her face turned from Draius so her words were muffled. "I wish that were true, Mistress."

"Why would you say that? You know that I'll never rest until the killers are found."

"Because Tyrrans have been murdered?" Maricie looked at her directly, raising her chin in uncharacteristic defiance.

"It doesn't matter to me who was killed. A murderer must be brought to justice. I should think you'd have more faith in me."

Maricie looked down and twisted the apron in her hands. "They say he was tortured. Who would do that?" She spoke so softly Draius had to bend down to hear her. Tears started down her cheeks.

Draius wanted to ask her where she'd heard that, when the City Guard had tried to suppress that information. But that discussion could wait.

"How did you know Tellina?"

"He was my father's cousin, in this lifetime." Maricie gulped.

"Really?" Draius was surprised. Sareenians had different naming conventions and Maricie had no connection to Tellina by name, but she might have the same lineage.

"My father's younger cousin, who had his weaknesses," Maricie said. "My father hopes his cousin will continue along the Way into the next circle of life. We pray for Tellina, and expect to meet him again."

"Why didn't anyone claim his body?" asked Draius, not really interested in Tellina's spiritual health. The Sareenian Church of the Way, which preached the Way of the Light, could ponder about his next life.

"My father was afraid to identify our family. After all, someone might be trying to kill our people."

She opened the box to show Maricie the brooch. The maid put a trembling hand over her mouth and her eyes teared again.

"Tellina gave that to his wife when they married. After she died, he always kept it near him. He was never the same after her death—I think it caused him to shun the Way."

Draius closed the box and handed it to Maricie. She pressed the maid's hand gently over the box, holding it in both of hers.

"Maricie, if your father wishes to remain anonymous, I won't identify him in my reports. But I need information to find Tellina's killer. Can you answer some questions?"

Maricie nodded.

"Did you know anything about his recent dealings, personal or professional? What he was doing after he moved his offices to Betarr Serasa, for instance."

"He would visit my father and they would talk sometimes, in the evenings. Since I visited on Fairdays, when I have the afternoon and evening off, I only saw Tellina once in a while."

"Did you see him this last Fairday?" Draius asked, hoping.

"He stopped by on the way to his office," Maricie said. "He was upset about something. He told my father he was breaking an oath, one he felt was ill advised. My father reminded him that keeping one's word is the Way of the Light, and the only virtuous way out was to be released by those that accepted his oath. Tellina seemed agitated by his answer, but would say no more."

"What time was this?" asked Draius.

"Hard to say, but I paid for a delivery right before he arrived and the carrier marked the time as half past four o'clock."

"And your father's residence is where?"

"On Palkka Street, several blocks into Keskil." The location was quite a long way from the Sea Serpent, in a tidy working-class neighborhood of Betarr Serasa where many Sareenians settled.

"Why was Tellina going into his office so late on Fairday?"

"In Sareen, one doesn't automatically get a day off from work every eight-day," Maricie said, almost proudly. "Cousin Tellina was used to hard work. He said he was putting in a claim with underwriters—best to do such paperwork when it was quiet."

Of course, Fairday night and Ringday morning would be quiet down on the docks. There would be no one around to hear the screams of a dying man.

"If you're willing, Maricie, I can leave your father out of this entirely by having you give a statement to the watch. I need to establish your uncle's whereabouts that evening."

Maricie probably couldn't write, but the watch could record her statement. Draius didn't add that Maricie's statement also removed Tellina from the list of suspects for the first murder. No one could have gotten to the Sea Serpent from Keskil in less than an hour, given the normal traffic on a Fairday afternoon.

"Did he mention stopping by the Sea Serpent earlier that day?" she asked the maid.

"No."

"Can you remember any more specifics regarding his discussion with your father? About his oath?"

"No—he was always private about his business."

"Did he ever mention the names of customers?"

"Never," Maricie said. "He felt it a matter of honor to be discrete. He was truly a good man, Mistress."

"Certainly, he was." Draius tried to keep the doubt out of her voice. "Did he have any close friends?"

"He didn't attend the Church, and I don't know anything about his friends. We were his family; we were closer than friends."

Yet his family apparently didn't know anything about his activities. While Tellina hadn't participated in the murder of Reggis, he was probably still a conspirator.

Maricie was tightly holding the box between her hands, almost like the supplicants that entered the Churches of the Way, of which there were many inside the sister cities due to the influx of Sareenians in the past ten years.

"On *your* honor, Mistress, you'll find these murderers?"

This was no time for hesitation, with those young, pleading eyes upon her.

"On my honor," Draius swore.

CHAPTER TWENTY-ONE

Toasts and Swords

Raise your drinks to salute those who gave their lives to protect Tyrra, and who go before us to shine in the Stars. May we earn our own place in the night skies by following them in glory and honor.

— *Traditional Tyrran Guard Toast, Origin Unknown*

"You look great, Ma!" Peri said from the doorway.

"Thank you."

Draius had to admit the City Guard dress uniform for women did look good, even if it wasn't functional. In an attempt to be feminine, it had a green kirtle that extended down below the tops of her boots. A vest of supple suede, with vents about her hips, went over the kirtle. On her chest, embroidered in gold thread, was the stylized phrenic head and horn. Maricie had ironed and starched her collar and slashed sleeves to perfection.

"Get my ceremonial sword, will you?"

Peri was happy to have a chance to take her ceremonial sword out of its stand in the downstairs front parlor. He came back upstairs with it sheathed, but swaying above his head. She grabbed it before he smashed something. The sword was a light ceremonial saber, with a barely sharpened blade. It wasn't intended for combat, but its length made it difficult for the boy to control.

181

She strapped the sword's sash over her shoulder and remembered the only times she had used this sword: Master Arvo's classes. He taught the fine points of Tyrran honor and swordsmanship.

"Never give point in a duel," Arvo would call out as they sparred, "because that's an assassination, not a proper contest. Always stop when first blood is drawn." Master Arvo had been fanatical about the intricacies and rules of the duel—but it had only taken one fight with a Groygan, to the death, for Draius to realize that Arvo's rules had to be thrown out in real combat.

Her rank and service medals were correctly aligned. Her unbound hair shimmered in silvery blond ripples down her back. When she looked in the expensive mirror that Anja had installed in her room, she thought she looked too young without her braids. There was no help for that; one didn't braid one's hair when wearing the dress uniform.

She twisted to the left and then to the right, watching the skirts swirl about her soft leather boots. After wearing breeches for so long, all that fabric twirling around her legs felt free and frivolously sensual.

"Da will be there too, won't he?" Peri asked, ruining her good mood.

"Yes, he will."

"I bet he'll look real handsome."

Yes, she couldn't deny that Jan was handsome. It wasn't his appearance that caused problems. He was exploitive and unreadable, unless one spent years studying him as Draius had. When Jan appeared to have a simple emotion, such as pleasure or anger, he could never be taken at face value. He was always manipulating, looking for the advantage and benefits for himself.

"You'll be asleep when I come home, so let me give you your good night kiss now," she said.

"I won't be asleep!" Peri protested. "Tell me all about it when you get home."

"We'll see." Smiling, she pushed him gently out of her room.

When he was gone, she made a last adjustment to her rank insignia and sighed. A whole evening would be wasted when she could be doing something useful. Tonight was the yearly Guard Festival and Awards. Every City Guard, King's Guard, and Naval Guard member would be there, except those required to be on duty or patrols. Even Betarr Kain City Guard might attend.

Today was Honorday and, by tomorrow, an eight-day would have passed since the murder of Councilman Reggis. The interviews with the people in the shops around Taalo's laboratory revealed that the apothecary had an apprentice. Unfortunately, no one had a name or lineage, only a description of a lanky male about seventeen years old.

Miina had the unpleasant duty of contacting every registered Tyrran matriarch to track down the Taalo's assistant, as well as trying to determine the apothecary's background. According to the interviews so far, Taalo portrayed himself as nunetton when he rented the shop from the Isan-Kolme—for much higher fees than he'd pay if he were attached to a lineage. They doubted he was missing entirely from matriarchal records, since he appeared to be "upper-city" educated. There was a chance a matriarch might remember him or, at least, remember paying for his education. Surprisingly, Miina approached this tedious work with good humor.

Draius exerted more pressure on the Purje-Kolme by petitioning the matriarch for Vanhus' business records. She wasn't following Anja's advice by keeping a low profile and she wondered when the matriarchs would blacklist her for being so impudent, but at least she had gotten results. For most of the day, she sat with papers and records collected for all three victims, trying to connect them. Each victim socialized in different circles and she couldn't tie Taalo to any of them. Worse, the apothecary still couldn't be found, even though the Pettaja clerks had managed to establish his habits: Taalo displayed interest in recently published scientific papers, as well as attending lectures promoted by the Royal Academy of Science. He also frequented certain bookbinders for the specially made paper he used in his chemistry experiments.

After fruitless hours in the office, Draius went to exercise Chisel in the stable ring. At least the fresh air helped clear her mind before she had to wash and dress for this evening's festivities.

"Draius, I'll have Cerin prepare the carriage and drive you." Anja called from the foot of the stairs.

"No thanks, I'll walk."

There had been a short but strong downpour after she left the stables, and the temperatures suddenly warmed. The streets were wet, and the evening was mild and sweet with early spring flowers. The Great Hall was only twelve blocks away and she would have a pleasant walk.

She entered the main square from the south, facing the Great Hall, and paused to admire the festival lights. Colored glass globes with candles were placed on ledges about the square, and light poured out of the tall, narrow windows of the Great Hall. The light reflected in puddles about the square. Laughter, punctuated with shouts, came through the open doors of the building.

As she approached the doors, a figure in green and gold pushed away from a pillar and came lightly down the stairs to meet her. It was easy to recognize the graceful movement and the coiled energy in each step.

"I suspected you'd be attending this alone," Lornis said. "You look too good tonight, you should have a protective companion." His hair was also unbraided and unbound. The shining mane swirled as he saluted and took her unresisting arm.

"As if I need protecting!" Draius laughed, feeling absurdly exhilarated. She didn't pull her arm away as they walked up the stairs. There would be no talk of death threats or magical charms tonight. "The only thing I'll need protection from tonight will be boredom."

"I am at your service, even for that." Lornis spoke gravely, although his eyes danced. They walked through the large doors together.

Noise and light clashed about the hall, almost making her head hurt. The City Guard dress uniforms were flashy, but the green and silver of the Betarr Serin Guard totally overwhelmed them. Here and there she spotted a blue uniform with gold braid on Betarr Kain City Guard. People in uniforms milled about the long tables, as friends greeted each other and searched for just the right seats. Barrels of lager and wine were stacked against the wall as busy barkeeps served drinks from the counter and kept the servers circulating with beverages for the tables.

Across several long tables, she saw Jan talking with Netta, apparently having a serious discussion. Netta's dark hair, such a contrast to her husband's, shone in the lamplight as she shook her head. She looked away, and her brown eyes accidentally met Draius's gaze across the room. For a moment, Netta and Draius measured each other. Then the woman looked down and Draius realized she'd been holding her breath. Jan moved away, apparently finished with the discussion. Looking about, Draius suspected that Netta hadn't brought her spouse, even though her Vakuutis-Nelja contract supposedly remained strong.

A watchman began beating a gong, signaling everyone to get to his or her seat and quiet down. Up on the dais sat Captain Rhaffus, as captain of the Betarr Serasa City Guard, looking uncomfortable in his position to the left of King Perinon. On the King's right sat the master of arms, Meran-Kolme Sevoi, resplendent in his silver and green uniform. On the other side of the master of arms was the captain of the King's Guard, as well as the captain of the Betarr Kain City Guard in his dress blue and gold.

Draius noted the absence of any Phrenii. So this would be a purely mortal affair. Besides, what harm could come to the King as he sat with practically every Guard member in the sister cities?

The dais wasn't crowded. Only the master of arms had his spouse sitting with him. Two of the captains were widowers and apparently planned to stay that way. No young woman had been selected to escort the King, opening up endless speculation. There were other noticeable vacancies on the dais: the captain of the Naval Guard and the harbor master usually attended, but they weren't here tonight.

Draius and Lornis found seats toward the back end of the long center table. Near the front of the same table, Jan took a seat next to his commander, the OIC of City Defense. She watched Jan smile politely and engage in conversation with his commander's spouse. Since Erik's fall from favor, he'd quickly cultivated other useful and politic friendships.

Draius and Lornis were sitting with a mixed compliment of King and City Guard. Across the table sat Bordas, the commander of the last border patrol she had been assigned to. The conversation was kept light, staying away from the threatening political situation: in response to Groygan military and naval build-up, the King's Council had increased import taxes yet again on Groygan goods. Tyrra now waited for the Groygan response.

She looked about at the crowd. The King's Guard executed military actions while the City Guard maintained defenses within Tyrra and provided the King's Guard with supplemental forces. Her throat tightened as she thought of the possibility of friends leaving and dying.

At her table, speculation started regarding the marked absence of any Naval Guard.

"Supposedly three ships of the line have left harbor within the past two days. Perhaps they're doing something about the piracy," Lornis said.

"Maybe they're training," someone suggested.

"It's best we mind our own business," Bordas said. That seemed to be the byword for the evening as everyone dug into dinner.

The food was simple but plentiful. Roasted pig was the main course, supplemented with heavy egg noodles, the Tyrran mainstay, and early spring vegetables mixed with last year's potatoes. Platters of candied and dried fruit were set on all the tables. No fresh fruits were yet available, other than what could be imported from warmer climates such as Sareen.

After most had been served their dinner, the program started. A watchman would beat the gong for silence, and an award or gift would be presented while the recipient (and often the presenter) stood red faced on the dais and shuffled his or her feet. The first awards were mostly fun and farce, such as the toy sword presented to a watchman who pursued a pickpocket with his sword drawn and tripped, breaking his weapon and his wrist. The man waved the small wooden sword with his splinted arm as he made his way back to his seat, where he and his comrades immediately precipitated a toast.

By the second break, Draius was weary of the noise and could not have stuffed another bite of food past her lips. Even imbibing conservatively with each toast, the evening was beginning to blur and feel like a ritual of endurance. The part she always dreaded was beginning: the serious awards. These were the career-advancing awards, prized by ambitious officers.

"Want to step outside for some fresh air?" Lornis asked.

She jumped up at his suggestion. They walked onto the back terrace that overlooked the public gardens behind the Great Hall. Others were trying to get some respite from the warm hall or, like her, trying to clear the wine from their heads. She and Lornis leaned on the stone balustrade, taking deep breaths of cool air.

"I'd trade this for all the wine inside the hall," she said in a low voice. Lornis nodded.

"Fine spring evening, isn't it, Draius?" said a voice behind her.

She turned to face Jan. "Yes, a fine evening."

"If you'll excuse us, Lieutenant. I'd like to speak with my wife."

Lornis nodded, but she saw a muscle twitch in his jaw. He backed away only as far as propriety demanded, still within earshot.

"What do you want?" she asked. Jan was waiting for Lornis to leave and that didn't seem to be happening. Given the wine she'd had, she didn't care who overheard their conversation.

"I've heard our contract is now the subject of discussion with the Meran-Viisi." Jan might have heard this from Anja, but Draius didn't think the matriarch would have confided in him. Had Maricie or Cerin listened at the door?

"I wouldn't say they're interested in our contract as much as they're interested in Peri."

"Yes, Peri is who we must consider. My son—who will *stay* Serasa-Kolme, even if they've re-used your cousin's name. On my Honor, I'll provide for him myself before I let the Meran-Viisi have him."

Picturing Jan with Netta, she released an explosive snort of laughter. "You? *You're* swearing an oath on your honor? You can't keep a contract, much less an oath!" She heard her words and her derisive tone, as if from a distance. It was too late to stop. The words were out of her mouth, and everyone around them went still.

Duels had been fought for such an insult. Now her mind filled with a glimpse of the *H&H* headline: *First Husband-Wife Duel Fought in the City Guard!* For a moment, her thoughts followed that bumpy road. She was good with the saber, but Jan had a better reach. The absurdity of the situation she'd precipitated made her hold back an uncharacteristic giggle of hysteria. *I've had too much wine. I shouldn't be talking with Jan right now, much less insulting his honor.*

Jan made an abrupt gesture with his hands, and through the corner of her eye, Draius saw Lornis make a small movement. Without thinking, her hand went to the Guard on the hilt of her ceremonial saber. Its sole purpose was dueling, after all.

"This is ridiculous, Draius. Keep your voice down." Jan lowered his own voice and held out his hands, palms up.

Draius took deep breaths, calming herself and building the wall up again, the wall that kept her feelings from overwhelming her. "I might be over-reacting, but so are you. I couldn't turn Peri over to the Meran-Viisi. It's not my decision to make and you know that. Why so much concern about this now?"

"Because *I've* been thinking about my son. Do you intend to sever Peri from the Serasa-Kolme, keep him from his cousins, his schoolmaster? How can you maintain the manner of his life without our resources?"

"You're being absurd. There's no question about Peri's support or education." Her jaw clenched. She and Jan were accustomed to a very comfortable life and they didn't pay for Peri's education. Traditionally, lineal assets funded the schooling of Tyrran children and supplemented their living expenses. Even if one lost their blood parents, no Tyrran child worried for their livelihood. Unless one was nunetton...

"What have you done, Jan?" Her tone was sharp. Had he cultivated Peri's fears, building up a nightmare of losing name, livelihood, and future?

"Nothing." His smile was angelic, but she saw the menace behind it. "Just remember that you may not always have the Meran-Viisi to fall back upon."

Perhaps Jan did know about yesterday's conversation with the matriarchs, because Draius might really have burned all her bridges with Aracia. If she had to petition the Meran-Viisi for Peri's education, she had no doubt Aracia would be harsh. The matriarch would require humility, perhaps even groveling, and she'd expect absolute obedience.

"I'm asking you again to withdraw your complaint," said Jan in a low voice. "You and Peri need me. One dalliance, one mistake, shouldn't cause our contract to collapse."

Why did he continue to lie to her? There had been many more than *one* dalliance; perhaps he thought the more he said the lie, the more likely she'd accept it.

The gong was beating insistently, calling them back to their seats.

"I'll think about it." Her tongue felt so thick and sluggish, she could barely get the words out. She turned away from Jan, trying to move decisively, but feeling sick to her stomach.

Inside the hall, Draius pushed her way quickly to the table and began to make apologies to her table-mates. "I'm feeling ill, so I'm going home early," she was saying to Bordas when Lornis caught up. She felt him standing close behind her. It was almost midnight, so "early" was relative.

"Are you well enough to get home?" Bordas stood as if he would escort her home on the spot.

"No, I'll be fine—"

"I'll escort her," Lornis cut in, with authority.

She pressed her lips together but said nothing, wanting to be out of the hall as fast as possible. Bordas's eyes flitted from her face to Lornis, and back again.

"We can get you a carriage," Bordas said.

"I'd rather walk, I—I think it's the wine."

Bordas and the others finally bid her goodnight. Outside, Draius wrapped her cloak tightly around her, irritated. "I didn't ask you to escort me!"

"No, but you don't seem yourself," Lornis said.

She moved away from him and walked quickly through the square with her long strides. He hurried to catch up. "Look, Draius, don't punish me because I'm offering you support and friendship."

They had left the square and were walking down Cen Sali Street, which ran parallel to South Dock Way and the river. She slowed down. "If you think you can help me, you're wrong. I'm trapped in a situation of my own making."

"How can you say that you're trapped?" He sounded exasperated. "This isn't Groyga, where women wear chains of ownership and are confined to their houses. You have plenty of options, not to mention two matriarchs willing to support you."

"Too bad I can't just stand on my own," she said bitterly.

"Everyone needs family. The matriarchs ensure the basic needs of life are supplied, and more. It's the Tyrran way."

Yes, it was. She often forgot that, because her father had taken steps to isolate the both of them from the Meran-Viisi after the Fevers. Her father didn't like to depend upon matriarchs, but he didn't leave her the means to be independent, did he? Then there was Jan. For some reason, he made her feel so helpless, so uncertain. She had to admit she was afraid of him;

she knew his vindictiveness. Her biggest fear was he'd wound Peri in an effort to hurt her. And it'd work.

Her best defense was to push the decisions on to someone else. "Lady Anja will find a way to work things out."

Lornis grabbed her arm and jerked her around. They faced each other in the middle of the deserted street. He grabbed both her shoulders tightly and she couldn't move. He was much stronger than she expected. "How can you be so competent in your work, yet so completely helpless in your personal life? From what I've heard, you haven't had a *marriage* for years!"

She was surprised by his vehemence. "Who told you that? Berin?"

"All you two have left is your contract, which is pretty obvious to anyone. Berin says you've been stagnating for erins. He thinks your matriarch would support whatever decision you make, if you'd only *make* one!"

She pulled away. "Isn't that the Tyrran way? To let your matriarch decide? And, for your information, I've made a written complaint but I have to stop there. I can't be the one responsible for ending our contract."

Lornis could never understand her relationship with Jan. For a moment, Draius longed to tell him about the dirty, little secrets that she kept for all these years. She wanted to trust him, anyone...

"Are you afraid of Jan? Do you fear you'll be separated from Peri? You should talk to Lady Anja about Peri's future. Perhaps she'll make him favored." He was referring to the common practice of matriarchs raising promising children, taking direct control and calling them "favored grandchildren."

Now he presumed too much.

"By what right do you give me advice about my son? Why are you so interested in my affairs?"

At her venomous tone, he stepped back with surprise.

"Why don't we examine your life? How does a Kulte-Kolme from the plains suddenly become a Betarr Serasa Guard officer, without going through the appropriate training?"

The muscles of his jaw clenched and he didn't answer.

"I thought so. We can critique my life, but yours must remain off-limits." She continued walking south along the street.

"Do you still love him?" Lornis asked abruptly.

The question stunned her, and her anger drained away. *Why is he asking me this?* She turned back. They had drifted near the mouth of an alley while talking. The street gaslight near them had gone out and she couldn't see his face.

"You once loved him, didn't you?" His voice seemed to float on the air, disembodied from the shadow of his shoulders and head.

This was the question she'd been avoiding, ever since Jan's public betrayal. She'd wrapped herself in anger and wounded pride, leaving no room for introspection. "I don't know if you ever stop loving someone. But love isn't the point. Not with Jan, because he always gets his way."

"No one *always* gets their way." Lornis's voice was so soft she had to strain to hear him.

Her back was to the alley. She was so intent on their conversation that she didn't hear movement—until heavy hands pushed on her back, throwing her forward. She stumbled and fell on the street stones, flat on her front and barely shielding her head with her arm. Her breath was knocked out of her and she heard scuffling.

She pushed herself back up to her knees, her chest heaving for air, seeing three bodies tangling with Lornis. She reached for her long knife, and only felt her ceremonial saber. *We're not armed for street thugs!*

"City Guard—we—we're protectors. Be off—off with you." Her warning came out in gasps and didn't have the effect she hoped.

Street thugs fear the Guard, but one of the three attackers turned away from Lornis with a grunt, or perhaps a stifled laugh. He, by his voice, muttered something that sounded like "only protectors for the *named*." He stepped toward her with a sword, *not a knife*, held ready in his right hand.

She drew her saber as she tried to stand, but stepped on her skirts and staggered. From the edge of her vision, she saw the man's left arm moving, aiming for her head with a small club. She ducked sideways. The heavy blow glanced off her shoulder.

She tumbled down again. Sharp pain shot about her shoulder, but luckily, not on her sword arm. The man who hit her turned back toward Lornis, while she rolled and regained her feet. Her saber was now free and she lunged, slashing at the back of his legs. The man grunted and turned as she propelled herself toward him. With all her weight, she drove the blunted, but not impotent, point of the saber deep into the soft area of his side. He screamed and dropped his sword as they both slammed into the alley wall.

The man was big and he thrashed, hitting her face with his elbow. She stumbled backward as he crumpled. He rolled against the wall as he went down and she yanked at the saber, which was not designed for thrusting.

She felt her saber break. She was left holding the hilt with a handspan of blade.

"*Watch!*" she yelled, her lungs now working. "Ho! Watch! Help!"

They were only blocks away from almost every watchman in the sister cities, but where were the ones on duty tonight? She heard only sounds of moans, grunts, and scuffling, but no beat of running feet.

She and her attacker ended up just inside the alley. Beside the groaning man, she saw an *H&H* soaking in a gray puddle as her mind continued to record meaningless details. In the street, Lornis's saber flew from his hand and skittered along the cobblestones. He jumped forward under a raised sword to grapple with an assailant. The other attacker moved around to the side, then melted away into the darkness.

Were they withdrawing? She took a step toward the mouth of the alley where Lornis struggled with his remaining foe. From the corner of her eye, she caught a spark of light. A match? A covered lantern down the alley? She turned.

The flare of a matchlock touching a powder pan was followed immediately by the flash from a muzzle. The shot deafened her, the alley walls focusing the sound. She was a great target, outlined against the dim light of the street, but she felt nothing. She turned to see Lornis fall, taking the man he was grappling with down onto the stones with him. The man squirmed to the side as Lornis fell on top of him. The assailant got to his feet, apparently unharmed from the shot.

Draius now faced Lornis's opponent, her sight hampered by bright powder flash. The man circled, only a shadow, and she moved to keep him in front of her. He held a sword designed for thrusting and his arm was moving—she balanced on the tips of her feet—

"No! Not the woman!"

The command came from behind Draius, barely discernible through the ringing in her ears. The man's thrust stopped. He turned and quickly ran down the empty street to the south, dodging into another alley.

She looked back over her shoulder. The alley was empty and the body of the man she'd gored was gone. Lornis lay at her feet, moaning softly.

She knelt beside him. He had a gash down his face that was bleeding heavily, and a deep cut down his leg. More serious, however, was the bullet wound entering his back and opening his abdomen in his left front side. She heard gurgling sounds, perhaps his breath, perhaps the wound.

"Lornis. Hear me. You're going to be fine." She knew she lied, and tears squeezed out of her eyes. She put her hands over the open part of his torso to try to staunch the blood.

"Help!" Surely someone heard the powder gun? She kept yelling so hard, her vision grayed. "Guard officer wounded! Ho, watch!"

At last, after forever came and went, she heard the belated pounding feet of the watch.

CHAPTER TWENTY-TWO

Healing

It's a terrible burden to live with these godless people and their monsters, the soulless creatures that run about the streets. Even the Tyrrans are afraid of them. Only the children can touch them, and only because they don't know any better. The adults won't acknowledge the creatures until they are needed for something, like healing. Even then, there are legends that "phrenic healing" will allow the creature to own the person's soul. This is a laughable concept from a godless people who don't understand the afterlife. If their souls go nowhere but to the stars in the night sky, as they believe, then what does it matter? What I wouldn't give for time in the temples of Giada and Falcona, under the warm Groygan sun.

—Report by Ambassador Velenare Be Glotta to the Groygan Council of Lords, in the Tyrran Year 1471

"The Phrenii have been called," Captain Rhaffus said.

Draius stiffened. *Lornis is dying.*

The nightmare continued. She helped take Lornis to the Betarra Hospital and then made her statements to the watch. She tried to see him, but wasn't allowed. Gaflis, the Guard physician, treated her shoulder and told her to go home and get some sleep.

Rest at this point was impossible. After going to change clothes and wash off the blood, she was back in the captain's office, gingerly sitting in one of his chairs.

"Don't you need the consent of his family for phrenic healing?" Draius felt her panic rise. There was nothing more revered, or feared, than the capability of the Phrenii to heal. According to legend and superstition, their healing didn't come free—especially to adults.

"I already told Gaflis he could call them, if needed." Rhaffus hesitated. "I'm sure of Kulte-Kolme approval."

A blanket approval for phrenic healing? Her body might be numb, but her intuition was more sensitive than ever. She'd worked for Captain Rhaffus long enough to know he was hiding something.

"Why did you let Lornis test to lieutenant? You've never allowed that before."

Rhaffus didn't answer.

"Don't I deserve to know? After all, I had to take him as my deputy," she said.

"Did he perform adequately?"

"Of course. He was exemplary." She winced at the past tense. "But I think I should know why he's different. Why the special treatment?"

Rhaffus hesitated.

She added, "I've already seen Jhari single him out," which seemed to convince Rhaffus. He nodded, but insisted she keep the information to herself. She agreed.

"The Kulte-Kolme matriarch came to speak with me personally. He's her favored grandchild."

She waited. So Lornis had the special attention of his matriarch—she wasn't surprised. But this wouldn't be enough to influence the captain, and neither would the wealth and influence of the Kulte-Kolme.

"Although he was initially trained in the family business, he wasn't suited for it. She moved him about. Before the age of eighteen, he apprenticed with a local astronomer, as well as for the Borough Guard."

"He also worked for a locksmith and a chemist. Granted, he's talented. So?"

"She couldn't contract him until she had placed him in an occupation, and he had such strange and versatile talents. She finally called for Jhari to do a reading."

The matriarch had *called* for a reading, and from the aspect of the Phrenii with the most prescience. Although not individual, each of the creatures displayed a phrenic power more strongly than the others. She remembered the words that Jhari had used, when the creature had encountered Lornis in the upper city.

"Jhari did a reading when Lornis was twenty-four, and predicted that he has an important role to play in defense of the sister cities. Lornis will keep Betarr Serin from falling." Rhaffus muttered the words as if he had learned them by rote.

Draius gaped. The great sister cities of Tyrra couldn't *fall*. They were the oldest cities known to mankind, built with the power of Tyrran engineering and the guidance of the Phrenii. The ancient streets and walls held echoes of powerful magic. "Fall to what? Disaster? Invasion? The Phrenii could prevent either, so what did they mean?"

"You know the answer to that question." Rhaffus shook his head. "The Phrenii don't know the details, or they can't communicate them. Since the sister cities have never 'fallen,' this was obviously a reading of the future. I don't think Lornis knows the specifics and Kulte-Kolme Enkali has told no one else but me. Now I have told you."

Draius chewed her lip. Lornis knew he faced a special fate. Nothing else explained the attention from the Phrenii, or the fact he was still unmarried; how could Lady Enkali contract him when he had such a destiny hanging over his head? She'd be obliged to reveal the phrenic reading during contract negotiations—and such a future could only be seen as a curse, an impediment to the success of the contract, to the conception of children.

"Of course his matriarch let him move to the sister cities. I started him with you in Investigation, but he will be assigned to City Defense eventually. He may get there naturally, because that is where he must be." Rhaffus stared at her, defiant. "It's not his time to die, not from some meaningless street brawl. After seeing his matriarch give him up to his destiny, I know she would allow phrenic healing."

For a moment, Draius wondered why Enkali hadn't gone to the master of arms, but it would be more difficult to merge Lornis into the King's Guard. Besides, city defense was executed under the City Guard, using defense plans created by the King's Guard.

A watchman came in and whispered something to Captain Rhaffus, who grinned in an unpleasant manner. "I've had Andreas hauled in for questioning. Now I might get some answers from him."

Andreas was in a foul mood, having been rousted from his bed and still in his nightclothes. The watch had probably been under orders to drag him through the streets regardless of his state of dress. The captain would spare no consideration for his nemesis.

"What's this about, Rhaffus?" Andreas glowered and crossed his arms. "If you're offended by my critique of the Guard yesterday morning, well, I'll challenge you before the King's Justice." He stood defiantly in front of the captain's desk and looked ready to march in front of a magistrate, even in his nightshirt.

"Not everything is about your silly paper," Rhaffus said.

The editor sullenly shot his chin out. Rhaffus pointed to Draius, who was sitting to the side of the door.

Andreas turned and his mouth dropped. "What happened to you?"

She knew how she looked. Her left arm was bandaged to her chest in a sling to immobilize her shoulder, although Gaflis thought nothing was broken. The left side of her face was black and swollen, her left eye barely open. The right side wasn't much better, being red and scratched. However, she could at least see out of her right eye. She had soaked her face with cool water, but the swelling had not gone down.

"Officer Draius had two attempts upon her life within this last eight-day," said Rhaffus. "Luckily for her, Officer Lornis was there the first time, but now he's under the care of a Guard physician and his wounds are serious, possibly mortal."

She looked down at her boots. *This time, it was Lornis who was lucky that I was there.* Although her bruises looked bad, she was only superficially hurt, almost as if the attackers had been careful to—

"What does this have to do with me?" Andreas turned pale.

"Do you know the penalty for attacking or killing an Officer of the Guard, Andreas?" Rhaffus asked.

The penalty for harming an Officer of the Guard could be the loss of a limb. The penalty for the murder of an Officer could be death, and all individuals involved could be deemed responsible. The King's Justice was harsh in these cases.

"Surely you don't think I have anything to do with this!" Andreas was white.

"You were the first to say I might be in danger," Draius pointed out.

"But that was only a teaser! I had no evidence! And I had no idea there was any danger to you when I printed that poem." If the circumstances were different, Andreas would have appeared comical. He buckled so easily when his own skin was at stake.

"You withheld information from us when we talked to you on Millday, didn't you?" she asked.

"I answered your questions." His tone was sullen.

"But you could have provided more information. You could have told us about the people Reggis went to *after* he left your society." Draius was guessing, but saw she hit the mark. At this point, Andreas would never ask to be questioned before a magistrate: if he was linked to attacks on City Guard members, no judge would protect his "expression of opinions" as support for withholding evidence.

"I didn't think it important! Besides, you didn't mention Taalo!"

"But Reggis mentioned him, didn't he? Does Taalo lead some other society or group? Was Tellina in it?"

"I told you I'd never heard of Tellina before." Andreas regained his composure. "I don't know much about Taalo, but Reggis mentioned his name when he said he'd found some people who put action behind their principles. He acted like all we do is sit around and talk!"

Rhaffus cleared his throat. "If you had cooperated with us, Andreas, we could have prevented the attacks last night."

Her eyebrows shot up, causing a twinge of pain. She felt sure Andreas wasn't involved with last night's assault, although the incident gave the captain grounds to question him. Captain Rhaffus walked around his desk to stand beside Andreas, who swallowed convulsively and looked at his feet.

"Where is Taalo now?" Rhaffus asked.

"I don't know." Andreas kept his eyes down. "I have leads out searching for him, but he's gone underground. *Deep* underground."

"Figuratively or literally?" she asked. There were tunnels under Betarr Serin, and the current Betarr Serasa was built over an older layer of the city that ringed the harbor.

Andreas glanced at her, perhaps to check if she was poking fun at him. "I meant that figuratively. No one knows where he might be."

"Who left the poem at your paper?"

"I never saw anyone. I told the truth. It was tacked to my door."

"Does the handwriting look familiar to you?"

"No," Andreas answered.

"Anyone else you know who might be associated with Taalo?" She watched the editor hesitate.

"There's a clerk here in the City Guard headquarters who might be involved with Taalo. I saw them speaking together, at least an erin ago. His name is Usko."

The captain shot Draius a look and she nodded: yes, she'd deal with this. The clerks who worked for the City Guard were not true Guard members, given the propensity of the Pettaja lineages to swap the clerks around as if they were a Sareenian guild. But many members of the Guard would think they were betrayed "by one of their own." She'd have to keep this quiet. However, she now understood Usko's strange reaction to Taalo's name.

"We think a group of conspirators is using your society for recruitment," she said. "We'll need names of people who were dissatisfied, or who only came to a few meetings before dropping out. They're all potentially involved in this treachery."

"I can give you nine names that meet your qualifications." The editor was now the epitome of cooperation.

"Thank you for being honest with us, Andreas. Now, if you'll excuse me." Draius winced as she struggled to her feet.

Captain Rhaffus still had more business with the editor. As she went through the door, he was starting the what-I'm-going-to-do-if-you-publish-anything-about-this threat. This time, Andreas might take the captain seriously.

Although she was satisfied Andreas provided honest information, his answers didn't address the nightmare of last night. Captain Rhaffus had ordered inventories be done in all Guard armories. All known gunsmiths were being questioned. This was a serious incident: the first case of criminal use of a powder weapon inside the sister cities. Carrying guns was prohibited within Tyrran towns, although they were allowed outside the city walls for hunting. They were considered overly expensive, less accurate than longbows or crossbows, and too noisy for serious hunters. In general, guns were frivolous and faddish, of interest only to collectors who could afford them.

She hadn't been seen the weapon used last night, but the flash indicated an amateur had loaded the powder. Currently, the Tyrran Guard was moving to muskets with serpentine locks and it seemed unlikely that it'd been one of those; they were in short supply and much more expensive than the old hakabuts. The hakabut was heavy with a hook on the end of the barrel for holding, aiming, and controlling the recoil. The weapon was designed to be fired from behind the defensive walls of a city or ship, not standing and from the shoulder. It was also available in more countries than just Tyrra: the Groygans made a version they called *harguebus* and the Sareenians called their versions *arguebusier*.

Draius found Ponteva had arrived early for his shift. No one else was in the office, so she told the grizzled veteran everything she knew regarding last night's attack. She also told him about the connection between Taalo and Usko.

Ponteva started growling.

"Take Usko into custody. I'll need to question him, so just confine him and—I mean it—don't hurt him," she admonished Ponteva.

"I'll restrain myself, ser. How is Officer Lornis?"

"Last I knew, he was alive, but Gaflis is sending for the Phrenii."

Ponteva nodded, obviously understanding the implication. One didn't call the Phrenii until death was imminent. If the Phrenii arrived before the moment of death and the patient had the will to live, the creatures could heal them. There were just those pesky side effects that everyone whispered about: the crippling empathy, the loss of your soul, and other, even worse, superstitions.

Lornis's condition was foremost in her mind; questioning Usko could wait. Draius left the office feeling confident that once the clerk arrived for work, Ponteva would take him into custody. She waved down a coach and told the driver to take her to the hospital.

The air in the hospital was sharp with bitter medicinal herbs. She found Gaflis in a hallway between wards, speaking in low professional tones with an orderly. She stood a discreet distance away until he noticed her.

Once he finishing speaking, the doctor walked over. His face always molded into a bland expression of reassurance, but she caught the crinkle of stress at the corners of his eyes. "Did you get some sleep?" he asked.

"A little. I feel better now." She blatantly lied. "How is Officer Lornis? May I see him?"

"I don't think so." The lines on the edge of the physician's eyes deepened. "He lost a lot of blood. We tried to stop the bleeding and stitched up what we could, but his wounds are deep and the damage is extensive. He never regained consciousness. Dahni is with him now."

The words hit her and opened a yawning well of fear and panic. She leaned against the wall, while Gaflis watched her with increasing concern. "But will it be worth the price?" Her voice rose.

Gaflis motioned for her to lower her voice and walk with him away from the ward. "The Phrenii can save him. I've seen them heal before, and I assure you I've seen them work wonders. I've heard the superstitions, but they're absurd." He stopped at the sounds of ringing hooves on marble, coupled with tinkling notes.

Draius watched the bright-eyed Dahni walk down the hall toward them. Superstitions! *We all swear by the Healing Horn, yet we fear that healing, afraid to become indebted to the creatures.* Her head filled with the well-worn phrases: "Saved by magic, owned by magic! Phrenic healed, but never the same! They heal your body, but own your soul!" *My mother didn't want elemental healing and she got her wish.*

Dahni's green eyes pierced her, then the creature turned to Gaflis. She looked down, ashamed of her thoughts. Saving Lornis's life was important, given the prediction she'd learned from Rhaffus.

"Lornis is asleep. The bullet is gone and the tissues appear to be healing, with no Darkness. He will need several days rest. Where is his family?" The creature assumed the family had given their approval, otherwise how could the Phrenii have been called?

"Captain Rhaffus has been given approval for any type of healing by the matriarch," Gaflis replied. "To notify her, we've sent a messenger by horse to Plain's End. The news will get to her faster than the mail coach."

Draius watched Gaflis, who seemed *too* smooth. It was unwise to lie to the Phrenii, or to withhold information.

"We're in your debt again, Dahni. If you'll excuse me, I'll check on the patient." The physician quickly bowed his head to the creature and left her standing there, wondering how Gaflis could be on a primary name basis with the Phrenii.

The creature turned its attention to her, but kept an appropriate distance. "We have more information for you, Officer Draius."

"Yes?" She watched Gaflis enter the ward.

"There was another attempt last night. The same male as before is attempting to wield a shard of the Kaskea."

"You're sure?" It was a habitual response, but rhetorical. *Of course they're sure.* "Do you know who he is?"

"He attempts to hide his identity from us, which is a sure path toward madness. If he drops into true rapport with us, his mind may break from the stress."

She suppressed a shudder, but still avoided looking at Dahni's face or eyes. "When you have information regarding his identity, will you notify me?"

"As a matter of course," the creature replied gravely and turned away.

"Officer?" The timid question at her elbow caused her to jump. A young orderly stood beside her. "Norsis is down in the morgue. He'd like you to identify a body, if you're well enough."

Draius knew the way to the morgue, where the coroner waited. There were several bodies covered with sheets, lying on wooden tables worn smooth by years of scrubbing. A sharp caustic smell similar to concoctions Maricie used on laundry day filled the room, not quite covering a semi-sweet, rank odor that she naturally flinched away from. "What body do you want me to look at?"

The coroner took a solemn look at her face, shook his head, and quietly clicked his tongue.

"I'm fine," she said impatiently. "Gaflis has seen to my face and shoulder. They will mend."

The coroner gestured at one of the covered bodies. "This floater was found this morning, down by the docks. He has a stab wound in his side that could have come from a saber. He has slashes in his leg, as well."

"You think he's one of my attackers. If so, I didn't see his face."

"That's not the point." Norsis pulled back the sheet to show her the battered head and face of the corpse; the rustle when he replaced the sheet seemed loud in the small room.

She gulped, but her voice was steady. "When it comes to size and weight, he's similar to the man I wounded last night."

"His face and head were battered after death. Before he was thrown in the canal, he was stripped." Norsis pointed to the body's lower right arm. "He has calluses and indentations that indicate a long use of wrist guards and sword work. This man was a professional."

"You think someone's trying to hide his identity?"

"I can't make assumptions, I only record facts," Norsis said. "Motives are your business."

Their eyes met, but neither of them said the name. *Haversar.* It was the signature "death rite" of the most powerful criminal in the sister cities, but why would someone who worked for Haversar be interested in jumping a couple of Guard officers in an alley?

Draius, unfortunately, knew more about Haversar than she'd like. Something didn't make sense here: he always kept a low profile with the Guard. "It wouldn't be wise to jump to conclusions. Not yet."

"Not when someone may have usurped the famous signature." Norsis nodded. "For instance, consider this floater who I classified as nunetton. He was found in the canals two days ago."

The coroner went to another table and pulled back the sheet. She wasn't ready for what she saw: only a boy, with his head and face bashed up. After wincing, she forced herself to look more carefully and saw he was more than a boy, perhaps sixteen years old—old enough to never touch the Phrenii again. The body was bloated.

"Can you tell when he died?" she asked Norsis.

"Hard to say. As early as Fairday, as late as Kingday. What's unusual is the age—can't be more than sixteen."

Yes, that was strange. Usually only the hardened, experienced criminals warranted disfigurement upon death. In theory, this meant the criminal was notorious enough to be recognized by his or her face.

"Stranger still, he's a tradesman. Or more likely apprenticing to be one." Norsis showed her the fingertips of the corpse, which were blackened. "This looks like solution of silver nitrate. The discoloration is harmless, but the solution is quite useful. It's made from—"

"This could be the missing apprentice to the apothecary, the aspiring chemist." She remembered Taalo's discolored hands. "If we could only find someone to identify him. How long can you keep him here?"

"I shouldn't keep his body any longer. He must be wrapped and burned as nunetton, with no one to light a funeral flame. Too bad." Norsis shook his head.

"Can't you keep him just a day longer? We still might get him identified."

Grudgingly, Norsis agreed to keep the cadaver one more day.

She had one more subject to talk about with the coroner, remembering "only protectors for the named," the muttered words burned into her memory last night. "Norsis, how complete are your records? Do you record every body that comes here? All the details?"

Norsis had never shown surprise in the past four years of their working acquaintance. Now his face elongated and his eyes widened. "Are you asking me if I keep records on nunetton, Officer Draius?"

She hesitated. The forgotten nameless were supposed to be just that: forgotten and nameless, bereft of support and help, beyond anyone's concerns. Most Tyrrans thought nunetton chose their path consciously, an entrenched belief reinforced by the Tyrran matriarchy. Neither Erik, nor any OICs of Investigation before him, had ever asked Norsis to tally the bodies of nunetton going through the morgue of the sister cities.

"This may involve more than normal murder," she said cautiously. "Something evil may have been loosed, and this evil may prey upon nunetton."

"What can be worse than the evil mankind deals to his own brethren?" Norsis asked. "But it's not unseemly to be concerned about the nameless, especially lately. I've recently seen some markedly strange bodies."

"Any examples?" She glanced about the morgue.

"No, not here, not now. I'm referring to six nunetton, and all within one eight-day in the previous erin. I'd never seen anything like it. Their throats were slashed, and all their blood seemed drained from them. Like empty husks..." His voice trailed away, then he shook his head. "But they were nunetton; nobody would be interested, would they? What could I do?"

"Well, I'm interested now. Do you have any drawings or notes?"

"I can send you my summaries. Meanwhile, see if you can find someone to claim this poor young man." Norsis carefully replaced the sheet over the body.

Draius bid him goodbye, her thoughts in turmoil. What role did the strange nunetton deaths play, if any? And the apprentice's death was made to look like it was caused by Haversar, which could be dangerous. If Haversar found someone mimicking his methods, he might not appreciate the homage. Even criminals had a sort of honor code.

As she found herself a coach, she tried to avoid the memories, and the facts, she couldn't tell anyone. Haversar certainly *did* live by a code, and he owed life-debt to someone. Her thoughts quickly skittered away from that possibility. She shouldn't jump to conclusions...

When she arrived back at the City Guard Headquarters, the watch shifts were changing and the watch commander drew her aside. Several muskets were missing from the Guard armory located at the stables, managed by Horsehead. Whether this was the result of an accounting mistake or a theft, no one yet knew. There was no sign of a break-in, but the watch shifts had been doubled and given orders to be on the alert for the missing powder guns.

Horsehead might have come under suspicion but many decades of service to the Guard kept him from being a serious suspect. She thought about the other City Guard Officers who had access to the armories; inventorying supplies for wartime fell under the Office of City Defense.

The watch commander wanted to issue her a musket.

"What would I do with that?" She didn't want to lug the heavy weapon everywhere.

"The captain is giving all officers the option of carrying a powder weapon, if they need protection. The watch is *required* to openly carry muskets now."

"The King's Law—"

"Changed, ser," the watch commander said. "We got the edict from the King only an hour ago."

She watched the activity, seeing the watch check out muskets, as well as powder and bullets. Previously, powder weapons had been optional but rarely carried. The muskets, powder, and bullets now added to the knife, club, and sword the Guard already carried. "We need all this against our own citizens?"

"The King and his captains are making a statement that the Guard are not to be fired upon." The watch commander looked sideways at her, and she caught the implication. Guard Officers, *especially Meran-Viisi*, shouldn't come under attack. For a moment, she wondered if King Perinon would have reacted the same if only Lornis had been the victim. She hoped her cousin would be more objective than that.

Refusing the offered musket, Draius walked toward her office, trying not to limp. Miina and Ponteva were waiting, glowering about Usko's treachery.

"He's locked up, separated from the petty criminals. The watch is under orders to treat him well. Not that he deserves it," Ponteva said.

Draius gingerly sat down. She was so tired...

"Usko may know where the missing muskets are," Miina said.

She shook her head. "I doubt he knows anything about that. Let him rest in a cell over Ringday—questioning him will wait. I need you two to get more background on Vanhus."

Was it already Fairday afternoon? An eight-day had passed since the murder of Councilman Reggis, and they had made such little progress. Miina, Ponteva, and Draius spent time exchanging facts and notes, trying to organize their meager leads.

When Draius left work for Anja's house, she paid the driver an extra tenth to get her home as fast as possible. As she climbed down from the carriage, she grunted. Her injuries became more painful with every passing moment.

"You have a package from Lady Aracia," Maricie said, as she gently helped Draius out of her cloak and belt.

The package contained the Meran lineage records she'd asked for. Predictably, the curt letter accompanying the package admonished her to protect the privileged information.

Draius didn't feel like digging into the records. Instead, she went to the kitchen where Peri ate a light meal of bread and cheese after his lessons. There could be no hugging until her ribs and shoulder were better, but she spent a quiet hour talking with her son in the warm kitchen that still smelled of the day's baking. Then she went upstairs, crawled on her bed and fell dead asleep.

CHAPTER TWENTY-THREE

Second Markday, Erin Three, T.Y. 1471

I heard about the attack on Officer Draius and her deputy from my employer. Until that point, he'd had me under guard and I wasn't allowed to read the *H&H*, nor could I hear any criers.

"Why didn't your lackeys finish the job? *She* should be lying in the hospital, not her deputy." The woman was irritating; how could she survive both my charms and hired street toughs?

Maybe she had a protective benefactor. I'd never really believed in ancestral intercession—but after forcing the dead to give up their secrets, I've found I have much to learn about the afterlife, whether it be the Tyrran's "Path to the Stars" or the Sareenian's circular and incremental "Way of the Light."

"*We* had nothing to do with it. But whoever attacked them has thrown the City Guard entirely off our tracks. They're busy issuing powder weapons to the watch and inventorying their armories." My employer rubbed his chin.

"But the Guard has detained my contact. He's been comprimised," I pointed out.

"The important distinction being *your* Guard contact. Not mine." My employer's teeth flashed white through his beard. "The Office of Investigation and their OIC aren't losing sight of their prime suspect, which is you. However, this attack created smoke on the battlefield, as they say. We're taking advantage of the situation and moving our operation again."

I tapped my pen against the inkwell. True, the clerk had been a source of information, but little more. I made sure he only went through me, and only knew my name. That meant I was still an outlaw that couldn't show my face on the streets and I required my employer's protection, facilities, and even his conspirators.

Placing my pen carefully on the blotter, I asked casually, "So we're going to try again tonight?"

"It's our only sensible avenue to finding the lodestone, isn't it?"

I suppressed a satisfied smile. There was an air of desperation about my employer that I'd never felt before. He had driven us to test the Kaskea through the night and into the early morning hours, pushing everyone to exhaustion. I didn't know how much longer his assistant could attempt to wield the Kaskea and yet hold off the Phrenii when they attempted to enter his mind.

But he was no concern of mine. My employer, his men, his assistant of diluted Meran blood, they were all expendable tools toward finding the lodestone. Once I knew its location, I'd be gone. There were risks, of course, to continually weigh and watch. For instance, I worried the Phrenii would find us before we find the lodestone, but I also used this concern to swell my employer's paranoia and hate of the creatures.

"This seems a piss-poor path to place our hopes upon," continued my employer. "I thought the Void was supposed to show us what we needed to know."

"We've already surpassed the extent of Nherissa's instructions. We can pull several people into the Void behind the wielder—surely that counts as progress." I had discovered, unfortunately, that we were probably in what the sorcerer's notes called the "Blindness," so I had to perpetuate the little lie about walking the Void.

The Blindness was still useful as the source of metaphysical Sight. But it wasn't the Void, the realm where sorcerers had walked hundreds of years ago. Instead, it was home to dreaming minds and hidden predators who stalked us, growing bolder with every trial. My employer thought they were the Phrenii and I didn't disagree, although I knew better.

"I wonder if this is worth the risk. We wander around in murkiness and hope to see clairvoyant flashes. What good is there in being able to see anything in the real world, but only if one has already visited it?" my employer asked.

"We were able to check the Groygan embassy by having a marker delivered in a gift," I pointed out. "So we now know they are not hiding the lodestone."

"Which I already knew, because I watched the ship leave harbor. No one could have removed the lodestone from the hold before departure."

"But they could have put in about the Delma Islands and brought the lodestone *back* into Tyrra." As I said this, I realized we would have heard of destructive rain, lightning, fire, and earthquakes happening somewhere if that had been the case. The Phrenii protect this realm and the lodestone would cause outbreaks of elemental storms if it were anywhere on Tyrran soil. I'd have to figure out a way to steer our searches in the Blindness outside of Tyrra's borders. This needed more thought and research.

My employer frowned. "Well, at least we're sure the lodestone is not inside the sister cities."

"Only because we've used the Void," I said. Best that he not realize we'd wasted time and energy searching inside Tyrra; even with its limitations, using the Kaskea shard to travel the Blindness was still our best option.

"But this is taking much too long! We need better Sight."

"Then I need fresh pain or death. With that, I can make more charms, give us more power."

He was silent then, rubbing his beard in thought. I waited. I'd convinced everyone that my charms increased the ability of the Kaskea wielder, helped others follow him, and hid us from the Phrenii. The last was a lie, because only the charm *I* wore had that ability.

"No snatching for a while. The manning of the watch has increased, their schedules have changed, and they're now carrying powder weapons. Without your Guard contact, we'd be taking too much of a risk."

"Even with nunetton?" I asked.

"Well, that's different. I'll see what we can catch." He was tired and grumpy from lack of sleep, as were we all.

CHAPTER TWENTY-FOUR

Confession

CITY GUARD OFFICERS ATTACKED

Two City Guard Officers were attacked Honorday evening by four unidentified men on the normally peaceful street of Cen Sali. Officer Kulte-Kolme Lornis is in critical condition at the Betarra Hospital, rumored to be suffering from gunshot. Officer Serasa-Kolme Draius was wounded, but is ambulatory. She did not deny this attack might be related to the murders of multiple citizens and a Sareenian. Little headway has been made in the investigation of those murders and concerned citizens are calling for results.

— *The Horn & Herald, Second Markday, Erin Three, T.Y. 1471*

Her watchmen leaned against the wall of her office and frowned at Usko, who slumped in a chair in the middle of the room. As far as Draius could tell, the clerk hadn't suffered any physical abuse, but his clothes were mussed and he smelled of sweat and fear.

"Officer Draius!" Usko burst out as she walked in. "I assure you, I had nothing to do with the attack on you and Officer Lornis!" He started to rise from his chair, but sat back quickly as Ponteva moved toward him.

Draius opened her shutters to the spring morning, braving the street noise so she could benefit from the fresh air. She winced as her right arm pushed against the shutter: an entire day of rest meant she no longer needed her arm bandaged to her side, but her shoulder and limb were still tender and healing. She'd slept through to late afternoon on Ringday, until Peri timidly knocked on her door. The entire household had tiptoed around all morning and afternoon to allow her to rest, and she was grateful to Anja for that.

While she knew Usko had nothing to do with the street attack, she had no inclination to put the clerk at ease. He was involved with Taalo and a mysterious group of people who had gotten away—for the time being—with several murders. If they could put a clerk into the Office of Investigation, she wondered just how deep the tendrils of this conspiracy grew.

"If you're innocent, you can tell me what you were doing on Honorday evening." She turned back to the clerk, who looked tousled and mousy, not like a snake hidden within the rocks.

"What do you mean?" Usko's expression teetered between relief and dismay.

"You know why you're here. You have an alibi for Honorday evening, but to use it you must pay the price. You must tell me about Taalo, because you've been identified as his accomplice. You can be charged with the other attack on my life." She watched Usko carefully as she talked.

He blanched slightly. "If I cooperate, can I keep this job? I might have abused my position, but that's nothing, right, compared to the people you want to catch?"

"Don't be ridiculous." Ponteva's words came through a clenched jaw.

"I'm not negotiating for the King's Justice. That's up to the magistrates." Draius waved Ponteva quiet. "Tell us about Taalo and why he attacked me."

Her neck muscles twitched at the memory of the constriction around them. Desperate to find an explanation for Taalo's "weapon," she'd had the pouch examined by mortal experts. Four members of the Royal Academy of Science, as well as two reputable apothecaries, couldn't explain how the charm worked. The purpose of the contents of the pouch had baffled everyone, but not the Phrenii. Too bad the magistracies of King's Justice wouldn't consider their testimony.

"I had nothing to do with that. *You*, ser, were the one who directed the analysis to his laboratory." Usko's voice was resolute, but his gaze slid away from hers.

Draius stared at the clerk with narrowed eyes until he squirmed in his chair.

"I don't know any details. If Taalo is behind this, then you know his methods." Usko looked down, avoiding her eyes.

"Methods?"

"Magic, of course!"

"Not the murders," she said with grim persistence. "The murders were not done by magic."

"If you want to believe that." Usko sounded like a sulking child. He rubbed his palms on his vest, his head bowed.

"I don't need convincing. The *Phrenii* told me that *mortal weapons and mortal evil killed those men*." She mimicked the singsong voice of the Phrenii, giving her words authenticity and making more impact than she expected.

Usko's head snapped up and his eyes went wide. His face became ashen. "The Phrenii know?" He whispered, but she heard him clearly in the small room. "But Taalo said..."

Draius wryly wondered whether she should start using the Phrenii more often as an interrogation threat. She decided to throw everything at him. No mention of the Kaskea; she didn't want to talk about magical relics in front of Miina and Ponteva. But she could make veiled threats.

"The Phrenii know more than that. For instance, they reported your activities on Honorday evening. What were their words? Yes, they said an attempt to 'enter their circle' was made, and they would know the perpetrators if they encountered them. They also mentioned a 'sure path toward madness.'"

Raw fear flared in Usko's eyes. "But—but, I only watched the door." If his face became any more paler, he'd surely faint.

"I can call the Phrenii. They sounded interested in your activities." She gestured to Ponteva and, although the grizzled watchman raised his eyebrows in surprise, he looked ready to do her bidding.

"Wait! No! I need protection!" Usko's voice cracked.

She had to promise to not call upon the Phrenii, plus assure him that the Guard could protect him from his cohorts, before Usko would talk. Once the clerk was ready to tell his entire story, he seemed to find some sort of relief. His hands relaxed and he laid them symmetrically on his knees.

"I first spoke with Councilman Reggis last fall. We were both newly-inducted members of the Society for the Restoration of Sorcery," Usko began. "I found the councilman polite enough, although he didn't make a point to be friendly with me, a lowly clerk.

"Reggis sporadically attended the meetings, and by the end of last year, I rarely saw him. Then, one evening in false-spring he showed up, entering the meeting late. I was becoming bored with this group of academicians, so I wasn't paying attention to the speaker.

"That night the councilman caught my eye. He seemed nervous and excited, and I saw him staring at me. I was uncomfortable and looked away. Several times during the evening, I found him looking at me again. After the lecture, he steered me away from the socializing would-be sorcerers. His eyes had an odd shine to them.

"'Usko,' he said, 'You clerk for the City Guard, right?'

"'Why, yes,' I said, flattered that he remembered my name, let alone my occupation and where I worked.

"Reggis looked around at the others suspiciously as he pulled me toward the door. 'How would you like to encounter real magic?' he asked. Through my sleeve, I could feel his hand shaking. I wondered if he was fevered, or worse, and asked if he was well.

"Reggis smiled mysteriously at me. 'Of course I'm well,' he said. 'Come with me tonight, and I'll show you something these fools only dream of!'

"I was intrigued, so I agreed to go with him. We left the SRS meeting and headed down toward the wharves. Those strange false-spring storms had started and they were shaking the cities. If it hadn't been for the periodic lightning, I would have lost Reggis in the dark. When we got into the warehouse area, he turned off the street and wound his way into back alleys until I couldn't tell which way was riverside and which was harborside.

"He stopped in back of a warehouse and banged on a door. I would have asked him where we were, but the thunder and rain prevented me.

"The door opened and Reggis pulled me inside. The warehouse was almost empty. In the center was a gray-haired man illuminated by a lamp on the floor. Beside him was a lone, large crate, taller and wider than the man himself. To the side of the warehouse, in the darkness beyond the lamplight, were three or four cloaked figures.

"A dark-haired man let us in and he closed the door behind us.

"'Who is this?' the man asked Reggis, raising his voice above the thunder. By his accent, I could tell he was Sareenian.

"'Someone we need,' replied Reggis, brushing the Sareenian aside and pulling me toward the lamplight and the man in the center, beside the crate.

"Reggis introduced me to the gray-haired man. Up close, he was shorter than I am, reaching my nose. We could only speak between the thunder that rattled the windows and seemed to shake the ground—you remember those storms. He extended a thin hand and gripped mine with surprising strength. 'A clerk with the City Guard!' he exclaimed, his eyes glinting. 'Where do you work?'

"'In the Office of Investigation, commanded by Officer Meran-Kolme Erik,' I answered.

"'An idiot, but he still bears watching,' the little man replied blandly, then introduced himself as 'Taalo, apothecary, chemist, and magical antiquarian.'

"'Antiquarian?' I wondered how Taalo differed from all the theoreticians with whom I'd just spent another boring evening.

"'Restorer of magical relics,' Taalo proclaimed with a wave to the crates and the rest of the warehouse. 'Can't you feel it?'

"Now that he mentioned it, I did feel something. I'd been uncomfortable ever since entering the warehouse, but I had attributed it to the strange events of the evening. My skin was crawling, and the hair on my head and neck crackled, making my scalp tingle. I looked around.

"'You feel the magic, don't you?' Taalo giggled, making a strange, high-pitched sound. He gestured toward the large crate. 'I can show it to you, but you mustn't get too close. It killed seven of the excavating team, and two of my analysts.'

"Taalo motioned for me to stand beside him in front of the large crate. I noticed that Reggis and the other figures moved to the far side of the warehouse. As I came closer to the box, the crawling sensation on my skin caused me to shake and I felt nauseous. Taalo reached up to a rope I hadn't noticed, one that went overhead to a pulley mechanism and to the front panel of the crate. He pulled on it and the front of the crate began to fall forward with a creaking noise.

"'See the end of the Phrenii,' Taalo said a bit too dramatically, or so I thought. I felt an overwhelming sense of doom and I suddenly did *not* want to see inside the crate. The front of the box fell on the floor, kicking up dust. What was inside was so powerful and dark it pulled at my mind. I fell to my knees, retching. I heard Taalo cackling.

"'It often affects people this way. You'll do better next time,' Taalo said, his voice in my ear. I could hear vomiting behind me; I wasn't the only one affected by whatever was in there.

"As I heaved up my dinner and tried to crawl backwards, away from that thing, Taalo kept speaking, 'With this, we can destroy the Phrenii and mankind can control magic again.'"

Usko paused and Draius waited. Ponteva and Miina looked annoyed; they probably thought Usko was lying. Like all Tyrrans, including herself, they'd been raised with the belief that the Phrenii were immortal and indestructible. She, however, had just had those childhood myths crushed by the Phrenii themselves.

"Look, Officer Draius, this must sound quite unbelievable to you. I know you don't believe in the restoration of magic." Usko shifted in his seat uncomfortably, looking at his feet.

"I believe your description of these events," she said, ignoring her watchmen's expressions. "What's hard to understand is why a councilman, an apothecary, a Sareenian shipowner, and a clerk conspired together, and to such ends."

"I can only tell you what happened, not why," Usko said. "My motives, in the beginning, were only to expand my knowledge. I can't speak for the motives of others."

"So what was in the crate?"

"Darkness."

She frowned. "You emptied your stomach for nothing?"

"I didn't say there was nothing in the crate, I said there was *Darkness*, the *cursed* kind. It writhed like a mass of snakes I couldn't quite see." The clerk's voice strained and cracked. He rubbed his knees. "And I will swear this by the Healing Horn of the Phrenii: what was in that crate can suck your soul away from you."

"As well as your blood?"

Usko's eyes widened at her question. "Taalo said he'd done experiments, but only on nunetton."

The room was quiet, except for the sounds of the street traffic wafting in from the window behind Draius. Suddenly the spring air seemed chilly, and she moved to close the window, cutting off the noise from outside.

A knock sounded at the door. Everyone started, and Miina left to attend to the visitor.

"Did Taalo describe what was in the crate?" she asked.

"He said it was the lodestone, a charm that lay hidden and protected for five hundred years."

"Did he show you any proof?"

"I had to take his word, since I'm not qualified to evaluate magical relics," Usko said. "They were going to ship it off. For all his bravado, Taalo couldn't control it, which was causing dissension within the group."

"Explain." Draius leaned forward.

"It sounded like everyone wanted it moved further away from the Phrenii and their power, to stop the storms. The question was where to send it, and I think the councilman wanted to do something different. Taalo said rudely that the councilman's *friends* had been out-voted and that he should shut up."

"They believed the lodestone was causing the false-spring storms?"

Usko cocked his head. "What else could have caused them?"

Draius saw Ponteva roll his eyes. She drummed her fingers on her desk. The false-spring storms had shut down much of the shipping in and out of Tyrra, as well as up and down the Whitewater. They were unusual enough to cause scholars to search historical records and no one found similar storms recorded in written Tyrran history. The *H&H* even attempted to interview the Phrenii, but reported the information they received as "obtuse."

She decided to move on; whether the lodestone caused the storms and flooding was irrelevant to her investigation. "What did they do with the lodestone?"

"Shipping the thing out of Betarr Serasa without attracting attention proved to be difficult. The harbor master's office reviews all incoming and outgoing cargo declarations. We needed false manifests and falsified customs forms to avoid a harbor inspection. There were also specific problems with transporting the lodestone. It couldn't be placed near people and it has strange effects on other materials. It needed a large compartment all to itself and because the storms had limited the ships that could safely leave harbor, cargo space was dear. Taalo told me there was much discussion regarding the shipping, how much it would cost, and of course, where to send it and who could be entrusted with it."

"Where *did* you send it?" she asked. *Could it be this easy?*

"Taalo had me prepare paperwork for five destinations: Betarr Kain, Suellestrin, Illus, Forenllas, and Chikirmo. He said the decision would be made at the last possible moment. I recall seeing Reggis arguing with Taalo, and I heard words about 'our Groygan contact.'"

"And you don't know the final destination?" She didn't need to see Usko's agreement.

"They were careful to hide things from me. But they couldn't hide the name of the ship. It was Sareenian, named the *Danilo Ana.*"

"What about names of people? You've only mentioned the leader, Taalo, and the councilman."

"I wasn't allowed to hobnob with the inner circle. They said that would protect my identity." There was an undercurrent of bitterness in the Usko's dry tone. "And you're making a mistake, if you think Taalo is their leader."

She motioned for him to continue.

"While he showed me the lodestone, Taalo would glance at another figure, as if for support or approval. I saw him practically flinch when the man gestured at him. Big, broad, tall fellow." The clerk stood up and showed them the approximate size of the man.

"What about his voice?"

"He was careful to hide his face and head with his hood, and he stayed in the shadows. I never heard him speak." Usko couldn't provide any more information about the leader; no sense of lineage or occupation could be gleaned from his description. As for other members of the conspiracy, he had no names and could barely provide basic information like heights, weights, and genders. Apparently, there was a woman, perhaps two, who Usko thought might be merchants.

Draius took a deep breath and mentally ticked off another dead end. "Well, let's establish some relationships between the victims." Maybe Usko might now prove his worth.

"I never met this Vanhus fellow, and all Sareenians look the same, don't they? The only Sareenians I met were associated with shipping the lodestone, which left port almost two eight-days ago."

She checked her calendar, moving her fingers over one eight-day, then another. "Do you remember exactly when it sailed?"

"I think it was Third Kingday." Usko sounded hesitant. "I remember thinking how miserable the weather was, and how I pitied the Sareenian captain, having to travel with the lodestone."

"What happened after the ship sailed?"

"We all know that answer: the storms stopped tearing the cities apart."

Draius pressed her lips together. Usko was being purposely obtuse. "I meant, what happened between the members of your conspiracy? Some of them soon came to tragic ends."

"Well, nobody bothered to tell *me* about the situation, but I could see things were going badly. I saw Reggis arguing with others and I wondered whether these people had the best interests of Tyrra at heart."

Draius exchanged a glance with Ponteva, whose eyes were narrowed. She agreed: it was a little late for Usko to profess allegiance to Tyrra and King.

"So you think the murders were the result of conflict over the destination—essentially control of the lodestone?" she asked.

"Maybe, but there were other problems. The ship may have been lost at sea, so the Sareenians were upset about the cost of fitting the ship."

"Could the ship's crew have stolen the cargo? What about pirates? And what about your cohorts at the destination; can they be trusted?"

"I don't know. They don't know, either, or they wouldn't be so frantic about finding the ship."

"And Honorday evening? When the Phrenii reported the attempt to enter the phrenic circle?"

Usko pressed his lips together. "My 'cohorts,' as you call them, only entrusted me with guarding a door."

"Who was present on Honorday?" She wondered if it was pique at being left out of the "inner circle" that was causing Usko to open up and turn on the others.

"Since Reggis is gone, the only one I ever meet is Taalo—but I think he's fallen from favor. As for others, perhaps ten people arrived. They protect their identities, even from each other. When they finished, one person was carried away."

"Did you see what happened that night?"

"As I said, I'm only allowed to tend the door. But every evening since Honorday, the result has been the same: someone collapses, but I'm not told any specifics." Yes, Usko was bitter about his status in the conspiracy.

"Can you tell us the location of this warehouse?"

Usko gave her a wry smile. "Unfortunately, I can only guess. I meet Taalo in the market square and I get blindfolded."

She glanced at Ponteva, who nodded. He would work with the clerk, trying to get any clues as to the location of the building.

"Could you tell if anyone was armed?" she asked.

"No. Never thought about it."

She tried another tack. "You know how some Guard look when they're without weapons. They're fiddling with their belt, their sword and knife hands seeking those weapons. When they have their arms, they often rest their hand upon them. Anyone behave like that?"

The corners of Usko's mouth lifted in sour amusement. "Officer Drai-us, most of these men are feeling for their money-purses, not their weapons. I suppose I've seen one or two of the robed figures 'fiddle,' as you say."

So the attack on her and Lornis still pointed straight at Haversar, but why? Haversar ran his organization with a brutal, pragmatic outlook entirely oriented on profit. Anything stolen by his people had to be saleable on the streets. No one who worked for him would dare identify him to the Guard, so few people in the Guard knew what he looked like. Draius did—she'd seen Haversar once when he was meeting with Jan—and loyalty to her husband had kept her mouth shut. Haversar was big enough to fit Usko's description of the leader, but surely he wouldn't be involved if there wasn't any likely profit.

She shut away thoughts of the attack and focused again upon the clerk. "What other information did you give Taalo? He couldn't have been only interested in your ability to forge customs documents."

"Oh, nothing of consequence. I think they were testing my loyalty. They asked for watch schedules and other meaningless items, such as manpower reports."

"You fool!" Ponteva couldn't contain himself. Usko cringed, confusion on his face.

"You might have thought those schedules meaningless, but they were probably pretty helpful to the conspirators," she said. "You've betrayed King and country with your actions."

"But—I never meant—"

"What's done is done, but perhaps you can remedy things. Tellina's body will be released today, so Ponteva will take you immediately to the morgue. Let's see if you recognize him as a member of the conspiracy."

"That's unlikely, ser." Usko blanched; although he worked for the City Guard, he had never been around corpses. However, Draius had no compassion for the clerk. She dictated what Usko would do in the coming days: he would remain under covert Guard custody, in hopes that Taalo would contact him again. He would continue to go home and go to work at the regular times, and he would be constantly watched.

When she finished and opened her office door, Miina had a message for her. "Someone stopped by to see how you were doing, a sickly looking fellow named Wendell. He waited for a while and eventually left."

She'd thank Wendell for his concern later. Meanwhile, she gave orders that Miina and Ponteva would be responsible for Usko, with the help of the rest of the watch. Above all, she stressed, the appearance of normalcy must be maintained so the conspirators wouldn't suspect that Usko had confessed.

Draius penned a note for Perinon, which read:

> *Sire, the existence of the lodestone has been confirmed through an eyewitness. This eyewitness supposes the object was shipped out of Tyrra on the Sareenian ship Danilo Ana, on the Second Farmday of Erin Two. Destination of the ship is still unknown.*
>
> *—Your faithful Officer of the City Guard, Serasa-Kolme Draius.*

She marked it with "For the King's Eyes Only" and sealed it with an official King's Law seal. As she gave the note to a runner, she wondered what Perinon would do with this information. Lately, the King had been showing a propensity for abrupt decisions.

For a moment she wondered whether her cousin was already wandering into madness. After all, the strain of the Kaskea was real. Mielis was only one example of several kings who had broken from that strain, albeit the most famous one.

She rubbed her neck as she indulged in a few wistful memories of running about the streets of Betarr Serasa with her cousins on imaginative quests and battles. Would Perinon ever laugh like that again? For that matter, would she?

CHAPTER TWENTY-FIVE

Postures and Facades

Tyrra has been established longer than mankind can remember. She was sequestered safely behind her magic until the Fevers, which had no regard for magical walls. In 1456, King Valos dismantled the Lightning Wall of the Phrenii, and the Mapped World clearly saw the complicated manner of Tyrran governance. The Kingship carries the authority of a hereditary principality, while the matriarchy selects who holds the Kingship, as well as enforcing a mysterious control throughout the populace. Networks of elected officials and administrators, who shift and change over time, alleviate the threat of treason. All this creates a state that is easily held, and almost impossible to overcome through disaffection.

—*To Have and Hold Power, Avo Cabaran, T.Y. 1471*

It was time for Draius to give King Perinon her report, unwelcome as it may be. The Guard in flashing silver and green said she'd find the King in the great Council Hall, although no formal session of the King's Council was in progress. Lightly bounding up the stairs of the Palace of Stars and through the stone archway, she kept her mind on her task—no time for memories, good or bad, today. Turning right into the corridor for the Council Hall, she regretted her haste. Two Groygans, wearing red and yellow uniforms of the embassy, were lounging in front of the chamber doors, which appeared to be new.

It was too late to turn back without losing face. Draius slowed down as much as she could while still looking purposeful. Unfortunately, there was no other reason to be in this hallway other than to go into the great hall. The Groygans pushed away from the wall with sinuous motions and stood in front of the doors, blocking her way. Through the closed chamber doors came the sound of raised voices, but she couldn't distinguish words.

"Honor, look. It's *far fintemila*," said the Groygan on the right, identifying himself as lower ranking by his words. He had bright yellow eyes and his skin was a sickly orange, the result of getting less exposure to the sun than he did in Groyga. He bared his canines at her.

"All I see is the offspring of cats," she said, addressing the higher-ranking Groygan. The younger one had called her a girl-pretending-to-manhood, which she had heard before. Likewise, her return had little sting, being a traditional jibe at the Groygan eye shape and elongated, slit-shaped pupils.

They were just going through the motions, posturing. She'd purposely addressed the senior of the two, who would now have to respond to her insult, weak as it was. As this older Groygan looked her up and down, she knew he was the more dangerous of the two. He'd been addressed as "Honor," so he was an Honored Sword of some rank. His bronze body looked battle-hardened and his posture screamed for his sword, which he wasn't allowed to wear outside the Groygan Embassy. The long blade on his ceremonial knife, however, almost went beyond his diplomatic rights and could be a formidable weapon. Her hand drifted to the hilt of her own long knife.

"Our women don't give birth in the fields, ride a-straddle, or manage property and money. They don't pretend to be men." The younger Groygan spat a gob, defiling the marble floor. She continued to ignore him.

The Honored Sword was taller than Draius and he came closer to stare into her face. She kept herself staring coldly into his foreign eyes. He moved to her side, which would constrict her primary weapon arm. She moved with him, face to face, purposely turning her back on the younger Groygan. The Honored Sword's mouth twitched into an unpleasant smile, and she returned it.

"No, De Garra, we should pity her. She's probably sterile, like most Tyrran women. Let her play at manhood, since she can no longer fulfill her purpose." The Honored Sword had a smooth voice and spoke impeccable Tyrran.

She was shocked, on several accounts. The Tyrran language was taught and known throughout the Mapped World, but Groygans she'd previously encountered had spoken it with strange inflections. Their guttural accents were heavy and identifiable, like De Garra's, and she had never *heard* a Groygan who could pass for a Tyrran. Then there was the nature of the insult, which worried her and although she'd never admit it, cut her deeply. Never before had any Groygan touched upon the shameful problem of the Tyrran matriarchy: the dwindling birth rate. Since Tyrrans never talked of this, how did this Groygan know? Was their situation obvious to strangers?

"My son is nearly old enough to learn the sword." She clenched her teeth. A warning sounded inside her head: *don't get emotional, don't get carried away.*

The Honored Sword cocked his head in a very Tyrran gesture. "Well, good for you," he said heartily, crossing his arms over his chest. His tone was casual and condescending. "And he probably has a good amount of Meran blood. What's your son's name?"

His hazel eyes with the narrow pupils flicked over her blond hair, her gray eyes, and her dusky skin: all the indicators that showed her Meran lineage—which was usually irrelevant to a Groygan. Draius was unsure how to respond, because the Stars would fall into Darkness before she'd give her son's name to a Groygan. Names were unique within each Tyrran generation, which this Groygan probably knew.

The doors behind her opened with a thump, banging against the walls and releasing the smell of freshly carved wood. It took strength to make those heavy doors fly open, and Draius had to ignominiously scamper out of the way of Groygan Ambassador Velenare Be Glotta. Velenare swept by without giving her a glance. He was broad, tall, and twice her weight. He could have knocked her into the marble wall without noticing.

"*Prendergi, Be Lottagre,*" said the Ambassador in a deep, guttural voice to the Honored Sword. Although Velenare was the first Groygan Ambassador to adopt Tyrran styles in clothing and hair, there was no doubt that *his* voice was Groygan. The Honored Sword and De Garra immediately fell in behind Velenare as he strode down the hall.

Trying to salvage her pride, Draius glared at the back of their three heads. Groygans typically had hair color that couldn't possibly pass for Tyrran: Velenare's hair was flaming red and De Garra's was a shocking orange, but the Honored Sword had dark muted bronze locks that were left long, in the Tyrran tradition. De Garra kept his hair disgustingly short and spiky, but then De Garra had no chance of being mistaken for a Tyrran in the dark—

She was caught flat-footed as the Honored Sword looked back at her before turning the corner. His eyes caught hers in a knowing, amused glance. Then he *winked* at her, and went around the corner.

She was infuriated. The King's Guard at the door let her stalk into the King's Council Hall. As soon as she realized that Sevoi was speaking, she backed up until she stood near the doors.

"We can't give in to his pressure. We had every right to conduct the raid into the Auberei Islands, and we had the blessings, even the encouragement, of every Sareenian state." Sevoi was the oldest man in the room, having been the master of arms, the commander of the King's Guard, for over thirty years.

"Turning over Rhobar might appease them, and we wouldn't lose face by doing so." Councilman Muusa had been recently appointed to the King's Council as a temporary replacement for Reggis. He was a thin man of average height and he looked agitated.

"You're wrong, Councilman. They've already swallowed Gosleir, with no protest from us, or anyone else. Giving them Rhobar would be tantamount to admitting Groygan influence now extends over the Auberei Archipelago," Sevoi said. "Rhobar doesn't come under Groygan jurisdiction, and as for whom he's wronged? He's extorted ransom and tribute from the Sareenians, and he's attacked and raided both Tyrran and Kitarran ships. Everyone is out for his blood."

Draius glanced about the room, noting Sevoi, Lady Aracia, Muusa, Perinon, and Perinon's ever-present Guards. The Phrenii were absent. Perinon looked haggard, as Sevoi and Muusa argued in front of his chair. Lady Aracia was an icy presence standing near the tall windows, removed from the argument.

"Groygan ships suffered from Rhobar as well," Muusa said.

"So Velenare claims. But I suspect he fears Rhobar will be exposed as a Groygan privateer, not just a common pirate," Sevoi said.

"We can't go back to the days of the Lightning Wall, when we symbolically cut ourselves off from the world," Muusa said.

"The Lightning Wall was *more* than just a symbol, Councilman." Perinon waved the ring that had the sliver of Kaskea. His gesture was languid and like Aracia, he didn't seem engaged by the dispute.

"What if Groyga interprets our raid as an act of war, Sire?" Muusa ran his fingers nervously through his thin beard. "They could stop trade, they could claim—"

"Sire, the King's Council shouldn't have raised taxes on Groygan imports." Aracia's cool voice cut across Muusa's and everyone in the hall looked at her. "I must remind you, gentlemen, that our productivity has not increased since the Fevers and our population still dwindles. We have developed wondrous and comfortable inventions, but we must exchange our mechanical advancements for food, clothes, and labor. We now need Groygan *food* to sustain ourselves, to stay alive. Capitulating on the matter of the pirate and appeasing Groyga, Sire, may be a matter of survival."

Aracia's words rang like a death knell. In the following silence, she bowed her head to Perinon and completed a grand exit; this time Draius couldn't have spoiled it. There was silence as they waited for the most powerful matriarch in Tyrra to leave the hall.

"Sire, Velenare surprised us during an informal meeting and I take full responsibility for that. I will immediately adjust the training of the King's Guard. But his demand to hand over Rhobar cannot be accommodated without offending Sareen and Kitarra."

Muusa muttered something under his breath. The argument had stalled, without producing workable options. Perinon dismissed him with a wan gesture and Muusa walked out. He then noticed Draius near the doors and motioned for her to come forward. After she bowed her head, Sevoi gave her a nod.

Draius was still piqued by her exchange of insults with the Groygans. "Sire, Master Sevoi, I met—encountered—Ambassador Velenare. He has an Honored Sword here, doesn't he?"

"Orze Be Lottagre," Sevoi said. "Yes, we know about him. He has significant military experience, both as tactician and strategist."

"He can pass for Tyrran, if he wants." As she said this, she felt a little foolish.

"It's impossible for a Groygan to pass as a Tyrran." Sevoi frowned.

"True, under daylight when one sees his hair color or his eyes. But I saw him in profile against bright light. His hair is long enough for Tyrran braids and in the dark, if he hid his eyes from direct light, no one would mark him as Groygan."

"We watch the Groygan embassy continually. He can't wander around the cities without our knowledge." Sevoi shrugged.

"I bet matriarchs still maintain their emergency passages into the tunnels. Sevoi, are we sure my brother closed the embassy to that warren under the plateau?" Perinon joined their conversation for the first time.

He was referring to his brother Valos, who was King only a short time and who established the embassies after the Fevers. Similar to the Groygan embassy in Betarr Serin, a Tyrran embassy had been created in Chikirmo, although their activities were extremely constrained by the Groygan Council of Lords.

"I don't remember exactly what was done to that estate before we gave it over to the Groygans. I'll check the records, Sire." Chagrin rolled off the master of arms.

She took a deep breath. Now it was her turn. "Sire, the embassy may be involved in other affairs as well. I came to give you a full report on our progress." Although finding a traitorous leak in the City Guard and confirming the lodestone had been smuggled out of the country might not be deemed true *progress*.

As she gave her report, she could tell Perinon wasn't impressed. His light gray eyes were bleak and chilling, without hope. They looked familiar, like hers had looked this morning in the mirror.

"Your source confirmed that the Groygan embassy is involved, that the lodestone was shipped to Groyga?" Sevoi asked.

"He only heard others speak of their 'Groygan connection,' and the port of Chikirmo was one *possible* destination. It's probable that Tellina's company did the shipping, and I'll soon confirm that."

"It's important to track down this 'Groygan connection.' Reggis was our prime negotiator for trade—could he have been a traitor?" Perinon asked.

"I don't know. Our source says the decision regarding where to ship the lodestone caused a split in their organization, and could be the reason Reggis was murdered. But I cannot confirm whether Reggis was a traitor to King or country," she said.

"I see why you're suspicious of Lottagre." Sevoi's face sagged. "If he can get out of the embassy unseen, he wouldn't be noticed on the city streets. He could have easily participated in this conspiracy."

"One more important point. The *Danilo Ana* hasn't put into any expected ports, so piracy is quite probable. Yet another reason why Velenare might be desperate to get his hands on Rhobar—that brash pirate leader might know where the lodestone rests," she said.

"Yes, Velenare is desperate. He even threatened to put an embargo on wheat, which we import heavily." Sevoi looked thoughtful.

"Well, he won't be getting Rhobar. Admiral Ahjo has him in chains and he'll be brought here to the sister cities." Perinon tone was sharp; he was finally showing some energy. "Meanwhile, let's cover other routes the lodestone could have left by—just in case the *Danilo Ana* was used as a ruse. Sevoi, speak with all the embassies and ask for their cooperation in stopping the smuggling of items banned for export. Keep it vague, whether you're speaking with Groygans, Sareenians, even Kitarrans, and remind them of our treaties in the matter of antiques, artifacts, or items of historical significance."

"Yes, Sire. I'll also send a messenger to our embassy in Chikirmo. They can watch for the ship and anyone who tries to pick up the cargo." Sevoi looked uncomfortable, and even though the King gave him a nod of dismissal, he lingered. He glanced meaningfully at Draius, then hesitantly added, "About *artifacts*, Sire..."

"I've made my decision." From the look they exchanged, this followed yet another disagreement she wasn't privy to, and she hoped to keep it that way. Perinon then waved Sevoi away, as well as the anonymous foursome of King's Guard, leaving her alone with him.

She waited. Decision, dismissal, even anger would be better than Perinon's brooding silence. After all, the City Guard let one of these conspirators operate within their headquarters for many erins. Now that she was alone with the King, she noticed how bad his face looked: drawn and tired, with dark circles under the eyes.

"Any mention of the Kaskea?" Perinon asked finally.

"Our source says Taalo never spoke of the stolen shard, but we can assume that since he has Nherissa's papers, he has it as well. And he's probably behind the probing the Phrenii have felt within their circle."

"We have learned, to our surprise, Cousin, how distinctly we feel the 'probing.' It disrupts our sleep with visions of blood."

She raised her eyebrows. Was Perinon using the royal "we" or the phrenic "we"? Was he losing himself, his individuality, within the phrenic circle?

"The man attempting to use the Kaskea doesn't have the education of this Taalo you've described," Perinon said. "Others push him into the Blindness with necromantic charms and blood—which is the wrong way to use the Kaskea. They are only making it harder on the wielder and, although he has Meran lineage, he's barely holding on to his sanity. He's only attempting this out of loyalty and fear."

The *Blindness?* There was so much here she didn't understand, but before she could begin to even frame a question, she heard ringing tones behind the doors. The heavy doors swung open, pulled rather hastily by outside Guards, and Mahri entered. Apparently the creature could choose to be silent, or it could forewarn its approach. The doors closed behind the creature as it walked down the hall to take a position behind the King's chair, giving her time to think.

"Since this is so risky, what do they hope to attain?" Right now, procedures were not as important to her as motives.

Mahri answered her. "They hope to attain the Void, to search for the lodestone."

The creature's words fell past her ears like the soft pattering of rain: just as soothing, and just as incomprehensible. *Attaining the Void,* to search? With the assurance of someone who could later remember every word, she tried to understand the gist of the sentence. "Can't you prevent them from entering this 'Void'?" She threw the question into the air, not knowing whether the wielder of the Kaskea, or the Phrenii, would answer it.

Perinon regarded her strangely, then his expression changed, becoming softer. Perhaps he sensed her frustration and when he answered his tone was sympathetic. "Few people would understand in this day and age. The Phrenii *are* the portals to the Void, which is the source of life-light magic. Unfortunately, they can no more prevent their use as a portal, than a door frame can prevent its door from opening."

"Using *that* analogy, I would suggest that doors can be difficult to open when they become tight in their frames, particularly during the summer. Can't you make their access just as difficult?" She directed her question to the creature behind Perinon.

Mahri cocked its head, regarding her with sparkling, faceted, golden eyes. It was impossible to tell what the creature was thinking, but Perinon's mouth pursed, like he was holding back a smile.

"You are very perceptive, Officer Draius, which is why you were chosen."

What did the creature mean by that?

Mahri kept speaking. "When we feel this man, we attempt to know him, to determine his motives, his background, and his identity. We are *difficult*, as you would say. But the more we press him, the more chance he will break and if he embraces madness, we fear the effects on another mind connected to us."

Another mind. There could be only one. She glanced at Perinon, who looked down at the ring on his tightly clenched fist. She became intensely aware of his dilemma. *He's already had his mind laid bare to the Phrenii, and now he must suffer some unknown criminal threatening his sanity. How he must hate being bound to that thing!*

The hard desperation on his face made her step backward. She kept her own expression blank. The last thing she wanted to show was her pity. "Our source is under house arrest, Sire, with my watchmen following him. The conspirators will contact him and we'll find the stolen shard."

His mouth quirked; he'd noted her overt optimism. "I have confidence you'll find it, Cousin, but I took measures to ensure the remaining shards are protected. I had them returned to my care."

She nodded, cautiously. The rumors of his "measures," particularly his unlikely magical powers and the humiliation of three Pettaja lineal matriarchs—just as unlikely—had spread through the streets like oil filming over water. However entertaining the gossip had been, she didn't give the story credence when it came from the Pettaja clerks helping in her office. She waited.

"I've decided to disperse the remaining shards to guardians I trust. Sevoi, even though he has criticized this scheme of mine, has still agreed to carry one of the shards." Perinon paused. He fumbled inside a vest pocket, being dressed casually today, and pulled out something on a chain. He abruptly held it out, silver links dripping over his fingers. "I'd like you to take custody of another one, Cousin."

"Excuse me? Are you cra—" She bit back the words, which came out with a sharp tone one should never use with one's sovereign. This was the reason for his addressing her as *Cousin*. He was hoping to take her back in time, and he did. For a moment she saw the young Peri, before he was Perinon, before he was King, wheedling an extra sweetmeat from the big-hearted baker near the square. He managed to feign fatigue for sweets back then, being altogether too cunning for his seven years.

"Draius?" His voice was low. "Will you protect one of the shards?"

She jerked her head up sharply, caught between past and present. This was her *King*, although he was *asking* her, not ordering her to do this. Was there any difference, coming from a sovereign? She looked at Mahri, a creature who could only incite shame, remorse, and guilt within her, and felt her stomach heave. Bile pushed into the back of her throat. "I can't," she said. "I can't bind to them."

"You don't have to. Besides, I don't think it's possible. I am the only one connected to them, the only one in rapport. This is a charge to protect the shard, nothing more."

"The master of arms." She looked at his hand, seeing a locket, not a gray shard. "He doesn't approve, because I'm Serasa-Kolme?"

"Sevoi doesn't want to disperse the shards so widely; he'd rather keep them all in the Royal Armory." Perinon cleared his throat. "And it's not the change of lineage. He doesn't approve of using City Guard, rather than King's Guard. But you're my cousin, I grew up with you, and I know you."

He continued to hold out the shining jewelry, all wrought in silver, the noblest metal even if it might not be the most valuable. She hedged. "I have more Meran blood than Sevoi, perhaps as much as you, Sire. Will I interfere with the circle, the phrenic mind, just like the conspirators?"

Perinon shook his head, but it was Mahri who answered. "The shard is protected by silver, making it difficult to touch. Even then, the mind that wishes rapport must volunteer, as well as exhibit great need, purity of motive, honorable purpose, steadfast heart—"

I get the point. *I'm safe from qualifying for rapport.* Ignoring the rest of the creature's monologue, she took the chain and locket. The links were well formed, tight, and strong. The locket was obviously crafted by a master artisan. It was flat and circular, as wide and high as her two thumbs. She fingered the raised Meran-Viisi emblem on the face, the constellation of major stars, caressing Cessina last of all. Pressing the small catch at the side, she popped the locket open and looked carefully at the flat shard of the Kaskea inside. Its color and texture was like slate and it was wired against the back of the locket. Mahri was right; it'd be difficult to accidentally touch the shard, if that was part of the bonding process.

"Keep it with you at all times, Officer Draius. Keep it safe." Perinon now formally charged her with her duty.

"Yes, Sire." She snapped the locket shut and put the chain about her neck. Her bruised skin quivered as she laid the cold metal around her neck. The locket slid down her breastbone to rest hidden underneath her collar ruff and uniform vest. *I'm simply exchanging one madman's charm for another*, she thought, and suppressed a hysterical giggle. She waited—and felt nothing. The locket might have held a lock of hair, rather than a piece of the most powerful artifact in Tyrra.

With a sigh of relief, she bowed. Perinon made a gesture of dismissal, but Mahri decided to impart another lecture and she had to pause.

"The lodestone must be found, Officer Draius. It is still capable of un-making us, and it holds the power of much torture and death. The pos-sibilities are endless if it falls into unscrupulous hands. The future it will bring fills our nightmares."

As the creature spoke, Perinon's face twisted, perhaps from memories of phrenic visions. She didn't bother to answer the creature—the lode-stone was no longer retrievable by the City Guard and if the Phrenii didn't realize this, then it'd be up to the King to deal with them.

She pushed open one of the high doors and paused to look back at Perinon, King of Tyrra, Holder of the Phrenii's Promise. He slumped in his chair and looked far older than his twenty-four years. She saw little resemblance to the cousin she'd seen crowned in haste, except the feeling of estrangement that he often radiated even before he suffered the bond of the Kaskea. *Not everything should be blamed on the Phrenii*, she thought as she walked out of the Palace of Stars.

• • •

After Draius left, Perinon stared down at the floor. He could see the pity rolling about in his cousin—after all, Mahri had been standing beside him. He hated seeing the pity, but the determination he saw might just help her capture the group he privately called necromancers.

Above all, he didn't want to continue to lie sleepless through the night to forestall the nightmares, the strange minds entering his dreams, and the terror experienced by someone lost in the Blindness and refusing help...

With a start, he realized he had some free time. His secretary was not in sight, meaning there were no pending appointments and he was left alone with Mahri, with his Guards outside. This was the closest thing to privacy that he could have.

Rapport had advantages. When he wanted to think, or have quiet, Mahri would know immediately and retreat. The creature faded from his consciousness, and Perinon reached for the book he had been carrying surreptitiously in a pocket. He opened up his slim copy of *To Have and Hold Power*.

The author, Avo Cabaran, now languished in a Forenllas prison because of his previous publiction. His protector, Lorenz Dimoni, had been killed and while the Dimoni family still held Forenllas, Lorenz's successor was offended by Cabaran's *Discourse on Forenllas*. That work exposed the power and corruption of that Sareenian City-State, as well as the church.

Cabaran's works were banned in all the Sareenian City-States, regardless of which family was involved. Urbano Dimoni, who held Forenllas, was said to be a despot and tyrant, while the Danta family of Illus and the Seguira family of Paduellus were considered benign. Of course, the rest of the world only knew this from Cabaran—a man who could bluntly write things like "Sareenians are irreligious and corrupt above all others" and "our Church and her representatives set the highest examples of immorality."

Cabaran's latest publication examined the means by which principalities held rule over men. He blatantly analyzed how countries or states could be held, whether they were obtained through arms, good fortune, or wickedness. Cabaran enumerated the desirable qualities a ruler should have; he encouraged sovereigns to arm their people, to exhibit liberality rather than tyranny, and to avoid being despised and hated. Perinon thought the reason the book truly shocked the world came in a late chapter, where Cabaran stated that it was unnecessary for a ruler to actually have all the good qualities he expounded, but the ruler should *appear* to have those qualities. A head of state should always *appear* to be merciful, faithful, humane, religious, and upright, but above all, a ruler should be flexible and when necessary, use duplicity to maintain power.

Perinon grinned. This was no surprise to him. He noted all the names of leaders the author listed in the chapter, but at the end of that section

Cabaran wrote, "There is a ruler of the present time, whom one is not allowed to name, who never preaches anything but peace and good faith, while to both he is hostile."

To whom was Cabaran referring? Perinon closed the book and tapped the cover. Then the answer dawned. Cabaran was referring to the Sareenian Church of the Way, with a leader, kingdom, and subjects, yet abstract in its borders. Perhaps the church, which had expanded significantly into Tyrra in the past few years, bore some examination.

Onni comes. Mahri entered his mind like a cool spring breeze wafting through a window. He looked about and slid the book back into his cloak pocket. Mahri wasn't in the room. Onni appeared at the door and cleared her throat.

"Yes, Onni, enter."

She dragged her feet a bit as she came to present herself. Onni was ten years older than Perinon, but she showed an innate timidity whenever she spoke with him—despite Aracia's attempt to eradicate it. Onni's eyes were clear, almost peaceful; a recent change, and Perinon knew the cause. He was closer to the dealings in his household than Aracia realized, so he was well aware that Onni had recently taken a lover, a man of her own choosing and acquaintance. Perinon hoped she would remain childless for a while, because once she bore a child, Aracia would end her happiness.

"Lady Aracia wishes to inquire after your health."

The fact that Aracia hadn't bothered to ask him herself while she was in his presence meant she knew Perinon's excuse of stomach pains earlier that morning was false, merely a way to avoid his Markday breakfast with her. Due to his nightmares and sleeplessness, he'd been too tired to deal with her.

"I'm better now, thank you, and thank Lady Aracia for her concern."

Onni nodded vaguely. She looked like she was carefully choosing her next words; she was coming to the point of her visit, per her mother's directions.

"The Lady wishes to know if you were pleased with Rauta-Nelja Cella."

Perinon pressed his lips together. Aracia was pushing him already? If he gave her any indication he wasn't considering a contract, more young girls would follow. Moreover, he *was* pleased with Cella, but for the fact she was so young and they would have to wait to marry.

"Tell the Lady that I've asked Cella to design new gates for the Meran-Viisi residence and I must evaluate the design before paying any fees to the Rauta-Nelja. I must consider how those gates will stand the test of time, and whether I will appreciate them when three years are past."

Onni wrinkled her brow. She knew her mother and Perinon spoke around her using codes and metaphors. Aracia would understand his meaning, if Onni repeated the words verbatim.

Perinon chuckled after the girl left the room. Aracia held up Cabaran's writings as examples for Perinon to follow? Well, she had better be prepared to deal with the results of her suggestion.

CHAPTER TWENTY-SIX

Second Hireday, Erin Three, T.Y. 1471

We have made progress, of a sort. As several of us pushed through the Blindness, one man had a flash of Sight regarding the *Danilo Ana*. How I wish it'd happened to me! He saw no storms about the ship, but clouds still hung dark and heavy over her. Black smoke rose from her deck and from a hole in her stern.

Since time doesn't always run true in the Blindness—or "Void," as I've incorrectly called it—the member who caught the glimpse felt it'd happened in the recent past. Obviously, this vision pointed to piracy.

"Our Groygan contact ruled out piracy." My employer rubbed his beard.

"You assume the Groygans control the piracy in the Angim. That may not be true." The individual who pointed this out always keeps his hood close, but most of us knew his name and where he worked. He walked away to take up a muttered conversation with the lucky seer.

"And the Groygans now shun us. Lottagre hasn't attempted to communicate with us for almost an eight-day," I said.

My employer didn't have any answer for that, other than a quiet grunt of doubt.

I watched our members clean up our hysterical "wielder" of the Kaskea. Still babbling, the pasty-faced fellow's eyes rolled up in his head and he became docile enough to carry away. With a nod toward the party of four, each struggling with a limp appendage, I added, "You know he's not strong enough. We're in desperate straits and we'll have to push him. If he breaks, he could reveal all of us to the—the—" I hesitated to complete the sentence.

My employer clapped his big hand over my shoulder, squeezing it painfully. "He's been a faithful employee and friend to me. For years."

"I'm not denying that." My words came out in a squeal and he loosened his grip. I rubbed my shoulder, looking away momentarily to hide my surge of anger. He'd pay for manhandling me. Later.

"I trust him." His voice was deeper than usual and his eyes were bleak.

"This isn't a matter of trust." The words hissed through my teeth. "Nor of loyalty. It's only a matter of time until his mind breaks, not his will."

He looked thoughtful. "You're right about the strain. Maybe we should take a day off. I'll buy him a pint tomorrow evening, as a respite."

Take a day off? Once again, my employer didn't understand. No amount of rest could help his assistant; the man had, inherently, a weak mind. I took a deep breath to calm myself. "I—*we*—need to be the first to find the lodestone. Do you think it wise to take a break now, when we're closing in on the ship's location? They say Rhobar operates under Groygan letters of marque, so those islands may soon be swarming with Groygans."

"There's no reason to panic yet." His face set stubbornly, but I detected a hint of desperation in his voice. "Those islands are like a rabbit warren. Look how many ships the King had to use to capture him."

"But it's no coincidence the King sent the Naval Guard after Rhobar! Why would His Majesty suddenly show so much interest, if not for his cousin—I tell you that City Guard bitch is closer than you think. What if the *Phrenii*—"

"I thought your charms could hide us from them."

"We're protected because—" *Because we're skulking around in the Blindness, you fool.* I'd almost said too much. I was the only one with a charm that protected me from the creatures' ken and I'd had no chance to test it. My words twisted, mid-sentence. "The charms protect us, but they weaken over time. At the least, get me a way to harvest fresh pain or death and I can bolster all of us, including the wielder."

He watched me silently for a moment, then nodded. He must think I was chafing at my confinement, even though I understood the necessity. The City Guard searched for me everywhere, questioning everyone who might know me or have seen me. It's a shame my charm didn't kill Officer Draius, although she's much less threat than the creatures who are portals to the Void, who can walk the Void as naturally as breathing. Soon it'd be too late for my employer and his cohorts. The Phrenii were coming for them, and my goal was to find the lodestone's location before that happened.

CHAPTER TWENTY-SEVEN

A Contract Breaks

FAMED PIRATE RHOBAR CAPTURED BY TYRRAN NAVAL GUARD

In a courageous raid, the Naval Guard captured Frisson Rhobar and destroyed his hideaway. Rhobar used the Auberei Archipelago as cover for twelve years, performing outrageous deeds, such as ransoming a Noble Light of the Church of the Way and extorting "protection fees" from Forenllas and Paduellus. But no more. The Naval Guard shut down Rhobar's posts, burned his ships, and delivered him to Tyrran magistrates in chains. Rhobar's deeds have been wildly romanticized, but they are still punishable by hanging. Our King has suggested the magistracy show leniency, provided Rhobar confesses his crimes. This makes our young King popular with Tyrran women but Sareen and Kitarra are outraged, claiming they've borne the brunt of Rhobar's crimes. The Groygan embassy has been silent on the matter.

—*The Horn & Herald, Second Hireday, Erin Three, T.Y. 1471*

O n Millday morning, Draius stopped by the hospital and found Lornis could have visitors. Indeed, one sat beside his bed, a petite woman with light brown hair. Her features and color were similar to Lornis's.

"One of the few cousins I have in the sister cities," Lornis said. "Leija, this is Draius, my commanding officer."

"How are you feeling?" Draius sat down beside the bed, opposite Leija.

Lornis's brown eyes were wide and trusting—almost childlike. He'd lost weight, making his chin, nose, and cheekbones more pronounced. Half his face was covered with green and blue bruising, a mirror image of the bruises on her face.

"Better, much better. When can I start work?"

She laughed, hiding her unease. What changes does one see after phrenic healing? Lornis seemed energetic for someone who recently had a bullet blow his gut apart and a blade slice his leg open. What about the hidden transformations, the ones everyone feared? "Gaflis has hinted you might be able to leave tomorrow."

"Good!" exclaimed Lornis. His enthusiasm reminded her of Peri.

Draius turned toward Leija. "I wanted to make sure—I mean, most people don't want—"

"Magical healing?" Leija smiled. "Don't worry. We accept it, on occasion. We're one of the few remaining fundamentalist lineages."

"Good. I mean, I'm glad they made the right decision, for you and your family." Draius exhaled in a silent sigh of relief. Some people wouldn't be able to live with the decision Captain Rhaffus made.

"And, on this occasion, we're grateful they called the Phrenii," Leija said, patting Lornis's hand. She stood, giving him a look Draius couldn't interpret. "I must leave you now, but I'll be back tomorrow morning."

After Leija left, Lornis put his broad hand down upon hers, which was resting on the bedrail. She jumped.

"Are you afraid of me, Draius?"

She paused. An urge to be honest, rather than tactful, overwhelmed her. "Somewhat, I guess."

"Because of the healing?" He watched her.

She dropped her gaze and struggled for words. "I've grown up with the stories and I half believe them..."

Her voice trailed away while she looked down at their hands. His were broad, with short fingers, contrasting with her slender ones. "My mother refused healing while she was conscious. She believed she wouldn't be the same afterward, and she died because of her beliefs. So, instead of changing *her*, it was my father who was never the same. I swayed between hating my mother for being too strong and leaving us, and hating my father for not being strong enough. Near the end, he called the Phrenii for healing, but not soon enough to save her. If he wasn't going to keep his promise, why couldn't he have called them sooner?"

Her perfect recall tortured her again. Resentment twisted in her gut. Meran-Viisi Sades had died from the Fevers, her blood and skin burning. Afterward, her only daughter Draius was expected by the matriarchy to "carry on," as all Tyrran women were. Draius's father been allowed to grieve and weep, without rebukes to "stay strong," even though *he* had let Sades depart for the Stars before her time. Young Draius wasn't allowed grief; she was chided for her tears, even during her mother's funeral pyre.

Lornis's hand tightened on hers, bringing her thoughts back to the hospital room.

"I'm sorry." His voice was hoarse and full of emotion. He looked ready to cry.

She pulled her hand away and silently berated herself. Lornis would be sensitive, emotional, and full of empathy after the phrenic healing. And, for some strange reason, she'd bared her emotions to someone she had known less than two eight-days. This wasn't like her; she hadn't confided these feelings to anyone, certainly never to Jan.

"Well, when you feel yourself again—" she began.

"I am myself, except there's a fire inside my body. I'm really hungry, more so than normal."

"The Stars save us, then. Tyrra could barely feed you *before* your healing." She shook her head while watching him carefully. Would he still be able to do his job, which demanded detachment?

"Don't look so worried," he said. "If I can get to work, have you got anything for me to do?"

"I'm going through the evidence again. I need to confirm that Tellina's ship carried the lodestone out of the sister cities, and by the Horn, I'm going to connect Vanhus to this whole thing. Not exciting work, and nothing physical."

Lornis nodded and closed his eyes. "I'll be there," he said, his voice strong. Then he suddenly dropped off to sleep and started gently snoring.

She quietly left. She rode Chisel today, so she took the horse back to the stable ring and put him through his forms. She had to protect her injured shoulder, which was healing, but not at the phenomenal rate that Lornis's wounds were. The mild spring weather and exercise cleared her head, but her aching shoulder made her turn Chisel over to the stable boys when she was finished. Someone else would have to unsaddle and groom the horse.

By the time Draius got to Guard Headquarters, it was afternoon. She nodded to Ponteva when she entered her outer office, where Usko worked under his watchful eyes.

She'd had the Meran lineage records delivered and, with some trepidation, she opened the package. Most Tyrrans learned at a young age not to poke into the business of the matriarchy, so she didn't know what to expect. Inside the package was a bound book that was more than a handspan thick, filled with ledgers.

The ledgers could have been financial records for a business, except they dealt in people. There were incoming and outgoing columns, as well as other columns with obscure purposes. Moving forward from the back of the book, which was still empty, she found the year and erin of her marriage, where she was listed under "Outgoing." On the date of her birth, she found her name entered as "Incoming" with numbers and symbols in the fourth column. Curious, she turned to the year and erin of Peri's birth. His name was an entry in the third column, with more obscure symbols and numbers in the fourth column.

The pages had no legend. She doubted Lady Aracia would translate the symbols and codes, but from a practical viewpoint, she didn't need to understand them to follow the records. She learned the first number in the fourth column would track back to the ledger entry of the parent, so she understood the relationships well enough. The symbols might indicate terms of contracts between lineages, which were irrelevant for her purposes.

There were references to people outside the Meran lines, even when there wasn't a contract. Comfort clauses often produced healthy children and, while they welcomed every child, matriarchs had a duty to hunt down each child's parentage.

She picked a date 30 years in the past and started grinding away. Once in a while she ran into a surprise: someone she hadn't known she was related to, or the marriage of some distant relative. She was still absorbed in the records when Ponteva knocked. Evening had come. Usko was going home and he'd be following the clerk, hoping other conspirators would make contact. Two other watch members would keep an eye on Usko's apartments throughout the night.

• • •

Without making a conscious decision, Draius found herself walking toward the City Guard barracks that evening. After entering the hall for the officer rooms, she stood at Jan's door and hesitated, putting a hand on the dark panels. The wood felt smooth, worn by years of oil.

With perfect detail, she remembered another barrack door, one she had been directed to with sly smiles and hints. That door had also been dark, oiled wood, but through it she heard the sounds of her husband and another woman having sex—Jan would later protest no *love* was involved. She'd finally opened the door a crack to peek inside. She didn't know why she did that. Was she a glutton for punishment, or did she *really* need to verify Jan was inside?

Once the scene was burned into her memory, she'd never be free of it. The room was a single berth and she had a clear view of the bed. Jan lay on his back, straddled by Netta's lithe body, her long dark hair falling forward over her full breasts and down onto his chest. Netta was petite, and his hands on her hips looked large as he guided her movements. There were gasping words, light laughter, but what came back to Draius's mind for review again and again, would be Jan's face and his radiant freedom—a look she'd never seen before.

She'd left the door ajar and fled, having to go back through the crowded common room. Her face burned as she hurried through and some of the knowing faces held pity, while some held satisfaction, for Jan had enemies. It was hard to hide secrets within the Guard. Since Jan was meeting another Guard woman and using the barracks for his trysts, he might as well have conducted his affair outside in the public square.

She took a deep breath. Jan would say this was all in the past and finally, she would agree. It wasn't because she could forgive him—she doubted she ever would, for any of his liaisons. But she now knew the answer to the question Lornis had posed to her: *Yes, I can truly stop loving someone.*

She tapped on the door and opened it when Jan called out. He was sitting in a chair reading. He looked up, surprise running across his face before he set it into a warm welcoming smile. *He was hoping to see me, but he'd rather have chosen the time and place.*

"Come in, Draius," he said, standing.

She stepped inside the room, closed the door, but remained leaning against the doorjamb.

When Jan saw she wasn't going to come any further into the room, he sat down again and put his book aside on a knee-high tobacco humidor, now performing its only role since he didn't care for pipes. The officer rooms were simple but elegant, fulfilling the needs of most single officers. There were two leather chairs, a desk, and a sideboard with several stocked flasks. The door to the bedchamber was closed, but she knew officers of Jan's rank usually had a comfortable bed and bath, with bells to ring housekeeping and valet service.

Jan's eyes flickered over her face, but otherwise he called no attention to her injuries, as she expected. She didn't say anything and the room was silent.

"Do you need something? Is Peri okay?" Jan sounded awkward, a rare event. He never liked to be the first to speak.

"Peri's fine. I wanted to discuss the attack on Lornis near the Great Hall several nights ago."

"Ah, I heard about that. Those ruffians certainly had balls, attacking Guard officers like that."

"Those *ruffians* went out of their way to avoid hurting me. They were well trained and armed with short swords. Not typical thugs." *And if you were a typical husband, you'd have rushed to my side to make sure the mother of your son was unharmed—but you didn't have to do that, did you?*

His expression altered only slightly, and she might be the only person who could have recognized the change. He was wary. By the Horn, she'd half hoped she was wrong.

"So what are you insinuating?" Jan got up and went to the sideboard to get a drink and in that action, betrayed himself. He hardly ever drank hard spirits. There was one exception: when he was nervous about his performance, such as before a Guard competence test, he would have a bit of distilled liquor to calm his nerves.

It was a sad commentary on their marriage that she only knew her husband due to her acute observation skills. He poured himself a finger of brandy and savored it. She stayed quiet while he finished the drink, gathering her thoughts and playing the waiting game she'd learned from him.

"There are rumors of Groygan spies walking about our streets, looking like Tyrrans. Surely you're not falling for that drama." His voice was smooth and confident—he was ready to play the game.

That's the difference between you and me, Jan. My life, and my son's life, are not games. Aloud, she said, "No, these were professionals. I had to kill one of them. That might not mean much to you, but it does to me, even if he was nunetton. Especially when his body showed up in the canals bearing the mark of Haversar."

Something flickered in his face, too quick to assess, when she spoke that name. *Haversar:* a name rarely mentioned between them. A name one always avoided speaking when on the streets. No one else within the Guard, except Draius, knew the history between Haversar and Jan. And very few in the sister cities knew that Jan saved a friend from drowning when they were both only eight years old, a friend who eventually dropped his connections to family and lineage, became nunetton, and took the anonymous name of Haversar.

"So? You got rid of some canal scum." Jan flicked his fingers dismissively.

"I know Haversar owes you life-debt."

"Are you accusing me of being involved in the attack?" He exploded off the chair, but she was ready. Another part of the game: react violently, suddenly, and make her back down.

She held her ground. "Those men had weapons training, as well as a new musket from some Guard armory. The captain is trying his best to ignore those facts because he hopes there's no Guard involvement."

"The captain's focused on the murders, as you should be." Jan calmed down in a heartbeat, performing the seesaw of emotions that used to bewilder her. His mouth twisted in a sneer. "You don't think the captain *expects* you to succeed, do you? Can't you see that you're fated to be nothing more than a sacrifice to public opinion, someone to blame?"

She paused, but she didn't take the bait and become sidetracked. Stepping away from the doorjamb, she started pacing the woven carpet. "Not everything revolves about my case, and that's where I made my mistake. I first assumed the focus of the attack was *me*, but these men were more intent on harming Lornis."

"They were thieves. Of course they went for the man first, that's how they operate."

"They weren't common thieves. *Thieves* don't jump City Guard members openly on the streets. *Thieves* use knives, not swords, and they try to rob you. That's the whole point for them. No, these were hired killers and they were after Lornis, not me."

He was too good at controlling his reactions—she couldn't tell if she hit the mark.

"Why'd you do it, Jan?" Her tone was cool and measured. When she finally put everything together, her anger burned. By now, it was restrained, manageable, a tool to be used. She'd learned from her husband and now, above all, she needed to maintain control. "What did you tell Haversar? Of course, your hands were never sullied by any arrangements and I'm sure you only intended to frighten, not harm me."

"You sound as hysterical as the *H&H.* Why not accuse me of being a Groygan spy, too?"

"I already know the answers." She continued on, ignoring his words. "Why? First, this attack would impress upon Lady Anja how much danger I'm in, and how risky my position as OIC of Investigation can be. If I was scared by it, that'd be an additional reward, but this was mostly for Anja's benefit."

She watched his face. No reaction. She continued. "Second, it'd make me appear incompetent. If the captain could be convinced to remove me, or even if I resigned my position as OIC, another bonus for you. Third, when Lornis was gone—"

"Are you accusing me of jealousy?"

"No. Unfortunately, I know you." Her tone was bleak. "With Lornis out of the picture, there's one less officer with the experience to compete for the positions you crave."

He didn't answer.

She didn't mention there had been a flaw in Jan's plan, but not due to poor logic or execution. He couldn't know that Lornis had a special fate, predicted by the Phrenii. He couldn't know the captain was committed to keeping Lornis alive, as well as keeping Lornis in the City Guard.

If she were facing anyone else, her accusations might be absurd. But this was Jan, who destroyed the careers of others, who exploited weaknesses until lives were in ruin. She remembered Kapeli. Poor Kapeli, who'd ended his life due to shame and an incredible gambling debt, all arranged and exploited by her husband. Kapeli had been nice enough; too bad he had been promoted at Jan's expense...

"Is attempted murder now another one of your tools? Your—" She stopped. Swallowed hard. She was about to say, "Your morals have become skewed." But what about *hers?* Little by little, she'd watched and accepted Jan's moral slips, sometimes even justifying them. Darkness had crept up on her and she'd slid into the morass herself, where she could think like Jan and easily put attempted murder into his perspective.

Outside, the light patter of spring rain started. Jan stood and closed the window while she felt paralyzed, her thoughts racing.

"This is all supposition," he said. "Would you drag these accusations out into public and sully the Serasa-Kolme? Do you want Peri to see his father brought before magistrates, based upon his mother's unwarranted suspicions?"

She leaned against the wall, feeling the familiar nausea of defeat. They knew each other so well. He knew she'd considered all options and had already decided against public action. Otherwise, she wouldn't be confronting him—which meant she had no higher moral ground to stand on.

"What have I become?" she whispered. All in all, she was sure Jan hadn't intended for anyone to die. That was an excuse for *his* actions; what were the excuses for *hers?* For doing nothing? Lornis was right when he hinted at her duality: not only did she lack competence in dealing with Jan, she also had a different moral code. Everything could be black and white when working, while her personal life was composed of many shades of gray. Now her two lives had smashed into each other.

Jan looked uneasy. Self-recrimination was probably the last thing he'd expected from her. Lowering his voice, he said, "You've been under a lot of stress. With the murders and all the trash being printed in the *H&H,* I can see why you might have jumped to these strange conclusions — which no one would believe."

"I won't—" she choked, then managed to gain control of her voice. She glared at him. "I won't do anything publicly, for Peri's sake, but this can be a matter for matriarchal justice."

Anja. The matriarch who had the power to dissolve their contract was young enough to know Jan's background. Although Anja would probably never admit it, she knew about Haversar, and matriarchs were committed to maintain lineal honor.

"You're really going to end our contract? Over this?"

"Can't you see how serious—" She took a deep breath and started over. "You know there's usually something that ties people together? Well, there's nothing between us any more. No love, no loyalty, no respect, no friendship, not even a shared set of moral values. I don't understand you, if I ever did. *And I'll never trust you again.*"

Instead of responding in kind to her emotional outburst, he calmly sat down. "True, we've drifted apart. But I've been trying. If you'd try, we could rebuild our lives."

"There's no marriage, no trust, nothing but ink upon paper. What do you suggest we build upon? And will you continue to seek comfort from other women?"

"Probably, but that's not my fault. You've become colder than the ice on the Cen Cerinas mountaintops." His dark blue eyes were level; now he was speaking the truth.

"I am what I am *because* of you. I must look into my own heart, yes, but so should you. When will you admit, even to yourself, that your affair with Netta was different?"

He shook his head. "Leave her out of this. We're talking about us. You know that Peri, and you, belong to Serasa-Kolme."

You mean we belong to you. She gritted her teeth. Like possessions that, if lost, would cost him honor. But she had to remember that Anja, as a matriarch, would take the same position. The difference would be that

Anja would consider Peri's needs first. "I don't want to put Peri into Aracia's hands any more than you do. But it may be in his best interest."

Jan's eyes looked dead, lifeless as a corpse, making her shiver. "I'll fight any attempt to change Peri's name. He's my son and he'll join me in the Serasa-Kolme constellation."

Provided you can live with enough honor to reach the Stars, she thought, but this time she didn't have wine loosening her tongue. She wouldn't take the risk, right now, of insulting Jan's honor.

"You have no proof," he added, after a pause. She knew that dangerously calm, calculating tone.

"Anja's not a magistrate, so I don't need proof. I can't let your behavior taint Peri and I think she'll agree." Her voice shook. "And I won't protect you any longer. No one else will, either. Norsis already knows Haversar is involved in my attack; he just can't fathom why. You'd better make sure that musket is never found, because it *will* connect you to Haversar and when that happens, I won't do a thing to help you."

"I can't be accountable for Haversar—"

She stopped him with a chopping motion of her hand. "I won't listen to any more protests, because even *you* can't tell when you're speaking the truth any more. And, Ancestors forgive me, I won't say anything about this to the captain, although you've changed our cities by giving criminals powder guns."

"I didn't do that." Jan's answer was automatic and had a small ring of truth, but she no longer cared. She opened the door, her form making a long, thin shadow into the hallway.

She paused and turned back. "This could be for the best. This will free *you* to be with Netta."

"Netta hasn't been able to have a child." An emotion flickered quickly over Jan's face. Concern? Pain? Who would know? She'd never seen true emotions from him, not even in the beginning of their marriage.

"Goodbye, Jan." She closed the door and stumbled down the hall. She didn't expect him to follow, and he didn't. She left the officer barracks as fast as she could.

Outside, the light rain had stopped. The air smelled clean, purified of smoke and soot. Her chest tightened as she strode down the gaslit street, avoiding people who were taking their evening walks and enjoying the mild weather. After passing a man and woman strolling arm-in-arm, chattering to each other, she withdrew into an alley and leaned against the cold stone. Her body tried to sob, her chest heaved and her throat constricted, but she couldn't cry. She hadn't had true tears since... She hadn't cried since her mother's death.

There was no sense grieving the loss of something she'd never possessed. When she started walking again, she moved slowly, feeling old and infirm. Her shoulder throbbed. She craved warmth, so she headed toward light, food, and friends.

CHAPTER TWENTY-EIGHT

Safe Passage

In this hermitage, Sorceress-Apprentice Lahna tries to teach us elemental magic and searches for answers. Why can we no longer reach the Void? The Void sits high above the world, and is the source of elemental magic. Between the Void and the solid world is the Blindness: the realm of dreamers and monsters. We can still wander the Blindness but since Cessina's death and the breaking of the Kaskea, no one can reach the Void, save he who is bound to the Phrenii.

—*Meran-Nelja Pilas, tentatively dated T.Y. 1048*

"By the Horn, I need a beer." Draius lowered herself gingerly into one of the Sea Serpent's chairs.

Berin's rumble could be heard throughout the common room. Patrons at nearby tables turned and looked, maybe wondering whether the sound was laughter, or something more ominous. Although she hadn't expected to find Berin and Wendell at the pub on a Millday evening, she was grateful to see their faces.

"You look worse than I imagined," Berin said. "The *H&H* didn't exaggerate that attack. No wonder you're swearing."

"Are you well, Draius?" Wendell poured her a glass of ale from their pitcher, his hand shaking a bit. He slid it over to her and she took a sip.

The ale was stronger than the lager she intended to order, but at this point she didn't care.

"I'm doing better than you, it would seem." She noted Wendell's pallor. He was also sweating, as if he burned with a fever. Her lips parted to ask him about his visit to her office but his eyes widened in alarm, like a trapped animal facing a predator.

She paused and Wendell quickly picked up the conversation. "I feel fine. I'm more concerned about your health and welfare."

"My health is fine, my welfare is—well, that's a different story." Draius sighed.

"More ale!" roared Berin. The order bounced off the back wall and reverberated around the room.

As if everything could be solved by more ale, more lager, or more wine... Berin was lucky to have a simple life, and such a loyal friend and employee in Wendell. She raised her glass for another sip, while she looked at Berin's assistant. Quiet, efficient Wendell. Always staying in the background. To her surprise, he was one of her distant cousins. Wendell's birth had been marked as an outgoing asset of the offshoot Meran-Nelja line in Aracia's records.

"So you're tired of being chased around by thugs." Berin's voice boomed and carried through the room, and when Draius didn't respond, he tried, "Or, perhaps, this is about Jan. What's that ambitious manipulator done now?"

She winced. Although her old friend was surprisingly perceptive, he didn't understand the complexities involved. He wasn't a man who could see shades of gray and he'd never been subtle in his support. She remembered his enthusiastic cheering when she won the Cavalry Seat Horsemanship competition at the age of sixteen. Her father had been too busy to attend, but Berin had managed. She'd been both embarrassed and grateful for his loud support then—and she felt both those feelings now. But she could never tell Berin everything about her husband. Would she even be able to tell Anja?

"You're already tracking backwards down the trail, aren't you? Changing your mind?" Berin's voice became deeper in a futile attempt to be quiet.

She glanced at him, startled. She *had* been wavering about carrying through her threats.

"I know you, girl." He pointed a beefy finger in her face. "You came in here full of resolve, didn't you? Now you're starting to justify his actions, and making excuses."

"So first I'm a woman, but now I'm a girl? I don't want to talk about it."

"Hmm. So, how's your lieutenant?" Berin quickly changed the subject, knowing just how far to push her before pulling back.

"Lornis appears healthy enough after the phrenic healing. The physician says he can start working in a day or two."

"Amazing," Berin said in a sour tone. "He was almost dead a couple days ago. Just think what *our* physicians could do with the knowledge locked up in those creatures."

She frowned. Berin's viewpoints about the Phrenii were not uncommon—one only had to look at the letters to the *H&H* to find others with the same opinions—but she wasn't in the mood to listen to him this evening.

"It's not the Phrenii's fault that they can't teach our physicians," she said. "They say mankind can't work without pictures, but they never think in pictures."

"Five creatures can't take care of an entire country of people. We learned this, to our detriment, during the Fevers. If they could train our hundreds of physicians—"

"Since their methods are magical, how can mankind learn them? For Lornis, at least, we should be grateful they have such methods! The Guard nearly lost a most valuable man—" She stopped. Even on this subject, she now held secrets. The captain said no one else could be told about Jhari's foretelling.

Berin cocked his head. When she didn't continue, he sat back and sighed.

"Look, let's not hash over one of the oldest arguments in history. Instead, let's hope your lieutenant has some spine left after the healing, so he doesn't burst into tears at the sight of a criminal."

She didn't answer. When did Lornis become *her* lieutenant? As if he'd become her responsibility. That hit a tender nerve, since she was responsible for the attack, in a way. She stared into her glass, watching a tiny bubble at the bottom slowly lose hold and lazily float to the top. She realized how tired she was, and how emotionally drained. There was no spark of energy or committment left within her.

Silence reigned at their table. Berin took a deep pull at his ale, and then held his empty glass up, sighing.

"Where is that girl?" Grumbling, he got up. Berin stopped the serving girl at the counter, where he started berating her, at top volume, on the quality of service. This time it wasn't Raivata serving them, but a docile, round-faced girl who looked more suited to the farm than the pub.

Wendell had stayed quiet, but after Berin left the table he reached out and laid a hand on her arm. "Draius, you must be *very* careful." His mouth twitched and his eyes had a feverish intensity.

"Of course."

"I mean you must be wary of everyone. It would be best if you found a different job."

"Is that why you came to the office? To give me warning?" She moved her arm away from his hand, and saw a flash of fear go through his eyes before he deliberately looked away.

"I only stopped by to check on your health." Wendell looked down, withdrawing as Berin came back to the table carrying a pitcher of ale.

"I'm going to have a talk with Mainos about that girl," Berin said.

"Unfortunately, I must say good night. I'm still fighting a chill." Wendell got up and bowed, before putting on his cloak and taking his leave.

Draius watched him go while sipping her drink. "How long have you known Wendell?"

"He's worked for me several years now. Hired him after you and Jan left for Betarr Kain."

"Did you know him before that?"

Berin's forehead wrinkled while he stroked his beard. "I guess not. We were introduced through a mutual friend."

"Do you know he's Meran?"

"His lineage is Purje-Kolme, but half this city can trace their blood back to a Meran line. Why?"

"No reason. But if I were you, I'd make sure he got to a physician. You don't want to lose a good employee."

"No, I don't. But I'm concerned about my long-time friend right now. I think you are in need of some entertainment. The carnival is setting up in the market square for Ringday—let me take you and Peri. It'll get your mind off your problems."

"Peri would enjoy that." She smiled, remembering a younger Berin who took a gangly adolescent girl under his wing. At sixteen, she had few friends and her father, a King's magistrate, benignly ignored her. He pulled her out of the Meran-Viisi lessons with her cousins and arranged for the best tutors that could be found in the sister cities, but they couldn't replace a young girl's need for family and friendship. Berin offered her that friendship without any conditions; he'd never shown any need for deeper involvement and she'd never wondered, never wanted to know, why.

When Draius came home, she found Peri and told him about the carnival on Ringday. He was so excited she worried about his concentration in his lessons and hoped Anja wouldn't get a message from his tutor.

"I can't wait till Ringday. Will there be magicians, will we see magic?" Peri asked.

She laughed. "The magicians you see in the carnival aren't using real magic. Only the Phrenii can do that."

"Then why are they called magicians?"

"They're sleight-of-hand artists, meaning they play tricks with their quick fingers. Now you need to get ready for bed."

Peri couldn't go to sleep immediately, having more questions. She answered them, calmed him down, and eventually he drifted off. After that, she went downstairs and found Anja in the front parlor working at her desk with a lamp. Financial records were spread across the desk and Anja worked though columns of numbers.

The young matriarch looked up.

For a moment Draius paused in the doorway, uncertain. Then her resolve hardened. This was the right thing to do, especially for Peri. She could no longer ignore Jan's behavior, not if she wanted to respect herself, and keep her son's respect. In a way, she knew this moment would come ever since she sat down to the comfortable meal with Lornis, Peri, and Anja, when she had noticed the relief of Jan's absence, before the charm started tightening... She rubbed her neck, then quietly closed the parlor doors behind her for privacy.

Anja was still waiting.

"I wish to speak with you, as matriarch for my family."

"Of course." Anja put aside the records and picked up a folded piece of paper: the one that, more than two eight-days ago, Draius had pushed under the doors. That formal complaint had seemed courageous at the time, but now she knew it was a cowardly postponement to the decision she had to make.

"I wish to dissolve my marriage contract." There was nothing she could add to soften the words. Anja motioned her to a seat, which she took. Her legs felt shaky.

"Is your decision final? Is it based upon calm reason?" Anja asked. "Jan's a stable and handsome man who cares for his son and has the resources of the Serasa-Kolme behind him."

"He does care for Peri. But he has no sincere feelings for me, nor I for him. We will have no more children." She'd made the biggest threat she could make to a matriarch. Anja's eyebrows tightened. Her dark blue eyes, so similar to Jan's, remained cool and her fingers began a slow drumming on the edge of the desk, sounding like hollow footsteps.

"Jan professes otherwise. Perhaps you need more time. The sting of betrayal and humiliation will fade eventually."

She flushed. "I admit Jan's last affair hurt my pride more than my heart. But there's more involved here than betrayal. Or love lost." To suppress the tremor in her voice, she carefully chose her words. "I don't agree with the... approach Jan uses, in his life and in his career. He walks the edge of ethical behavior and stretches the law to suit his actions. I don't want Peri to learn from him, or mimic him."

Anja became still. She stared at her fingers on the edge of the desk while she asked, "Can you provide examples of inappropriate *behavior*, beyond his infidelities?"

Draius took a deep breath. "For his actions in Betarr Kain, I have support that would be acceptable to a magistrate. I have a letter Jan used to harass—" She might as well be honest, since she was betting her life on Anja's response. "Actually, Jan *blackmailed* a fellow officer, a rival who had fallen into debt. For his behavior here in the sister cities, I have only suspicions. However, I'm certain that Jan's criminal contacts arranged the attack upon Officer Lornis and me."

"Are you intending to use this as leverage against the Serasa-Kolme? Perhaps bypass my arbitration?" Anja still hadn't moved.

"No, of course not." She didn't want Anja to think she was also resorting to blackmail. "I don't want Peri to *ever* learn about this. I'm trying to say that my regard for Jan isn't entirely the result of my hurt pride. My honor requires this, as does my self-respect. I suspect you have your own resources—look into Jan's activities yourself, if you choose."

If you dare, Lady Anja. The room was quiet for a moment as their gazes locked.

"Then I ask you to keep this to yourself until I've had time to do that," Anja said firmly.

"Certainly." When Anja didn't look convinced, she added, "On my Honor, Lady."

Anja leaned back and crossed her arms. "I'll be honest. It's unlikely that Vakuutis-Nelja Netta will have any children. Thus, contracting her to *any* Serasa-Kolme asset would be unwise, particularly to Jan, who has already successfully fathered a child. My best bet is to see you and Jan reconciled."

She felt a pang of pity for Netta, but shrugged it aside. "I will abide by your decision, Lady, but I promise you we'll *never* reconcile."

"Very well." Anja sighed and picked up a pen on her desk. "I'll look into your concerns. Do you wish Lady Meran-Viisi Aracia to be your advocate?"

"No, I don't need Meran-Viisi involvement. I'm not asking for lineal changes—both Peri and I should remain Serasa-Kolme."

"Really?" Anja asked. "Why should *you* stay Serasa-Kolme?"

"You said I could be useful, that I could be valuable—" She stumbled over the words.

"If you left the City Guard? Are you thinking of quitting, Draius?"

"Not quitting, never that." She raised her chin. "But if circumstances don't change, I may lose my position and perhaps even my commission. That's simply the price for failure."

Anja smiled and her face softened. Draius was surprised how young she looked, but then quickly reminded herself that Lady Anja was a matriarch. *Never* trust someone who's trained to run a lineage, someone who was raised to sacrifice anything and everything for her bloodline and "assets."

"Don't let your failure in marriage taint your professional work," Anja said. "And don't let Jan affect your confidence. From what I've seen, you're quite suited for the Guard. You just need to change your circumstances."

After those strange words, Lady Anja dismissed her.

•••

It was after noon on Fairday. Draius and Usko were the only ones in the outer office when Lornis arrived. His skin was pale and while he carried a cane, he didn't use it. His uniform, as always, was pristine and after he settled himself in a chair at the table, he gave Draius a dazzling smile.

"Well, at least your spirits are high," she said.

"I feel better than I look. Does that make any sense?"

Usko kept his gaze down and ignored their conversation. Perhaps the clerk felt guilty about Lornis's condition, suspecting the conspirators had been involved in the attack. *Well, a healthy amount of guilt isn't a bad thing, especially if it helps him cooperate.* Unfortunately, thinking about the attack caused her own pangs of guilt and she glanced down at the table, also avoiding eye contact with Lornis.

"Miina is on watch duty and Ponteva's making one last attempt to identify Taalo's apprentice." She gestured at the piles of papers. "Usko and I are looking for information on the *Danilo Ana*, the ship that carried the lodestone out of port."

Usko cleared his throat and adjusted the spectacles on his nose so they were precisely straight. "We discovered that Tellina was filing a claim for the *Danilo Ana* with Vakuutis-Nelja underwriters. This was risky for Taalo and the other conspirators, so that may be why they murdered Tellina."

Shipowners often insured their cargoes with underwriters. It was an advanced form of gambling: underwriters bet the losses would be minimal and their income would cover them, while ship-owners gambled that compensation for losses would make up for payments. What was ludicrous was that the most common cause of loss to shippers in these days was piracy, and piracy wasn't covered any more. Only when cargo was lost to "natural tragedy during safe passage" could a claim be made, and then multiple forms of proof of value were needed to make the underwriters pay off.

"They didn't want Tellina to submit the claim because it would bring unwarranted attention to the ship?" Lornis asked.

"Tellina was risking exposure of the conspiracy so he could recover the cost of the vessel." Draius hoped she'd never have to explain any of these details to Maricie.

"What he was doing was doubly deceitful," Usko said. "Underwriters require a legal assessment of the cargo and written guarantees that nothing dangerous is being transported. Tellina couldn't truthfully provide an assessment or such a guarantee."

"He doesn't sound like a follower of the Way of the Light," Lornis said.

She looked sharply at him. There was more naiveté in his voice, and his words, than she liked. "People often have misplaced loyalties." She winced and looked away from his wide brown eyes. This hit closer to home than she liked, and her voice became harsher. "I've heard that Groygan thieves favor the goddess Erina, yet the Mistress of Time doesn't condone thievery."

Her voice became strident, and she felt as guilty as Usko looked. The clerk shuffled papers into piles, keeping his head bowed. Lornis cocked his head and looked at her quizzically—she was suddenly reminded of Dahni. For a moment she panicked. How much empathy could Lornis have from the phrenic healing? Could he read her mind? What followed was bitter accusation. *I wouldn't be in this position, if not for Jan.* There was only one reason to keep her knowledge about the attack within the Serasa-Kolme, as Anja requested, and that was for Peri's well being.

"Officer Draius and I are searching for a possible Groygan connection," Usko said in a quiet voice, bringing Draius back to the business at hand.

"The fact that the conspirators are convinced the ship went down strengthens my suspicions that the ship sailed for Chikirmo, and that Groygans may be involved," she said.

"How did you make that connection?" Lornis looked bewildered.

"Rhobar controlled the pirating around the southern Angim, and the King's Guard is convinced he did his deeds with Groygan knowledge. Not necessarily as a privateer, but they feel Rhobar couldn't have operated as freely as he did without Groygan blessings."

"Ah. You think the conspirators had a Groygan benefactor, someone with enough authority to give the ship safe passage. That's why they think the ship is still out there," Lornis said.

"That's my guess." She was pleased, almost irrationally so, that the healing hadn't dulled him. "Meanwhile, I need you to figure out where Vanhus fits in this whole thing. The Purje-Kolme matriarch is already pestering the captain for the return of these records." She dumped a pile of papers in front of Lornis.

"Yes, ser," Lornis said cheerfully, making her eyes narrow. How was it possible for him to be in such good humor, when faced with that pile?

Lornis set out paper, pen, and ink for notes, and started. There was quiet in the office, save for the scratching of his pen and murmured comments as Usko identified something he thought Draius should read.

After several hours, the lieutenant gave a little whoop and looked at them with a bright smile. "I found the connection. Taalo said they lost 'seven of the excavating team,' is that correct?" Lornis asked Usko.

"Yes, I believe that's what Taalo said," the clerk answered cautiously.

"Vanhus wasn't only involved in imports and exports. He also ran exploration teams. Over a period of five erins, he paid out *seven* death compensations to various lineages, and each compensation is noted as an 'excavation accident.'"

Draius harrumphed. She'd looked through that same pile a day ago, and hadn't caught the significance of the death compensations. Lornis found the connection within hours. Her ability to hold onto the details was slipping, with everything else. "So Vanhus worked for the conspirators, possibly to find the lodestone. But why kill him?"

The door opened, and all three looked up as Ponteva entered. "I still have no name or lineage for the apprentice, and I've gone to every matriarch within the sister cities to check for missing persons. Norsis had to send the body to the anonymous pyre operated by the hospital."

She'd been hoping for more; now she only had her theory that the boy was killed because he knew too much. She didn't think Taalo was the bash-in-the-head type. She easily pictured him with knives, using scientific precision, but she couldn't see him wielding a club. Taalo probably had someone else take care of his apprentice.

"How sad for the boy." Lornis shook his head. "To have no one by your pyre, no one to call your ancestors to lead your way to the Stars."

She'd never considered herself spiritual. However, she was affected by Lornis's words and not wholly because of the death of a nunnetton. She hadn't attended her father's pyre; by the time she'd received the letter from Meran-Viisi Nuora, he was dead. It was 1465 and although her father had been ill, he hadn't been expected to die—he was only 79 years old. Now she wondered who had been at the pyre to sing for her father. He had transferred to the Meran-Viisi from the Meran-Kolme, so Draius had placed his ashes into the Meran-Viisi reliquary with hardly a thought. Worse, she didn't remember mumbling a request to her ancestors for his safe passage.

She came out of her reverie to notice Lornis watching her. *By the Horn, what is he doing to me?* She had half a mind to ask him to leave the room. Instead, she looked out the window to see the clouds flaming from the sunset. She dismissed everyone and Usko, still under arrest, left with Ponteva.

Lornis stood up a bit stiffly, using the cane. "Well, I need more rest and large quantities of food." His tone was light, but he looked tired.

"Are you feeling well?" Draius asked.

He paused. "Are you asking as my commander, or as my friend?"

"Does it matter?"

He looked at her carefully, and she dropped her gaze. "It probably matters more to me than it does to you," he said softly.

"Look, Lieutenant—"

"I know I make you uncomfortable, but it's not me. It's you. You're hiding something and it's going to crush you. I'm warning you, because I—I care about you."

She was speechless while Lornis made a dignified exit. After he left, she mechanically filed away the evidence important to the case in a marked box.

Twilight softened the streets as Draius left the office. She hailed a carriage, but paused before giving the driver her home address. Changing her mind, she said, "The Meran-Viisi reliquary, and hurry."

Since her intentions were obvious, the driver did his utmost to get her up the plateau and to the reliquary in Betarr Serin before the stars came out. She tipped him well before hurrying through the arches into the place where 700 years of Meran-Viisi ancestral ashes were kept.

All reliquaries were open to the night skies, and inside there were about thirty people getting ready for star-rise. Not everyone went to the pubs on Fairday evening; some went in pursuit of spiritual peace. She seated herself cross-legged upon the mats laid out on the stone floor, and looked up as the stars became visible. While the Meran-Viisi constellation slowly rose in the spring night, she sang with the others as her ancestors came into sight.

"Reach to the Stars, o soul who now wanders. Strive for the Stars, for home, family, and peace."

As the familiar chant continued, Draius watched the clear night sky. Under her breath, she recited her ancestor's names as she looked to each point of light. *Although this is belated, Father, I wish you safe passage on your journey. May you find peace and your own place in the firmament.*

Suddenly a star flared across the night sky, so bright that Draius saw the trail after she closed her eyes. There were murmurs within the reliquary; something important was happening. The Star Watchers, in consultation with the Phrenii, would have to interpret this portent.

CHAPTER TWENTY-NINE

Second Fairday, Erin Three, T.Y. 1471

Last evening, I thought we lost our wielder, but he pulled through. This time, however, we barely had any time to look for the lodestone before he collapsed. I attempted to speak with my employer about his unsuitable assistant.

"If he goes mad?" I asked. "What will we do?"

"I have contingencies," was the answer. "Leave it be, since you have a different task. We must deal with the clerk. He's under watch every hour of the day and we'll have to do it remotely, with charms. Can you do it?"

My heart was beating fast. Yes, I could do it, but... "I'll need specialized charms, powerful ones. I'd have to make more."

"I figured that." My employer motioned for me to follow. He grabbed a lamp to light a musty hallway. As he led, our footsteps creaked on cracked floorboards. At the end of the hallway was a door. My employer unlocked and threw it open, holding the lamp high.

"Can you do anything with *that?*" His deep voice reverberated in the close hallway and room, and caused a pile of rags in the corner to flinch and twitch.

I took the lamp from my employer and stepped slowly into the room, which held nothing to help the boy who huddled in the corner. He looked to be as young as ten, or perhaps as old as twelve years. His face was a patchwork of green and yellow bruises.

"What's your name, son?" I asked in a friendly tone. I've always been good with children, so I got the desired effect. The boy looked at me with hope.

"Sk—Skuva, ser," he stammered. "Can I go now?"

There was no doubt he was nunetton. No one, even a child, in this situation would have withheld his lineal name.

"In a while, Skuva. We'll release you, never worry." I kept my tone reassuring.

After I closed the door and we walked back down the hall, my employer said, "He's only a nunetton pickpocket, but he's young. Are you too squeamish to use him?"

I knew my employer's disdain for the forgotten nameless, but I also knew his own lineage was dying. He might as well be nunetton himself. "Why do you ask?"

"You told the boy he'd be released."

"Oh. The release I speak about is the release of his soul to its journey. Subjects should always have hope, so they hold onto their life tightly, making their pain more powerful."

My employer grunted. "I never cease to be amazed by your ruthlessness."

I had been thinking the boy's youth would add new points to my collection of data, making my numbers more reliable. I got a bit huffy. "I merely maintain scientific objectivity."

"Whatever you say. But use the nunetton *slowly*. It's getting more difficult to snatch subjects for you. Something in the wind has made them scurry into their holes."

I raised my eyebrows as we parted. It wasn't the "wind" the nunetton feared, or even the rumors of disappearances. An oppressive pall hung over the sister cities, as if every inhabitant drew in their breath for strength, holding it, in fear of what was coming. This went for the elementals as well; they hadn't been seen roaming the streets in their phrenic form, followed by children, for several days. I wondered whether they hid inside the Void and searched for the Lodestone. No doubt, they also searched for us.

From behind, I saw my employer's huge shoulders were hunched. I believe he also hears the footsteps of doom following him, and he's become desperate. When our group meets, there's always an undertone of hopelessness and failure. Others must feel this also—and I've planned accordingly. My notes and minimal effects have been packed for days.

I'm ready to leave. I just need to know where to go.

CHAPTER THIRTY

Murder By Magic

I send this to your Lordships by fastest ship possible, because timing is crucial. Last night, a star sped across the Tyrran sky and might have been seen from Groyga. While we know this to be a whim of the gods and not subject to interpretation, the Tyrrans are atwitter because their Star Watchers have predicted an important decision for Tyrra. This can be used to my Lords' advantage: the populace will be easily distracted by any proposal we make, regardless of how distasteful the proposal may be for Perinon and his Council. As always, I remain your servant, dedicated to Groygan expansion.

—*Letter from Ambassador Velenare Be Glotta to the Groygan Council of Lords, in the Tyrran Year 1471*

Ringday dawned with a clear sky and Draius lay dozing, trying to resist the morning light. She heard Peri downstairs chattering to the staff, Maricie admonishing him for being in his nightshirt, followed by the sound of bare feet running up to his room. Pushing her head deeper into the down, she tried to keep the rest of the world outside of her warm safe cocoon. The house and Anja and her servants were starting to feel like *home*.

She took her time getting out of bed, washing, and dressing. She reached for her civilian clothes, glad to forgo the usual uniform. The weight of the ever-present locket plus shard was becoming so familiar she barely noticed it.

Peri was so excited about the carnival he couldn't sit and eat his breakfast. Anja finally gave up and let him leave the table. She and Draius continued to eat in silence, the previous night's discussion regarding Jan lying heavily on them.

Draius was busy worrying about her future. Anja had decisions to make, because Jan's actions caused ramifications beyond their contract and there was the entire Serasa-Kolme lineage to consider. Anja had the power to take Jan's lineal name from him and ostracize him—the most extreme punishment possible. On the other extreme, Anja might do nothing. Draius couldn't make a guess as to what awaited her and Jan; the matriarch's inscrutable Serasa-Kolme face didn't give her any clues.

Draius and Peri walked to the market square since the weather was mild. The streets weren't muddy, only moist from a light spring rain. In an erin or two, summer would be entrenched and walking through the streets would be a choking experience as carriages raised the dust.

Peri skipped here and there, humming. As always, he was full of questions. "Do you think the Phrenii will be at the carnival?"

"I don't know." The creatures hadn't been seen much lately; everyone remarked upon that. However, there would be children at the carnival, many without adult supervision, because they should always be safe within the sister cities. The children might attract the Phrenii—and vice versa.

"Will they come to see the sleight-of-hand tricks?" Peri stumbled over the unfamiliar words.

"No, the Phrenii probably aren't interested in that."

Peri bounced on to other topics. "Why do carriages have springs under them?"

"So they can carry passengers safely over the holes in the streets."

"Can we travel up the Whitewater with Da this summer?"

She paused. Luckily, she didn't have to answer Peri because the crowd at the Canal Street intersection diverted both of them. People lining both sides of the street blocked their intended path. "What's going on?"

Peri was craning his neck and jumping this way and that to get a better view. Surprisingly, he answered her. "I think they're transporting Rhobar up to Betarr Serin. Our tutor talked to us about this."

Hmm. She raised an eyebrow, embarrassed that her young son knew more about what was happening in the cities than she did, and she was City Guard.

"They're coming!" Peri raised his arm and pointed southward. The reason he could see the procession was that the King's Guard had chosen to transport Rhobar in an open cage on a wagon platform, making him visible above the heads of the crowd. Tyrra was making a point, ensuring that the entire Mapped World knew that the rumors were true: Tyrra has captured the pirate Rhobar and crushed his band of thugs.

On either side of the platform rode a line of King's Guard to keep the crowd back and the prisoner secure. Draius saw Bordas riding beside the wagon team, but this wasn't the time to wave or call out greetings. There were four mounted Guards to each side of the wagon. The use of King's Guard also made a statement: Rhobar wasn't just a criminal—he was a threat to King and country. Where he was being taken, no one knew, but there weren't any magistrates in his future.

"Ilke said he's dashing and handsome." Peri looked up at the passing figure, whose wrists were manicled to the cage.

Draius had to agree with Ilke. Even more surprising was the presence the pirate exuded. He kept a calm, noble demeanor, despite the shouted insults and occasional rotten vegetable hurled his way. He didn't ignore the crowd, but rather tried to make eye contact, smiling every once in a while. She wondered if he was acting or if he had really so easily accepted his situation.

"Do you think he's handsome, Ma? Some of the girls say he's too pretty to be evil."

Peri's question pulled her out of her reverie. "Ah. Well. Darkness and evil hides in all sorts of people—so attractiveness has nothing to do with honor or character. Some even think that darkness hides more readily behind an attractive face, but I think it's best to judge a person by their actions and decisions, not their looks."

"But Ilke says they're going to torture him for information. Is that the right thing to do?" Peri asked, as the crowd dispersed and they continued toward the market square.

The "right thing" was relative; was it the *moral, ethical, honorable, correct,* or just the *expedient* action to take? Did the security of the Tyrran people, the Phrenii, and the King override all other considerations? After seeing Rhobar herself, this was an awkward issue that she didn't want to explore—not with her young son on a Ringday when she was off duty. Again she was saved. They turned the corner and the carnival came into view. Peri couldn't contain himself and started leaping along with glee. She stretched her legs to keep up with him.

"What's your hurry, boy?" boomed a voice to the side of the market square. Berin strode over to them. He grabbed Peri, swung him around, and then hoisted him up on his shoulders.

Peri squealed. "I can see everything from here," he said when he got his breath back.

And Peri *was* determined to see everything. No booth could be passed without inspection, no game untried. She was glad she brought a handful of tenths, which she broke into pithes for playing the games. She was weary of all the variations of ring and basket tosses by mid-morning, but thankfully the performances started. There were three small stages set about the square and the acts would rotate to each stage. They saw many amazing feats: a juggler, three astounding acrobats, and a sword swallower. Although Draius assured Peri that no real magic was involved, she herself wondered how they did some of their tricks.

There was an intermission at mid-day so the food merchants could sell their wares to the hungry crowd. They had mutton-on-a-stick and fried bread covered in sugar. She hoped Peri wouldn't get sick later, but that was the chance she had to take.

Ponteva found them as she made Peri wipe his hands on one of the large handkerchiefs she had the foresight to bring. "Ser, I have unfortunate news," Ponteva said in an undertone. "Usko's dead."

"Did Taalo show?" Her attention was diverted from her son's greasy hands and back to murderers and smugglers. She'd hoped the conspirators would try to clean up their leak, and she wasn't a bit surprised that Usko didn't survive the confrontation. *Hmm—only a couple of eight-days as OIC and look how cavalier I've become with other people's lives.*

"Uh, no," said Ponteva. His eyes flitted to Peri meaningfully; he was uncomfortable making the report in front of the boy.

Peri, however, realized that his carnival day might be quickly brought to an end. "I don't have to leave, do I?" He was winding up for a negotiation about whether he could be left at the carnival on his own, and with how much money.

There were no Phrenii to be seen at the carnival, so there would be no safety net for an inquisitive child. Draius stopped Peri short with an abrupt motion of her hand. He knew his mother well, and his face crumpled.

"I know we usually consider the streets safe, Peri." Thoughts of strangers with powder weapons flitted through her mind. "But times are changing and you're growing up. Besides, the Phrenii aren't here—"

"Why can't I stay with the boy?" Berin asked. "I can have him home before the sun sets."

"Please, Ma?" Peri brightened as he saw his Ringday salvaged.

This day wasn't going the way she'd planned, either, but Peri would still be able to see the magicians perform. So, after foisting all her handkerchiefs on Berin and admonishing both of them to be gentlemen, Draius left with Ponteva.

•••

There was nothing the watchmen could do to prevent Usko's death and they protested this several times as they told Draius the story.

Ponteva and Miina had kept Usko under observation throughout the previous evening. Usko carefully stayed within his ordinary routine and they followed him home to his flat near the edge of the market district. Miina was stationed near the front stoop of the opposite building, and another watchman was positioned in the back alley, where windows to Usko's third floor flat of rooms could be seen. Nothing happened until late evening, when a packet arrived. Usko had tipped the courier, and gone back into the flat. The lights in the flat went out at an appropriate bedtime.

Ringday morning, the clerk didn't come out to pick up his milk. By mid-morning, when Ponteva and another watchman came to release them, Miina voiced her concern regarding the souring liquid. They went up to the third floor flat and knocked. There was no answer. The four watchmen broke in, then found Norsis and Draius as soon as they could.

Usko's body was sprawled face down, and looked as if he was trying to crawl toward the door of his flat. Gold tyr coins, more than Draius had ever seen, lay about the clerk and his mouth was *stuffed* with them. His open eyes were cloudy with dust and his face showed terror and disbelief.

"You heard nothing and no one entered the flat?" Draius asked for the third time.

Miina shook her head, white-faced. She was probably feeling shock and guilt, as well as working on very little sleep.

"Miina, have the watch notify the Pettaja-Kolme," Draius said. "But they must make it clear that there'll be no access to the body, or these rooms, until we're finished."

Miina looked relieved as she left. Draius also released the other watchman who had stayed through the night.

"Where's the packet that was delivered to Usko?" she asked.

She examined the leather parcel carefully without touching it. It lay on the other side of the body, opened, and with untied twine about it. There might have been coins still inside it, but no one wanted to touch the parcel to check. The courier had been questioned, but couldn't provide any information. He was a professional messenger: the packet and fee for his services had been left at his advertised drop. The man supposed, from the packet's weight, that it contained gold—so he was also honest.

"Amazing that someone would be foolish enough to leave that much gold at a courier drop," Ponteva said.

"He was being paid off," the other watchman said.

"I doubt he choked himself voluntarily with these coins," she said. "What have you found, Norsis?"

The thin coroner was listening to their conversation. "You're right, Officer Draius. A man would choke and vomit if he attempted this himself. Also, the tyr are packed so hard into his gullet that I'll only be able to remove them by cutting open his body."

"Is it possible someone used a tool to push the coins into him?" She stared at Norsis, who shrugged with one of his thin shoulders.

"There's no evidence of any tool use, or that anyone else was in this room," he answered.

She looked around the room again, memorizing the neatness. "How odd," she muttered to herself.

"Officer Draius, you better come see this." Ponteva stood at the street-side window, his eyes wide.

She went to the window and looked down. Three of the Phrenii stood on the opposite sidewalk, and they were all looking up at the window where they stood. She noted the faceted eye colors: green, blue, and brown. Water, air, and earth. Dahni, Jhari, and Sahvi. Healing, prescience, and influence. Fire was the missing mundane element, representing the aspect of protection, because Famri was stationed in eastern Tyrra to be close to the Saamarin and the Groygan border.

Every one of the Phrenii near the sister cities was here except the keystone—then Mahri, with the golden eyes, trotted down the street and stood in front of the other three. Spirit had arrived and the phrenic circle was functional. It was an unprecedented confluence of the elementals and children were quickly gathering. She drew in her breath sharply.

"Why are they here?" Ponteva rubbed his sparse beard nervously.

She was spooked also, having never seen more than two of the Phrenii in one place before. "I think they want to speak with me."

Ponteva shot her a glance. *Better you than me*, his face said.

The children had become a mob by the time Draius strode onto the street. The combined power of the four Phrenii caused everyone's hair to lift and move, affected by some unseen and unfelt breeze. The air tingled against her face and there was ringing in her ears. The effect on the children was extraordinary: they were chattering, squealing, laughing, running around the creatures, stroking them with their hands, and laying their cheeks against the luminous coats. There were more children here than Draius had seen at the carnival. She waded through them to stand in front of Mahri, a careful pace beyond the reach of the creature's horn.

"Officer Draius," Mahri said, lowering its head. "We are reporting the use of the phrenic circle last night."

She didn't have to ask for what purpose. *But why did they wait until now to tell me?*

"It took all our aspects to track down the focus. We thought it necessary to provide you with a location, but we found you here already."

She hoped Mahri was merely following a logical thread in the conversation, rather than reading her mind. "My clerk Usko was murdered last night. We had watchmen observing the rooms, but they never saw anyone enter or leave."

"You will not find any indication of a physical presence," Mahri said. "This time they have truly done murder by magic."

"*Who* did this and how did they do it?"

"The Meran who wielded the Kaskea went mad. These people are experimenting with new-found power from their necromancy, and are learning quickly." Although Mahri didn't appear to be raising the volume of its voice, she could hear the creature clearly above the children.

"What about the King? Is he safe?" she asked. Was Perinon still sane?

"We insulated the King from the madness while the perpetrators focused their will from the Blindness to trigger a necromantic charm. They must have already positioned it."

She didn't fully follow the creature's words, but she'd have the leisure to go over them again and again, since they were entrenched in her memory.

"They risked traveling the Blindness for this, so we are sure you will find such a charm." Mahri gestured with its horn toward Usko's rooms.

"And the people who did this? Do you know any names?"

"We know the Meran who wielded the Kaskea, and he despised himself for not being stronger. Before madness took him over, we know he called himself the 'Mouse.'"

She bit back a frustrated retort. After all, these creatures were not human and they were probably incapable of understanding human idioms. "He was *calling* himself a mouse because he despised his weaknesses or timidity. This won't help me find him."

Mahri cocked its head to observe her better with its glowing gold eyes. She felt a thrill of fear: she didn't intend to offend the creature.

"'The 'Mouse' is *whendal* in the ancient tongue," Mahri said in a clear and lilting voice. "In this, we are certain."

Wendell. A name was unique within a generation. In the back of her head, memories started crashing together, making a landslide. "I stand corrected, Phrenii. You've been quite helpful." She bowed and gave the ritual farewell words she learned to give to the Phrenii as a child, "You have served us well."

"We remain to serve." Mahri responded with the phrase used by the Phrenii for the last thousand years.

Draius turned and grabbed her hair as it floated in front of her face, tucking it firmly under her cloak. She started back to the apartments, not bothering to watch how the Phrenii dispersed the mob of children.

"Officer Draius." Mahri's voice stopped her. She was turning back as the creature continued, "We also know this: a child's life hangs in balance."

She'd left Peri with Berin, and Wendell was Berin's employee and friend. She stumbled. Her chest tightened. Running, she took the stairs to the flat three at a time. She had to get the arrest order out, then get to Peri.

The watchmen were wide-eyed when she returned. Few adults, other than the King, ever faced multiple Phrenii and spoke with them.

"What did they say?" Ponteva asked.

For a moment, she hesitated as her mind raced. Should she go outside the King's Law? Who could she trust, who could she ask to follow? If only Wendell was involved, then she was panicking for no reason. She'd known Berin for years; he wouldn't endanger Peri, would he? *A child's life hangs in balance.* She'd let her people deal with Wendell, while she dealt with Berin. "Ponteva, get the watch and arrest Purje-Kolme Wendell."

He immediately left. She wondered what shape Wendell would be in, considering the Phrenii thought he was insane.

"Norsis, I have other business to attend to," she said. "I trust your usual thoroughness when recording observations and examining the body. The Phrenii say you'll find some sort of necromantic charm—"

"Are you well, Draius?" Norsis cocked his head.

She was dressed in civilian clothes and without any weapons. Glancing about, she noted the dead clerk's desk, his instruments of trade arranged carefully.

"I must entrust you with a letter." Duty, always on her mind, was now a hindrance. She reached for pen and paper and wrote a short message. After signing, she blotted the paper carefully and folded it several times. Then she addressed it, and sealed it securely with Usko's wax and seal. This seemed to take forever, because she couldn't keep her hands from shaking.

"Be sure to deliver this tomorrow—*unopened.*" She handed it to Norsis, ignoring the questions on his face. There should be nothing unusual about delivering a note on Markday, when offices and businesses opened. Unfortunately, she wasn't sure she'd be seeing the usual bustle of the beginning of the eight-day.

Then she ran from the building and hailed a coach. By the time she was home, dusk was settling on the streets.

"Stay here. I'll need you again," she said to the coachman. He tipped his hat, looking bored.

As she let herself into the house, Anja stepped down the stairs. "Really, Draius, I don't approve of you keeping Peri out so late. It's past time for his evening bath."

Her worst fears were confirmed. *I've been such a fool. This is all my fault.*

CHAPTER THIRTY-ONE

Coercion

Information obtained from Illus allowed naval vessels to surprise Rhobar's main post, but he had more stationary guns than expected. Defensive bombardment sunk four of our large galleys, although most crew survived. Fortunately, the majority of Rhobar's galleys with heavy guns were caught in port and trapped. Loss of Tyrran life was minimal, and confiscation of Rhobar's assets has more than made up for our destroyed ships. As for the ship my liege searches for, the *Danilo Ana*, we found no evidence of it in Rhobar's ports.

— *Initial Report from Admiral Purje-Nelja Ahjo, Erin Three, T.Y. 1471*

In a city where children are safe to roam the streets alone, in a country where every child is precious and considered to be the future of Tyrran culture, the use of a child for coercion is unthinkable. Anja's first assumption was obvious: Peri was playing somewhere, and wasn't aware of the time.

"I'll send Maricie around to his cousins," Anja said, as Draius pushed past her on the stairs.

"No need," Draius called over her shoulder. Cold fury built, fueling her body and steadying it. Her hands no longer shook, and she changed her clothes in record time.

Before she put on her shirt and vest, she fingered the locket hanging about her neck. Perhaps she should leave the Kaskea here in Anja's house. She opened it, stared at the shard thoughtfully, and nearly dropped it when it suddenly flared with a green light. But, just as quickly, it was gray again. It still looked like a piece of slate, no matter how she turned it in the lamplight. Did she just imagine the flash?

She snapped the locket shut and left it around her neck. The weight against her breastbone was almost comforting. Besides, the charge to protect the Kaskea shard wasn't part of this investigation, the investigation that had put her son's life in jeopardy. Even though her resignation from the City Guard now rested in the coroner's coat pocket, she'd made a pledge to her King, her *cousin*, and the shard should stay with her.

When she came back downstairs, she wore her field clothes, which had no insignia so they didn't really qualify as a uniform. Her saber hung at her hip and her short knives were stowed, two tucked inside her boots and one under her left arm.

"Where are you going?" Anja looked her up and down. Maricie stood behind Anja, her hands nervously rolling the hem of her apron.

"Maricie, make sure the coach stays," Draius said with cool precision, remembering her transportation. The maid bobbed her head and left immediately. Anja moved to block the door, arms crossed, waiting for the answer to her question.

"Peri may have been abducted."

"Why? Who would do such a thing?" Anja's facade cracked; for the first time in Draius's memory, a Serasa-Kolme face looked frightened. Kidnapping a child was beyond Anja's capacity to comprehend.

How much should she tell Anja? Berin only needed her, so involving Anja would complicate the process of getting Peri back safely, possibly endangering the matriarch as well. Keeping her tone calm, Draius said, "This is my fault. I didn't see the signs, and I trusted someone I shouldn't have. This has to do with the murderers I've been tracking."

There it was: Peri was in danger because of *her*, because of her job, and because she hadn't allowed herself to see the truth about Berin. Anja's dark blue eyes accused her, but there was nothing to do now but accept responsibility, and do whatever it took to get Peri safely back. There would be no talk of money, because demanding ransom in exchange for a child was heinous and she knew Berin didn't need it anyway. For a moment, she felt overwhelmed by the betrayal, from someone she'd known for years—

"Then we must call the watch." Anja turned.

"No!" she cried, stopping Anja mid-step. "Let me find out what they want, otherwise Peri may be harmed."

"But the watch—"

"*My* first priority is Peri's safety, but that's not the watch's priority. Their duty would be to apprehend criminals." *I can't depend upon others when it comes to the safety of my son.* She'd never felt so alone.

Maricie was holding the door open and she could see the waiting coach. She needed to get out of here. "I want your word that you won't call the watch until I get back with Peri. *Please*, Lady Anja." Her voice cracked and she clenched her jaw. If she could hold onto her anger, then she could keep away the dark dread that threatened to swallow her.

Anja just tightened her lips into a thin line.

Draius had no more time to argue and went out the door. As she hopped into the coach she told the driver to go to the City Guard stables, as fast as he was able. The stable hand on duty didn't question her need for her horse well past the supper hour. She saddled Chisel herself, ignoring the pain in her shoulder, and was quickly on the streets.

Chisel was a weapon, trained for cavalry use. The warehouse district off the wharves was rough, but no one got in her way as the 18-hand-tall horse carried her through streets and dark allies, hooves clattering on cobblestones or thumping on clay. Shadows skittered out of the horse's way and melted around corners.

She slowed to a trot when she came to the street where Berin kept his main office. She turned the corner and looked down the alley. At the end of the passage, a shack jutted out from a larger building. Figures clustered around the wooden steps of the shack, dressed in dark clothes, but there was too little light to discern numbers.

Taking a deep breath, she drew her saber quietly and urged Chisel forward so that he leaped into canter, then a gallop. On the packed clay ground, the sound of his hooves thudded and echoed off the walls. The figures at the end of the alley looked up and scattered in alarm. She counted eight individuals fleeing to the shelter of either side of the steps while she bore down on the center figure: a broad, tall fellow who didn't flee like the others.

She brought the horse skidding to a stop short of Berin, while his cohorts scampered out of her range. Chisel stamped and snorted, causing Berin to move around to the near side of the horse and away from her sword arm. He reached up and tried to grab Chisel's bridle, but she kneed him over so Berin missed. He slowly lowered his arm.

"I thought you'd be here earlier." His distinctive voice carried throughout the alley.

"It took time to clean up the mess you left last night." She kept her saber ready. "Where's my son?"

"Lower your sword, Draius. You can kill me right here and now, but that won't get you your boy."

"I want Peri." She kept Chisel sidling from side to side, in case Berin tried to pull her from the saddle. She lowered her saber hilt to her thigh to keep from fatiguing her arm.

"You think I'd keep him in my office? No, getting off your horse and agreeing to help me is the only way you'll see him." Berin waited, impassive, while she decided what to do.

Dark figures crept closer, out of the alley shadows, and formed a wide circle around her, her horse, and Berin. There was silence as the circle started closing. If they thought they were threatening her, they were wrong—she felt the quick rise in Chisel's hindquarters and heard the soft thump of his hoof hitting a body. A cry of pain, and the circle hastily expanded. Meanwhile, she kept her attention on Berin.

He ignored the others as well. Taalo—there was no mistaking that mop of fuzzy gray hair—stepped out of the office to stand behind Berin. Her throat tightened.

"I give you my word, on my Honor, that I will resign my position and leave the City Guard," she said. "No one will find out about your actions from me—if you give me Peri, unharmed."

Taalo snickered. "As if we would believe you."

Berin raised his hand, making the small man flinch. "I'd take that pledge on your Honor, if that was what I needed. But I need something else from you."

Her heart sank. She'd convinced herself that she didn't know him any more, but she was wrong. She could still see the same Berin, which was painful, but now she saw the man who would take whatever actions necessary to exact revenge upon the society and creatures who allowed his family to die. He'd never been more "wind than weather," as he often claimed. There were deep and turbulent storms under his easy-going facade, as well as unbending purpose fed by desperation. Worse, she heard the dead undertow within the currents of his voice; the sound of a man trapped by his own struggles, a man who'd already made the decision to sacrifice himself—and possibly her and her son.

Taalo smiled as he watched her.

"So you're running out of Meran blood?" She was rewarded by surprise on his face.

"Draius, this is the *only* way you will see your son again." Berin said and she recognized the finality in his tone. She'd seen this stubbornness before, and knew he was as immovable as stone.

A child's life hangs in balance.

There was no point in delaying longer, so she sheathed her saber and dismounted, leaving a rein to trail on the ground.

"You understand that we must ask you to disarm," Berin said.

She took off her sword and secured it to her saddle. "There," she said.

Berin's laugh made her wince. "Do you think I'm stupid? That I haven't seen what you wear to the field? You have three more knives on you—two in your boots and one in a sheath under your arm. Take them off."

She took off the other three knives and put them in a saddlebag. When she turned back, a figure was whispering to Berin.

He shrugged in response. "My colleague is worried about your horse. We must find a place to confine it."

All her weapons were now on Chisel, and the horse was a means of escape for herself and her son. However, she'd naively thought Peri would be at Berin's office.

"Don't bother." Draius threw the rein that ground-tied Chisel back over his neck. She stepped back and gave the horse a command, using a sharp whistle.

Chisel snorted and whirled, causing figures to scatter again. He picked up speed, unchecked, and pounded down the alley and turned back onto the street. Draius knew that no one could stop the horse until he was back at the Guard stables. At some point, someone would question his riderless presence.

"That won't help you." Taalo giggled, a high, quick, almost snorting sound. "No one will find you where you'll be going."

"I want to see my son. *Now.*" She glared at Berin, ignoring the little man.

Berin and Taalo led her into the office, while the other figures moved away down the side alley. They kept their faces hidden from Draius, which was a good sign. If they hid their identities, then they might release Peri. Berin closed the door and the three of them were alone in the office, which was minimally lit by a candle. Even in the dim light, she could see the office was stark, containing only a battered chair and a bare desk. If Berin managed his ledgers here, he kept everything inside the desk drawers.

"My son?" Pointedly.

"He's at another location, where we'll be going in a moment or two," Berin said as he lit a small lantern and adjusted the wick. His voice was loud in the tiny room, causing vibrations in the old wooden structure. "We'll have to blindfold you."

She snorted. "What good will that do?"

"You may suffer the inquisition of the Phrenii. The less you know, the better." Taalo's eyes were bright and he seemed excited, his small body practically quivering.

Did they expect her to use their stolen shard of the Kaskea? She fought the impulse to touch the locket; its weight suddenly pressed on her breastbone. A shiver ran down her back as she remembered the prohibitions about attempting use of the Kaskea without supervision of the Phrenii. Hoping to divert them, she mustered up the most acidic tone she could. "Wendell is in custody by now. Is he so insane that he can't be questioned? How many people will you hurt? How many will die in your quest for revenge, Berin?"

Regret covered his bearded face, slowly dissolving into stubborn resignation. "Contrary to what you may think, I *am* trying to do this with minimal loss of life."

"So the deaths of Reggis, Tellina, Vanhus and numerous nunetton are 'minimal loss of life'?"

"Disagreements, rather, which gave us a fortunate amount of power," Taalo said.

"And killing Usko was punishment? Or was his murder an experiment?"

"Quiet!" Berin's sharp command caused the apothecary to withdraw as far as possible to the other side of the small office. "This is not an opportunity for you to ask questions, Draius. You must be our channel to the Void tonight."

"Why don't you just slice me open, scatter my blood about and draw symbols with it? You can do anything to me, as long as you release my son." She was losing control, exactly what shouldn't happen. She took a deep breath to push down the fear and nausea rising in her stomach.

"You're more valuable alive and pumping out blood," Taalo said from his side of the office. Berin shot Taalo a look, and the apothecary pressed his lips together. The little man liked to talk too much.

"I won't help you murder more people." She looked at Berin with challenge.

"Tonight we search for a powerful artifact, not a person."

"The lodestone?"

"That doesn't concern you. If you help us tonight, Peri will be free to go home tomorrow morning."

"Release my son *now*, and I'll give you all the cooperation you need." She watched Berin's face carefully.

"No. Throughout this process, I want you to remember that we have Peri. The boy cannot go home until—until you're finished."

Until they run out of my blood? Until I'm insane and no longer a threat? She knew when Berin was hiding something.

"If I come through this evening sane?" she asked. "What then?"

Berin nodded, seeming relieved. "I'll be candid. We need to pull a lot of power through you, more than we've ever attempted before. It's likely that if you live, you'll be... affected. But consider it a fair trade for your son's life. He will be taken home tomorrow if you cooperate."

Could he really hurt my child?

When she continued to hesitate, he added, "Make no mistake, it *is* his life you're bargaining for, Draius. Although I'd find it distasteful to kill the boy, there are others who won't have such qualms. I have people at my command who would kill Peri without compunction."

"Believe him," Taalo piped up, unable to stay quiet. "He had my young apprentice killed, over my objections."

She saw the sharp glance Taalo sent toward Berin's back, full of hatred, disdain, and fear. For a few moments, there was silence in the office.

"I'll cooperate." Her voice was heavy. "But only if I can see Peri."

Berin shook his head, but she was adamant. "If you want my assistance, you must let me see that my child is unharmed."

"Very well, you'll see that he's healthy and safe. If you work with us tonight, he'll go home tomorrow. You have my word."

She wondered if his word was still reliable, but she had a gut instinct that it was. It was strange how criminals could be fickle regarding their morals: Berin might murder without any pangs of conscience, but his word could still be honored. Of course, her own honor wasn't gleaming at the moment; she'd just agreed to help these criminals.

She thought about her note, and then shrugged away her hopes for outside help. She'd purposely delayed its delivery to give her time to retrieve her son.

Taalo blindfolded her and tried to disrupt her sense of direction by turning her around several times. They took her through alleys between the warehouses near the docks and at times she heard water lapping and smelled canal water. In the back of her mind, she kept track of the turns, but the rest of her thoughts were for Peri.

They were several blocks southeast of Berin's offices when she heard a door open, felt their footsteps go over wooden floors, then over stone. Now their footsteps echoed within a large structure and she smelled rank, still water.

They removed the blindfold and her heart sank again. Taalo had been right; no one would find her here. Betarr Serasa was not as old as Betarr Serin, but it had been in existence for more than 600 years. Many parts of the city near the canals had sunk, been forgotten, and built over by newer structures. This was one of those forgotten places; behind her was an opening that had been chiseled through the wall of a modern warehouse. They stood above an ancient quay that accessed a murky and forgotten feeder canal. The damp walls were stained with black and green growth that glowed eerily from the lamp held in Berin's hand. The stains showed how often floodwaters had filled the entire lower quay area.

"Where's Peri?" she asked.

Berin motioned for her to go down the stone step to the dock, then over the small feeder canal on a bridge that looked new. On the other side ranged stone arches in a row, through which she saw light. Stepping through an arch with Berin and Taalo, she entered a long, large hall lit by lamps hanging on the columns that supported the arches. Perhaps, before it was built over with more modern facilities, this was a holding and loading area for the canals. Twelve robed figures were congregating and milling about in the center of the large space, speaking to each other in hushed tones. Several looked up when she entered and made efforts to hide their faces inside their hoods.

Berin took her across the stone room to a new wooden door, which he quietly opened. Motioning Draius to keep quiet, he took her into a small room divided by a curtain. He kept a heavy hand on her shoulder to ensure her silence, although she had no intention of letting Peri know she was near. If the boy didn't believe Berin's story, whatever it was, then he would be dead.

He drew aside the curtain to let her peek. On the other side Peri was lying on a bench, apparently asleep, his chest moving in shallow breaths. A woman sat with her back to the curtain, so Draius couldn't see her face. She was stout and probably strong enough to handle Peri, should he try to resist.

Overall, her son seemed safe for the moment. She drew a deep breath as Berin pulled her away from the curtain. Back in the loading area, a large wooden chair with armrests and a high straight back had been moved to the center of the room. Taalo stood beside the chair and motioned to her to sit in it. Berin moved away to consult with the robed figures.

"You never told me what happened to Wendell," she said to Taalo. *Maybe Ponteva has already found him.*

"Unfortunately, he killed himself." Taalo grimaced, showing gray teeth. "Hung himself this morning when we weren't watching. This time we'll be more careful."

*So they'll ensure I won't harm myself. I'll become some insane beast in a cage,
carefully fed, watered, and bled.* It took all her will not to back away from the
chair. Her conversation with the Phrenii at Nherissa's tower suddenly re-
played in her head, when she noticed fear in Dahni's voice. *The murderers
have assumed the Kaskea resembles a necromantic charm. They taint our bond
with blood and pain.* Taalo might know how to make necromantic charms,
but he didn't understand how the Kaskea bonded man to elemental.

"With your skin color, you should have Meran blood. So why aren't
you volunteering? Not willing to take the risks?" She continued to stall,
knowing she was baiting Taalo. After going through the Meran-Viisi
records and the matriarch interviews, she knew the apothecary wasn't
Meran. Lornis and Miina thought he'd left his lineal name behind when
he was younger than marrying age and before the Fevers, making his lineage almost impossible to pin down.

Taalo's eyes narrowed. "Regretfully, the Kaskea rejected my blood.
You do me wrong, Officer Draius, to think I have no courage."

"Perhaps—but we all know your sense of humor."

Taalo barely came to her shoulder, but that didn't affect his confidence. His chest swelled up like a bird trying to impress his mate. "You're
referring to the rhyme I submitted to the *H&H?* Yes, I authored that."

Berin had turned away from robed figures pointing in an animated
discussion, apparently trying to decide who went where within a circle
drawn on the floor with slaked lime. He was behind her, waiting.

"Did you know this morning that you were going to do this?" She directed the question to Berin.

"I never wanted this, but I try to plan for all contingencies." Berin's
voice bounced off the walls, even in this huge room. "Please, Draius, sit in
the chair. I could have someone force you, but that would be undignified."

Draius kept a calm outward face, but inside, her anger and fear almost
made her shake. She sat in the chair. The high back came above her head
and her forearms naturally rested on the wide carved. Taalo immediately
started to tie her arms down to the chair.

"I've already given my word that I'll cooperate. Why tie me?" she said bitterly, pulling her arm away.

"The first time Wendell used the Kaskea, two people had to hold him down to keep him from harming himself or others. It's more efficient to immobilize you from the start."

While Taalo tied her limbs tightly to the heavy chair, she stared at Berin, letting all her anger and hatred at his betrayal blaze from her eyes. "Having me use the Kaskea will get you nowhere. I might have Meran blood, but I have no training. Wendell tried several times before he wielded the Kaskea with any results. How can you expect me to do better?"

Taalo responded. He seemed unable to let her questions go unanswered. "Not to worry, Officer Draius. We're just piggybacking on your blood. We're the ones who have experience and training." His eyes moved to glance slyly at Berin's back. "Besides, we know how to remain hidden from the Phrenii."

Taalo was lying. She didn't know why, but she didn't have time to puzzle about it as she called, "You give your word that Peri will be released, regardless of what happens tonight?"

She watched Berin, wanting one last reassurance from him, but she didn't get it. He made a sweeping motion with his arm and didn't even look at her. "Get her blood and prepare the circle."

Several robed figures were at the edge of the lamplight, fussing over something that she couldn't see. Others stepped into the circle in front of her. Some appeared to be meditating, keeping their heads bowed. Berin took something out of his pocket and handed it to Taalo. Neither took any special care with the object and when Taalo put it around his neck, she could see the small piece of slate wrapped in silver wire and suspended from the string. It was a shard from the Kaskea, having a similar triangular shape to the one inside her locket—laying all five pieces together would create the original round form.

While Taalo searched through a bag near a small brazier, she wondered if there was any way to use one shard of the Kaskea *against* another.

No, it wasn't possible, at least from the little she'd learned. The only point she knew for certain, from the Phrenii themselves, was that Taalo was going about this all wrong. As Dahni said, blood and death magic were anathema to them, and to the use of the Kaskea.

When Taalo turned around, she recognized what was in his hands. She knew the brass spring-loaded lancets only from diagrams in her history lessons, because the Phrenii had stopped bloodletting long before the Fevers. In Taalo's other hand, which he protected with a wrapped rag, was a heated silver cup for suctioning out the blood and collecting it.

She strained against the bonds but she couldn't move her arm away as he nicked a vein. Blood welled immediately and he put the cup over it. She drew in her breath as the metal burned her, but didn't make a sound or give any other indication of pain—that would only satisfy the little savage.

Taalo efficiently scraped the cup against the nick, cauterizing it as he captured the blood with the small cup. He held the shard of Kaskea over the vessel and then dipped it into her blood. A humming noise sounded. When he held the shard up, dangling in front of her eyes, it began to glow green.

"This didn't happen before." There was uncertainty in Taalo's voice as he looked inquiringly at his leader.

Berin looked around at the other figures, then shook his head, frowning. "Maybe the Kaskea is adjusting to her. She has stronger Meran blood than Wendell."

Taalo nodded. He leaned forward to whisper in her ear. "If you reach the Blindness and encounter the Phrenii, resist them. The woman has orders to kill your son if anyone disturbs our ceremony."

Behind him, she saw the figures at the edge of the lamplight bring forward a wooden frame and orient it within the circle. On the frame was bound a gagged boy, only a year or so older than Peri. The child's eyes darted around, terrified. Multiple recent wounds marred his midriff. There was blood splattered on his ragged breeches and muffled grunts of terror came through the gag as he jerked his head.

A child's life hangs in balance—this wasn't just about Peri, or her.

"You nameless bastards," she yelled, jerking at her own bonds. Her arms were tied tight and the chair was too heavy to move.

"Ah, if I had a tyr for every time I was called *that*." Taalo smiled and turned back to the circle.

No one else acknowledged her outburst. Her mind raced as she watched the robed figures settle about the circle, surrounding the boy, Taalo, and Berin. *No one knows where we are.* Taalo picked up a long thin-bladed knife, not a kitchen implement or defensive weapon, but one intended for surgery.

What can I do? She suddenly saw Mahri, standing behind Perinon's chair. *The mind that wishes rapport must volunteer... it must exhibit great need, purity of motive, honorable purpose, and steadfast heart.* She heard Taalo say something and Berin, perhaps, make a deep, satisfied grunt as she closed her eyes. Her mind filled with a vision of Dahni, standing beside the canal as she and her cousins swam.

Hear me, Dahni. A child will die tonight. Find us.

The locket pressed down on her breastbone. It felt so heavy; it was going to crush her. She gasped, snapping her head against the back of the chair as her vision went white.

She heard Taalo's shout of surprise and then *nothingness* invaded her, smothering her, filling her ears, nose, and mouth. She tried to scream, but heard only a sizzling sound that rose to a roar. She spiraled—upward? Downward? Vertigo.

• • •

Perinon was tired and not in the best mood when he ordered the prisoner to be brought to him.

"We can do this tomorrow, when you're rested, Sire." Sevoi must have sensed his fatigue.

But tomorrow he wouldn't feel any better than he did today, not if he continued to be pursued by madness and nightmares whenever he tried to sleep. He glanced about, petulant. Where were the Phrenii? He'd requested they be present when he questioned the pirate.

Frisson Rhobar looked to be over thirty years of age, and was handsome enough to cause women to swoon. His skin was the same value as Perinon's, but while the King's skin had gray, dusky Meran coloring, Rhobar's was the warm brown of a Sareenian. Even though his black hair was held in pragmatic Tyrran braids, he *was* Sareenian, and Perinon had to remind himself that this man was already into his middle age. Rhobar would have a shorter lifetime than the average Tyrran—made significantly shorter by his vocational choices.

"I'm honored by your attention," Rhobar said with a smug smile, even though he had his arms bound behind him and a manacle about his neck.

Perinon signaled his Guards, who jerked Rhobar off his feet and pushed him onto his knees. The King had encountered enough smugness for one day, having recently met with Aracia regarding the costs for the new metal gate. The design Cella had drawn was beautiful and when he saw it, he knew his wooden gates would have to go. The cost would be substantial, but Aracia didn't attempt to negotiate a different figure with the Rauta-Nelja, which irritated him even more than her attitude. Sure, he was attracted to Cella, who wouldn't be? Yet something inside of him resisted; he couldn't yet give in to the matriarchal machinations.

"Where are the Phrenii?" he muttered, and Rhobar's eyes widened. The pirate probably thought he was calling on the creatures to perform some sort of arcane torture.

Well, he'd have to get through this without the enhanced insight he'd have from the creatures. He stood up, and the King's Guard positioned behind Rhobar forced the pirate's head down in respect.

"You owe your life to me." Perinon walked close so Rhobar would have a good view of his boots. "You're not hanging from a noose today because *I* intervened. Do you understand?"

Rhobar didn't reply, his head still forced down by the Guard. Perinon gestured. The Guard took his hand away and stepped back.

"Do you have any code of honor?" Perinon continued. "In Tyrra, we would say you owe me life-debt."

Rhobar muttered something.

"What was that?" This time, Perinon grabbed Rhobar's hair to pull his head back, so the captive would have to look up at him. He was tall, so the pirate's neck stretched and his eyes rolled upward.

"I suppose I can thank you for the view from my prison cell." Although it seemed difficult to grin when one's head was pulled backward, Rhobar managed.

"You don't value your life?" He let go of the man's hair.

"Of course, but I always want more. A character flaw, I suppose." Despite being roughly treated by the Naval Guard, Rhobar still had spirit.

"I want the *Danilo Ana*." Perinon watched carefully, noting the flash of recognition in Rhobar's eyes.

"The *Danilo Ana* must be a talented woman. Everybody wants her." Rhobar kept his tone light.

"So your Groygan masters asked you to find her, perhaps for plunder?"

At Perinon's words, Rhobar attempted to stand, but was kept on his knees by the King's Guard. "I have no masters! I am my own man and I make my own decisions. Yes, she could have brought us gold, but the *Danilo Ana* was cursed. She was listing to her port side when we found her, and her crew killing each other in madness. *I* chose to scuttle her, and *I* let her sink to her peace."

Perinon believed him. "But not before confiscating her cargo?"

"We saw nothing of value on that cursed vessel."

Rhobar must not have discovered the lodestone, or perhaps the lodestone's evil aura had actually repelled the superstitious pirates. Perinon changed the subject, pacing in front of Rhobar. "So what would be the payment for your life-debt to me?"

Rhobar gave a short laugh. "I have nothing, thanks to your Navy."

"You have your life—ah, but that's mine anyway, isn't it?" Perinon stopped pacing and looked down at the prisoner.

"Are you playing a game with me, ser? What's your point?" Rhobar asked, his eyes narrowing.

"The point is I can use your life as I see fit. And I wish to use your life for the benefit of my Naval Guard and my country."

"Sire—" Sevoi hadn't been forewarned of his plans, and the master of arms now saw where he headed.

"I can be paid to do anything." Rhobar's brown eyes were sly.

"Therein lies the problem, Sire! He's worse than a hired mercenary." Sevoi couldn't contain his outrage.

"Our naval tactics can be vastly improved by this man. If he proves himself trustworthy, I might commission him," Perinon said to Sevoi.

"But he can never be trusted!"

"Oh, but he can," Perinon said. "He can, because otherwise he'll be turned over to either the Sareenians, the Kitarrans, or the Groygans. Which would you chose, Rhobar? The Sareenians and Kitarrans call for your blood, while the Groygans want you silenced. Last time I checked, they all call for public execution as punishment for piracy. Some still disembowel their prisoners alive, don't they?"

"Times have changed, if Tyrran royalty must resort to coercion." Rhobar's lips twisted. "And, all the while, looking down your nose at the *barbarians* in the rest of the Mapped World."

"I'm merely pointing out your choices." Now Perinon was using a light tone. "And they're the only choices you have. You can live a long life in the service of Tyrra, or have a much shorter life with the barbarians."

"Only if he pledges fealty in front of the Phrenii," Sevoi argued, ignoring Rhobar. "They will show you his true allegiances."

"Of course." Perinon turned to face Sevoi. "But consider this: once he's publicly working with our Naval Guard, it becomes doubly difficult for him to seek refuge with anyone, even outlaws. No one would trust him."

Sevoi looked dubious. "I can't see anything good coming of this, Sire, but—"

Perinon staggered and gasped. Someone was using the Kaskea, some-one different, with Meran blood as strong as his. "The Phrenii. Get wa-ter…"

Sevoi jumped forward to guide him as he fell backward into his chair.

"Get him out," Sevoi ordered, pointing to Rhobar. "Send for the secre-tary, tell him the King's walking the Void."

"Wait! Give me a chance!" Rhobar shouted at Perinon, who ignored him. Rhobar continued to struggle against the King's Guard as they pulled him from the room.

Perinon held out his hand, looking at the ring that held the Kaskea. The shard glowed with a bright, golden light.

Someone familiar uses the Kaskea. She does not hide her identity. Inside his head, Mahri's voice was cool and smooth. Perinon suddenly *felt* the mo-ment, many years ago, when he'd been afraid to jump into a deep part of the canals. He felt his cousin Draius grab his hand with a firm grip as she laughed, pulling him to the edge. He felt the exhilaration of fear when he jumped, the splash of coldness, and the canal water closing above his head as he sunk deeper than he had ever been. Yet Draius kept her hold on his hand, helping him rise.

He opened his eyes and saw his secretary hurry in with a pail of water.

"Be ready." Perinon clenched his ring hand into a fist and dove into the Blindness.

CHAPTER THIRTY-TWO

The Void

They say when sorcerers learn to walk the Void, their apprentices stand by with pails of water, in case their clothes start to smolder. Now that our King learns to walk the Void, we hide his burned clothes from the populace as well as any other elemental effects of rapport with Jhari. Strangely, the Phrenii can transit to and from the Void without adverse effects—perhaps because they are portals, and made of the same life-light as the Void.

—Toimi, Historian to King Ruusu, T.Y. 523 (converted to New Calendar)

Lornis rubbed his stomach contentedly as he went through the barracks common area and headed for the officer rooms. For the first time in days, he felt he'd finally eaten his fill, although he'd devastated the Sea Serpent's provisions.

As he opened the door to his suite, he heard a measured tread coming down the hall. There would be little reason for Ponteva to be in the officer quarters, but he waited patiently for the watchman to approach.

"Ser, there's been strange developments," Ponteva said quietly.

Ponteva's tone made his skin prickle. They were standing in the hallway that connected to all the rooms for officers that held ranks less than commander. There was little privacy here. Lornis motioned for the watchman to follow him into his small sitting room, and closed the door.

He hadn't heard the details surrounding Usko's death, but he heard them now. It was strange enough for the Phrenii to show up, together, to speak with an officer of the City Guard, but Ponteva further questioned Draius's behavior following her encounter with them. "The commander was distressed, ser, by what the Phrenii told her. She then sent me to arrest Purje-Kolme Wendell."

Wendell? This could only be the same Wendell who worked for Berin, who was seemingly attached to his employer's side. But if that wasn't strange enough—

"Wendell is dead, ser. Had to break in, and we found him lying on his bed."

"What?"

"Hung, according to Norsis. Said Wendell was placed on his bed *after* death. Having to process yet another body on Ringday ticked Norsis right off, so he gave me this message to deliver. Said he didn't have the time."

Ponteva handed Lornis a note. The seal was unbroken and the hastily scrawled words were in Draius's hand: "Deliver to Officer Lornis on Markday morning."

Lornis hesitated. "Should I open it early?"

"Not for me to decide, ser." Ponteva's voice became prim. "Commander Draius is *usually* precise. On the other hand, she seemed unnatural this afternoon."

"Hmm, yes, there is that."

A timid knock at the door made both men whirl around. The knock was singular, and wasn't followed by another. Lornis stepped forward quickly and flung open the door.

Maricie had been turning away. "Ser?" She glanced at Ponteva, standing behind him.

Before the phrenic healing, Lornis often had propositions from women who hoped for children, a contract with a rich lineage, or just a night of pleasure. Maricie, however, was Sareenian and wasn't raised to be as agressive as Tyrran women. Besides, she was quite young.

"It's about Master Peri, ser," Maricie said. "He's gone missing."

"Oh." Lornis flushed, embarrassed by his assumptions. "Did Draius send you?"

"No, ser. Mistress Draius and the Lady had words. About the safety of Master Peri." Maricie twisted the fabric of her apron. "Then Mistress Draius left and Lady Anja sent me to get Master Jan. Which I did, ser, some moments ago. He's already left at the Lady's direction."

"Why call upon me?" Lornis asked. His curiosity fought with his sense of propriety; he should probably stay out of an internal Serasa-Kolme matter.

"Mistress Draius said something about the 'murderers.' If Lady Anja treats this as a lineal matter, those that murdered my father's cousin may never be caught. As it says in the Book of Light, *Justice is required for all souls to progress along the Way.*" Maricie's liquid brown eyes narrowed and glittered in the lamplight.

Lornis said nothing. He looked down at the note in his hand and broke the seal. The note read: "I am tendering my resignation as OIC of Investigation, as well as my commission with the City Guard. If I'm unavailable on Markday morning, you must look to the ancestral stars who have lost their followers." Draius had signed it with her full lineal name.

Lornis grimaced. "Are you willing to interfere in matriarchal matters, Ponteva? I think Draius and her son are in trouble—far beyond the reach of matriarchal justice."

"I'll follow your decision, ser." Ponteva's voice was steady, like a rock. "And that'll serve as my excuse, as well. *You're* the one who could lose your career."

"I wasn't meant for politics anyway." Lornis looked at Maricie. "Tell me everything you know."

•••

Voices called, whispered, screamed. Draius was deafened.

"Rise, rise," urged one voice.

She struggled to look around and was wrapped tightly by the blinding fog. She panicked. *Where am I?*

The same voice cut through the rest, a familiar voice. "Relax and float upward, like when we dove into the high canals."

She tried to look around and was engulfed again by the sizzling and crackling noise of millions of thoughts and voices, the roaring whiteness. She clawed at her eyes and ears, trying to clear them. *Didn't they bind my hands?*

Who are you? She tried to call, but every time she did, she was overwhelmed by the sounds.

"Don't use your senses, cousin. You have no body here."

Peri—Perinon? For a moment she panicked, and the roaring whiteness took her over. Then she relaxed and glimpsed white mountains, fading through fog. This gave her hope, so she forced the languor, remembering when she and her cousins jumped into the high canals on the north side of the city, where the water was clean, and they would let their bodies float lazily up to the surface and light. Before the Fevers forced them into adulthood...

The whiteness cleared, like stepping up through fog onto a crystal mountainside. She could spread her senses out and felt outlines take shape. The world lay below her: the two cities, the bay, the sea, and the mountains. All of Tyrra was an image made in white, with sharp lines. For a moment she felt peace, and saw a small pulsing golden light in the city halfway up the mountain. Focusing on that light, she felt a dizzying effect of magnification when she drilled through the fog, the walls, everything, to Perinon's chair. But this was a world of white marble, with no man or woman or creature to be seen.

Cousin! When she tried to call to him, she disappeared back down into whiteness and noise. Fighting it exhausted her. But, when she rested, as if floating, the white vista came back to her. Was she mad?

"Madness comes from resistance. Don't try to talk, cousin. You don't hear my voice, but rather my thoughts and emotions."

She could sense so much more about Perinon. There was inexperience and fear in him, as well as uncertainty. She could feel fleeting emotions and catch glimpses of his memories: his father dying during the Fevers, his elder brother Valos ruffling his hair before he left on the hunting trip that ended his life, his mother retiring from public life to die. He had suffered many of the same sorrows as she. Could he feel the same from her?

"Your mind is very open, a surprising contrast to your physical self." Amusement faded to caution. "Only the portals may speak here. One will come for you and you must remain open to them, or your mind will break."

The Phrenii? She'd forgotten this was their domain. She went tumbling down through whiteness and for a moment, she was back in the warehouse again, straining against the bonds while a small gray man held up a dripping knife. There was chanting and screaming. Was she screaming? Then she was smothered in roaring, sizzling whiteness again.

With effort, she tried to regain the peace she'd felt before. *No moving, no speaking, just rest, just float,* she repeated internally to herself. The calm surrounded her and took her memories.

• • •

The vista was pure white, unsullied by color. She watched the cities, sharply outlined, sitting above the layer of fog. Through experimentation she drifted to places she knew, places she must have visited before she came here, but only represented here in light. She didn't know how long she'd been in this place, and she didn't care.

The creature approached her. She knew this one and its beauty. It represented water, and the life-light contained within that element.

"You are Draius. The 'Little One,'" Dahni said.

My name?

"You are an officer of the City Guard. This can happen to those who first drive through the Blindness and step into the Void; they must learn to remember. Remember your life, Draius."

She struggled to remember, because this creature thought it important.

"You have a son named Peri. You are wielding the Kaskea and you must learn to control it, not have it control you."

Memories came back in a rush, almost crushing her. The pain caused her vision to fog up and for a moment she was in the blinding, choking whiteness.

"Do not sink into the Blindness." The clean, cool words caught her. She relaxed and when her vision cleared, Dahni was still there.

"Yes, you remember." Dahni sounded sad. "And you remember that you are afraid of me."

She cried now, not caring about the suffocating fog. She cried for the loneliness of her life, for all her mistakes, and for Peri. She cried for her father's grief, and finally freed, she cried for her mother's painful death. She felt sadness and pain coming from Dahni.

Why do I have to remember?

"You have responsibilities. I cannot allow you to forget them."

She had thought the Phrenii incapable of understanding human feelings, but the emotion she now felt within this creature was astonishing. Every human soul encountered was remembered and catalogued; every soul lost was mourned for an eternity. There was more grief within this creature than Draius, the person she remembered, could ever contain.

"I am the element you are bound to. You will only see me when you enter the Void and, in the solid world, we are in rapport."

She struggled with the words, the thoughts, the questions she wished to ask this creature. *Where am I?*

"We call this existence the Void and it shows the shape of the world," the creature said. "The Void is also more than that, much more, but it will take time to teach you."

She remembered Berin, Taalo, the others. *Criminals use me as a channel to the Void. They threaten the life of my son and another child.* She finally released her despair, her fears for Peri's life, the unknown boy's life, her sanity, and her hopeless situation.

She felt Dahni absorb all her fears, examining each. "You have carried others into the Blindness, the layer which separates the solid world from the Void. These others get glimpses of insight into the solid world. But they mistakenly think they have reached the Void."

Can't you stop them?

"I cannot. I am part of, and portal to the Void. I cannot travel in the Blindness. But you can stop them." The creature dipped its horn to indicate a downward motion.

Draius tried to *look* where Dahni pointed and only succeeded in blinding herself. She dispersed the fog easily and tried again, this time extending her senses. By straining, she forced her senses downward and she now knew the layer under her was thick, but could be punched through to see into the solid world below. It was thick enough to have *things*, unnatural creatures, moving inside. Some circled and swam like sharks, others appeared to take linear paths.

"It is dangerous to wander in the Blindness, where there are hunters," said Dahni. "The people who used you for entry can never ascend above the Blindness, unfortunately for them."

Hunters? She concentrated on one of the large swimming things, but it kept sliding out of her grasp. Her mind shuddered.

"The predators, those that feed upon sleeping souls, are the hunters."

She extended her senses further down into the foggy Blindness. Concentrating and finding a specific something, or someone, was like dredging for the last small piece of meat in a bowl of thick stew. She pulled her senses back.

What about my son? This black fear ate away at her.

"Perinon prepares the King's Guard and they are coming to rescue you and your son. I will lead them to you."

Panic came over her. *No, they'll hurt Peri if their ceremony is disrupted. I didn't give you my location or my permission to do this.*

"And what about the other child?"

She didn't have an answer, suddenly ashamed, but still wanting to protect Peri.

"By rising to the Void you have showed your position." Dahni gestured with its horn and suddenly they were in the sunken quay. Or rather, they were in the Void's elemental representation of the place that she'd just left—with no living creature in it. There were outlines of the chair she sat in, but now there was only a pulsing green light where her body should be.

"I ask you once more, Draius. Who will save the other child?" Dahni dipped its horn again, so she extended her senses to the reality below. There was green light below the Blindness and by concentrating, she was suddenly *there*. She saw her body tied to the chair, her head lolling forward. The robed figures were seated and holding hands. In the center of their circle she saw the boy bleeding, lethargic from blood loss, but still alive. For how long?

Sickened, she rose and dove again, this time to the small room at the side of the stone quay. She now saw Peri, lying on a bench in sleep. The woman, younger than Draius originally thought, still sat watching him. The woman's head was nodding. She was falling asleep, although she'd periodically stir and look to the curtained opening. A knife and an empty glass lay on the bench beside her.

She rose back up to the Void, to find Dahni waiting.

Can't you do something for my son? Use your magic?

She felt despair as Dahni shook its head in answer to her questions. "I must abide by the rules of time. I travel as fast as I can in the solid world. *You* must make a choice and take action. The men search the Blindness and I cannot reach them. You must find them yourself."

If I disrupt their search, they promise to harm my son. What do you see?

"I cannot see all the consequences. But if they find the lodestone, Tyrra will fall."

The finality of Dahni's statement startled her. It seemed unlikely that her action, or inaction, could cause the collapse of Tyrra. *Isn't it enough to save Peri and the other child?*

"We sit upon a pivot in time," Dahni said patiently. "If these men find the lodestone tonight, war will take Tyrra by surprise. We need to delay this, because Lornis is not yet ready. *In this, we are certain.*"

Even though the idea sounded absurd, Dahni used the ritual phrase which meant the Phrenii were sure, absolutely sure. What the creature left unsaid disturbed Draius more.

War is coming, no matter what? she asked.

"Yes," Dahni said. "It is only a matter of when. By your decision you can make it happen later."

Still Draius hesitated. Wandering blind among all those creatures terrified her, but if she could find Berin or Taalo, she might be able to divert them. But what would happen to Peri? Could she even save the other boy? Of course, what would happen when Tyrra went to war, as the Phrenii predicted? How much death could result if they were unprepared? Uncertain, she teetered between all the possibilities.

Will you be there with me?

Dahni knew what she meant, replying with an intense regret that she'd never suspected the creatures could feel. "No. You will not sense me in the Blindness, but you will have an advantage. I can arm you with knowledge before you go in."

Knowledge didn't feel as useful as a cold blade, but it was the only weapon she had. She reluctantly made her decision. *I'll do what I can.*

"You will have the element of surprise. The others think you are insane and can be no threat to them."

She could only agree with that assessment: she was mad to try this.

"They do not realize you have independently used the Kaskea. They also do not realize you can move to and from the Void *and* the Blindness. Right now, they use necromantic charms to link themselves, in a chain, back to their bodies. Anyone cut off from that chain will be adrift."

How do I go down into the Blindness?

"If you want to go, you will get there," Dahni replied. "*Feel* for the hunters, because you may not survive an encounter with them. They are attracted to strong emotions. Remember, you can find safety in the Void because they cannot rise above the Blindness."

She felt Dahni's anxiety and concern.

I will search for them. I'm not sure what I'll do if I find them. With that ambivalent decision, she dove for the Blindness without a plan, and without a hope.

• • •

It seemed like she'd wandered the Blindness forever. The sizzling and roaring that surrounded her no longer bothered her; she'd learned to filter out the random thoughts and dreams of others. When the hunters swam past, she shied away and made her mind go blank so they couldn't sense her. She could feel their hunger as they glided and slithered around in the Blindness looking for prey, searching for thoughts and emotions. Fear excited and attracted them.

Eventually she felt a thread of familiarity, the memories of a bushy beard and a hearty laugh. She followed the thread, feeling a presence with a different flavor: the person she never knew, a person with suicidal desperation. Focusing upon Berin, she followed him in his sweeps.

Like a string of beads, she could feel others trailing behind him. Taalo held on to Berin, then there was another she didn't know, and another, and another—she counted six souls strung along, the lifeline back to their physical bodies.

She circled them like a hunter, while she decided what to do. The way the conspirators chained themselves together reminded her of a children's game called Fortress, where she held hands with her team and tried to withstand an attacker taking a run at the line of defenders and breaking them up. Usually the attacker was given time to size up the defensive wall and try to determine where it was weakest, looking for a smaller child that might not be so strong, or trying to break off an end defender. To offset that, each team tried to intersperse weaker and smaller members among the stronger ones.

But she had no way to judge the strength of the links in this chain, and she suspected she'd have only one chance to make this work. In the end, she made the same decision as if she were eight years old and running against defenders that were all stronger than her. She chose to try to break off the last person in the chain: Berin, who ranged out front and only held on to Taalo. Perhaps the fear and hatred she'd seen in Taalo's eyes would aid her, weakening the link between him and his leader.

She dove at the tenuous glowing line that held them together, moving deliberately and keeping her mind on cutting the connection. She hit the link and like a blow to her mind, felt the thoughts of both men. The Blindness momentarily cleared below the three of them, exposing the sight of a ship's hull breaking upon rocks that stood like a fence against a desert shore. The *Danilo Ana* had reached the end of her journey.

No! Like the hunter she pretended to be, she tore into the link, ravaging it. Perhaps it was her fear, perhaps the aura of doom that rose from that hull helped also, but the link glowed and finally snapped. Berin floated away from the chain and she felt him reaching—but they were more inhibited than she was, because she blocked Berin from Taalo with a thought. Berin thrashed.

Then Taalo and the others that made up Berin's safety chain were gone, so suddenly she was shocked. Berin also stopped moving. He floated in the Blindness and she felt him casting his senses around. She hadn't thought to shield herself from Berin, like she had from the hunters.

"Draius!" Berin's thought came through the Blindness like the crack of a whip. He sensed her.

Berin, there are bigger issues than your revenge. War is coming. As her mind flickered to Dahni's words, she felt him become enraged.

"Those creatures let my family die!" She heard his thoughts as speech, but he seemed incoherent with madness. Perhaps the interminable time spent wandering around the Blindness had unhinged him, or maybe this was magnified frustration and rage. Berin rushed her and she felt the collision of two minds occupying a point where only one mind should be.

And you abducted my son! Her bitterness formed a poison cloud as she struggled with him, buoyed by her own anger. Berin's mind felt like a sharp knife digging into her. She pushed back in the same manner and felt him give way. Suddenly, she knew she was stronger than him here.

Their struggle attracted hunters and she felt them circling, waiting, hoping to feed after they weakened each other. There'd be no end, and no reasoning with Berin now. She knew that. One creature passed close, brushing her mind with inhuman hunger and malice. She screamed soundlessly at the touch.

She began to fight differently, trying to contain Berin. It was harder to hold onto him than to strike out, but they wouldn't live through this if she didn't get them both out of the Blindness—quickly. She tried to pull him into the Void where the hunters couldn't go, but he tied her to the Blindness like an anchor. She'd lose him if she fled to the Void.

She again changed her tactics abruptly, heading for her body and hoping to get Berin back as well. She dove, holding him close to her and shielding him from the hunters like a child in her arms. She took the things by surprise; they swooped after her in pursuit. Berin struggled, but it was becoming easier to constrain him. What saved them were the hunters fighting among themselves to be the first to get to their prey. She felt one come close, only to be headed off by another; they started ripping each other apart. She tried to ignore them while she rushed toward her physical body.

With a shock that felt like dropping into ice water, she dove into her body. Shards of light and sound buffeted her, until she realized that she was receiving her senses from her eyes and ears again. She struggled to remember how her eyelids worked. Cool water drops fell on her face as she remembered how to breathe. She smelled smoke, heard rain sizzle. Rain? Wasn't she under cover?

She was alive again. The falling drops melted into mist as she opened her eyes, squinting against the light. She was surrounded by violence and chaos.

CHAPTER THIRTY-THREE

Payment of Life-Debt

I chose this solitary life, so I approach my death with only pen and paper as my companions. I helped my master hide a powerful evil and unfortunately, we couldn't anticipate the tools men would invent, nor what ends powerful men would employ to find it. Now I know what my master tried to hide from me, even upon his deathbed. I will not have peace in death. I will be pulled from the Stars and tortured for my knowledge, and when men unearth this evil, the phrenic circle will be broken and savage warfare will erupt...

—The Prophesies of Sorcerer-Apprentice Lahna, from the private Meran-Viisi Library, tentatively dated T.Y. 1071 (New Calendar)

Figures fought in and around the stone arches, and out onto the quay. Lantern light cast garish shadows of grappling shapes onto the walls, columns, and ceiling. Berin lay near her feet beside the boy, who still breathed shallowly. Draius coughed from the smoke. Something hot weighed on her chest and her clothing smoldered, but luckily, she was soaking wet. Actually, everybody, *everything* was wet and the puddles about the quay reflected the lamplight. She was still strapped in the chair while everyone fought around her, ignoring her. She felt like a bubble of air, caught between rocks as a waterfall roared past her.

Robed figures clashed with ruffians, but ruffians who were skilled with weapons. The back of a tall, broad-shouldered man to her left looked familiar, and when he pushed away a robed figure to get room to use his sword, she recognized Jan. He was using his service saber, and his moves and stance were familiar.

Farther away, a man with long brown braids was pulling a robed figure off a smaller individual. The smaller person twisted and, with a petite hand and arm, thrust a long dagger into the chest of the robed attacker. Miina and Lornis? What were they doing here?

She looked around while she struggled to get her arms out of their bonds. Her limbs were weak and lethargic; she seemed to be moving in molasses, while the struggling forms around her sped up. The entire Office of Investigation was here, but none wore the City Guard uniform. She caught sight of Ponteva, fighting doggedly with his back against a wall, facing two berserk opponents.

Her dreamlike state ended as two men fell across her chair. She screamed as they crushed her right arm into the wood of the armrest, bending her wrist the wrong way. The man on top stabbed the lower man's chest while she was squeezed against the back of the seat. She felt the impact of the knife as it ground between the bones in his chest and she stared into the victim's crazed face, his hood thrown back, as he died. The man on top pushed himself upright and she looked up into cold gray eyes. *Haversar.* He turned back to the fighting, leaving the body lying across her body, with warm blood seeping onto her lap and legs.

She arched her back to push away the heavy limp corpse, trying several times before it slowly rolled off of her. It fell onto Berin's legs. Berin still didn't move. She was soaked with the man's blood and she no longer smelled smoke, only gore.

All of Berin's followers were fighting with a wild frenzy, otherwise they wouldn't have had much chance against trained Guard and Haversar's men. She finally got her left arm free, but she couldn't move her right hand without feeling sharp, grinding pain. Something was broken. Fumbling with the knots using her left hand, she felt the brush of power on her skin. It raised prickles on her neck. Could everyone feel that? What was causing this insanity?

Someone had to save Peri! Disregarding the agony, she viciously pulled her right hand free of its bond. She tried to stand, kick her feet outward, but found her lower legs were also tied to the chair. Fear clutched her, gave her nausea. The woman watching Peri—what would she do?

"Jan!" She had to be heard above the clanging weapons, shouts, grunts, and screams. "Jan!"

Jan's opponent crumpled to the ground, and he turned toward Draius.

"Peri! Over there!" She pointed with her good arm toward the small door. Jan nodded as the figure on the ground reached up and clung to his leg. He slashed downward, hitting the back with a dull crunch. She turned her attention to her bound feet, knowing that Jan would do whatever was necessary to get to their son.

The power in the room still tickled her skin and as she fumbled one-handed with the bonds, she cast about with her senses, just as she had done in the Blindness.

Suddenly she was galloping down the streets of Betarr Serasa. The air was clean from the rain and the night sky was clear, shining with her people. Behind her flashed the silver and green of the King's Guard, as well as Perinon, pushing his horse to keep up.

We are coming. The voice in her head was Dahni's, the view of the world she saw came from the creature's eyes.

"Draius?" Lornis knelt beside her chair, his hand on her knee. His face was lit by green light, making his cheekbones sharper than normal.

"Are you hurt?" He looked at the blood, trying to see if it came from her wounds.

She could only shake her head. How long had she been caught in that vision? The fighting had stopped and the quay seemed unnaturally quiet. Crumpled bodies lay scattered about, and she heard faint moans. The smell of oil from capsized lamps overwhelmed the smell of rain, smoke, and blood. The blood on her lap and thighs was drying. One of Haversar's men was freeing the nunetton boy and binding his wounds. The boy looked to be unconscious, but alive.

Jan stood near, holding Peri across his arms. Peri's head lolled against his chest in deep, unnatural sleep. Jan stared at Draius, or more specifically, at her chest. She looked down and saw the locket front had burst, or perhaps melted. The Kaskea shard flared with bright green light. As she watched, the light faded until the shard looked like a dull piece of slate again.

A movement behind Jan caught her eye. Haversar bent over a robed figure and cut its throat. Several of his men were looting other bodies.

"Jan, stop him!" she said. "He hasn't the right to mete out King's Justice."

Jan looked at her for a moment, and then jerked his head toward the wounded nunetton boy. "He hasn't the right, after this was done to one of his own?"

"If any of these people are alive, we need information from them. Believe me, they'll pay for this. Necromancy is punishable by worse than death."

Jan considered her words for a moment. He leaned over Berin's body and gently laid Peri on her lap. She gasped as she moved to hold him, pain shooting up her from her right wrist, but she hugged her son fiercely with her good arm. Other than the deep sleep, he appeared to be unharmed.

Jan walked over to Haversar and they argued in low tones. Haversar's men stopped rifling among the bodies.

"The King will soon be here with his Guard," she called.

Both Jan and Haversar jerked their heads to look at Draius.

"How do you know?" Haversar's voice was low and dark, chilling her.

"I saw them passing through the marketplace." Then, when they looked unconvinced, she added, "I saw them through Dahni's eyes." She knew what that meant, and why people now drew back from her.

Lornis stopped untying her ankles and nodded toward Haversar. "It's only through his help that we were able to find you. His people know many of the forgotten places."

"Do you know who he is?" Draius asked.

"I've a good idea. But I'm not going to worry about that now." He went back to untying her bonds. Only Lornis seemed to be unaffected by her obvious rapport with the Phrenii.

Haversar's men melted away, carrying the boy and two of their wounded with them. If the men died, they would be found floating in the canals, stripped of everything. Depending upon their notoriety with the King's Law, their heads might have all identifying features removed or smashed: a symbol of service to Haversar, of a sort.

This left only the small group around Draius and some twenty bodies on the floor. The door and stairs on the other side of the canal suddenly exploded with green and silver. *The King.* Everyone but Draius went down onto one knee.

Dahni slipped through the door, down the stairs, and over the bridge. The creature started making its way to Draius, stepping daintily over bodies.

"Battlefield protocol, everyone," called Perinon's crisp voice. Everyone stood. Ponteva, Miina, and Lornis stood to one side of Draius, all looking studiously at their feet. Jan stood on the other side.

Draius still had Peri on her lap and, unfortunately, one leg still bound to the chair. She watched Perinon examine the quay littered with bodies, then look carefully at the group about Draius. Miina shivered, and everyone's wet clothes were stained with blood.

"Quite a bit of carnage for the four of you," Perinon said. He apparently discounted Draius, still trussed up in the chair.

"Yes, Sire," Jan said.

Trust Jan to give the easy lie. Her staff members all carefully examined their boots.

Gaflis appeared, with his assistant, and they attended the wounded. Dahni now stood in front of her. Jan, Ponteva, and Miina all moved back, away from the creature, while Lornis knelt again to remove her remaining bonds.

"We know you well," Dahni said, looking at Lornis.

"You healed me," Lornis replied. "My eternal gratitude, Phrenii."

"We remain to serve," came the ritual response. The creature looked into her eyes. "We can heal you also, Draius."

"No healing. What—?" She bit her lip and took deep breaths as she glanced from person to person.

As soon as Dahni came within a couple paces, her eyes saw more than the superficial skin of those around her. She looked down to her lap and saw Peri shining with innocence. She looked at Miina and also saw innocence, but it was virginal and not at all childlike. Feeling like she'd violated Miina's privacy, she looked away. Ponteva had both darkness and light coiled within him, the darkness like tree roots, necessary for strength, and the light radiated loyalty.

Jan also had a coiled darkness, dangerous and self-serving, with few glints of light. Somehow, Draius knew the glints of light were for Peri and not for her. Last, she looked down at Lornis. She could see that some of his light came from Dahni, from the healing. The light shining from him was intense. He had smudges of darkness also, but not a disturbing kind like Jan's.

All mortals are a struggle between light and darkness; their nature is made clearer by our presence. Dahni's voice was inside her head. The creature moved back and the effect faded.

She looked up and saw Perinon staring at her. Their gray eyes met. With a shock, she realized why Tyrran kings fought so hard to marry for love, and it had nothing to do with pleasing the romantic inclinations of the populace. What would it be like to marry a woman who didn't care for you, when you had to see her feelings so blatantly every time the Phrenii were near? And the Phrenii were always near the King. She wouldn't be able to stand looking at Jan, day after day, seeing the dangerous darkness inside him and knowing how little he cared for her.

"Take this thing off me." She swallowed hard and almost choked. "I don't like what it's doing to me."

Lornis reached to take off the Kaskea, but Perinon's bitter laugh stopped him.

"Taking it off won't change anything, cousin. The Kaskea is bound to you and you will feel its effects even if you throw the shard into the deepest part of the sea. No one else can use that shard until you die." The finality of Perinon's words hit her like a hammer, more effective because she felt the truth in them.

Jan lifted Peri off her lap and Lornis removed the rest of her bonds, but she couldn't move because both her legs were numb. Gaflis started splinting her lower arm and pain shot up to her shoulder.

Dahni was suddenly in her mind, softening her pain.

"No. Stay out. No healing." She felt Dahni fade and the pain spike again.

Berin mumbled something. Gaflis had examined him and pronounced him singed, but unharmed, and now he was regaining consciousness. His eyes were unfocused as he struggled to sit up. Lornis and Ponteva drew their weapons and circled to stand behind Berin's large shoulders.

"Back?" Berin whispered, turning his head to take in the view of the sunken quay. Miina stepped forward to stand in front of Draius while Jan stepped back, still holding Peri.

"We are arresting you under the King's Law," began Ponteva, fulfilling his watchman duties and starting to drone the specific articles.

Berin struggled to his feet, ignoring Ponteva, his eyes on Draius. At full height, Miina didn't even reach his armpits and he could look directly over her head and into Draius's eyes. Berin had no weapon, but Miina still held her long knife ready.

"You think I'll gratefully owe you life-debt." Berin's voice, spiteful, echoed off the stone. His attention was upon Draius.

"No, there's nothing between us." She looked away from the dark maelstrom of sorrow, hate, and envy that Berin carried for the Phrenii. "Not any more. What madness possessed you?"

"Not madness. Retribution. Did you know my *last* cousin, Ilves, died while you were at Betarr Kain? He had a cancerous growth in his belly and he refused phrenic healing, but not the support of a physician. Do you know how these creatures advised his physician?" Spittle flew from Berin's twisted lips; his tone was venomous and she shook her head in answer. "They advised *poison.* They told the physician to give Ilves draughts of slow-acting poison! Can you believe it? The physician ignored their absurd advice, but Ilves still died in pain as the growth ate his other organs."

She opened her mouth to answer, but never did. No one was ready for Berin's move, and his intentions were so overwhelmed with hatred that she, as well as the Phrenii, were surprised. The big man leapt sideways and twisted, *away* from Ponteva and Lornis, *away* from Miina and Draius, straight at Dahni. He moved fast, his large body committed and unstoppable.

No one knows how much the Phrenii weigh. By all appearances, Berin weighed three times that of the translucent and delicate Dahni. Dahni's horn whipped up in defense and when Berin's body hit it, the creature staggered backwards. Berin laughed, taken immediately by the phrenic madness. Blood bubbled out of his mouth. He fell forward onto Dahni as his knees buckled, causing the horn to push out of his back.

Both Dahni and Draius screamed. Blood gushed from Berin's chest onto the face of the creature, who tried to shake off the impaled body. Perinon dropped his sword, covered his face, and crouched.

The scream from the Phrenii was eerie and unworldly. All but Draius and Perinon were mesmerized, watching silently as the creature tried frantically to pull its horn out of Berin's body. Draius continued to scream. She clawed at her face and eyes. Perinon moaned and collapsed onto the floor, frantically wiping his face. A Guard finally knelt and tried to keep Perinon from harming himself.

Miina grabbed Draius's forearms, even though one was splinted.

She struggled, ignoring the pain. "Berin, no! Get the blood off! The blood!" Her sight blurred and she retreated to white chaos.

CHAPTER THIRTY-FOUR

Changes

The training of a matriarch is brutal, and I'm not referring to long hours spent studying records or the lineal business. A matriarch must make decisions in a pragmatic, heartless manner, and be ready to sacrifice all for her family line. I was taught this when Nuora dissolved my first contract because I was childless. "Love" can't overcome our dwindling birthrate. There is one exception: he who wears the Kaskea must be given allowance to find love, although this secret we keep close.

—*Meran-Viisi matriarchal records, made by Lady Aracia upon her replacement of Lady Nuora, T.Y. 1465*

Lornis tried not to fidget, gripping his hands tightly behind his back. He admired Jan's calm demeanor, considering they faced a terrifying sight for any grown man: three matriarchs sat at the table in front of them. Lady Meran-Viisi Aracia, Lady Kulte-Kolme Enkali, and Lady Serasa-Kolme Anja all bore expressions of disapproval, in varying levels of severity. He and Jan were being taken to task, and this had been important enough to call his matriarch Enkali into the sister cities.

"We called you here to address the issues of Draius and her son, as well as your parts in her rescue." Aracia spoke first. As matriarch of the oldest constellation and the lineage of the King, she carried the most power of the three.

Lornis looked down when Enkali's bright eyes focused on him. He didn't want his grandmother to see the emotion within him, the frustration and pain of watching Draius lie comatose for almost an eight-day.

"We've consulted the Phrenii," Enkali said gently. "They say Draius will recover, and they feel she will be sane when she wakes."

Relief flooded through him, loosening his clenched fists. It'd been questionable whether Draius, Perinon, or even the Phrenii, would recover from Berin's death. King Perinon's "illness" was noticed by the *H&H*, but never connected to the sudden lack of Phrenii about the streets. The Phrenii *disappeared* for several days, while Perinon and Draius both lay insensate. When they appeared again, the King recovered, but not Draius. The Phrenii insisted upon abiding by Draius's wish and had not applied any of their healing.

Lornis raised his head to meet his grandmother's eyes.

"Peri will sleep better, hearing that news," Jan said.

Lornis winced. Peri had been at his mother's side every morning, staying until his father came to take him to afternoon lessons. The boy had been wracked with grief and guilt, feeling he was to blame for his mother's situation. Lornis didn't know if Jan tried to alleviate some of Peri's guilt, but he'd tried whenever he stopped by the hospital room. He couldn't tell if he'd helped the boy, or made matters worse.

"One of our decisions is to promote Serasa-Kolme Perinon to favored grandchild," Aracia said. "The Serasa-Kolme will finance Peri's education, while he will be marked in Meran-Viisi records as possible heir for the throne, in the event the King has no suitable children within the next fifteen years."

Lornis couldn't get any hint of the underlying conflicts by looking at the women's faces. Anja's face mirrored the bland expressions of the other two matriarchs, although she looked like a young girl next to the wizened Enkali. This was undoubtedly the result of heated negotiations, due to the money involved. Regardless, this was a boon for Peri, who would now receive the education of a Tyrran king.

"Draius and I are honored. You won't be disappointed in Peri." Jan bowed.

Jan didn't give any other indication of his feelings, but Lornis remembered the public argument between him and Draius. He'd wanted the boy to remain Serasa-Kolme but, if King Perinon didn't have sons, Peri would eventually have to become Meran-Viisi. Perhaps Jan could overlook the lineal name change, if his son became King.

"There is the matter of your marriage contract," Anja said.

"My indiscretions are over," Jan said. "In any event, we can append mitigating clauses to the contract, for either Draius or myself."

Lornis examined his boots, not wanting to see Jan's face. Did Draius really approve of comfort clauses?

"Contract clauses no longer matter," Anja said. "Draius asked to have the contract dissolved and since she now wears the Kaskea, we must abide by her feelings."

"She must now go with her heart," Enkali added, and Aracia nodded.

Were the matriarchs speaking of love? Lornis and Jan glanced at each other, their eyebrows raised. Matriarchs spoke of family obligations, of setting aside one's feelings for the good of the lineage, and of sacrifices—never of love. The men waited for more explanation.

"I don't understand," Jan said, breaking a moment of silence.

Enkali and Anja looked at Aracia.

"The Meran-Viisi understand the burden of wearing the Kaskea." Aracia's voice was tight. "It will be impossible for Draius to live within an arranged marriage."

Jan shook his head and opened his mouth, but Anja cut him off.

"You will be as clear as a window to her. There will be no more children if your contract stands." Anja's tone was curiously flat, as was her expression, but something in her face caused Jan to close his mouth.

Lornis continued to examine his feet. His left toe was scuffed, so he'd need to buff that boot when he got back to—

"Lornis." Enkali's voice made him snap his head up.

Here it comes. I'm going to be punished for interfering in Serasa-Kolme business. He hoped he wouldn't be moved back to Plains End, away from the sister cities. Besides, he wasn't stupid: everything changed after Enkali had consulted Jhari. While he didn't know the details, he knew he had to be *here* in Betarr Serasa.

"You must abide by whatever Draius decides."

What else would he do? Confused, he noted the humor in his grandmother's quick brown eyes. Realization slowly dawned. *Draius is free to be with whomever she choses.* If he got out of this matriarchal tribunal with career, lineage, and body intact—he'd be going courting. And, if Jan wanted to mend his relationship with his now-previous wife, he'd have competition.

Aracia interrupted his gleeful reverie. "Lady Anja will address your involvement with criminal elements of, shall we say, unsavory reputation?"

"The Guard often uses criminal sources of information. Without Jan's source, we'd never have found Draius—" Lornis snapped his mouth shut when Jan gave him an unfriendly glance.

He didn't get around to saying that Anja appeared to already know that source, a man with cold eyes who Lornis didn't want to remember, or ever want to see again. He suspected the man was a career criminal, and a very powerful one. When Anja had reluctantly accepted aid from Lornis, as well as from Jan's source, she'd applied the condition that "the watch and the City Guard cannot be formally involved."

Lornis had explained the conspiracy concerning the Sareenian ship *Danilo Ana*, a councilman, and Berin—with possible Groygan interference. Apparently the pickpockets and small-time street thugs that skulked outside the control of matriarchs and the King's Law had suffered from the strange activities of this conspiracy. They had gathered impressive intelligence on their own, but needed the extra pieces of the puzzle, brought by Lornis. The man with the cold eyes knew all the dark corners of the sister cities, including the forgotten places.

"Of course, saving Draius and Peri does mitigate your punishment." Anja's eyes were only for Jan. Lornis stepped back, happy to be left out of her frigid gaze. This was matriarchal justice, but about something other than the rescue attempt.

Jan tensed and stood taller. "The life-debt is paid. There is nothing more between him and me."

"Ensure it stays that way," Anja said. "Otherwise, I will remove your name and all Serasa-Kolme support."

Lornis stepped back further. This was an extreme punishment. Aracia and Enkali stared off into the air. Watching another matriarch clean her own house even made them uncomfortable.

"As it is, you remain Serasa-Kolme. I'm reinstating *half* your disbursements and allowing you to see Peri, provided you remain a proper model for him."

Jan looked down, his jaw clenched. Lornis willed him to say nothing. This wasn't the time to argue with his matriarch, not with the Meran-Viisi and Kulte-Kolme watching. After a moment, Jan nodded and looked up to meet Anja's eyes. Some agreement passed between them, although Lornis doubted this would be their last words on this subject.

Surprisingly, there was nothing more. Lornis felt the tightness around his chest fade. There hadn't been any punishment, at least for him—and Draius was now free.

•••

When Draius woke, she saw a white ceiling above her and smelled the herbs and concoctions used in the hospital wards. Her head felt fuzzy but her body felt whole. She wriggled her toes and fingers, feeling the heavy splint on her right hand and arm. She knew, without looking, what creature stood beside her bed. The memories came rushing back: the horn driving through Berin's heart and the blood gushing onto her face.

"We killed him." It was an accusation, full of anger that could be directed nowhere.

"Yes," Dahni replied. "Berin acted on impulse and we were distracted. Unprepared."

Before she'd been bound by the Kaskea, she would have thought the creature's answer was callous. Now she felt the crushing weight of Dahni's sorrow, shepherding generation after generation of Tyrrans to the Stars, and still not immune to the loss of an individual soul. She hadn't known the Phrenii mourned so deeply. She couldn't keep hold of her anger, not when she compared it to that immense pain.

"The Phrenii never kill," Dahni added.

"I know," Draius whispered, her throat constricting. Even during war-time the Phrenii only supported Tyrra with non-lethal magic. They never participated directly in battle.

"Now we are tainted by blood and death. We are changed."

"Changed how?"

Dahni didn't answer. She sensed the creature couldn't explain how. Perhaps the Phrenii were being overly dramatic, because throughout Tyrran history they had provided battlefield *support*. The phrenic elemental powers, which the King could direct, were used for distraction or blockading, not as weapons. However, those elemental storms might have indirectly hurt or killed *someone*.

Elemental storms? She looked at Dahni's eyes, green, representing water and healing. "Where did all that water come from? The puddles, the wet clothes on everyone. And I'm sure I felt rain when I came out of the Blindness."

"You were out of control, pulling our power, but we allowed it because you were defending yourself. You can do that only with our permission."

"Will I be able to heal, too?"

"We do not know. The King has only been able to channel our elemental powers, not our abstract ones." Dahni was referring to their powers like prescience, healing, influence, protection and the power to command loyalty, inherent in Spirit, otherwise known as Mahri.

She changed the subject. "How long have I been here?"

"Almost an eight-day. Your body needed rest from the shock. We did not heal you, because you did not give us permission." The creature almost sounded motherly, if that were possible.

"Where's Peri?"

"At his afternoon lessons. The sleeping draught the criminals gave him did no permanent harm. Your matriarch sends her regards, with a message that your son will be her favored grandchild."

Draius raised her eyebrows. She was relieved to hear Peri was safe, but Anja's message had interesting ramifications. Dahni watched her with bright green eyes.

"Have we said something unexpected?" Dahni asked.

She finally put her finger on what bothered her. "Why are you plural now, when you were singular in the Void?"

"Our individuality will ultimately un-make us, or so the prophecy goes. This is why we only allow ourselves to be singular within the Void, and only to you, Little One."

As usual, she filed away the words that didn't make sense and picked only one puzzle to attack at a time. Glancing down at her long frame in the bed, she said, "That's twice you've referred to me as 'Little One.' I'm definitely not small."

Dahni cocked its head. "We apologize. The term *dra'us* translates to 'Little One' in the old language. It is easy for us to make mistakes with names."

"Well, that language has been dead for over 600 years—long enough time to learn a new one. Please don't call me that any more." She petulantly adjusted her sheets.

The creature didn't say anything, but she felt a tickling in her head.

"Are you laughing at me?" She glared at Dahni. Struggling up to a sitting position, she leaned back against the iron frame of the bed so her head was nearly on the same level with the creature's bright green eyes.

"We do not laugh," the creature said, using a grave tone.

She glanced around the room, which seemed so normal. She just didn't feel normal. "My life will never be the same, will it?"

"No."

"Will I always know exactly where you are? Will you always be in my mind?"

"Yes."

The Phrenii never lied, and they apparently didn't waste words.

"What does it mean to have two mortals using the Kaskea?"

"We do not know. Two mortals have never, at the same time, been in rapport with us."

"At least we've settled that." Draius felt the tickling in her head again. "You *do* have a sense of humor."

"Maybe we do, but it is still true that we do not laugh."

She heard the sound of a throat clearing. Lornis stood at the door, hesitant to disturb their conversation. Since Dahni was close, she could see his feelings shining out of his body. They were so bright they almost hurt her. They were frightening, as well. *Of course I'm scared. I've never experienced honest concern for my well-being—or maybe I've never believed it possible.*

Dahni sensed her discomfort and backed away as Lornis came in the room. "We will be near, if you need us," the creature said delicately.

"Of course you will." She couldn't help the sarcasm, but she was grateful when Dahni finally left the room. She could look at Lornis and breathe without her heart racing.

He came to stand close beside her bed, looking like he'd never been near the brink of death. Just like the first time she'd met him, his City Guard uniform was immaculate.

"I'm glad you're awake and well. I came to tell you that I'm transferring. The captain only meant for Investigation to be a temporary assignment for me."

She nodded.

"I'll be transferred to City Defense and working as liaison to the King's Guard." Lornis had found his place.

She had to say something. All those secrets were gnawing at her. "You'll be working for Jan. There's something you should know—"

"I know more than you think." He cut her off, perhaps to save her from an embarrassing confession. He told her about the matriarch's rulings, and how Jan was being punished for his criminal "connection."

She took a few moments to absorb everything. Her contract with Jan was dissolved, not due to Jan's behavior, but because she now wore the Kaskea? The situation was rather absurd. She sighed and wondered what marriages were like in other countries. Was life going to be easier or more complicated, now that she had more control?

One aspect of Lornis's story mystified her. Why did the matriarchs punish Jan in front of Lornis? Perhaps they wanted to make the punishment more embarrassing, and to give Lornis leverage over Jan.

Unfortunately, Lornis still didn't know what Jan was capable of doing. She caught his arm, and held on tightly. "There's more."

Lornis looked at her strangely and slowly sat down on the side of her bed.

Now everything poured out—once she started, the words came rushing out. All Jan's manipulations that she'd discovered, but didn't tell anyone, poured out now. What Jan had done to Kapeli, encouraging the man's gambling. How she'd come across a letter Jan was writing to him, a letter of blatant extortion, a threat to expose the gambling and the debts. How Kapeli had committed suicide rather than shame his family—yet she had done nothing. Then there was the attack; she was sure Jan had asked Haversar to have his thugs kill Lornis. She even suspected Jan had provided Haversar with the powder weapons.

"I'm sorry I didn't tell you any of this sooner." When she finished, Lornis was silent. His long hair was unbraided and some of it fell on the bed, brushing her hand. She stared at the hair, rather than looking into his face. She'd probably just destroyed any future friendship, or more, with him.

"Thank you for telling me now, but it's not my place to judge you. That'll happen when you face your ancestors, hopefully after a long and honorable life. My thoughts are that you did the best you could, given the circumstances. You had to be loyal to the Serasa-Kolme. Jan was your husband and you loved him." There was a slight rise of his voice at the end of the sentence that she had to answer.

"I *did* love him. No longer." She still looked away from his face, not wanting to chance rejection. His hair was shiny and felt silky against her hand. She slowly wound her fingers into the strands.

"Jan loves his son, that much is obvious. I'll be safe working for him. In a way, we're bound together and we'll never be rid of each other." Lornis's voice was wry as she felt him lean forward. She closed her eyes and felt his breath on her hair as he continued, "But he was a fool to push you away, while I can only dream of having someone as loyal and generous as you."

His lips brushed her forehead as his words trailed away. She felt her heart thumping as his lips trailed down the left side of her face, touching her temple, her closed eyelid, her cheek, the corner of her mouth... Oh, it took so long before his warm lips touched hers and then they were kissing, her good hand buried in his hair. She wanted to devour him, taste all of him. His chest pressed down on hers and—

Jan is here to visit you. Dahni's cool words cut through their rough breaths, fragmented murmurs, and the warmth spreading through her body. She pushed Lornis away.

"Early warning," she gasped.

He caught her hand and held it tight. "What?"

"Jan will be here soon. Tell me about the investigation. What happened to Taalo and the others?" Sounds drifted in through the window. There were crowds gathering in the street and faint music playing from far away, but getting stronger.

"We've gotten confessions that name Berin, of course, as the organizer and leader. Taalo and his apprentice killed Reggis, then the conspirators got rid of the apprentice because he was a liability. After that, Berin and Taalo get all the blame for killing the Sareenian, Vanhus, and Usko. They're easy to blame, because one is dead and the other—" Here Lornis dropped the other boot. "Regrettably, Taalo is missing. He escaped, perhaps through the canal tunnel. It appears he was packed and ready to abandon his cohorts. What a disloyal wretch."

A movement caught her eye. Jan was standing in the doorway, his gaze going from Lornis to Draius. How long had he been standing there? She hoped she didn't look too flushed. Lornis still held her hand, but she didn't pull it away. After all, her marriage contract to Jan had ended.

"What about everything stolen from the Royal Archives? The Kaskea shard and the—the lodestone?" She decided to ignore Jan, who silently leaned against the doorframe.

"We think Taalo still has one shard of the Kaskea. The Meran Sword of Starlight and tapestries have been found, and some proscribed documents remain missing—probably with Taalo. The good news is that the King has confirmation the lodestone was lost at sea."

She wasn't so sure, considering the shipwreck she'd seen from the Blindness. But there'd be time to talk to Perinon about that, as well as the Kaskea shards. And, knowing her cousin, he'd chase after that stolen shard—no matter where Taalo went. She felt about her neck, knowing what was there, knowing it would be there until the day she died. The shard of the Kaskea was now wrapped in silver wire and suspended from a heavy chain. It lay quiescent until she lifted and held it, when it flared with green light. She dropped it hastily.

"The King says it'll take some practice on your part to control the Kaskea and its effects," Lornis said. "And about Berin..."

She waited. Jan stayed where he was, looking bored.

"His pyre is scheduled for this evening, and the Meran-Viisi will officiate at the Tarmo-Nelja reliquary. After the interment of his ashes, they'll close and seal the lineal reliquary."

This was a surprising twist. As Starlight Wielder for the Meran-Viisi, King Perinon would light Berin's pyre. More than Berin deserved, since he wanted to unmake the Phrenii and as a result, tear apart Perinon's sanity. But, as the last Tarmo-Nelja, perhaps it wasn't enough.

"The Tarmo-Nelja are no more," she murmured.

"Yes, they are certainly 'the Stars that have lost their followers.' May I offer you my company this evening, for the pyre?" Lornis still held her hand.

She glanced at Jan, who raised his eyebrows and looked away. The silence grew uncomfortably. But if Lornis has the courage to ask her right in front of his future commander and her former husband, then she should have the courage to answer. "I'd be honored to go with you tonight."

"Thank you." Lornis squeezed her hand before letting go.

"I told Peri to watch the parade while I checked on you." Jan looked awkward, perhaps for the first time since she'd known him. He pushed away from the doorframe. "I'll go get him."

There's no love in his heart for me. That didn't sting any more. She finally noticed the sounds coming through the open window: the gathering crowds, the anticipation, singing, and merriment.

"A parade?" She glanced at Lornis.

He smiled, lighting up the room. "Oh yes, there's a celebration. King Perinon has been contracted to Rauta-Nelja Cella, with the marriage scheduled in two years. As a magnanimous wedding boon, the King dropped charges against the pirate Rhobar—that fellow who's so popular with the women. Then, in a similar gesture of goodwill, the King's Council dropped taxes on Groygan goods."

"Are you sure it's only been an eight-day? The council never moves that quickly."

"Remember, that portent from the Stars promised a significant decision. When the Groygans made a proposition to reduce their forces near the Saamarin, in exchange for us dropping taxes on Groygan goods, the council jumped at it. They want to be part of history as we move into true peace and prosperity."

"True peace and prosperity," she repeated in a whisper, thinking back on Dahni's warnings of warfare and a changed world. She could almost believe that future had been thwarted and, if she closed her eyes and willed it, she might hold onto this daydream for a short while.

Peri is here, Dahni's quiet voice said in her head.

"Ma!" Peri ran across the room to climb onto her bed and throw his arms around her neck.

"Peri, be careful." Jan stayed at the door.

"It's okay," she said. "I'm fine."

She hugged Peri tightly to her side with her good arm, rubbing the top of his head with her cheek. The future could wait. She took a deep breath and immersed herself in the feel and smell of her son.

"Dahni says you're better. Do you want to come home?" Peri's voice was muffled as he pressed against her shoulder.

Home. "Yes, I'd like that," she said.

CHAPTER THIRTY-FIVE

First Millday, Erin Four, T.Y. 1471

I had a harrowing time, longer than an eight-day, hiding about the docks before I could find passage out of Betarr Serasa. Not only was the City Guard hanging about, I had to worry about every thief and beggar, even the supposedly blind ones, recognizing me. Never again will I underestimate Haversar, or the breadth and power of a city's underworld.

Luckily, I've been taken under the wing of a Sareenian merchant who deals in hand-made trinkets and toys—I didn't pay much attention to details, given the circumstances. He got me on a ship, disguised as his apprentice. He represents the Sareenian desert tribe we first approached, the ones who say they dabble in necromancy. They're uneducated in the art but I can teach them.

Once I've paid back the merchant and saved enough for passage, I'll be heading across the Angim to Groyga. There I'll offer my services, either as apothecary or necromancer. Unlike my late employer, I have no qualms about serving Tyrra's traditional enemy. I'll find a benefactor with the resources to explore the southeastern shores of the Angim.

Based upon the position of the sun, the desert shoreline, and the barrier rocks that look like teeth, I'm sure I can find the *Danilo Ana* wreckage.

And with it, we'll find the lodestone.

FROM THE AUTHOR

Thank you! I hope you enjoyed *A Charm For Draius* and the world of the Broken Kaskea.

If you have a moment, please help others enjoy this book, too. Lend it or recommend it to friends, readers' groups, and discussion boards.

The next novel in the Broken Kaskea series will be *Souls for the Phrenii.* Want to know when it will be released? Visit my web site at Ancestral-Stars.com and sign up for my release announcement email list.

If you're interested in military-flavored science fiction, please take a look at one of my other series, the Major Ariane Kedros Novels:

Peacekeeper (Roc/NAL/Penguin, Overseas: Cajun Coyote Media)

Vigilante (Roc/NAL/Penguin, Overseas: Cajun Coyote Media)

Pathfinder (Roc/NAL/Penguin, Overseas: Cajun Coyote Media)

Mercenary (Cajun Coyote Media, est. 2016)

ABOUT THE AUTHOR

Laura E. Reeve began writing science fiction and fantasy in the fifth grade, leading to a lifelong obsession for building worlds. Along the way, she spent nine years as a US Air Force officer, holding operational command positions and having the opportunity to escort Intermediate-Range Nuclear Forces Treaty inspectors. Her civilian jobs have ranged from Research Chemist to Software Development Lead. She currently lives in Monument, CO with her husband and a Shiba Inu who runs the household.

Visit Laura's author web site at **ancestralstars.com** or her art stock web store at **ccm.ancestralstars.com**.

CPSIA information can be obtained at www.ICGtesting.com
Printed in the USA
BVOW08s1913190516

448778BV00004B/71/P